A PARCEL OF ROGUES

James Findlay Sleigh

Livingston Press
The University of West Alabama

ISBN 13: trade paper 978-1-60489-297-0
ISBN 13: hardcover 978-1-60489-298-7
ISBN 13: e-book 978-1-60489-299-4

Library of Congress Control Number 2021946099
Printed on acid-free paper
Printed in the United States of America by
Publishers Graphics

Hardcover binding by: HF Group
Typesetting and page layout: Taylor Donato
Proofreading: Tricia Taylor, Joe Taylor, Robert McKean
Cover Design: Joe Taylor
Cover photo: Photographer unknown

Dedicated to Pat Donnachie
who believed when others didn't.

6 5 4 3 2 1

A PARCEL OF ROGUES

The English steel we could disdain,
Secure in valour's station,
But English gold has been our bane;
Such a parcel of rogues in a nation!
—Robert Burns

CHAPTER 1

Gourlay and his old crony, McMinn, sat on the kerb sharing a Woodbine and taking in the yellowish early morning sun. Despite a mildish hangover, McMinn was in one of his rare expansive moods. "Best perr Ah ever had." He pulled up his trousers' leg and extended his foot to show the pair of elastic-sided boots. "See, these are made for cripples... That's whit the elastic's for... Tae make it souple... Look at thae soles... Hardly ever wore. A cripple disnae get aboot as much as ither folk, an' if he does, it's mebbe in a wheelchair, so they nivver wear them oot..."

He sucked on the last of his cigarette and blew the smoke skywards. "Ah wis especially lucky; these yins were made for a valgus foot... Ye ken whit a valgus foot is?" Gourlay shook his head. "Weel, it's a kinda club foot," continued McMinn warming to his subject, "except that it turns inward... Like this..." He got to his feet and hirpled round to demonstrate. "See how the foot is turned in like? An' so they're only wore a wee bittie on the inside o' the sole... Like new an' only three bob!"

Gourlay smiled and the admiration in his voice was not feigned. "You're a fund of useless knowledge McMinn. How is it ye ken what a valgus foot is?" Pleased, McMinn flicked the stub of the cigarette onto the cobblestones, tugged at his ear and smiled widely. "It a' startet when Ah went doon tae the library tae return some books for an auld biddy. It wis wan o' thon bluidy cauld days — fair freezin — an' here if the library wisna a' warm an' cosy. There's nuttin' tae dae there but read, an' Ah've been reading ever since... Even startet teachin' masel French, Spanish and German."

"Izzat a fact?" said Gourlay, impressed. "Let's hear ye speak some German."

McMinn rubbed his stubbly chin with the back of his hand and pondered deeply for a moment, cleared his throat noisily, then enunciated in his gravelly voice, "Er, Gooten Tag. Wie geht es Ihnen...?"

"Jings! That's great, so it is!" exclaimed his pal slapping his knee. McMinn lowered his eyes modestly. There was a pause. "Er, McMinn..." began Gourlay in his most beguiling manner, "whit's the chance o' a sub tae tide me ower?"

To his surprise, McMinn was solvent. Obligingly, he produced a handful of change, and, selecting three half crowns, handed them to Gourlay.

"You should open a bank accoont, Gourlay. Wance ye get an accoont, ye can aye get a loan frae the bank... It's easy. Ye jist..." He tailed off as he caught sight of a thin, scruffy-looking little man in a boiler suit and checked cap hurrying along on the other side of the street.

Gourlay vaguely recognized him as an acquaintance of McMinn's who, rumour had it, had been turfed out of some order of monks or other; it seemed that he was in the habit of talking in his sleep, and one night had recounted some particularly salacious tale which had set his fellow monks all aquiver; the upshot was that he had received his marching orders.

Suddenly, McMinn called out, "Hey, Hector! Wait!" And without a farewell, he dashed off, leaving Gourlay to mull over this latest proposal for raising capital.

Later in the day, Gourlay found himself in a stately but somewhat run-down Victorian crescent. An emaciated woman in hair curlers was trying to drag a pram up the steps of one of the houses. It was heavily laden with a huge pile of newly-washed clothes wrapped in a striped sheet. He took hold of the front end of the pram to lend a hand, and immediately the harassed lady

JAMES FINDLAY SLEIGH

began heaping abuse upon him.

"Get yer filthy hauns aff or Ah'll cry the polis! Molestin' a puir wumman! Ye bastert ye!"

He made off with alacrity, yelling, "Fat tart!" at her over his shoulder — his favourite epithet for women of any shape, size or persuasion who upset him.

He wandered around somewhat aimlessly for a few hours, from time to time wishing he'd had the foresight to ask McMinn for a couple of fags — aimlessly, but very much on the *qui vive* for anything of worth which might perchance his way.

A pawnbroker's window caught his eye, and he marvelled at the great variety of dust-covered articles heaped untidily one upon the other: dozens of watches, some without hands, jewellery of all kinds, and, clenched tightly by a pair of false teeth, a well-worn wedding ring, parts of a motorcycle, a very dented tuba, several guitars — most of them sans strings — a budgie cage, a sporran, a pair of plimsolls... He looked up. Below the three balls were the words, H EN SH PIRO. *MON Y LOANED ON AR CLES OF ALUE.* He toyed with the idea of pawning his coat, but it was still very chilly in the evenings and doubtless the pawnbroker would be a tough nut to conclude a deal with. "A loan...! Goad! The bank! ..."

The bank was closing when he arrived. The teller at the wicket nearest the door looked up from his books at the breathless customer. "Yes?"

"Er, I'd like to open an accoont."

"If you'd just go over to the teller by the pillar sir — I've closed my books for the day... The bank closes in five minutes," he added in a tone which implied that sir had at least a sporting chance of completing a transaction. The second teller was a pretty miss with heavily lacquered hair and blood-red nails. As he approached she glanced at the clock on the wall behind her and gave a hint of a frown. "We close in less than five minutes."

"Yes... I'd like to open an accoont."

A pained expression clouded her face. "Certainly sir. What kind of account did sir have in mind?"

"Oh, a savin's accoont," said Gourlay, who liked the sound of it. "Aye, a savin's accoont."

After a while, having entered all manner of details into an oversized ledger, she produced a pretty green passbook with the bank's crest on the cover. "Now sir, how much would you like to deposit?" Her pen was poised.

"Two shullins."

A look of mild disbelief flitted over her heavily made up features. "Two shillings?"

"Well, make it hauf a croon." With some reluctance, he handed over the coin and received the pristine passbook appropriately annotated. "Now, who do I see about a loan?"

"A loan? That would be Mr. Harrison. Along the corridor there... First door on the right."

The door was marked   **E. HARRISON: MANAGER**. Gourlay peered through the frosted glass panel, but could see nothing. He adjusted his tie, gave each boot a quick polish on the backs of his trousers' legs, and knocked. No response. He knocked again, louder this time. Still no answer. He dropped to one knee and placed his eye to the keyhole, but all he could discern was part of the top of a huge desk.

"Can I be of assistance?" The refined voice behind him startled him, and as he straightened he grazed his nose on the door handle. Mr. Harrison was a dapper, bespectacled, grey-looking man in a grey suit.

Gourlay tried to forget his smarting nose. "Er, I've been sent, sent to see the manager."

"I'm Harrison, the manager. Do step inside." Courteously, he held open the door and Gourlay went in.

The office was well-appointed to a point just short of opulence.

A modest coal fire burned in a businesslike way. Mr. Harrison indicated a plush chair, and seating himself behind his great desk, extended a cigarette box, but then before Gourlay could take one, withdrew it and snapped it shut. He ran his eyes over the scruffy little man before him. "And how can I be of assistance my good man?"

Gourlay smiled wanly. He had long since learned to ignore the thinly-veiled condescension implicit, to his mind at least, in the phrase, 'my good man.' He took a deep breath. "Ah've come for to secure a loan."

The bank manager raised his eyebrows a degree or two, slowly removed his spectacles, and placed them on the desk with a distinct click. "Indeed?"

So far, so good, thought Gourlay. *At least he hasna said no yet.*

"Indeed?" repeated Mr. Harrison, as if he liked the sound of the word. "And what sum, pray, did you have in mind?"

"Oh, a paltry hundred or so to tide me over," said Gourlay crossing his legs, leaning back and attempting to adopt the bank manager's off-handed, slightly bemused tone.

"I see..." Mr. Harrison placed his hands together and made a little steeple with his finger tips. "What are your assets?"

Gourlay assumed a blank look.

"You do have an account with us Mr. er...?"

"Baines, H. Gourlay Baines."

"Do you have your account number to hand Mr. er, Baines?"

Gourlay produced his passbook and handed it over.

"Fine. Now, if you will excuse me for a moment, I will be right back," said Mr. Harrison and left the room.

As was his wont, Gourlay began to study his surroundings. His eyes lit on the cigarette box and it was but a moment's work to transfer half a dozen cigarettes to his pocket. Then he noticed a bowl of chrysanthemums on the desk. He wondered if they were real. He leaned forward to sniff them and was immediately overcome by a violent fit of coughing. He thumped his chest with clenched fist and looked around for somewhere to spit, but the room, despite all its paraphernalia, contained nothing suitable. Never one to be caught short in an emergency, he raised the ornate inkwell from the desk and neatly dropped a gobful into it. He replaced it and sat down and was still gasping for air when the manager returned. His face was not happy.

"How much did you say you had in mind to borrow again, Mr. Baines?"

Gourlay was about to say, "two hundred" when, noting the gravity of the bank manager's expression, altered the figure accordingly. "Let's say fifty quid."

"I don't quite know what your game is Mr. Baines, but I see that you opened an account with us only this afternoon. Isn't that so?" Gourlay nodded and wished that he were elsewhere.

"Mr. Baines, we do not hand out unsecured loans. Do you have any assets at all?"

Gourlay shook his head slowly. Mr. Harrison leaned forward and said heavily, "We, Mr. Baines, are a bank, not a philanthropic institution. I bid you good day."

Night fell over Glasgow like a cloak. The yellow light from the street lamps spilled over the streets and pavements, giving the passers-by jaundice. Gourlay jingled the two half crowns in his pocket and found the sound mightily reassuring; it was grand to be solvent. In the park by the Kelvin River he found a vacant bench and sat down to luxuriate in the last of Mr. Harrison's cigarettes. The nearby University clock boomed out seven times. A small mongrel dog approached him cautiously. Its reddish brown coat was matted and it had a dirty bandage made from an old handkerchief round the end of its tail. It sniffed his boots with discreet fascination. Gourlay was no dog lover; it seemed to him that on the slimmest of pretexts most dogs did their best to maim or dismember him. Over the years, he'd tactfully adopted a strict policy of laissez-faire regarding canines. He exempted no dog, because he'd found to his cost that there seemed to be an inverse law which said that the more innocuous it looked, the more lethal it turned out to be. The dog crept under the bench, lay down, and continued to examine the heels of his boots with an air of intense concentration. From time to time, it made a whiffling sound.

"Get oot o' therr!"

The animal looked up at him nose twitching. There was no malevolence in its eyes, and Gourlay immediately softened.

"Ach, it's you an' me against them, eh no, dug?" he said quietly and gingerly patted the dog on the head. The dog wagged its tail.

Gourlay stretched out his legs and put his hands in his pockets. The half crowns were still there. He felt rich and began to muse. "A good meal... Could aye give Andra the three bob I owe him... Naw, it can wait... A dram! That's it! Havena had a dram in ages... Whit's the name o' that wee howff up Garscube Road...?

"That's it pal," he said to the dog which lay sprawled between his feet, "I'm gonna hae a wee dram tae masel'!" The dog thumped its tail on the grass. Gourlay rose, stretched extravagantly, breathed in the night air — the damp night air permeated with the soul of the City — and strode off purposefully in his loping gait.

As he turned along St. George's Road to Cowcaddens, he paused to study the posters outside the cinema by the Underground: *Dance of the Maidens* and *The Curse of Drango* were playing. He shook his head. When he was a lad, he'd been inside when it was still a theatre and seen *Aladdin* for sixpence. He headed up Garscube Road, past several pubs till he recognized the one he was looking for. He went in. The ceiling was low and the whole place reeked of stale wine, beer, and cigarette smoke. The customers were all male, all small, and all very poor. He glanced around to see if he knew anybody. Each table in the seating area was sectioned off from its neighbours by a waist-high partition. The place was crowded, but he managed to squeeze into a vacant seat opposite two men. He'd scarcely seated himself when the barman brought over two tumblers, one containing cider, the other red wine. He fished out one of his half crowns and got one and six change. He downed the red wine. It was so wersh it drew his cheeks together, but he consoled himself with the thought that for five bob he could get roaring fou.

He studied his companions as he sipped his cider. The man directly opposite leaned out from the table at a precarious angle. He wore a filthy, collarless shirt and a grey bunnet. His friend had attained an advanced state of inebriation and was in a boisterous and receptive mood. "C'moan, Jammy," he cried in a loud rasping voice and nudged the leaning one with his elbow. "Drink up! Ye're fa'in ahint!" He indicated Jammy's untouched drinks and turned to Gourlay. "Ach, he's a wee bit aff colour this nicht is Jammy... C'moan Jammy, gie the man a wee bit song." By way of an answer, Jammy farted loudly, and quick as a flash his pal said in mock serious tone, "Ye've goat the right choon, but the wrang words therr... C'moan!"

Gourlay sipped his cider which was as sweet as the wine was sour. The diminutive man extended a grubby hand. "Ma name's John... Ma freens cry me Polka."

"Ah'm Gourlay," replied Gourlay affably.

"Pleased tae meet ye Gourlay. Whit'll it be? Same?"

"Naw, that's alright..."

"C'moan Gourlay... There's never a bird can fly on ae wing..."

Polka turned to face the bar and held up three fingers and the barman brought over three glasses of cider and three of wine.

"C'moan Jammy! Drink up therr!" persisted Polka loudly, then in a conspiratorial whisper which sounded like a growl, "Here's lookin' at ye Gourlay."

"Cheers," said Gourlay without enthusiasm and raised his glass. They drank in silence and Jammy farted again.

"D'ye come here often?" queried Polka bent on forcing a conversation.

"Time tae time," responded Gourlay easily.

Then for no reason apparent to Gourlay, the noise level, which had been quite considerable up till then, dropped suddenly. Gourlay's first thought was that the drinks had affected his hearing, and he shook his head violently and jabbed his fingers into each ear in turn. Polka, who was facing the door, tried to slip under the table his eyes wide with a mixture of fear and horror. Gourlay turned.

Filling the doorway, arms akimbo, stood a huge figure of a man who glared around with calculated belligerence. Conversation had now died away completely.

"Christ, it's Big Red!" husked Polka from under the table.

Even through the fug of smoke, Gourlay could see why the newcomer was so named; he must have been close to seven feet tall and his red hair, eyebrows and beard were so red that his massive head seemed to be on fire.

"Glasgow scum!" intoned the giant, and ran baleful eyes round the room. Pin-dropping silence ensued.

"Losh! He *must* be seven feet," mused Gourlay. "Nae man an inch under that could say that in a Glesca pub an' live."

"Bloody cowards," rumbled Big Red. "Hah! Do I smell the blood of an Englishman?"

As he strode into the room, Gourlay noticed with awe that his hair brushed the ceiling.

"Right, dwarfs," the voice boomed. "Light bulb. Ten bob."

Puzzled, Gourlay watched a variety of the bar's clientele stagger, march, hirple, or run up to him and press silver coins into the outstretched shovel of a hand.

"Enough!" said the big man imperiously and pocketed the

coins. He deftly removed a light bulb from a ceiling fixture, popped it in his mouth, crunched it, and promptly swallowed it. A great shout went up and men stomped, huzzahed, whistled and clattered glasses on the table tops. Big Red bowed deeply, wiped his bloody mouth, smiled broadly at the assembly, turned on his heel, and vanished into the night. There was a collective sigh of relief, then excited conversation broke out.

"In the name o' fuck, whit wis a' that aboot?" croaked Gourlay. Polka eased himself from under the table and back into his seat. His face was ashen. "That wis Big Red," he said simply.

"An' is he an Englishman or what?"

Remarkably, it was Jammy who answered. Big Red's visit had miraculously restored his powers of speech and a slight degree of sobriety. His voice was slurred and spasmodic. "Naw. He's a Scot... Offered tae crush Polka's heid like a grape, eh no, Polka? Ye mind o' that?"

"Aye. He had a dram taken ae nicht an' Ah must hae said something tae upset him... Bugger howket me up oot o' ma seat — wan bluidy finger, mind — under ma jaiket collar, an' dunted ma heid against the ceiling..."

"Ye stupit bastert ye! Ye cried him a big poof!" said Jammy with a mirthless, wheezy laugh. "Lucky we wisna a' killt... Goad, Ah mind the time Big Red..."

But he never got to finish his tale. A glass in each hand, a diminutive, glum-looking man approached the table and indicated the seat next to Gourlay. "Is that seat took?"

Gourlay examined the chair with exaggerated care for a moment then cracked, "Naw, it's still here!" The stranger was not at all amused. Gourlay moved into the corner seat and the man sat down. Silence reigned over the table. The man stared morosely into the middle distance and downed his wine in one big gulp. He belched, smacked his lips on his coat sleeve, downed his cider, and belched again. He removed his hat, laid it on the table, and catching the barman's eye, held up his index finger.

"You're fair knocking them back this nicht, Alec," said the barman.

"Aye," replied Alec flatly selecting a shilling from a handful of coins. The barman returned to the bar. Alec placed the coins on the table and began producing more from various pockets. Gourlay stared as he methodically began to arrange the coins into piles on the tabletop according to their denominations. Suddenly, he stopped and looked directly at Gourlay. "Whit are you starin' at?" he demanded. Gourlay busied himself with his wine. The table was silent but for the steady clinking of coins. He glanced across at Jammy, but he'd reverted to his semi-comatose state and looked so uncannily like a corpse that Gourlay shuddered. By way of attempting to enliven the proceedings, Polka nudged his partner in the ribs. "C'moan, Jammy, gie's a wee sang!" But Jammy was so far gone that he couldn't even raise a decent fart. "Aw, he's a rerr wee singer, Gourlay... You should hear him so ye should... He can mak' folk greet wi' his singin'..."

"Folk aye greet when Ah sing," said Gourlay with a poker face.

"Izzat so?" said Polka credulously. Weel, c'moan then... Let's hear you... Mebbe ye'll get Jammy here startet... C'moan! Aw, C'moan, Gourlay!"

Alec lifted his heavily-lidded eyes from his coins and rasped malevolently, "Aye, c'moan, Gourlay! You that's sae damn smart, c'moan, mak' us greet!"

Gourlay sensed the situation was rapidly turning dangerous and was alarmed.

"Aw. Ah'm no up tae it the nicht," he said, and coughed a little cough and tapped his chest meaningfully. Alec thumped the table so hard that some of the coins fell from their piles. His face had a tautness about it and Gourlay thought he could discern something distinctly homicidal about the eyes. "C'moan, Gourlay, you that's sae clever — C'moan, mak' us greet..."

"Er, Ah need the toilet," said Gourlay rising. Alec pulled him down. "Naw, naw, naw, Gourlay. You've tae gie us a song first. Isn't that right, Polka?"

Happy that Alec was picking on someone else, Polka nodded vigorously. Gourlay felt trapped. He stalled for time. He hummed a few notes and assumed a puzzled expression as if he were searching for the right key. He noticed that Alec's eyes were slitted and the expression on his face almost demonic. Then something brushed Gourlay's leg. It was the dog. Hoping to divert Alec's attention, he began showering lavish extravagant attention on the animal. "Hello wee dug! My, my! Ye must followed me a' the way from the park!"

But Alec was a very single-minded man. "Never mind the dug... Sing up!" he hissed and thumped the table again. The dog growled a low warning. "C'moan, sing!" insisted Alec. The dog growled again, louder this time. "Get oot o' therr!" said Alec, and gave the dog a swift tap in the ribs with his foot. The dog snarled, clamped its jaws on Alec's trousers' leg, and began worrying it with a muffled, "Aaargh! Aaargh!" gargling sound. Alec's eyes opened a fraction. He turned on Gourlay, and grabbing him by the lapels of his coat, pushed him against the wall. "Get yer damn dug aff ma leg!" he spat. Polka leaned forward, and to Gourlay's surprise, instead of coming to his aid, attempted to rain blows on his head.

Gourlay had had enough. In one swift movement he swept the hatful of coins off the table. Alex released him, and with the dog still hanging on grimly, tried to gather up his money, which had rolled all over the bar floor. The tinkling coins caused an immediate scramble among the more alert of the bar's clientele. The barman called for order, but in vain. Gourlay picked up a glass of wine, threw the contents into Polka's face, and departed the table with such alacrity that Jammy fell off his seat with a terrible thud and lay where he fell, quite still, his eyes glazed and staring.

Although intent on quitting the pub as if his life depended on it, Gourlay took time to scoop up some coins from the tabletop and pour a glass of cider on the neck of the nearly distraught Alec who was crawling about on the floor trying to retrieve some of his money. Gourlay headed for the door and set off down the street at the double with the little mongrel at his heels.

Putting a good distance between himself and the bar, he slipped up a close mouth, and under the soft greenish light of the gas lamp at the foot of the stairs, sat down to get his breath back. He counted the coins he'd picked up — thirteen shillings and seven pence.

"No' bad... No' bad... A rerr night oot for a shullin," he reflected as he pocketed the money and turned to the dog. "Here, wee dug... C'mere..." He patted its head. "You saved ma bacon son... Are you hungry?" The dog tilted its head to one side. "C'moan then. Let's see if we can get ye a bite."

He rose and went to the nearest door and examined it closely. The brass letterbox flap was shiny, and above it was a little tartan plastic plate bearing the name *Gowalski*. "We're in luck son," he said to the dog.

Through long experience, he had discovered that people who kept the brassware on their doors well-polished were more approachable than those whose brass was tarnished. He'd also found that people with foreign-sounding names were generally benevolent souls. He'd never been able to explain why this was so, but, to Gourlay, it was a fact, and as he well knew, 'facts are chiels that winna ding.' He rattled the letterbox flap.

After a long moment, a light came on in the hallway, and the door, held by a stout chain from opening more than a couple of inches, was unbolted and eased open. A woman's voice said, "Yes?"

Gourlay closed one eye and opened the other as wide as he could. "Er, could ye dae a blind man a favour? It's no' for me like, but for ma dug here... He's fair starvin'... Ah wis wondering if you could spare a few scraps...?" He could only see a part of the woman's face through the space at the door, but from what he could see, she looked as if she were a kindly body.

"For yer dug ye say?"

"Aye."

"Well, just a wee minute..." The door was closed and he heard the key turn in the lock; blind man or not, Mrs. Gowalski was taking no chances. Soon, she returned with a pokeful of scraps, which she passed through the gap in the door. "Good luck tae ye, son."

"Aw, thanks very much, Mrs. Gowalski."

The door began to close then was suddenly jerked open to the full extent of the chain. "Hey, if you're blind, how did ye ken ma name wis Gowalski?"

"Oh, ah, er... Well, they dugs they gie us are awffy clever... They can dae a' kind o' tricks... Ah wis especially lucky because this wan can read an a'..."

Mrs. Gowalski looked slightly nonplussed. "Oh aye. Well, goodnight, son..."

McMinn's attic room on St. Vincent Street was deserted, and there was no sign of the landlady. He let himself in with the key his crony kept planked on the sill above the door. Once inside, he shared out the scraps with the dog, eating the tastier morsels himself. Mrs. Gowalski had done them proud.

Before he left next morning, Gourlay left a note on the floor by the door.

Dropped in. But no sign of you. Sorry you were out.
See you later. G.
P.S. No sign of landlady either — did you finally
droon her in the Clyde?

He gave the dog some water, pocketed some stale biscuits he found in a tin on the mantelpiece, then they left quietly.

It was a glorious morning. Rain had fallen during the night, and the City smelled fresh and clean. Gourlay treated himself to a packet of five Woodbines and a morning paper. Seeing a tram rumble past gave him the urge to take a ride. The dog close at his heels, he strolled along until he came to a stop, and within a few minutes a green and orange Cunarder tram appeared grinding along on the crown of the road closely followed by half a dozen cars and a coalman's horse and cart. The procession ground to a halt. The conductor, hat pushed well back on his head, ticket machine slung low on one hip in the manner of an Old West gunslinger, eyed them coldly.

"Whaur ye gaun?" queried Gourlay.

"Ballieston."

"It says Broomhouse on the screen."

"Mebbe it does," retorted the conductor sourly. "It says India Rubber oan the tyres, an' we're no gaun there either."

"Tyres, my arse," mused Gourlay as he mounted the stairs. "Silly bastert's livin' in a fantasy world — thinks he's a bluidy bus conductor."

Late afternoon found the pair at the Gallowgate. The streets were thronged with shoppers making last-minute purchases, and trams and buses were all packed to the doors. At one stop he watched with intense interest as a stout woman in orange coat and plimsolls concentrated on getting a huge roll of linoleum onto the tram. He saw the conductor's smirk vanish and his jaw fall slack as she succeeded in doing the impossible; with superhuman effort, she rammed the roll up the stairs effectively isolating the top deck passengers from the rest of the world.

In front of a dingy second-hand clothes shop, a pavement artist had decorated the pavement with his works. Gourlay studied the first. It was a meticulously drawn portrait of a mountain. The colours were bold — the sky was a deep blue, the trees vivid green, and the mountain itself an improbable canary yellow. Underneath, in neatly chalked letters, he read, **A MOUNTAIN. ALL MY OWN WORK.** The next endeavour showed a bright red boat sailing on a mauve sea and it was entitled, perhaps not surprisingly, **A BOAT AT SEA. ALL MY OWN WORK.** Several art works farther on, sat the artist himself, head bowed, morosely contemplating the hat between his crossed legs; it contained an assortment of coins. The dog, obviously an impassioned critic, raised its leg and urinated. Gourlay watched fascinated as the red boat slowly dissolved into a scarlet river and was swallowed by the sea.

"Hey! Get that dampt dug the hell oot o' therr!" yelled the artist. Gourlay turned.

Alec!

Before he could make off, Alec, blood in his eye, leapt to his feet and now held Gourlay's collar in a vice-like grip. "So, it's you is it? You an' yer bluidy dug! Ah'll melt ye, ye wee bastert!" He raised his fist, but before he could clobber Gourlay, the dog fairly launched itself at Alec and set about shredding his trousers' leg. An interested crowd began to assemble, and a fat woman dealt the artist a tremendous blow to the side of the head with her handbag. Gourlay wriggled free and gave his adversary a swift, hard kick on the kneecap before grabbing the hatful of coins and slipping away into the crowd.

As he sped up a side street, the dog at his heels, he became aware that they were being followed, and what's more, although he was pounding along in top gear, their pursuer was gaining. He dodged up a close mouth, but despite his pleas of, "C'mere boy... Good dog..." the dog stood outside on the street, tail wagging. The man, a little, roly-poly fellow who resembled a clean-shaven Santa Claus, arrived puffing like a steam engine. "Ah, er, pech pech... Ah came for to thank you for, pech, standing up for wee Sam here," he wheezed. He's been missing for a week. He reached into his pocket and produced a ten shilling note. "Ah hope ye'll accept this." Gourlay did. "Bless you," said the little man, still trying to catch his breath. "Ah'm very gratefu'... "C'moan Sam, yer mammy'll be fair pleased tae see you again."

Gourlay tried to pat the dog which was jumping up and down with delight and making little rumbling sounds. "Cheerio Sam. It's been great knowin' you."

With a, "Losh, Sam, whit happened tae yer tail?" the master and the mongrel headed off.

Alone again, Gourlay counted his money. Twenty nine shillings and five pence, not counting an East African half crown.

On the street again, he crammed the hat into a litter basket on a lamppost and set off humming happily to get himself a nice cup of tea and a roll and bacon.

CHAPTER 2

A few days later, Gourlay returned to the bank armed with an itemised list of his assets which included an I.O.U. for ten shillings owed to him by Daft Harry, a tennis racket, a bicycle wheel, some hand-painted magic lantern slides of the Zambezi River, a Wehrmacht helmet, and a hub cap from a Bentley in addition to a number of articles of lesser value. By his calculations, his worldly goods were worth at least seventeen pounds, but he nevertheless entertained some doubts regarding the manager's understanding of the matter and prepared himself to accept graciously whatever amount Mr.Harrison was prepared to offer.

He entered the bank with some trepidation half expecting to be challenged at every step. But no one appeared to notice him. He rapped sharply on the manager's door with more confidence than he felt.

"Come!" called Mr. Harrison.

Gourlay went in extending before him like some talisman the list of his possessions. Mr. Harrison was pouring over a ledger. "Yes?" he said, without looking up.

"Ah've come aboot the loan..."

As if electrified, the manager leapt to his feet and in a low voice came straight to the point. "If you are not off the premises in ten seconds, I personally shall boot your arse from here to Galbraiths!" To reinforce his threat, he stalked to the corner of his desk. Gourlay retreated to the door. "It's no' fair," he whined, "This is a list o' my assets, an'..."

"Three seconds...! Pilfer my cigarettes indeed...!" said Mr.

Harrison advancing.

It's strange how the mind works when adversity threatens; at that instant, three things occurred to Gourlay: Mr. Harrison was an Englishman, Mr. Harrison dyed his hair, and Galbraiths was nearly two streets of hard kicks on the arse away. Thinking discretion was the better part of valour, especially when dealing with a lunatic, Gourlay hurled a few insults in the general direction of the manager's office, and moved off smartly.

Before leaving the building, however, he carefully wrote in block capitals on the back of a withdrawal slip: **THIS IS A HOLD UP. I'VE GOT A GUN IN MY POCKET. HAND OVER ALL YOUR CASH OR I'll BLOW YOUR FUCKING HEID OFF.** He placed the slip in the middle of a pile of blanks and sauntered out smiling smugly to himself at the thought of the chaos which would ensue when some unsuspecting customer presented it to a teller in the course of making a withdrawal.

That evening, he dropped in to see McMinn again, but again, the bird had flown. He let himself in and made himself comfortable. He was sitting on the edge of the bed leaning over removing his boot when he noticed a foot sticking out from under the bed. It was clad in a dark blue sock with a large hole in the toe. For a moment, he wavered, undecided whether he should try to leave quietly or face up to what could only be an intruder, then, his mind made up, he slowly raised his right leg and brought his boot down on the projecting foot with all his might. The foot immediately disappeared and there was a wail of agony followed by a string of horrendous oaths. The bed bobbed violently and the muffled, pain-filled voice of the intruder continued to utter obscenities and threats of the most blood-curdling nature. Heart racing, Gourlay poised himself either to flee should the stranger prove too much to handle or to dish out a good thrashing should he already be sufficiently incapacitated by the injuries already inflicted upon him. After a further brief period of swearing, growling and scuffling, a figure emerged from under the bed.

"Gourlay! Ye bastert!"

"McMinn! Whit in Goad's name were ye doin' under the bed?"

McMinn limped around the room, an expression of excruciating pain written all over his rugged features. "Ye bluidy eejot! Ye've cripplet me for life!"

"Jeeze, Ah'm sorry McMinn... Ah thought ye wis a burglar."

"Ye eejot ye! You could have speired wha it was first... Whit the fuck did ye hit me wi' onywey?"

"Just ma buit."

"Jist yer buit! Christ! It's a good job it wisna ma fuckin' heid that wis stickin' oot!" He sat on the bed making little moaning noises and nursing his injured foot. Gourlay clucked sympathetically, but despite himself couldn't suppress a guffaw. "Hey McMinn, ye'll no' hae ony trouble wearin' thae valgus buits noo!"

McMinn stopped rubbing his foot and glared at him. "That's no' the least bit funny, so wipe that smirk off yer face or Ah'll wipe it off for ye an' quick!"

"Alright, alright. Keep yer wool oan McMinn... Ah'm sorry..." There was a long silence interrupted only by an occasional low moan from McMinn.

"Hey, McMinn, remember whit you said about a bank loan? Well, Ah went roon tae the bank an' couldna get a penny oot o' them... Bluidy manager didna even gie us a fag... Sassenach bastert!"

McMinn sat on the edge of the bed cradling his foot. He gave his pal a long hard look. "That reminds me... Here Gourlay, how would ye like tae earn a few quid, easy like?" He hobbled over to the sideboard and counted out five one-pound notes from a cocoa tin. "Here, take it. There's plenty more for the askin'." Never a one to look a gift horse in the mouth, Gourlay quickly pocketed the proffered notes. "Jeeze, thanks McMinn... Whit's the catch?"

McMinn tentatively tested his injured extremity on the floor by the bed then sat down again.

"D'ye ken Big Red?"

"I'll never forget him," said Gourlay simply.

"Well, he needs some help wi' some diggin'."

"Diggin'?"

"Just."

"Diggin'?"

"Diggin," responded McMinn with a hint of irritation. He lowered his voice to the merest whisper. "Ah'm no' permittet tae say mair, but it's for Big Red. Ye'll be well paid... Keep the fiver as an advance like."

Gourlay rubbed his jaw reflectively. "O.K. But whit's the catch?"

"There's no bluidy catch. Ah tellt ye. We've aye trustet wan anither right? Since our army days, right?"

Gourlay nodded not knowing quite where McMinn was headed.

"Weel, gin ye trust me, whit wey dae ye keep speirin' whit the catch is?" he said heavily in his gruff voice. Not wishing to further aggravate his friend, Gourlay kept his peace.

"There's nae catch," continued McMinn. "Just some diggin' an' keepin' yer cakehole shut... No' as much as a peep to onybody." With that, he ushered a puzzled Gourlay to the door. "Ah've got tae get crackin'... Now, look, today's Friday, right? Meet me by the shell at Queen Street Station... Sunday, eight p.m. sharp. O.K?"

Gourlay spent much of the intervening time examining and re-examining the five one-pound notes. Time and time again he went over every word McMinn had uttered but could not make head nor tail of it. Two things, however, stood out clearly in his mind: firstly, he did have five crisp notes, and secondly, as he understood it, if he was prepared to do some digging, he would receive more. It was the thought of being the possessor of even more money that finally drove all doubts, suspicions, and hesitations from his mind and made him decide that he would indeed meet McMinn at the appointed hour.

By half-past seven, Gourlay was already at the station passing the time away by acting out the rôle of a top MI5 man engaged in tracking down an international spy. He lurked in the shadows and studied the scurrying passengers. But sadly, even to his fertile imagination, most of them looked innocuous enough, and not one of them gave him as much as a second glance. He was beginning to tire of the game when he saw him…

The man was well dressed, but unshaven, and carried a bulging attaché case. Gourlay turned up his coat collar, and trying his best to appear nonchalant, followed the man as he made his way to the newsstand and bought a paper. He thumbed his way to the sports section and began reading with an almost frightening intensity. Still reading, his attaché case under his arm, he headed for the Gents. Gourlay followed, the idea now firm in his mind that the man was searching the paper for a coded message. They stood at adjacent urinals, and when the man went to wash his hands, Gourlay was at his heels. The man turned on the tap, then without warning, reached into his jacket pocket, produced a long-bladed knife and in a single swift movement, leapt at Gourlay, grabbed him by the collar of his coat with his free hand, pinned him against the wall, and placed the point of the knife against his throat. "Whit the fuck d'ye want mister?" His voice was low, husky, and full of menace. "Clear oot o' here, an' fast, or Ah'll slit yer bluidy thrapple! Understand?" Gourlay understood implicitly and rushed up the steps as fast as his trembling legs could carry him. Safely at the top of the steps, he recovered enough of his composure and wind to call down, "You bastert! Ah'll get ye for that! You just come up here an' see!" However, he did not wait to see if his challenge was accepted and made off at a good clip.

He had gone but a few steps when someone tapped him on

the shoulder. The blood froze in his veins and he stood stock still expecting to feel the keen edge of a knife slicing his throat.

"Whit the hell's the matter wi' you?" said a throaty voice he immediately recognized.

"McMinn! Christ! Whit a fleg!" he husked rubbing his crotch. "Ah think Ah've peed masel'"

McMinn looked at him incredulously. "For Goad's sake Gourlay, pu' yersel' thegether! Whit the hell's the matter wi' you? An' ye've got a wee cut on yer chin… C'moan, we've got tae get crackin'."

He led the way keeping to the back streets and lanes, and now and then he would look about in the most mysterious fashion. Gourlay became a little disconcerted when he realized that from time to time they were retracing their steps. But in view of his pal's serious demeanour, decided not to ask questions. Finally, at a dimly-lit dead-end street that he did not recognize, they went up a close. McMinn rapped three times on a ground floor door and after a few moments it was opened by a small, grimy-faced man in a grubby boiler suit. They went in. Without a word of greeting, the man showed them into the kitchen which, used as he was to poverty, staggered Gourlay by its squalor. The windows were boarded up and light was provided by a single candle in an empty tin in the middle of the floor. The room was in such a filthy, run-down state that it could not have been lived in for many months. The floor was carpeted with a thick layer of earth and rubble. At a makeshift table made from piled up wooden boxes a huge man sat drinking tea from a jam jar: Big Red, the light bulb swallower. There was a silence. Gourlay stood feeling awkward as the big man examined him from head to toe. "So you're Gourlay eh?" His voice was neither friendly nor unfriendly. "I'm pleased to meet you… I've heard a lot about you from McMinn here… And this is Hector…" The man in the boiler suit nodded and Gourlay suddenly remembered why he looked familiar.

"Would you like a cuppa?" asked Big Red.

"Thanks..."

"And you, McMinn?"

McMinn shook his head. "Thanks. Ah just et."

The big man awkwardly poured Gourlay a jar of tea that looked, and to some extent, tasted, like tar. He sipped it in silence aware that all eyes were upon him. After a lengthy silence, broken only by a regular slurping sound as Big Red drank his tea, Gourlay felt it incumbent upon himself to say something by way of conversation. He looked about him from face to face, but could think of nothing to say. The silence weighed upon the room. "Er, nice place ye've got here." They looked at one another then back to him. Judging from their expressions he might as well have announced that he'd got leprosy. Then Big Red spoke up. "You've got to be bloody joking! This dump a nice place! It may be to you laddie — depends what you're used to. But after this job, you can say ta-ta to all that."

"The diggin' ye mean?" said Gourlay boldly.

"Aye. The diggin'. There's a pot full of gold at the end, my friend." He winked broadly at McMinn then turned to Gourlay again. "I'll explain as we go along, but right now it's time we did some more work... OK lads, let's get on with it... It's your turn topside, McMinn?" McMinn nodded. Big Red looked at his watch. "I'll be back at one. Keep hard at it lads... You too, Gourlay." He whispered something to McMinn, and left.

"O.K.," said Hector rising, "Let's go." He picked up a torch and led Gourlay to an awmry or cupboard near the door. On the floor, on top of a pile of earth, were some old newspapers and books. These he lifted, then poking his finger through a knothole, raised what appeared to be a trapdoor to reveal a gaping hole. The top rungs of a ladder rested against the far side.

"Right. I'll go first," said Hector, and disappeared down the ladder.

Somewhat reluctantly, Gourlay followed and found himself in a dimly-lit cellar the floor of which was covered to a depth of two or three feet with earth, bricks, and general rubble. In the far wall the bricks had been removed and through the gap there was what appeared to Gourlay to be an endless tunnel. Hector handed him the torch. "Keep on until you can go no farther. O.K?"

The tunnel was damp and smelly, and in some places so narrow that he had to crawl on his stomach. He had no way of judging how far he'd gone when suddenly it came to an end. Behind him, Hector's muffled voice came to him. "You'll find a basket and a little shovel. Start digging, fill the basket, and when it's full, pass it back to me."

Gourlay fumbled around and found both. He dug into the earth which was soft, moist, and smelled abominably. He didn't find the work too taxing, but after a while he began to feel stiff from the confined space and dampness. He wondered what it was all about and pumped Hector for enlightenment, but the latter kept his peace and told him he should ask Big Red.

By one o'clock Big Red arrived and called the weary and grimy pair to the surface. He'd brought several newspaper-wrapped servings of fish and chips and these he handed out to his men. After the hours he'd put in, Gourlay felt entitled to an explanation as to what was what. He cleared his throat. "Er, would ye mind tellin' me what a' this diggin's aboot? Whit are we diggin for?"

Big Red studied him closely for a moment, glanced at McMinn, and shoved a few chips in his mouth before answering. "Aye, surely Gourlay... We're headed for the bank. We're nearly there. It's easy. We dig our way right into the vault, and Bob's your uncle!" He looked round the grubby faces. "Mark you, lads, we've got to get a move on. I heard through the grapevine that Sanny Rutherford's supposed to be having a go at the same bank... He's in for a shock — the time he gets there, the cupboard'll be bare!" He handed Gourlay a bottle of Irn Bru. "Here, that'll put lead in your pencil...

Ah'm sorry it's not the hard stuff, but it's a policy of mine never to drink on a job... You're up top the rest of the night, Gourlay. O.K? Just keep your eyes and ears open and your mouth shut, and mind nobody comes in without the rap, rap, rap. O.K?"

The night passed slowly, and several times Gourlay dozed off. In his dreams, he was rich. He had his Bentley and lived in a big house. Bank manager Harrison fawned over him and offered not cigarettes, but cigars.

At seven in the morning, a very grubby Hector and Big Red came up from the depths. "Right lads. That's it for the day," said the Big One dusting pieces of earth from his beard. "We're all nackered. I'll see you at seven the night." His eyes fell upon Gourlay. "Oh, before you go, Gourlay... By my calculations, we're just about there, but I need you to double-check some measurements. When the bank opens at ten, could you go in and pace out the distance from the wall to the right as you enter over to the vault on the far side? You'll see it OK... The vault's just to the left of the foreign exchange wicket. O.K?"

Gourlay nodded.

Outside, he filled his lungs with the keen morning air and wandered around killing time. A little before ten, he made his way round to the bank, and to his horror, realized it was the self same bank which had turned down his request for a loan. There was no doubt about it; he could see Mr. Harrison conversing with one of the tellers.

His first instinct was one of self-preservation — just keep on walking and let Big Red and the others get on with it. On the other hand, he was five pounds to the good and there was the promise of more to come. He meandered slowly away mumbling to himself. A large yellow dog sniffed his boots. Suddenly, Gourlay's eyes lit up and he slapped his thigh, and he exclaimed, "That's it! That's it! Ye clever wee bugger ye Gourlay!" The dog backed away in alarm. "Thirty feet... Wha's tae ken the difference? Ah'll

tell then thirty feet. What's a few feet either wey amang freens?"
He looked about him in satisfaction; he had the whole day ahead
of him and money to indulge his every whim.

In Byres Road he went into a poshish restaurant for a bite
and a pot of tea and smiled blandly at the fashionably dressed
ladies about him. The waitress, a silver-haired motherly woman,
called him "Sir" and did everything in her power to please sir. He
watched as the ladies nibbled their gâteaux and Empire biscuits
and sipped their tea and was appalled to note the amount of food
left uneaten on their plates. He derived enormous satisfaction
from a glimpse he had through a gap in the screen by the kitchen
door of the waitress ravenously wolfing down a leftover Swiss
roll. He drank in the scene about him; it wasn't every day he was
privileged to witness the Kelvinside bourgeoisie at tea. He'd
heard McMinn talk of the 'pan loaf' accent of the West End of
the City, but had never noticed it before. But here, apart from the
waitress, they were all chattering away in peculiar accents and
manners that sounded to him like a roomful of Scots vainly trying
to sound like a roomful of English. There was a handful of slightly
uncomfortable looking and self-conscious husbands in attendance
'Yes dearing' and 'No dearing' left, right, and centre.

Leaving a shilling under his saucer, he left. The sun was
quite warm and he wandered about enjoying it to the full. Along
Sauchiehall Street he spent an age watching an elderly woman in
a rabbit skin coat leaning on a railing and playing a single note
on a mouth organ over and over again. He paid half a crown at
the Cosmo Cinema and saw an unutterably boring and bloody
Japanese film based on the Shakespeare's *Macbeth*.

At seven, he was back at the squalid little flat feeling fit and
rested. At nine-thirty, Hector's voice called out from the tunnel,
"Hey. We've hit a wall... We can't go any farther." Over a cup of tea
they gathered round Big Red and discussed the problem. Hector,
normally soft-spoken and taciturn, expressed the view that they

should simply forget the whole venture. But the big man would have none of it. He stood up assertively and threw the dregs of his tea onto the floor. Glaring at the faces of his grubby helpers, he exclaimed, "I'll get through the bloody wall myself!" He grabbed a shovel and disappeared down the ladder. Gourlay, Hector and McMinn looked at each other slightly shamefacedly then McMinn took the initiative. "C'moan lads, let's gie him a haun'."

They crowded into the tunnel. Big Red fumed and attacked the wall uttering such obscenities that Gourlay thought the bricks would collapse in a heap of their own accord. The big man kept hammering with the shovel until cracks began to appear. Sweating profusely, he grunted in satisfaction and handed the shovel to Gourlay. "Here... You have a go... I'm peched... You should be able to pry the bricks out..." They exchanged places.

Gourlay inserted the edge of the shovel into one of the cracks, and was about to begin levering when he stopped short. "Lissen!" From the other side of the wall came the muffled but distinguishable sounds of someone chipping the brickwork. Big Red pressed forward and placed a large ear to the wall. "Well, I'll be jiggered!" he said after a pause. "It must be that wee bugger Sandy Rutherford..." He turned to Gourlay. "How far did you say it was from the wall to the vault?"

Gourlay swallowed. "Er... Thirty feet," he replied with more confidence than he felt.

The big man looked pensive for a moment, then pulling a tape measure from his pocket, handed it to Hector. "Here, I'll hold the end. You nip on back... I've an idea." Hector crawled back along the tunnel calling out the footage as he went. "...23...24...25...26...27...28...29... That's it. 29 feet." Big Red wiped his brow on an earth-crusted hairy arm. "Christ! That's a piece of luck... Twenty nine bloody feet!" The light of battle in his eyes, he patted the soft earth above him. "We go up lads... We'll beat these bastards to the post!"

For perhaps an hour, they took turns digging and lugging the soil away until operations came to a sudden halt; a great slab of concrete barred farther progress. The big man was beside himself with excitement. "We're in luck lads! We just have to find a crack or joint, then a wee bit jelly, and Pouff! We're rolling in the lolly!" Almost frantically, he dug at the earth to reveal more and more of the concrete, and there it was — a joint. "Bring me my box of tricks," he commanded imperiously.

Hector fetched the box — a large, heavy, battered toolbox. "Right lads, watch the master at work!" He snapped his fingers. "Trowel... O.K... Gimlet... Trowel... Right... Spoon..." Soon, everything was to his satisfaction and they all retreated along the tunnel while Big Red unrolled detonation wires as he went.

Gourlay watched wide-eyed as he connected the wires to a battery and switch device. "Here, that's great Big Red!" he enthused, admiration in every word. "Wan thing though. How dae ye ken how much jelly tae pit in the crack?"

"Ha! That's skill my boy... Training, experience." He gave a great guffaw which echoed along the tunnel and caused pieces of soil to crumble down from the damp roof. "Training courtesy of his English majesty's Demolition Corps... Ye see, if that's the floor of the vault, then it'll be damn thick concrete — maybe a foot or eighteen inches — and in a case like that, you have to give it a good dose."

Gourlay nodded, and trying not to reveal his doubts, said, "But whit if it's no' the vault flerr?"

"Ach, there'll be a bigger hole than I intended, that's all. You're a worrier, Gourlay... It has to be the vault — Christ man, ye measured it yourself." Gourlay turned away looking glum and pensive, but no one seemed to notice.

"Whit aboot Sanny Rutherford?" queried McMinn. The big man curled his upper lip — or at least his fiery moustache quivered a little at the corner. "Pfff... What am I supposed to do?

Write him a letter telling him to clear off? Have faith lads! He'll get a bit shook up, and serve the wee bugger right for poaching on my territory... O.K. lads, hold tight, here we go!" He threw a switch and immediately, there was a violent explosion, the blast of which bowled them over. Big Red picked himself up. He was visibly shaken. "Holy Jesus!" he exclaimed in a hoarse whisper. "It wasn't supposed to be that big a bang... We've got to move fast... The polis'll be here in a jiffy."

They scrambled along the tunnel which was rapidly filling up with dust and smoke, and there before them, was a gaping hole through which a dazed and tattered, but otherwise uninjured Mr. Harrison had fallen. He was still seated in his now demolished and still smouldering chair, and had a silly little grin on his face. Bits of carpet, jagged pieces of concrete, and miscellaneous bric-à-brac from his office had accompanied him. Staggering about in the acrid smoke in the midst of the devastation, Sanny Rutherford and two black-faced companions shouted obscenities at each other. "Ye daft bastert! Ye must hiv unearthed a bluidy bomb!" cried one in a small plaintive voice. Coins, thousands of newly-minted glittering coins, were still cascading through the hole.

"Holy Jesus! Holy Jesus!" croaked Big Red dazed by the enormity of the explosion. McMinn was the first to regain his senses. "Let's get the fuck oot o' here!" he yelled, and scampered off up the tunnel. Hector and Big Red followed, and after scooping up as many coins as he could, Gourlay sped after them on all fours.

Later, at McMinn's, the two cronies held a post mortem, "It wis a' that Sanny Rutherford's fault," said McMinn. "If he hadna butted in wi' his stupit face, everything would've been hunky dory." Gourlay nodded sagely. McMinn looked pensive. "Aye. An' we went up at twenty-nine... That's only wan foot o' difference... Hoo the hell could we hiv endit up in a bluidy office? It's damn funny Gourlay... Ah thought the offices were at the ither end o' the bank... Here, it wis you that tellt Big Red it wis thirty feet..."

Gourlay lowered his eyes and held his peace. After brooding for a few moments, McMinn suddenly brightened. "Here, whit wis they coins? Ah didna get ony." Gourlay pulled one from his pocket and flipped it onto the table. McMinn picked it up and turned it over in his grubby fingers a few times. He peered at it and slowly spelled out "T—A—N—G—A—N—Y—I—K—A... Tanganyika!" He turned it over and on the obverse made out the words, *National Bus Company — One Token.* He made a wry face and then guffawed. "Here Gourlay, we're in luck. If we ivver get tae Tanganyika we'll can ride aboot oan the buses tae oor herts' content!" Gourlay shrugged then gave a little grin.

As far as Gourlay was concerned, that was the end of the affair. But it was not to be. Threats of recrimination darkened the air. Big Red, felt chagrined and humiliated in the eyes of his men and believed he was honour bound and obligated to re-establish himself as a great warrior and leader of men.

Sanny Rutherford, apparently little the worse for wear except that most of his hair had been burned off and there was a constant ringing in his ears, also thirsted for revenge. Slightly-built, he was obviously no match in single combat with the big man, but by all reports, he seemed to have a veritable army of cutthroats, cutpurses and ne'erdowells at his immediate beck and call, and if reports were accurate, intended to deploy them to his advantage in a face-off with Big Red.

McMinn, his ear constantly to the ground and acting as Big Red's emissary, interpreted the various signals and explained to Gourlay that a very nasty situation seemed to be brewing up. Diplomatic notes had been exchanged between the rival camps' protagonists, and the latest from the pen of the big fellow, to put it bluntly, was strongly worded. "Here's his note here." McMinn's attempt to hide his excitement failed miserably. He produced a folded sheet of cheap, lined notepaper. "Ah've tae gie this tae Sanny's man at seven... There'll be bluid spillt yet, Gourlay."

Gourlay studied the scrawled message and read it aloud:

To that fox-faced wee bauchle Sanny Rutherford.
Any more of your insults and I'll crush yer stoopit
heid like a grape.
Red.
P.S. If yer brains wis on fire, I wouldna piss in yer ear.

He read it over again and idly wondered why Big Red, who was well-spoken, wrote in patois... Perhaps an amanuensis had penned it for the big man. He shrugged, and handed the note back to McMinn.

The feud between the two men was one of long standing and had spluttered along in a desultory sort of way for years. But like two old dogs, Big Red and Sanny had done more baring of teeth, raising of hackles, and growling than actual fighting. Nevertheless, Gourlay felt that in a way he had been a catalyst in what might well turn out to be a major bloodletting between the factions. Big Red, for all his foibles and eccentricities, seemed to Gourlay to be a decentish sort and Gourlay did, after all, have five pounds that endorsed his view. He felt that he should confess; tell Big Red that he hadn't taken measurements in the bank and throw himself upon the big one's mercy. On the other hand, if his confession was to be taken amiss, who knew what the consequences might be? It was quite within the realms of possibility, Gourlay felt, that it could be his head that might end up being crushed like a grape... Another possibility occurred to him: essentially, he'd been sucked up into this mess and it wasn't really his quarrel, so why not opt out now and leave them all to get on with it? Then he remembered that it was through the good offices of his old pal McMinn that he'd become involved in the first place... Yes, upon reflection, he owed it to McMinn to act honourably. "You never tellt me ye kennt Big Red that weel afore."

"Truth is, Ah dinna. He saved ma bacon in a stushie a while back, an' since then Ah've run wee errands for him an' the like... Ah like him, but Ah'm feart o' him at the same time... Funny bloke... A wheen bricks short o' a full hod! He tellt me Ah wis nivver tae let on tae anybody that Ah kennt him."

"What for?"

"Nae idea... But he's awffy kind heartit so he is. See the money he gets in pubs eatin' light bulbs? He gies it tae puir folk."

"Get away!"

"It's true, Gourlay... Ah ken that for a fact." McMinn eyed the wag at the wall; it was just after six. The two sat in pensive silence. "Whit dae ye think will happen, Gourlay?"

Gourlay shrugged. "Ach, there'll be a fracas an'..."

"A whit?"

"Punch up, stushie, donnybrook, collieshangie... A few broken heids, a few bruised egos, an' an eternity o' ill feeling... It'll no' be the end of the world."

"But that Sanny Rutherford's a bad wee shite, Gourlay."

"You know him like?"

"Aye. Spiteful wee bugger... Big Red's mair nor a match for a dozen, but Sanny's a right wee schemer... Ye canna trust him..."

Gourlay asked to see the note again. Brow furrowed, he perused it for what to McMinn seemed an aeon. "Ha!" barked Gourlay suddenly.

"Christ! Whit a fleg! Ah'm a nervous wreck!"

"I've got it, McMinn! It's so bloody simple! Listen. You've tae meet Sanny's man at seven, an' hand ower the note?"

"Aye. So?"

"An' is Sanny's man givin' you a note?"

"Ah hae ma doots — mair nor likely, he'll ask me tae meet him in the morn, same place and same time, tae hand o'er Sanny's reply. Why?"

"Great! Here's whit we do... We simply tone down Big Red's

note... It's a' a matter of de-escalation..."

"Ah dinna follow," said McMinn screwing up his face.

"It's easy. A' the notes between them go through you, so a' we dae is tone them doon a bittie... A pound tae a penny Big Red an' Sanny will be bosom cronies by the end o' the week!"

McMinn expressed his doubts, but his pal's enthusiasm eventually won him round.

Thus it was that Big Red's original inflammatory epistle was reworded to read:

Sorry aboot yer lugs an' hair. I think I used
too much jelly on the job.
But whit were you doing down there anyway?
   Red.

The next day, McMinn received Sanny's response. Together, the pair poured over it, and after some doctoring it read:

Hearing is coming back slightly, and it looks like
Ah winna hae tae wear the wig much longer.
We were down there trying to do the shop next
to the bank.
          Sanny.
P.S. Next time, dinna use so much jelly!

As the days passed, the notes came more and more to resemble exchanges between old chums.

Good news about the wig and hearing.
Suggest we shake hands ower a dram.
I'll buy.
Aye,
   Red.

And back came the response:

O.K. Name time and place.
Suggest knives, axes, razors an'
the like are left at hame.
  Sanny.

The big man's reply, after a few alterations by the pair, read:

O.K. How about church hall at corner of
Byres Road and Great Western 7 p.m. on
Wed? Caretaker is a pal of mine.
Best wishes,
  Red.

Sanny's note culminated the transactions and had Gourlay and McMinn shaking each other by the hand:
Fine. See you then,
Truly,
  Sanny.

CHAPTER 3

And so it transpired that a motley mob of desperadoes sidled into the sacred building on a dreich mid-week night. The hall, which stood at the rear of the church, was nondescript, and identical to thousands of halls to be found up and down the land. High-ceilinged and utterly cheerless, it had been used by generations of churchgoers for their more secular pursuits: Sunday school parties, various prize givings, flower and pet shows, jumble sales and the like. Because it had a raised, curtained stage at one end, it was in demand by local amateur theatre groups. But this gathering was unique in its annals; the General Assembly itself could not have produced such a disparate flock of outlandish, kenspeckle individuals. McMinn, Gourlay, and Sanny Rutherford's factotum, a weasel-faced fellow who went by the name of Valentino and sported an outsized walrus moustache, were the first on the scene. They were greeted by the caretaker, Joseph, a burly man with wire-framed spectacles, who was much addicted to whistling syrupy melodies and waxing poetic about the love of his life — a tiny yellow canary also called Joseph. With a nod of thanks, he accepted the gratuity McMinn pressed into his hand, and, like a referee in a boxing ring, had a few words in the ears of the emissaries regarding the rules of the upcoming fixture.

"Right, gents. There'll be nae booze consumed oan the premises. Smokin's O.K. as long as youse use the receptacles provided for the butts. There's a late service in the kirk next door the nicht, so keep the noise doon in here." He gave a quick furtive glance around the room and lowered his voice.

"An' if the meenister happens by, tell him you're a drama

group haudin' auditions... Is there ony questions?"

"Do we lock up when we leave?" asked Gourlay.

"Good question, good question," said Joseph. "It's ma nicht at the Legion, but Ah'll be back roon eleven tae lock up... Er, hoo mony folk are ye expectin?"

McMinn and Valentino looked at each other.

"Aboot a dizzen," said the latter.

"Same here," agreed McMinn.

Joseph nodded, and whistling sweetly, disappeared through a door leading into the church proper.

The celebrants began to arrive in ones and twos, and after solemnly shaking hands with McMinn and Valentino, took up positions along the walls. Gourlay noted that by unspoken agreement the north wall seemed to be reserved for the Sanny Rutherford camp while the south one was Big Red's preserve. A small van arrived and two scruffs began offloading a vast supply of whisky and beer — courtesy of Sanny, it appeared. Not to be outdone in the hospitality stakes, Big Red's helpers arrived and promptly rolled half a dozen wooden kegs of ale into the no-man's-land in the middle of the hall. On top of the kegs they carefully, but ostentatiously piled several crates of whisky.

"Jesus McMinn! Just how many are expectit?" queried Gourlay.

"Well, Ah thocht mebbe a dizzen or so wad show up... But Ah had nae haun orderin' the booze..."

He glanced round the hall with apprehension.

"There's got tae be forty here already, an' it's no' even hauf six yet."

And still they came. From the twilit world of the City's seamier quarters, they came, sometimes singly, sometimes in groups. Barbers, tram drivers, barmen, men of no fixed abode, some with extensive criminal records, some not long out of prison and some still on the run, pals, followers and acquaintances of the above straggled in. As if in response to some latter day fiery cross, some had rallied nobly to what they perceived to be a sacred call, while others, motivated by somewhat less altruistic persuasions, turned up in the hopes of either a free piss up, a collieshangie, or with luck, perhaps both.

McMinn fussed about like a mother hen and desperately tried to get the members of rival factions to mingle, but to no avail; the mass of Sanny supporters along one wall glowered at the phalanx of Big Red followers ranged several deep along the opposite wall. A minority gazed misty-eyed at the stacked refreshments or fortified themselves with swigs from private stocks secreted about their persons, but a greater number in each camp grumbled to their neighbours or aired personal grievances to anyone prepared to lend an ear. An occasional catcall, curse, or obscenity would soar above the rumbling ranks to the vaulted ceiling. In the annexed church where God-fearing people were congregating, those blessed with acuity of hearing were disturbed by the ghostly and hellish imprecations and blasphemies which floated down and immediately resolved to live more chastely. The murmuring and subdued war cries increased in frequency, urgency and volume as the appointed hour approached. Gourlay, wandering in the vicinity of the refreshments, felt the mounting sound resembled a volcano about to erupt. He could see Valentino desperately wrestling with a diminutive man in a paper hat who appeared to be trying to rip the former's glorious moustaches off his face. Of McMinn there was no sign. He glanced at the clock on the proscenium — a few minutes shy of seven o'clock — and began to ponder what effect the entrance of the two leaders would have on the assembly. If they were perceived to be other than equals, he felt that the result could be calamitous... They just had to make an entrance together and be seen to be on the best of terms. But it could not be left to chance...

He hurried for the exit and pushed his way through the flow

of men coming in. On the pathway surrounded by a little knot of sycophants was an extraordinary figure; Big Red, towering above everyone, was kitted out in a tiny kilt. Stifling the urge to laugh, Gourlay went up to him.

"Gourlay isn't it?" boomed the giant.

"Aye. Can I have a word wi' you in private like?"

"Surely."

They stepped to one side.

"What's the problem Gourlay?"

Gourlay took a deep breath.

"Mebbe you thought a few folk would turn up the nicht, but there must be a coupla hundred packed in the hall therr. From a' the rumblings, my guess is that we're headed for a right stushie... It's like twa armies facing wan anither and waitin' for the orders tae charge..."

The kilted Goliath studied the smaller man for a moment.

"Oh dinna fash yersel Gourlay... No need tae worry. It's all in hand. I knew a crowd would turn up — that's why I sent so much booze. An' Sanny's well aware of the dangers. We had a brief word together earlier in the day and I have his word that his lot winna be the first to start any trouble..."

He placed a great hand on Gourlay's shoulder.

"But thanks anyway, Gourlay — I like a man that's thinking and alert. Now away you inside and enjoy yourself. Keep me posted on any developments."

He stalked off.

Whatever else he is, he's no fool, Gourlay thought.

Until then he'd looked upon the giant as an eccentric but simple-minded fellow. Now he realized that under the clownish mop of red hair lurked a canny mind. As he turned to head back into the hall a slight commotion at the end of the lane caught his eye; Sanny Rutherford and his bodyguards were descending from a battered blue van. Gourlay smiled at the incongruity of the two leaders — the huge man in the ridiculous mini kilt dominating the smaller, stooping figure. Apart from the fire-damaged bald patches, Sanny's pate sprouted a bristly stubble which served to enhance his already villainous appearance. His quick eyes missed nothing. Solemnly, the two shook hands.

"Aye aye Red," said Sanny laconically giving a wan smile.

"Nice to see you, Sanny... My man here tells me trouble's brewing in the hall."

"Trouble?"

"Aye. Apparently, they've lined up in two camps..."

"Nae problem. As long as we're seen tae be freens, there'll be nae trouble... C'moan, let's go in."

As they passed him, Big Red nodded in recognition and Gourlay felt proud.

As the two entered the hall, the hubbub died down and slowly a great roar gathered in intensity and welled up making the very rafters dirl. Above the racket sounded the thin squeal of an out of tune set of bagpipes. McMinn materialised and joined Valentino and the small party of henchmen and other courtiers as they made their way past the heaped refreshments and mounted the steps leading to the stage. The leaders went up together, and no sooner had they set foot on the platform then the curtain swung open and some spotlights came on revealing a nativity type scene complete with tatty-looking life-size papier mâché figures — the remnants of a recently-staged children's playlet mounted by the Kelvinside Ladies Ecumenical Strolling Players.

Centre stage was a long table and some chairs. When the platform party had arranged itself round the table, Big Red at one end, Sanny at the other, they waited till the roar had diminished to a few catcalls, cheers, oaths and hurled obscenities then took their seats. The big man and the small eyed one another, glanced from time to time at the assembled multitude, and then eyed one another again.

"You first," said Big Red in a hoarse whisper. "Say a few words..."

Sanny, who obviously had, as they say, 'a few drinks taken,' flicked his bloodshot eyes round the table. "Naw. You go first, Red."

Whether it was Sanny's bashfulness, innate sense of caution, a ruse, or observance of some obscure protocol, Big Red wasn't sure, but deciding that someone had to say something before the mob grew unruly again, he got to his feet. His chair fell back with a crash. He moved to the front of the table, paused, inclined his shaggy head toward Sanny, and cleared his throat.

"Friends... Friends..."

He raised his hands for an already existing silence. "We're a' friends here... Now, we've some of us enjoyed a rivalry for a while, but I'd like to make one thing clear: Sanny an' me might have had differences of opinion from time to time, but we're friends now for a' that."

He turned to Sanny.

"Right, Sanny?"

With much scraping of feet and a flurry of movement, the smaller man rose somewhat unsteadily to his feet and joined Big Red on the apron. The two stood in awkward silence for a long moment and the tension seemed to be enhanced by the quiet.

Gourlay, sitting beside a pensive looking McMinn, idly wondered how Mark Antony would have adjusted his famous oration to fit the needs of the present situation. Sanny ran his fingers over the burnt wasteland of his cranium, coughed lightly a couple of times, and with a last glance at his companion, began to speak. His voice was thin, even, tremulous, but easily carried to all corners of the room. "Aye. We're a' freens here... Even brithers... But even brithers fa' oot from time tae time, but they're brithers just the same..."

He ran a baleful eye over the ranks as if daring anyone to

challenge his words, but there was no response save for an inadvertent squawk from the bagpipes followed by a titter. Faint notes from the organ in the church next door wafted in and accompanied Sanny's words.

"Aye! So wi' ma brither's approval," and here he turned to Big Red who nodded, "we'll tak' a cup o' kindness an'..."

He never got to finish; the hall burst into life as everyone tried to be first in the queue for refreshments. A seething mass of bodies jostled for position, and fists, feet, elbows and even teeth came into play as men from both factions met and contested. A cask of beer, spigot wrenched out, jetted its contents over the combatants and Gourlay watched slack-jawed as a wiry little fellow with a flat nose downed the best part of a quart of whisky without removing the bottle from his lips. The din was ear-popping, and invective and empty beer bottles were soon being flung about with equal abandon. The platform party called in vain for restraint, but even Big Red's masterful bellowing was swallowed in the general hubbub. Gourlay clutched McMinn's arm.

"Christ, McMinn, if they rin oot o' booze, there'll be murder done... C'moan, McMinn, let's get the hell oot o' here while the gaun's good!"

"Take it easy, Gourlay. They'd have tae get past Big Red first... It's O.K. Have faith."

"Well, if you say so," said Gourlay doubtfully. "But just in case we need tae skedaddle, Ah noticed there's an emergency exit ahint the plaster cuddy... Saw it when we were settin' up the table an' that."

"Aye, O.K. Dinna fash yersel'... You're a worrywart Gourlay."

Gradually, as the liquor and beer reached the cracked lips and parched throats of those dying of thirst at the rear of the crush, the noise abated somewhat and a modicum of order prevailed once more. A bottle was passed up to the party on stage and speedily made the rounds.

JAMES FINDLAY SLEIGH

"If there's any booze left down there," roared Big Red, "Let's drink a toast..."

McMinn took a quick pull on the bottle and handed it across the table. "To friendship!" shouted the big man. He took an unsparing swig and passed the bottle to Sanny who raised it high and cried in an adenoidal voice, "Tae absent freens!"

Yells of "Friendship!" and "Absent Freens!" filled the hall. Sanny stretched up until he was almost on tiptoe and put his hands on the big one's shoulder. He put the bottle to his lips, gulped a couple of times, and handed the nearly empty bottle to the big man. Then, for no particular reason, someone on the floor called out "Scotland!" in a raspy voice, and like wildfire, the refrain was picked up by a hundred lubricated throats. A rhythmic chant and stomping — "Scot-land!" thump, thump, thump, "Scot-land!" — shook the building while cries of "Speech! Speech!" punctuated the racket. There was the sound of breaking glass followed by a deep rumbling sound as a massive wooden barrel cut a swath through the multitude and crashed against the stage.

"There's gaun tae be mayhem yet McMinn!" croaked Gourlay half rising from his chair.

"Ach, wheest Gourlay; this is gettin' interestin'... If this gets oot o' hand, we'll can be oot o' here in a jiffy..."

"Speech! Speech!" squawked a score of voices as the chanting and thumping continued. A burly man close to the stage had a bottle broken on his head, and Gourlay glimpsed a runt of a fellow crash his knee into the groin of a man wearing a canary yellow suit. But it was all in good fun; a sense of camaraderie still seemed to prevail. A maudlin sense of patriotism was very much in evidence. At a slight loss for words, and like a jazz musician vamping until the melody came round again, Big Red reached back into the dark recesses of his mind, and groping there awhile, came up with some half-remembered line from his schooldays. In a loud but monotonous and sepulchral voice he intoned:

"As long as a hundred of us remain alive we will never consent to subject ourselves to the domination of the English..."

Great huzzahs and cries of "Down with the English!" greeted his words. The giant roared, slapped Sanny on the back with exuberance which almost knocked him off the stage, downed the last of the whisky, and with a flourish and mighty yell, tossed the empty bottle high into the air. Whether the crowd thought he'd struck Sanny or whether people took the thrown bottle as some kind of ritualistic gauntlet was academic. But the resulting pandemonium was concrete enough. Sporadic fighting broke out in earnest while a whole gamut of assorted cries rang out: "Remember Bannockburn!... à Bruce!... The Alamo!... Fuck the Pope!... Fuck the English!..." and a lone voice crying in a hysterical falsetto, "Fuck everybody!" A shower of empty bottles and other assorted missiles clattered onto the stage. A plaster of Paris sheep had its head knocked off, and Valentino, crossing himself quickly, tossed what looked vaguely like the remains of a papier mâché donkey into the wave of men on the floor below. Something resembling a cricket ball with nails hammered into it hit Sanny Rutherford square in the face. He gave a shriek, put his hands to his bloody face, and toppled off the apron.

From a crouching position under the table Gourlay could see a great pair of hairy legs framed against a seething mass of bodies locked in mortal combat. With great kicks and flailing arms, the big man was roaring for order and repeatedly repelling those foolish enough to attempt to clamber on to the stage. One of Sanny's henchmen at the rear of the stage threw a papier mâché ox right over Big Red's head and into the crowd below where it was immediately trampled into fragments.

The lone piper screwed his pipes and played *Scotland the Brave* until someone slashed his bag with what Gourlay thought looked mightily like a bayonet. He glanced behind him. Valentino, eyes tightly closed, moustaches bristling, was about to launch the infant Jesus into the maëlstrom. But of McMinn there was no sign. Gourlay crawled to the front of the table, and peering over the edge of the stage he could see Sanny lying in a crumpled heap among the barrel staves. Big Red, who had leapt off the stage with a Tarzan-like yell, was now kiltless, his great white backside a beacon. He was roaring like a bullock whilst felling adversaries left, right and centre. A seraph with a beatific smile flew over the table and disintegrated when its flight was impeded by a little knot of warriors who were performing mayhem on all and sundry.

The door at the rear of the hall opened and caretaker Joseph stepped in followed by a boyish-faced minister. The "Fuck the English!" cry was taken up again, and howling like banshees, a pack of men, the big man in their midst, bowled over the astonished clergyman and stormed into the church. The hall grew quieter as more and more of the battlers headed through the doorway or vanished through the exit doors into the night. Gourlay heard the sound of glass breaking, shouting, then, topping the din, the frantic and irregular pealing of the church bell.

As the last of the stragglers disappeared, he surveyed the devastation. A score of men, *hors de combat*, but still more or less alive, lay on the beery, glass-scattered floor moaning and nursing their various injuries. A radiator lay at a crazy angle, water gushing out, and in a corner sat the dazed piper crooning over his wounded pipes. Gourlay crawled out from under the table, shook some fragments of glass from his hair, and with a last glance around, slipped off through the exit door at the rear of the stage.

Half way down Byres Road, he could still hear the bell, and, more faintly, the continuing sounds of destruction. After the noise and the smells of the hall, the night air was a tonic and he breathed it in gratefully.

"God! What a night! Where the hell did McMinn go? There'll be repercussions for this night's devilry," he mused, and pursing his lips, loped off to spend the night at McMinn's, which was closer to hand than his own place on Renfrew Street. A police car, lights flashing and horn blaring, roared past. He continued on his way whistling tunelessly and idly thinking that he must be about the only one, apart from McMinn perhaps, to have survived the night unscathed, when a giant dervish whirled by — Big Red! Cutting a peculiar figure in a purloined man's jacket, the sleeves knotted around his waist, scantily covering his nether parts, the powerful hairy legs were working like pistons. By the time Gourlay had collected his wits, the figure had vanished into the murk.

"Funny...Naebody's after him...Where the hell's he gaun in such a hurry?" He shrugged. "Ach, tae hell wi' the lot o' them."

Feeling peckish, he treated himself to a fish supper and a bottle of Irn Bru. He shook his head violently in an attempt to get rid of the donging sound at the back of his skull, but the net result was that a few slivers of glass fell into his chips. "Ach, to hell wi' the lot o' them," he mumbled, "bunch o' desperadoes."

McMinn was in his bed when he arrived some time later. "What are ye doin' in yer pit, an' wi' yer claes oan, McMinn?"

His crony stared at him. "Ah'm siek."

"Sick?"

"Sick tae death wi' a' the shenanigans. Christ man, Ah could've goat masel' killt... They're a bunch o' wild fuckin' animals so they are. Who needs it, Gourlay..? Haw, are you alright?"

"Hair's fu' o' broken gless. But Ah'm OK. Best place in a blitz is under a table..."

"Blitz is right! Fuck, hauf a dizzen German bombs wouldna hiv done as muckle damage as thon mob." He shook his head sadly.

Gourlay proffered the bottle. "Here McMinn — hae a swig."

"No thanks."

"Comin' doon Byres Road, Big Red passed me at a great rate o' knots."

"He wis here five meenits syne."

"What for?"

"Ach, he wanted tae borrow a perr o' breeks tae cover his hurdies. Said he couldna find his kilt..."

"Here, Ah will hae a swig..."

Gourlay handed him the bottle.

"Onywey, he coudna get intae ma breeks, so he took a sheet an' happit himsel' up in it...Bluidy daft if you ask me. Said if the polis stopped him he'd say he wis oan his way tae a toga party... Bluidy daft. Ran off mumblin' somethin' aboot an army an' a manifesto or somethin'..."

"An army?"

"Aye. He wis rantin' oan aboot a common enemy an' ha'en a sense o' focus or somethin'." McMinn tapped his forehead meaningfully. "The lights are oan, but naebody's hame... Here, did that mob break intae the kirk?"

"Aye. They a' left the hall an' went ragin' intae the church... The bell wis clangin' an'..."

"Ha! He wis tellin' me that the congregation took tae its heels...Damnable so it is, Gourlay...Auld codgers and auld biddies runnin' for their lives... He said he made a great speech frae the poopit an' got Hector tae ring the bell. Said it wis a proclamation... 'A nation reborn,' he said... An' look at ma bluidy table! The bugger broke it wi' his nieve. He wis rantin' oan aboot the Sassenachs an' got that worked up he broke the edge o' ma table...That wis ma mither's table..." he said mournfully.

"Wi' his fist?"

"Aye...Whaur will it end, Gourlay? A' this fechtin'?"

"Christ knows."

Gourlay sipped the last of his Irn Bru reflectively. "Who knows, McMinn?"

"So Big Red just took off in his sheet?"

"In *ma* sheet," corrected McMinn. "Aye. Shoutin' an' bawlin' a' the way doon the sterrs...Yodellin' something about staging a happening."

"A happening?"

"A happening, aye. Ma heid's still bizzin', Gourlay... He wis rantin' an ravin, thumpin' the table an' loupin' aboot as if he wis wud."

"Wud?"

"Whit wey are ye aye repeatin' me?" he growled McMinn, a slight edge to his voice. "Wud... Mad... Dae ye no' speak plain English?"

"Sorry, McMinn," responded Gourlay trying to hide a smile.

"A happening — that's what he said. He said it wis important that he demonstrate — that wis the word, demonstrate — that he wis capable of commanding the army."

"What army is he talking about, McMinn? Surely no' that clanjamfrie at the hall the nicht?"

"The same."

"Did he say what the happening was to be?"

"Naw... Ah've tellt ye a' Ah ken... Now, if yer bidin', could we mebbe get some shuteye?"

Gourlay removed his boots and generally prepared himself for a night's sleep at the foot of his friend's bed.

"Hey, McMinn..."

"Whit noo?" grumbled a voice muffled by several layers of blankets.

"Since when did ye take up the habit o' sleepin' wi' yer boots on?"

McMinn sat up, a pained expression on his angular face.

"Whit Ah dae in ma ain scratcher is ma ain business... But for yer files, Ah'm keepin' ma claes oan because Ah'm feelin' insecure... Gin that big lummock comes back the nicht, Ah want to be ready tae make a bolt for it. An' Second..." He held up two grubby fingers. "Second, Ah'm wearin' ma buits because Ah'm still breakin' them in... An' third, will ye turn off that fuckin' light an' get intae the bed!"

Gourlay did not sleep well. He was tormented by fragmentary dreams: A vast and ragged army assaulted Westminster... A half-naked Goliath hurled exploding statues of John Knox into the ranks of the enemy, and rows of bowler-hatted Englishmen, upper lips very stiff, wielded tightly-furled umbrellas to ward off the charging hordes... To add to his discomfort, McMinn would give a low moan from time to time and his legs would jerk spasmodically giving Gourlay a painful boot in the ribs...

CHAPTER 4

For Gourlay and McMinn the days drifted by in a desultory sort of way. In the normal course of events they'd have gone about their respective businesses with their paths crossing from time to time, but for the moment they both felt it would be wise to lie low until the incidents at the church blew over and were reduced to a few notations in a police jotter. Both were alert to the possibility that the various constables on patrol would be giving a second glance to anyone they felt might have any knowledge of the fracas. For the most part, the pair passed the time, occasionally joking and occasionally spatting, in McMinn's little flat. Happily, McMinn's sour-faced little dumpling of a landlady was spending her days, and some of her nights, nursing a sick relative in Paisley, so the pair cavorted around with a greater than usual sense of freedom. They discussed Big Red's cryptic remarks about a manifesto, a happening, an army, but could come to no consensus as to what it all might mean. McMinn remained unshakable in his belief that the big man was "wud," while Gourlay inclined to the theory that the hairy one had a master plan and that they'd soon be privy to it. "Dinna forget," he said, "they thought Joan of Arc was nuts too."

"So what?"

"Well, imagine for a moment that mebbe, just mebbe, the folk we think are nuts have insights denied to us who have sound minds..."

McMinn threw his head back and gave a loud barking laugh. "Folk are either crazy or they're no' crazy. That's a' there is to it."

Slightly miffed, Gourlay held his peace.

On the afternoon of the third day of his sojourn with McMinn,

Gourlay went out. Affecting a distinct limp by way of a disguise, he was wending his way along when he suddenly came face to face with a beefy policeman.

"Just a minute," said the constable.

"Who me?"

"What's the matter wi' your leg?"

"Ah've got a limp."

"I can see that," said the policeman phlegmatically. "Hurt it at that riot last Friday did you?"

Gourlay assumed his most guileless expression. "Riot? What riot? Ah wis born wi' a limp."

"Hmmph. Well, on your way..."

Happy to escape, he distanced himself from the officer as speedily as his pretended affliction would decently allow. He could feel the policeman's eyes on his back. Then came a yell, "Hey you! Stop!" He didn't. Using both legs to wonderful effect, he sprinted off up a side street with the policeman's cries and clattering boots on the cobblestones fading with every step. Safely away, he stopped to regain his wind. Bent over, his hands grasping an iron railing for support, he gulped in the brisk air and suddenly realized why the bobby had had second thoughts about him. "Fuck! Ah wis draggin' ma left leg when he stopped me, but hirpled awa' with the right... Oh, ye daft wee bugger Gourlay..." He shook his head.

He spent a tolerable afternoon whiling away the time in conversation with Wee Jummock, the attendant at the palatial gentlemen's toilet deep in the bowels of the earth below Charing Cross. Diminutive, hump-backed, and with a deathly pallor which matched the glazed tiles of his charge, he was inordinately proud of his little empire. His only view of the outside world was limited to the shadowy feet that trudged above his head over the tiny glass grillwork that permitted a modicum of daylight to filter down. But that bothered him not a whit. So protective was he of his gleaming aseptic tile, brass and oak world that he'd been known to launch himself like a tiger upon any fellow foolish enough to throw a cigarette end into a urinal. "Dae that again, friend," he'd hiss in his tinny voice, "an' Ah'll be roon tae your place tae piss in yer ashtray!"

His other great passion was his unbounded admiration for the Russian writer, Anton Tchehov. It seems that he'd once met an elderly lady who had attended school with the writer's sister, and infected by her boundless enthusiasm for the author, from that time on he'd been filled with an unquenchable thirst for anything connected with Tchehov's life and works. "You know, Gourlay," said the little man warming to his subject, "wan day Gorky went tae visit him an' keeked ower the hedge in the garden, guess whit he saw Tchehov daen?" Gourlay shook his head. "He wis chasin' sunbeams, tryin' tae catch them in his hat, an' when he caught wan he'd jam the hat doon on his heid an' smile... Noo whit dae ye think o' that eh?" And the little hunchback would smile joyfully at the recollection.

Darkness was falling as Gourlay cautiously made his way back to McMinn's. At the foot of the stair leading up to the flat he bumped into his pal. After exchanging pleasantries, they mounted the steps together. Gourlay thought he detected something that suggested suppressed excitement in his crony's demeanour. As McMinn clomped ahead of him he called out, "For Goad's sake McMinn, no sae fast... Ah'm fair peched, forjeskit... How is it that a' ma friends bide in attics?" he whined.

"That's no' true... Daft Harry lives in a basement... An' so does Jessie, wink wink!"

"Just as weel...Ah'd be too nackered tae lift a leg if she lived up as mony stairs as you," replied Gourlay sourly. "An' here, leave my love life out of it if you please."

On the top landing McMinn pounded violently on the door.

"Whit's wrang?" asked Gourlay. "Forgotten yer key?"

"Naw. Just want tae check the battleaxe is no' in." No landlady appeared despite McMinn's spirited assault on the door. They went in and McMinn closed the door behind him and began to yell a string of terrifying imprecations at the top of his lungs. As Gourlay studied his pal in goggle-eyed amazement, obscenities and bawled vilification, all addressed to the absent landlady, fell easily from McMinn's lips.

"Jesus Christ McMinn! Whit's the gemme?"

"Daft auld bag," husked McMinn quite enervated by his exertions. She's aye gi'en me a hard time, so Ah wait till she's oot an' get ma ain back... It's thera... therapeutic."

His ritual catharsis completed, he negotiated yet another flight of stairs with Gourlay at his heels and entered his little room. He swaggered over to a large sheet-draped object and beamed. "Guess whit this is?"

Gourlay rubbed his chin. "Ah've nae idea... Looks like a bluidy motorbike," he guffawed.

"It is! It is! How the hell did ye know? Look!" And McMinn swept the sheet away with the panache of a conjurer to reveal an ancient girder-forked monster of a motorcycle. A little pool of black oil had seeped into the ragged carpet underneath the machine. Excited as a schoolboy, McMinn proudly straddled the brute, pulled a lever here and there, and kicked it into life. The window panes rattled and Gourlay almost fainted at the unearthly roar of the engine and pungent white smoke which billowed out of the battered exhaust pipes. After revving the bike a few times McMinn switched it off and sat there grinning from ear to ear. "We'll, what do you think?"

"Think? Ah think you're oot o' yer fuckin' skull, that's whit Ah think," spluttered Gourlay. "Open the windae afore we're arsefixiated... Whit in the name o' the wee man possessed ye tae bring it up here?" he grumbled. "Where did ye get it?" He wiped his streaming eyes with his coat sleeve. McMinn dismounted, ambled over and whispered conspiratorially, "It's stole... Ah couldna leave it oan the street could I?"

"How the hell did ye get it up the stairs?"

"Ah got haud o' a bunch o' students an' tellt them it wis a prank — a practical joke against a pal. They thought it was such a 'wizard whiz' as they cried it, that they dragged it up nae bother."

Gourlay shook his head incredulously. "I still think you're aff yer heid...What the hell are you going to dae wi' it?

"Ah thought you'd never ask. Ah'm gaun tae the Hielans oan it... A tour o' the Hebrides. Ye fancy it, Gourlay? We can lie low for a whilie an' let Big Red an' the rest o' them get oan wi' it... What do you say?"

With his recent run in with the law still fresh in mind, it took Gourlay only a moment's reflection to decide that a spell away from the City was a grand idea. Swept along by McMinn's enthusiasm, he soon became as excited with the prospect of the trip as his crony. They decided to leave in the small hours of the morning. With luck, the landlady would not have returned, and between them they could easily manhandle the machine down the many steps to the street on their own. There were, of course, minor snags such as the fact that McMinn's only experience as a motorcyclist would be limited to practice sessions performed in the room. But McMinn was undaunted. With the bike on its stand, he assured Gourlay, and rear wheel spinning, it would be almost the same thing as being on the open road. And so, with much coughing, spluttering, and dabbing of watering eyes, he practised gear changes, braking, and signalling until, as he put it, "Ah'm ready tae face the rush hour on Jamaica Bridge." Another little snag emerged; Gourlay pointed out that the bike had no lights. Again, McMinn put his chum's mind at ease by explaining that two torches, one showing a white light, the other a red, would meet the legal requirements of the Road Traffic Act and satisfy the most discerning of policemen. And as for the licence and insurance, well Gourlay needn't trouble himself on that account either:

"Ye dinna need either till a polisman stops you," he explained with disarming logic. "And," he added with pride, "see that tax disc? Well, it's no' a tax disc — it's a label from a Guinness bottle! Ye'd never tell, wad ye?" His chest expanded proudly.

Gourlay smiled. "Well, well. And haven't you been the busy little bugger, eh?"

A little after three in the morning, the two intrepid madmen were rolling along the Great Western Road.

"Ah canna haud baith o' thae torches McMinn!" shouted Gourlay above the roar of the bike. "Ah need a haun' free tae haud oan wi'!"

"Ach, wance we're oot the City we'll no need the red yin," bawled McMinn.

The machine wobbled precariously on the tram lines.

"Jesus McMinn! I'm nearly off... Ah need tae hing oan... What'll I do wi' the red yin?"

"Stick it up yer bahookie," roared McMinn.

"Verra funny."

"Naw. Ah'm serious... Stick it under yer arse... Sit oan it!" yelled McMinn topping the clatter of the engine and rush of wind.

His arms round his chum's waist, Gourlay felt more secure. For the first time he began to notice how cold it was; the blast was making his eyes stream. He was full of admiration for McMinn's prowess as a motorcyclist. Getting started had been a problem, but now they were mobile, he was handling the machine as if he'd been born to it. It was many years since Gourlay had been out of the City and already he could almost smell the heather, the reek of peak smoke, and the tangle of seaweed on the rocky beaches.

The streets, glistening damply under the street lamps, were quiet. The only policeman they saw never gave them so much as a second glance as they roared by. Suddenly, the road grew dark; they were beyond the City boundary now and no street lamps shone. McMinn slowed the bike to a walking pace and cursed. The not unpleasant smell of hot engine oil reached Gourlay's nose. "Whit's up?"

"Ah canna bluidy well see, that's whit's up," whined McMinn. Gourlay peered over his pal's shoulder into the darkness.

"Hey, McMinn, you can make oot the road by the white line doon the middle!"

McMinn edged the bike to the middle of the road, and sure enough, the long dashes of the broken white line rolled reassuringly beneath them. "You're a genius, Gourlay!"

They began to pick up speed again.

"Hey McMinn, dae ye ken the 'Road tae the Isles'"?

"Aye. We're on it!"

"Naw. The song..."

McMinn's strident baritone aided by Gourlay's creaky tenor combined to create an imperfect but lusty duet which came to a faltering end when the pair ran out of words.

"Here, whit's the tango o' the isles onywey McMinn?"

"Five o' clock in the morning an' you want tae know whit the tangle o' the isles is! Questions, questions, aye questions... Here, have you got a fag on ye?"

"Naw."

"Damn. Ah'm fair gaspin'."

They were sweeping round a bendy road which runs round the shores of Loch Lomond. In the predawn light Gourlay made out a vast sheet of water to his right. As the light gradually increased, the water's surface changed from a deep purplish colour to a dull pewter. They were negotiating a bend when suddenly McMinn gave a shriek. Gourlay, his nose buried in his friend's back, saw nothing. He heard the squeal of a heavy vehicle's brakes and then felt the bike swerve violently, mount the verge, and careen down a bank into the chilly waters of the loch where the engine stalled and the machine stopped in a foot or so of water. There was a deathly silence but for the lapping of the waves on the bank.

"Are you alright Gourlay?" McMinn's voice was subdued.

"Aye... Fuck! Ah'm wet through and chittern wi' cauld... An' the sandwiches will be soaked... Whit the hell happened?"

"A lorry... Ah think it went off the road oan the ither side... Here, sees a haun' wi' the bike."

After much foul language and splashing about, they managed to lug the motorcycle and their gear up the bank and onto the road. The dark outline of a lorry could be discerned on the far side. They found the driver unconscious in his seat.

"Is he deid?" queried McMinn in a small voice.

"Naw. Just a dunt on the heid... He'll be O.K... Here. I wonder whit he's carrying?"

The rear doors were secured by an outsized brass padlock, but after a search, they found the key in the driver's jacket pocket. They stood in gaping awe at the sight of the lorry's contents; cardboard boxes of cigarettes were piled to the roof. Gourlay was the first to find his tongue. "Jesus! Fags! Oh, Jesus!" he croaked.

"It's an Act of God," husked McMinn reverentially.

"An' Ah wis tellt He died in 1916... But it's an Act of God right enough..."

"Whit is?"

"The fags... We were meant tae get them... Or some o' them at ony rate." Their wet clothes for the moment forgotten, they sat down on the grass verge to consider what to do about this grand act of divine benevolence.

"Let's take the whole bluidy lorry load," proposed McMinn.

"Dinna be daft... We'd never get away with it..."

A lone duck winged its way across the shining water. Gourlay rubbed his chin pensively. "Here, do you think we can get the bike started again?"

"Mebbe. We'd have to dry it oot first... Why?"

"Right then. That's settled... We'll just nick a box — it'll never be missed — an' be on our way."

"Naw," said McMinn soberly. "It's no good. Sooner or later, sonny boy in the cab there will wake up, report the accident, an' gin we're no' here it'll be like a hit an' run... An' the polis everywhere wad be efter us... Naw, it's no' good..."

There was a pause while Gourlay digested his friend's words. "O.K. McMinn, tell ye what. Let's nick a box, get the bike started an' head for home."

"Hame?"

"Aye. The polis would naturally assume we'd keep on going north, an' by the time they figure it oot, we'd be home... Just think, dry claes, a warm pit, an' as mony fags as we can smoke!"

Gourlay's seductive oratory shattered the last bastions of McMinn's reservations, and soon, the bike running again and the steely light of dawn silhouetting the dark hills around them, they were rolling towards Glasgow complete with a box of cigarettes.

"Hey Gourlay!" called McMinn over his shoulder.

"What?"

"How's about a fag?"

"You'll have to stop the machine then... Ah canna fiddle with the box an' hing oan at the same time."

McMinn brought the bike to a spluttering halt, and Gourlay carefully opened the carton. "Hey!"

"What's up?"

"There's nae fags... Feels like tools an' a jaiket or something..."

"Nae fags!" cried McMinn, despair in his voice. "Let's see."

He groped in the box, and sure enough, it contained only some clothing and some tools. "Aw Jesus!"

Gourlay shook his head in disbelief. "How dae ye explain that, McMinn?"

"It's a bluidy mystery." He shook his head sadly. Sitting astride the motorcycle in the cold morning light, his damp clothes sticking uncomfortably to his cold skin and desperate for a smoke, there was to Gourlay's mind only one logical thing to do. "That settles it; let's go back and pinch the whole lorry load."

"Ach, dinna be daft..."

"But why no'?"

"For Goad's sake!" whined McMinn in exasperation. "Even if the driver's still unconscious, an' Ah said *if*, if he's still oot, the polis wad be oan tae us in a jiffy... We'd never get away wi' it."

Gourlay gave a sigh of resignation. "Aye. Maybe you're right... Seems a bloody shame but..."

McMinn glanced round at his friend. "Tell ye whit. We can go back an' get oorsels a full box as a sort of consolation."

Gourlay brightened. "Great! Now you're talkin'!"

"O.K. Hing oan..."

"Here, whit aboot this box?"

"We'll take it back... Ah dinna mind being done for a carton o' fags, but Ah'd bluidy hate masel' if Ah wis done for a box fu' o' auld claes!" He kicked the machine into life, turned it round, and headed northwards again.

Back at the lorry, McMinn examined the driver while Gourlay replaced the box. "How is he McMinn?"

"Seems O.K. He's still breathin' ony road."

From his perch on the running board Gourlay leaned forward and studied the ashen-faced driver. "You know McMinn, this poor bugger needs medical attention."

"You mean a doctor?"

"Naw. A bluidy plumber, ye eejot! Lissen, we canna take him oan the bike, but suppose we were tae drive him to a doctor in the lorry... Think aboot it... Take yer time..."

After a moment's cogitation, a sly smile spread across McMinn's craggy face and he slapped his fist on his forehead. "Ye clever wee shite ye Gourlay! Of course! If we get stopped by the polis, nae bother... We wis just takin' him tae the nearest doctor... An if we're no stopped," he gulped in excitement, "If we're no' stopped, then a' the bluidy fags are oors!"

Chortling and guffawing at their cleverness, they hid the motorcycle in a clump of bushes by the roadside.

"O.K. Gourlay. See if ye can make the driver comfortable — prop him up on the passenger's side. Here, sees a haun'..." Gourlay studied the driver in the silvery light. A large lump on the forehead and some dried blood on his nose seemed to be the only evidence of his recent argument with the windscreen. He gave a groan as Gourlay moved him into an upright position. "He'll be O.K... Open the window a bit — fresh air will do him good... Here McMinn, can you drive this machine?"

"Ah've done enough drivin' for wan night — it's your turn."

The lorry started easily, and after a few crunching noises from the gearbox it lurched forwards over the grass verge with a bump which caused the injured man to groan again. "We're off!" grinned Gourlay. "Hing oan tae yer ovaries, McMinn!"

Above the hills, a light blue tint to the sky held promise of a glorious day. McMinn cleared his throat. "Here Gourlay, what do we do if the polis stop us?"

"They've nae reason tae stop us. But if they do, let me do the talking... We'll stick to the truth, or pretty close to it. If you're asked a question, just let on you got a dunt when the bike left the road. The polis are smart, see — that's how they catch folk out — they ask wan fellow a question then take the other aside an' ask him the same question. They catch them out because he hasna heard what his pal has said an' gives a different answer. See?"

Slightly baffled, McMinn nodded.

Gourlay whistled tunelessly through his teeth as he carefully negotiated the bends in the road. They had covered some four or five miles when he suddenly stopped whistling. "Jesus!"

"Whit?"

"Look!"

A few hundred yards ahead, standing in the middle of

the road, was a policeman. Even from a distance, he appeared dishevelled and grubby, and his uniform was ill-fitting, but he was still imposing. The lorry ground to a jerky halt. "Good morning constable," Gourlay called brightly.

"*Sergeant* to you!"

"Sergeant."

"Right. Into the lay-by here," he ordered. "And switch off the engine."

Dutifully, Gourlay parked on the spot indicated and the sergeant ambled over. "I've been expecting you," he said grimly with the merest hint of smugness in his voice and drew a little notebook from his tunic pocket. "I suppose you know the penalty for theft on this scale my lad?"

"Theft?"

"Mebbe naebody tellt ye that you canna go stealin' a whole lorry load of cigarettes on the King's highway?" said the policeman with heavy sarcasm. Gourlay's mind raced... Stolen! The only possible explanation was that they were in a stolen lorry, and the man with the bump on his head was a thief! Fast talking with full editorial licence was called for...The sergeant listened to his story in a bored sort of way, glanced at the injured man, asked a question from time to time, and scribbled hieroglyphs into his notebook which Gourlay noticed seemed to contain the names of racehorses and their betting odds.

"You say you were on a motorbike going north?"

"Aye."

"How long ago would that be?"

"Er, mebbe an hour or so ago."

"Did you have your lights on?"

"Emm... Not exactly... You see we had a spot of bother wi' them, and... They fused, so we were using a torch an'..."

"Hmmph. An' which one of you is the singer?"

"Singer?

"Aye. I've been in the bushes here since three this morning waiting for this lorry to turn up... I had a hunch it would be taken south... I was right, wasn't I?" remarked the policeman with a hint of smugnesss in his voice. "I heard the bike pass wi' someone singing like a lintie." He placed his notebook and his pencil back in his pocket. "O.K. Out you get... On your way."

Gourlay and McMinn looked at one another. They didn't have the cigarettes, but, amazingly, it seemed as if they might be off the hook. They climbed out of the lorry.

"Er, sergeant," began Gourlay deferentially, "you mean we can go an' pick up oor bike an' gear now... before it gets stole?"

"Aye. But I want you both back here within the hour," said the policeman easily.

"Yes sir! We'll be right back." Gourlay tried to hide his relief.

On the long hike back, McMinn kicked the grass verge in savage irritation. "Jesus Christ! Whit a mess! Wha would hae thocht the lorry wis stole already?

An' we've still got problems... If we don't show up wi' the bike, the bluidy polisman is sure to do us for havin' a stolen vehicle... An' if we dinna show up..." He drew his finger across his throat... He picked up a stone and threw it high above the trees bordering the loch. "You know, Gourlay, it's a damn funny thing... He never asked tae see your licence..."

They walked on in silence each following his own train of thought. Back at the bike they sat down to weigh things up.

"Ah say we take the bike an' make a run for it... Head north an' chance it... Whit dae ye say Gourlay?"

"Naw. Oor best bet is tae leave the bike here an' hoof it north until we can catch a bus or a train back tae Glesca..."

"Aye. Mebbe your right," admitted McMinn glumly. "Gin we dinna turn up, that sergeant'll phone ahead an' there'll be a bobby ahint every bush between here an' Crianlarich jist waitin' for twa eejots oan a motorbike... An' a stolen bike at that."

"What'll we dae wi' the bike?"

"Ach, it's no problem just as long's we're no akshully ridin' it... Still an a', we'd best hide it."

They gathered branches and bracken and carefully concealed the machine. This done, they sat down again, huddled against a cold wind blowing in off the loch. Suddenly, McMinn leapt to his feet with a wild cry. "Jesus Gourlay! Ah almost forgot!"

"Goad! Whit a fleg! What's up?"

"Ah nearly forgot... C'mere..." McMinn led his pal to a clump of bushes. "Look! Fags! Ah nearly forgot in a' the excitement... Ye've got tae hand it tae me Gourlay... It was damn smart o' me... A whole carton!"

"You're a genius McMinn!" exclaimed Gourlay ripping open the carton with trembling fingers. "Aw Jesus! Look! Ye glaiket bugger McMinn — it's the same carton we had afore — the wan wi' the claes an' tools! Fuck! There musta been twa thoosand boxes oan that lorry, an' you had tae pick the same bluidy wan!"

McMinn staggered around alternately moaning and kicking at stones with great violence, and over and over he mumbled something about 1916. Despite his own acute feelings of disappointment, Gourlay felt compassion for his crony.

"Here, McMinn..."

"Whit?"

"If it's ony consolation, Ah feel the same wey... It's been a hell o' a nicht... Let's go doon tae the lochside an' kick fuck oot o' the watter."

"Dinna be daft."

"Only a thought."

Despondently, the two friends concealed the carton beside the motorcycle, gathered their damp gear, and set off up the road. They had only gone a few hundred yards when the hum of an approaching car sent them scurrying into the ditch.

"Aw shite! We'll be bluidy weeks getting hame at this rate," complained McMinn.

"Ach, we'll can catch a bus at Arrochar... I think..."

They scuffled along in brooding silence oblivious to the beauty of the scenery around them.

"Hey, McMinn?"

"Whit noo?"

"Is there ony shops at Arrochar?"

"Whit wey?... Dinna ken... Probably..."

"Ah'm gaspin' for a fag."

McMinn gaped at him in disbelief, then whipping off his bonnet, began to beat him around the head and shoulders with it in mock ire. "If ye mention fags again, Ah'll bluidy well throttle ye an' chuck yer corp intae the loch!"

"O.K. O.K. Keep yer wool oan!... Here, McMinn?"

"Christ! Whit noo?"

"We're no' done for yet; we're still on the road tae the isles!"

"Oh, isn't that just wonderful! Ah canna tell ye how happy that makes me feel," said McMinn sourly.

They shared a very soggy tomato sandwich and trudged on in silence until the sound of an approaching vehicle sent them cursing into the ditch again. Gourlay got to his feet after it had passed while McMinn remained seated moodily studying his boots. A thoughtful look came to his rugged features. "Y'know, Gourlay. Ah canna get ower that bobby no' askin' ye for yer licence... It's damn funny the mair Ah think aboot it... An' did ye notice he was unshaven?"

"Aye. But he tellt us he'd been hidin' in the bushes hauf the nicht."

"True... But that wis two or three days' growth he had... An' Ah'll tell ye anither thing... A' the time he wis speirin' aboot this an' that, Ah couldna help but notice that he wis wearin' shoes, no buits... Whoever heard tell o' a polisman wearin' shoon? An' the wey he let us go back for the bike... It's like he wis glad to be rid o' us..."

"Whit are ye sayin' McMinn?"

"Ah'm tryin' tae say that he wisna a real bobby... Christ man, his uniform didna even fit!"

Gourlay looked thoughtfully at his pal. "You could be right... An' mebbe the claes in the carton were his!"

McMinn rose slowly to his feet and shook first one foot then the other with a grimace. "If we're right, thon bugger's off wi the whole lorry load o' fags... Makes ye think, eh no'?"

Gourlay cast a pensive look at the frigid waters of the loch through bleary eyes. "Bluidy well does... An' here's us, a couple o' honest, hard workin' blokes canna even raise a fag end between us!" He turned to his pal and curled his upper lip in a wry smile. "It's no' fair, so it's no'..."

CHAPTER 5

Back in the City after their truncated vacation, the weary pair dried out their clothes in a launderette where, to the great amusement of the female clientele, the manager, an acquaintance of McMinn's, allowed them to stand naked in his little cupboard of an office while they were waiting for the machines to work their magic.

Later, they treated themselves to the luxury of a scalding, chest-high soak at the Corporation—run George's Cross public baths. For sixpence you got a cake of yellow soap, a long-handled scrubbing brush with most of the bristles missing, and almost enough steaming water to swim in. They emerged, pores tingling, and bleached pristine white.

Back in the high-ceilinged room he called home, Gourlay had scarcely clambered into his bed for a much needed nap when a great banging at the front door drove away all thoughts and prospects of sleep. "O'Leary!" sighed Gourlay. "Just what Ah needed!" The landlord's agent, O'Leary, was in the habit of paying surprise visits to his properties every few weeks when he'd attempt to collect overdue rents and drive his tenants into various degrees of nervous and mental exhaustion. The term 'visit,' as Gourlay knew only too well, was a euphemism; generally, it took the form of an assault. Even now, as the roaring and battering at the door continued, he had visions of a Norman warrior armed to the teeth, mailed fist thundering on the door. No one else, understandably perhaps, seemed to be in any hurry to greet O'Leary, so he made his way to the door, unlatched it, and quickly leapt aside. The agent immediately charged into the hallway while the door swung violently on its hinges. He glared around belligerently, head lowered as if about to charge again, and cast a keen eye at Gourlay. "You're up to date with your rent," he stated flatly.

"That is a fact," said Gourlay with an inaudible sigh.

"Is Duncanson in?"

"Nae idea."

He felt sorry for the slightly-built, intense Art School student who lived in a state of dread at the very thought of one of O'Leary's visits. The Irishman pounded his fist against the student's door several times by way of a warm up, and not even waiting long enough to see if a response was forthcoming, took several steps backwards and with a wild cry flung himself against the door which burst open with a great splintering sound. Cursorily brushing a few fragments of wood from his shoulders he directed his attention to Duncanson's oil paintings which lay in a row at the foot of the far wall. They represented the culmination of three years' hard effort and formed the bulk of his work to be presented at the upcoming Art School Diploma Show. No art connoisseur, O'Leary savagely kicked some of the canvases to shreds then, with energy to spare, lashed out at the bed. That was a mistake; being in a constant state of penury, Duncanson had constructed the bed himself — a pile of bricks at the corners supported a sheet of plywood upon which rested a lumpy mattress. A serious fellow who by and large kept himself to himself, Duncanson, for reasons known only to himself, was in the habit of urinating into empty milk bottles and storing them under his bed. O'Leary's spirited onslaught caused the bed to collapse and the contents of a score or so of the milk bottles spilled over the floor. Eyes streaming from the pungent, ammonia-like fumes, and howling like some wounded beast, O'Leary stormed out of the room, bounded across the hall and clattered down the stairs. The air was blue with imprecations.

Gourlay closed what was left of the door and returned to his room mumbling, "Daft Erse bastert... He'll be the death o' someone ae day…" He returned to his bed and was just drifting off into a dreamless sleep when he heard McMinn's voice calling hoarsely through the letterbox on the front door.

"Christ! There's nae rest for the wicked!" complained Gourlay and got up muttering darkly. "Hey, what's the panic McMinn? Ah wis trying tae get forty winks."

"Never mind that noo."

He produced a crumpled piece of paper from his waistcoat pocket and handed it to Gourlay.

"It's from Big Red… He wants to see us at seven."

"Eh?"

"A hoose in the west end… That's the address."

"Whit time is it noo?"

"Efter six."

"Any idea what it's aboot, McMinn?"

"Nae idea… Somebody handed it in tae the landlady last night… An' Ah wis hopin' for a quiet night."

"Me too… I just got into ma scratcher… Ah'm fair puchellt. But we'd better show up… Ah get the feeling the big yin could be a good friend, but Ah'd hate tae rub him the wrang wey…"

The house, a massive Gothic monstrosity of a place, turned out to be closer than they had thought, so they arrived a full quarter of an hour ahead of schedule. With some trepidation, they crunched up the long driveway and knocked timorously on the iron-bound door. After a few moments it was opened by a large, unkempt man with a bushy beard. "Ah! Gourlay and McMinn isn't it?" He extended his hand. "Come away in gentlemen…"

"It's you Mr. Quayle!" began Gourlay.

"Call me Terry."

"Aye… Terry… We'd nae idea it was your place we were comin' to… We're a bit early."

"No problem, no problem at all. Big Red hasn't arrived yet,

so we'll just make ourselves comfortable, shall we?"

He ushered the pair along a hallway festooned with various flags, the stuffed heads of big game, Zulu shields and assegais, and various mementoes of the Boer War and they entered a magnificent room which, to Gourlay's surprise, was lit by gas. A cheery fire crackled in an oversize fireplace its orange glow slightly offsetting the blue-green gas light. The room was filled to bursting point with a great miscellany of Victoriana and almost every inch of wall space was taken up by portraits of whiskered gentlemen, diplomas, gewgaws and knickknacks. Quayle's grandfather, it appeared, had served with distinction in the Boer War campaigns and several mementoes recalled his close friendship with Lord Robert's son who'd been killed in a vain attempt to save the gun limbers at Colenso.

"Can I offer you a sherry?" enquired their host indicating a couple of massive bat-winged leather chairs.

Gourlay had met Quayle on several occasions after they'd struck up an acquaintanceship one summer's afternoon at a boating pond so was perhaps less surprised than McMinn at the genteel, bygone-age setting of the room. Quayle, with the aura of aristocracy-fallen-on-hard-times about him, blended in perfectly with his surroundings. One of those men powerful of intellect and wholly without envy or malice of any kind, he cut what is known in Scotland as a kenspeckle figure on account of several eccentricities in manner and dress. His habitual garb consisted of a French beret, black leather jacket, paint-spattered plus fours, puttees and white cricket boots. The latter he kept immaculate by dint of regular application of a paste concocted by himself and consisting of Fullers earth, chalk and flour. In wet weather he wrapped his feet in plastic bags held in place by pieces of string tied round his ankles. But despite his sartorial originality, Terry Quayle was not a man to be taken lightly; he was no buffoon. Gourlay admired him greatly and stood in awe of his encompassing storehouse of a mind. McMinn, almost engulfed by the overstuffed chair, sipped his drink and kept his peace as Quayle warmed his expansive backside at the fire and said Big Red would explain the purpose of the *tête-à-tête* when he arrived.

And so they whiled the time away talking of this and that. Or rather, Quayle talked and the pair listened to tales of Pictish symbols, women as predators, the Piltdown hoax, Madeleine Smith and Madame Bovary, mammoths, mastodons and sabre-toothed tigers.

"Aye. In these days, Britain wasn't an island you see; it was joined to France... The sabre-toothed tiger might well have stalked down what is now Sauchiehall Street."

"Naw! Izzat a fact?" exclaimed McMinn very impressed.

"Aye. Here, did you know that Sauchiehall Street was once known as Sauchiehill Street?"

"Naw! Izzat a fact?"

"Aye. Have another cheese roll, McMinn... Gourlay?"

They sipped their sherries and munched their rolls. And so the night drave on — there were no songs, but much clatter. No slouch himself when it came to the arcane and recondite, McMinn soon overcame his initial sense of awe and was soon contributing easily to the wide range of topics. But the hour approached and there came a mighty rapping to the door. "Big Red!" chorused Gourlay and McMinn. And so it was.

Himself came in — larger than life — neatly and conservatively dressed and carrying something long and narrow carefully wrapped in brown paper. He placed the mysterious package by the fireplace and solemnly shook hands with the three men.

"You'll join us in a sherry, Red?" asked Quayle.

"No' for me, thanks," he responded ambling over to the fireplace again.

Gourlay was struck by the chameleon-like character of

the man; each time he saw him it almost seemed as if he were meeting a different person; he did not appear at all out of place in the elegant, old-worldly surroundings, and Gourlay smiled to himself when he recalled the last time he'd seen the big man tearing down Byres Road in a state of undress. He noticed, too, that Quayle treated him with quiet respect. For a few minutes Big Red stared at the fire while the others fiddled with their drinks. The atmosphere in the room was expectant rather than tense. Then he turned and gazed at each man in turn. Whether it was the firelight or something to do with the crowning mop of hair Gourlay didn't know, but there was a distinct red cast to the big man's eyes.

"Now, I don't want to give the impression that I've seen the light, had a vision, or some revelation... No... In fact, I think I've been like a fart in a colander for the main part... But things have been bubbling and fermenting away in my noddle for years, and just a few nights ago in the kirk everything seemed to come together..."

He clapped his hands. "Now, a while ago, Terry here and I had a long talk, and he quoted a writer who said, 'Life everywhere is much to be endured and little to be enjoyed...'

"Johnson" added Quayle almost under his breath.

"Aye. Johnson. An Englishman, but a wise man nevertheless... And just for the record, Terry told me that five oot the six amanuensi who helped him put his dictionary together were Scots — Right Terry?"

"Right."

"Anyway, I was thinking about joy and endurance and things, and suddenly thought that in Scotland we know a great deal about endurance but not much about joy..." He spoke in a relaxed manner as if he'd been born to the lectern. To Gourlay, his words did not seem rehearsed, but he got the distinct impression that the thoughts and ideas had been formulating inside the big one's head for some considerable time. Listening to the voice, rich and low, controlled, even soft, he knew that if he chose, Big Red could make the rafters ring. "We need a common focus, a national focus, and by God!" he banged his great fist into an open palm with a loud smack, "By God! We have it already in the English! We're a divided nation — Glasgow/Edinburgh, Catholic/Protestant, Highlander/Lowlander, myself and Sanny even... Linguistically-speaking, a farmer in Aberdeenshire likely has more in common with a Dutchman than a Sassenach... But is there a better uniting force than a common enemy?" He paused and glanced around as if he half expected to be challenged. "To purge the English hence, my friends, we need an army the like of which auld Scotland hasn't seen since the days of Wallace and Bruce." He shot a quick look a Gourlay. "What do you say, Gourlay?"

Gourlay's mind raced. He recalled the North African campaigns against the Afrika Korps... Columns of marching men... Tanks... Planes... Guns... The dust and flies... And above all, the comradeship and sense of purpose... "It sounds great, a great idea... But if we march against the English, we'd be outnumbered ten to one... Would we no' be annihilated just?" The big man threw his head back and roared with laughter which was so full of good humour that the three joined in lustily until the whole room seemed to shake.

"No, no, laddie! We'll not be marching against them... We can't win in a pitched battle, but by God! We can make the buggers squirm by other means... Make it so uncomfortable for them in Scotland that they'll pack their bags and leave. You see, Gourlay, we're talking about units or cells... Bands of men harassing the English. Right, Terry?"

Quayle put his unlit pipe in his pocket and nodded.

"Right. We've looked at English history," he said in a confidential tone, "an' what we've learned is that the only lesson the English understand is when their wallets are hurt... They're damn good on the battlefield because they're too thick-headed to know when they're beaten..." Big Red bobbed his head a couple of times. "Aye. They're a nation of shopkeepers... Folk of the cash register... Outwith lines of wee Johnny Keats you were quoting the other day... Something about a wee Shakespeare — an' he might have been a bloody committee — they've produced very few folk with vision or originality when you consider how many of them there are... I think there are about ten of them to one of us..." He turned to Quayle with a wide grin which displayed his very white piano key teeth. "Here, Terry, what about those bird eating peas...?"

"Oh aye..." Quayle sauntered over to a massive bookcase, selected a slim volume, and opened it at a page marked by a slip of paper. "This is good," he smiled turning to face the company... Lissen..." And he began to recite in an exaggerated English accent:

I had a dove and the sweet dove died;
And I have thought it died of grieving:
O, what could it grieve for? Its feet were tied,
With silken thread of my own hand's weaving;
Sweet little red feet! why should you die —
Why should you leave me, sweet dove! why?
You lived alone on the forest tree,
Why, pretty thing! could you not live with me?
I kiss'd you oft and gave you white peas;
Why not live sweetly, as in the green trees?

"I kiss... I kissed you oft... And gave you... gave you white peas!" cried Big Red his huge frame convulsed with suppressed laughter. "White peas...! Jesus! Even on a bad day, Burns never wrote anything half so bad... Sweet little red feet!" he roared aloud in a veritable gale of laughter. "It makes you puke!" His bellowing laughter was so infectious that they all began to titter and laugh, and just as the laughter began to subside, McMinn began to bray and the sound was so odd that everyone burst into roars of laughter again.

"Anyway," said Big Red brushing away the tears from the corners of his eyes, "Wilde, Shaw, Scott, Stevenson, Behan, Burns, Barbour, Fergusson, Swift, Byron... All Scots or Irishmen — not an Englishman among them..."

"Byron?" queried Quayle eyebrows raised.

"Aye. His mother was Catherine Gordon from Aberdeen — and he went to school there."

"Debatable..." said Quayle quietly.

"What?"

"C'mon Red, let the English have Byron!"

"Hmmph... Anyway, the English interest in Scotland has aye been self-serving — they're here just for what they can get out of it by way of profit... So, if we can make it unprofitable for them to be here, mark my words, they'll leave... So lads, let me ask you straight: are you interested in forming a unit?"

"What would it cost us?" piped up McMinn after a short pause.

"Cost? In money?" asked Big Red in surprise.

"Aye."

"No cost — in fact, we'd hope each cell, each unit, would raise funds to help the whole movement — the army as a whole..." Then, catching McMinn's puzzled look, "You see, the army would consist of many different cells..."

"Each one autonomous, but loosely integrated with the whole," added Quayle helpfully.

Gourlay and McMinn looked slightly nonplussed. Were they getting into something which was way above their heads? It struck Gourlay that the simplest thing to do would be to bend with the wind, so to speak — go along with whatever this daft scheme Big Red was espousing. He looked at McMinn who was intently studying his fingernails. "Er, can me an' McMinn hae a private word thegether, Big Red?"

"Surely, surely."

Leaving the pair to mull things over, Quayle and the big man quietly left the room.

"Whit dae ye think, McMinn?" Gourlay asked as the two closed the door.

"McMinn smiled wryly. "Ah'd say they're planning a big job — mebbe a bank or something."

"How's that?"

"Sam Johnson, that Quayle wis quotin', also said that patriotism is the last refuge o' a skellum!"

"Ach, dinna dazzle me wi' yer littry allusions, McMinn; Ah speired a simple question."

"O.K. O.K. Keep yer wig oan! Ah'm just saying' that a' this bletherin' aboot an army is maist likely a cover up for a really big job, a heist."

"Aye, mebbe..." Gourlay's face puckered. "But what have we got tae lose? I say let's go along wi' it — we can aye get oot quickish gin we get in ower oor heids... Dinna be sweir."

McMinn chewed this over for a moment before responding. "O.K. Whit the hell... seems reasonable tae me, Gourlay..."

Then, as if on cue, Big Red and Quayle returned.

"Well, gentlemen — what is your decision?" asked Quayle easily.

"Ye can coont on us... We're your men," said McMinn simply.

"Good lads!" Big Red came over and shook hands with them. "Good lads!"

In a few strides he was at the fireplace where he quickly unwrapped his package. Gourlay's eyes widened as he beheld an absolutely gigantic, gleaming sword. As the big man approached, sword in hand, he shrank into his chair.

"You first Gourlay... Here... Kneel down," boomed the sword wielder. Meekly, slightly scared, slightly embarrassed, Gourlay complied.

"What I have here," intoned the big man, "is a replica of the sword of Sir William Wallace — the real one is safe in Edinburgh; no man living is fit to wield it..." From his kneeling position, and feeling somewhat ridiculous, Gourlay peered up. The sword, the handle of which Big Red was extending towards him, was at least six feet in length. With Big Red steadying the weapon by its blade, Gourlay took a firm grip of the enormous handle.

"Right Gourlay, repeat after me..." and he began to intone:

My first allegiance is to Scotland. My second is to my comrades. On pain of death, I will betray neither. I shall not rest till the English are purged from the land of my birth.

With a little prompting, Gourlay managed to stutter out the words in a small voice while McMinn and Quayle, looking for all the world like mourners at a funeral, stood with heads bowed. McMinn, in turn, stumbled through the oath. There were handshakes all round then Quayle replenished the glasses with whisky and proposed a toast: "To Scotland!" he said simply.

They drained their glasses in contemplative silence, then after some pleasantries, Big Red got down to business.

"You two and Quayle here are the nucleus of a cell. Task one will be to recruit new members. Sound them out, and try to go for variety — you want brains as well as brawn... Task two: Get to work! That means raising funds for the Army and spreading the good word... There's really only one rule: If it's good for Scotland, then it's right... Are there any questions?"

Somewhat abashed by the speed of things, the pair were slow to respond, and sensing their slight perplexity, Quayle said quietly, "The lads'll need a while to think things ower Red..." He turned to the two cronies. "Don't you worry. Nothing's going to happen overnight; it'll take months, even longer to form a proper cell... Take one day at a time... And remember, I'm your man — I'm always here if you need me. If you find a likely recruit, check him out as best's you can then arrange for me to meet him... And, as Red just said, if you keep in mind that if it's good for Scotland then it's right, then you'll not go far wrong... You're bright lads, I know it, so be circumspect in all your dealings with folk that aren't members of your cell; as the Bard says, 'Keek through every other man wi' sharpened, sly inspection...' And never forget for one moment what the English did to Wallace — they'll string you up by the balls if they're given half the chance! Discretion, discretion is the keynote..."

Several questions were birling around in Gourlay's head, but he thought that some of them might sound silly on this solemn, even historic, occasion, so he momentarily kept his peace. He looked across at McMinn who seemed to be lost in thought... the long silence was beginning to make him feel uncomfortable, so he framed a question or two. "Er, a couple of questions..."

"Go ahead, Gourlay," said Big Red with an easy smile.

"Who'll be in charge o' this Army?"

"Ah! Well, that has to remain a secret... The whole idea of cells is that they function more or less independently... For the time being, look upon Quayle as your Number One... OK?"

The big man turned to Quayle who said without hesitation. "The National Army for the Liberation of Scotland — N.A.I.L.S. for short..." Gourlay opened his mouth to speak, but before he could utter a sound, McMinn spoke up. "Whit did ye mean when ye said tae look for a variety of recruits?"

"Just that, McMinn — variety," said the big man. "The greater the variety of types and skills within a cell, the greater its chance for survival and success... We'll need members frae a' the airts — even Edinburgh."

"An' how many folks tae a cell?"

"Another good question," said Big Red running a hand through his flaming mop and turning to Quayle. "What would you say Terry? Ten?"

"Even less — if the unit is too big its cohesiveness could be lost... Six to eight would be ideal I'd say. But don't worry about that, McMinn," he continued, "as soon as a cell gets too big to be manageable, we just split it... Oh, and on a big operation, you might have half a dozen cells co-operating under a single command... You see lads, the idea of cells is that the army as a whole can never be wiped out... There'll be commanders, but no single chap in any cell could name them or even identify the members of other cells, because he doesn't know who they are. It's a safety device... I'll be your cell's resource man, but that's all. The cell will normally make its own decisions in the democratic way. O.K.?"

"Well lads," broke in Big Red, "I've another wee group to see, so I'd better be pushing off... Terry will answer any other questions you have..." As he began wrapping up the sword he caught Gourlay's curious look. "Beautiful, isn't it?"

"That it is? But how did ye come by it?"

"Quayle has a pal who works for the Museum of Antiquities — his specialty is armour and the like — and he made this in his spare time... Having made it, he wasn't quite sure what to do with it and gave it to me when he got wind of what we were up to... Said it would be the perfect symbol..."

"Yes," added Quayle. "And we'll be giving out miniatures to a' the cell members... You can wear them ahint your jaiket lapel... They'll be ideal for identifying fellow members o' the Army... Maybe we'll have some gold ones made and award them for special services rendered, eh Red?"

"Aye. That's a great idea... But you'll have to excuse me gents; I really have to get going." Solemnly, he shook hands with Gourlay and McMinn, and with a nod and smile for Quayle, slipped off into the night.

It struck Gourlay that his departure was as if a light had gone out somehow. Even allowing for his considerable physical presence, the man had an aura, a charisma... There was no ignoring him. And what a multi-faceted man... Was this soft-spoken, gentle giant really the same man who ate light bulbs and laid dozens low in the church with his bare hands? He certainly was an enigma... Lost in these musings and speculations, Gourlay was barely aware that Quayle had filled his glass and was holding it out to him. McMinn stood up and wandered over to the fire. "Ah dinna mind tellin' ye that Ah'm feart o' Big Red... An' him wi' that bluidy great sword! Who needs an Army? We just need tae point him towards England, gie him a wee shove, an' leave him tae his ain devices!"

"Heart of gold," said Quayle. "He's really a very gentle soul."

"How did ye come tae meet him, Terry?" asked Gourlay sipping his sherry.

"Ha! It's a long story," said Quayle sitting down and removing his cricket boots. "We ended up in the same school... In England..."

"Naw! Izzat a fact?" interrupted McMinn in a loud voice.

"Aye. My Dad was in the Colonial Service — in Africa — and I was sent to a boarding school in England where my uncle's folk lived... That's one reason my accent sometimes makes me sound like an Englishman... And after Red's father died, he was shipped off to some relative in the same area. Well, I got kicked out of the boarding school, and when I finally settled into this Secondary Modern school, there was Big Red — they called him Jock, of course... Well, as the only two Scots in a school chock full of Sassenachs, it was natural that we'd gravitate to one another..."

"Wis he a big laddie when he wis a boy?" queried McMinn.

"No. In fact, at one time he was smaller than I was, even though we were about the same age. But he was a right tiger..." Quayle leaned back in his chair, lit his pipe, and smiled to himself at old memories.

"I had this conker, a Scottish one, but it had been to Rhodesia and back and was all dried out — it was black, and like a chunk of iron. In England, it smashed all the English boys' fresh off the trees conkers to smithereens... They held a counsel of war and decided that my chestnut wasn't a chestnut at all and were trying to chuck me and my conker into the village pond... Wicked bunch of English snots too... They meant business. Well, Big Red came to the rescue... broke one lad's nose and threw three of them into the pond... Hell of a stushie about it... Caned by the headmaster... Irate parents threatening lawsuits, the whole business... But though he became something of a hero to the younger lads who knew what it was to be bullied, it never went to his head — the adulation I mean... Always very fair was Red, and still is — no side with him... As kids, the pair of us came to detest the English for their superior ways... A strange people... No soul... Ach, drink up, lads an' to hell with them!"

"And when did he come up wi' this idea of an Army?" asked Gourlay.

Quayle sucked noisily on his pipe. "Well, it's difficult to say exactly... He's never forgotten the way he'd been treated by the English schoolboys — kids can be pretty cruel — and the whole school, teachers an' all, were aye very condescending... An' his stint in the regular Army did nothing to endear him to the southrons... Imagine being that tall, and wi' his accent — it must have been like being back in school again — not a one dared to say anything to his face, but you can imagine the scheming and conniving behind his back..." Quayle attempted without success to relight his pipe. "But I think the notion of an army of Scots had something to do with the fracas at the kirk hall — you'd know more about that... I wasn't there. But something clicked in his noddle..."

"An' whaur does wee Sanny Rutherford fit into a' this?" asked McMinn after a pause.

"Sanny? As far as I can make out, he's all for the idea. But I hardly know him — Red's dealing with him... But the last thing we need are factions... Sanny will have to make up his mind..."

"Shit or get off the pot?" broke in McMinn.

"Aye. He can't sit on the fence — he's either for us or against us..."

"Anither thing, Terry," said Gourlay, "did you ever hear tell of a happening?"

"Quayle looked puzzled for a moment, then smiled suddenly. "Oh *that*! Aye... Well, it's important to get the right kind of publicity in any new venture... Red came up with the idea that once the units are formed we'd need to stage a happening — something that would announce to the world, and to the English in particular, that we are a viable force... But nothing concrete has been planned yet. We'll be looking for ideas, so if you get any notions, pass them on..."

The drinks, the warm room, and the substantial talk had all taken their toll of the pair. Gourlay noticed that his pal looked bleary-eyed and he himself felt that a good night's sleep wouldn't go far wrong. Only Quayle, sucking contentedly on his unlit pipe, looked as if he were ready for an all night session of drinking and conversation. Gourlay rose. "If ye dinna mind, Terry, McMinn an' me are fair wabbit... It's been quite an evening, an' we've plenty tae think oan..."

After handshakes all round and 'thank yous' from Gourlay and McMinn, the little gathering broke up and the pair crunched off along the driveway and into the soft Glasgow night.

CHAPTER 6

Apart from Duncanson's attack of hysterics when he saw his ruined paintings, life at his Renfrew Street abode was uneventful for Gourlay and the days passed quietly. Of McMinn there was no sign, and he presumed that he too was lying low and still recuperating from the recent excesses.

Gourlay studied himself in the mirror, pulled a few horrendous faces, then turning his head and rolling his eyes to their fullest extent so that he could see himself in profile, decided that he had a noble face. "Gie me a beard and Ah'm the dead ringer of Abe Lincoln," he mused. He opened a window, and to his surprise found that the air was warm, almost balmy; could summer have come at last? On the gutter above his head, two pigeons strutted and warbled. One (he assumed it was the female) stood quite still staring into space while the other (without doubt the stupid male) stuck his neck out and did a showy little dance until, overstepping himself, he fell off the gutter and winged his way to safer courting grounds. The faint, thin sound of a dance band came to his ears from the rear of the Locarno Ballroom across the street.

Leaving the window open to catch the evening breeze, he sat on the edge of the bed and tried to remember the words of *T for Texas,* an old Jimmie Rogers' song which had been running in his head... 'T for Thelma, that gal that made a wreck out of me...' He pulled up his trousers' legs and examined his wiry legs. "Hello wee legs — my, ye're awffy peely-wally lookin'... An' me a sodger an' a'!" For a few moments he marched up and down the little room in an elaborate goose step. The affair at Quayle's already seemed distant and dreamlike. Was he really a member of some great invisible Army? He rather fancied the idea, but deep down wished that a uniform came with the position. "Whoever heard tell o' a sodger withoot a bluidy uniform tae his name?" he muttered.

He decided that he really didn't care about the English one way or another; they were like a bump on the head or some other minor affliction... One got used to them much in the manner that a dog gets used to his fleas. He mulled over the notion McMinn had put to him as they'd strolled from Quayle's, that any nation living adjacent to the English for a couple of thousand years would be, willy-nilly, reduced to a state of nervous exhaustion. "Sure enough, he thought, the Welsh have a row of mountains separating them, and the Irish have their sea. But poor Scotland, exposed to English rapacity, had become a playground for them... We're bought an' sold for English gold right enough... What was that word Quayle used to describe us? 'Emasculated'... That's it... We've lost our balls... Aye, maybe the English are to blame... Might as well blame them as anybody else... Aye!"

He studied himself in the mirror once more. "Maybe I had ancestors who fought and died for independence... But where has it got us? We've got Wallace's sword, an' Bruce sits on a big bronze cuddy on Bannockburn field. Hmmph. An' McMinn says the statue was made by an English sculptor... An' we have oor ain crown jools back... But the Stane o' Destiny is still in Westminster... An' it's oor fuckin' stane!" he bawled at his reflection.

A gentle knock at the door shattered his reverie — Duncanson. "Are you alright in there, Gourlay?"

"Oh, er, aye..." And then a thought occurred to him. He opened the door to the student and came right to the point. "Eh, Duncanson, what do ye think aboot the English?"

"The English?"

"Aye."

"My father is English."

Gourlay coughed a little cough and held his peace.

"It's not the English I think about," continued the student, "it's the Irish... Look what that Fenian bog man did to my paintings! I'm probably going to have to repeat my final year at Art College, and I'll not get a grant... Bloody great Irish pillock..."

Gently, Gourlay closed the door. "Ach, Ah couldna see him as a freedom fechter onywey..." He yawned extravagantly and prepared himself for bed.

The bright morning sun woke him as it slanted through the grimy windows onto the bed. He sat up, stretched, yawned, scratched his tousled head and peered through tired eyes. The slated roofs glistened in the hard light, and far beyond the City limits, the hills looked young and inviting.

Towards mid-morning, McMinn arrived carrying a pair of boots laced together. "A braw day, Gourlay — ye should have been up oors ago... It's gaun tae be a stoater so it is... It's warm already... Here," he said, holding out the boots, "Try them for size..."

Sitting on the edge of his bed, Gourlay dutifully put on the boots and laced them up. He put his weight first on one foot then on the other and studied each boot in turn. "Aw Christ, McMinn, Ah canna go aboot like this... It's stoopit..."

"Therr a real handsome perr... Ach, ye'll get used tae them nae bother..."

"Mebbe," conceded Gourlay. "But naebody, Ah mean naebody, walks aboot wi twa left buits."

"Ten bob for baith o' them," enticed his friend.

Earlier in the week in passing the time of day with his pal, the Rabbit, McMinn had got onto the subject of what his one-legged chum did with the unused boot or shoe when he bought new footwear. The Rabbit had explained that sometimes a shop would sell him one shoe or boot, and use the other for display in their window... It all depended... But usually, he had to buy the pair.

"Ye should find anither lad wha's missin' his right leg,"

McMinn had helpfully suggested.

Apparently, the Rabbit had shrugged and explained that was easier said than done and that he'd have to find a man missing his right leg or foot and needed a size nine for his left foot... Additionally, he'd explained, that the potential purchaser would have to like the same style in footwear as him...

McMinn was about to abandon the subject, but the Rabbit had added a post script: "Hech, an' wi' a' my weight on the wan foot, Ah have tae be very fussy... Need a good solid sole an' that... Ah usually buy the same kind." He had then raked around in a cupboard and produced two identical brown boots saying, "It's a helluva waste, but what can ye dae...?"

McMinn rubbed his jaw. "Size nine...? Tell ye what, Rabbit — Ah think Gourlay taks size eight... Maybe they'd fit him... Maybe he'd buy them. Wi' these being a size bigger than he takes, mebbe them being for the left foot wouldna matter."

"Ten bob an' they're his."

Thus it was that Gourlay came to be trying on two left boots, size nine.

"O.K. Tell ye what, McMinn... Ah'll wear them the day an' see how it goes... They're certainly a very nice perr, nae question. Ah still think it looks daft, but Ah'll try them..."

"Ony chance o' a cuppa, Gourlay?"

"Surely." He lit the gas ring and clattered around preparing a pot of tea and some toast.

McMinn sat on the edge of the bed. "So what have you been up to, Gourlay?"

"Aw, this an' that," replied his friend. "Here, what happened? Cut yersel' shavin'?" Gourlay asked, noticing for the first time that McMinn was wearing a largish elastoplast under his chin.

McMinn fingered it gingerly. "Naw. Some shite pulled a knife on me in the Gents at Central Station last night."

"Weel-dressed bloke carrying an attaché case, unshaven?"

"That's him," said McMinn in surprise. "Hoo did ye ken...? Wee shite went for me an a' for nae reason... Ah wis ha'en a piss an' speired of him what he thought aboot the English, an' he went for me, the bastert... But he'll leave folk alane in the future."

"Howzatt?"

"Ah broke his wee fuckin' face, that's why... Wee shite!"

"Haw, McMinn?"

"That's me."

"Are ye thinkin' o' invitin' ony meenisters tae join the cell?"

"Naw... Whit wey?"

"If ye do, ye're gonna have tae clean up yer langwich — ye've an' awffy foul tongue in yer heid!"

"Hmmph. Must be the company I keep! But you're right, Gourlay — it *is* awffy, innit? At school if we wis caught sweerin', we got oor mou' washed oot wi' thon yellow soap..."

"Well, ye'll can start up a swearie box, an' ye'd be able tae retire on the proceeds in nae time at a'," guffawed his pal.

"Mebbe... Here Gourlay, Ah've been doon tae the Mitchell Library an' did some work oan oor army..." He produced a crumpled sheet of paper from his inside jacket pocket and handed it to Gourlay. "Read that." Gourlay smoothed out the sheet and began to read aloud in an affected bass voice:

"—A candidate must compose at least one song

—be a perfect master of his weapon

—a good runner and fighter

—he must leap a tree branch as high as
   his forehead, and get under a branch no higher
   than his knee

—he must not refuse a woman without a dowry

—must offer violence to no woman

—be charitable to the poor and weak

—must never refuse to fight nine men of any
   other race should they set upon him

—no Fienne must go back on his word, though
    it cost him his life..."

"Now then, what dae ye think o' that?" asked McMinn. "It's the code of the old Celtic warriors, the Fienne."

Gourlay looked thoughtful for a long moment. "It's verra nice McMinn... It's kinda like poetry innit?" He studied the piece again and suddenly guffawed. "Haw! That's me tae a tee... a perfect master o' ma weapon!"

"C'moan Gourlay, be serious."

"Sorry..." He perused the paper again. "Fecht nine men o' ony ither race... That's a bit much innit?"

"Isn't ony Scot is more than a match for nine Sassenachs?"

"Mebbe..," admitted Gourlay with a wry smile. "But suppose it wis nine Blacks that jumped oan ye; whit then?"

McMinn scowled and gave him a morose look. "Mebbe ye want an addendum that says ye've tae fight ony nine men unless it's Africans? Dinna be daft."

"Sorry McMinn... But what's the idea o' the piece onywey?"

"Just an idea. Ah got tae thinkin' aboot Big Red an' oor oath, and thought a wheen elaboration might be in order." He indicated the paper. "It's supposed tae be the code the Fienne lived by... It wis just an idea," he added lamely.

"We've enough oan oor plates McMinn. Big Red's oath is fine... What we need tae get crackin' wi' is some conscriptin'."

"Aye... But I'll keep this code for Quayle; it's the kind of thing he'd like... Er, did ye have anyone in mind?"

"Huh?"

"Tae conscript?"

"Naw... I tried Duncanson next door, but he's a fart, a dreamer — useless. How about you?"

"Nah. Nothin' doing so far... Weel, as Ah said, Ah did try that eejot in the Gents an' near got ma thrapple slit for ma pains!"

"Mebbe he wis an Englishman!"

"Aye, mebbe," concurred McMinn sourly.

They munched their toast and sipped their tea reflectively, or rather Gourlay sipped while McMinn slurped his from a cracked saucer.

"You know," said Gourlay, "what we should do is draw up a list of folk we know an' see if any of them are suitable... What about the Rabbit for instance?"

"Aye... I was sizin' him up when we were bletherin', but what use wad a wan-leggit man be in oor Army?"

"Thats' no' the point McMinn... It's no' as if we'll be daen ony marchin'... It's attitude that coonts, an' ony expertise he has... What's he good at?"

"The Rabbit? Hoogmagandie, shaggin' — how de ye think he got his nickname? Funny the wey wummen throw themsels at him... Christ, if ye've got ony money or a big dong, ye've got it made — an' the Rabbit hasnae ony money! Oh, Ah saw him near brain a fella wance... Gave him a hellish dunt oan the heid..."

"Wi' his dong?"

"Naw! Wi' his crutch for Goad's sake! Wi' his crutch!"

"Hmmph... Weel, whit aboot Hector then?"

"Hector's a different kettle o' fush... Ah ken him weel... He can read Latin..."

"Oh, that's a great asset that is! C'moan McMinn, be serious."

"He's already a pal o' Big Red's."

"So much the better... he's worth checking out I say."

"Aye, O.K. Ah'll do that then."

"You know, McMinn," said Gourlay after a pause, "ye think ye ken folk weel till something like this crops up... Near everybody Ah ken is Scottish, but Ah've nae idea to what extent they're really aware of their national identity, or whether they give a damn about that... Ah'll hae tae gie it some thought, take it under avizandum... Ither than that, Ah'll just keep ma een peeled for suitable folk..."

McMinn tilted the saucer and drained the last of his tea and smacked his lips loudly.

"That wisna a bad cuppa... What are ye up tae the day?"

"Nuttin much... It looks like a braw day ootside, so Ah'll mebbe take a wee dander aroon an' try oot the buits... They're no' bad at a'... But thae elastic-sided wans o' yourn look verra comfy."

McMinn looked down at his feet. "Aye... Well, Ah'd best be off, Gourlay... Catch you later, eh?"

"Aye. O.K. Cheery bye the noo, McMinn."

As McMinn stepped out the door Gourlay called after him, "Hey, McMinn!"

"What?"

"Watch oot for thon nine Africans!"

The day was sunny, even hot. In the parks, pale-skinned children romped, guzzled ice cream sodas, got red-lipped from sucking endless iced lollipops and made merry as only children can. The menfolk took off their jackets, rolled up their shirt sleeves and placed handkerchiefs (carefully knotted in each corner) on their heads in token recognition of summer. Women, hardier than men, made even fewer concessions; they sat in little groups, quietly perspired together, and kept an eye on their offspring. Occasionally, one more daring than the rest would remove her shoes with a shy smile and little sigh of relief and complain sheepishly of painful bunions or simply explain, "Ma feet's fair bilin'."

Gourlay, still wearing his heavy winter coat but hatless in deference to the hot sun, marvelled at the pleasantness of everyone — everyone, that is, except the hot and harassed tram conductors. Inside the trams they were allowed to remove their caps and most of them wore lightweight jackets and trousers. But despite this and the open windows, the interiors became unbearably hot and the poor conductors sweated and fretted as they went about their work.

Everyone seemed to be out in the streets and the trams were so busy that Gourlay managed to pass two fare stages before the unsmiling conductor finally got round to him and stood beside him jingling coppers in his left hand and calling, "Ferrs please, ferrs please" in a thin nasal voice. He took the tram up Maryhill Road, and on leaving, deftly extracted the vehicle's copy of the Corporation Tramway Bye Laws and Board of Trade Regulations from the specially-constructed little compartment above the door. He clomped through the streets in his new boots alternately humming tunelessly and reading the Bye Laws aloud in a bass tremolo:

12 — *No person shall bring into or upon, or convey or cause to permit to be conveyed, in or on any car, any bundle of clothing, or article or thing, tending to communicate any infectious or contagious disease, any dead body, or any article of an offensive or dangerous character or of...*

"In the name o' the wee man! Ony deid body...! Who in the name o' fuck wad want tae take a deid body oan a caur?" He rubbed his jaw reflectively. "Either some daft gowk did try it wance, or the mannie that wrote this shite wis aff his nut." Chuckling to himself, he put the booklet into his coat pocket and resumed humming. A small, snottery boy with holes in his pullover fell into step with him and eyed him from head to foot with hawk-like scrutiny.

"Hey mister!"

"What sonny?"

"Baith o' yer boots are the same."

"So what's it to you?"

"Ur you glaiket mister?"

Gourlay raised his fist. "Ah'll gie ye glaiket ye wee nyaff! Piss off!"

Whistling happily, the boy wandered off leaving Gourlay muttering, "Fou of piss an' vinegar! Wee nyaff..."

Passing a newsagent's, he treated himself to five Woodbines and a bottle of Irn Bru and headed off bent almost double as he attempted to examine his boots as he walked. Then catching sight of the silver glint of water beyond some derelict factory buildings,

JAMES FINDLAY SLEIGH

headed over to investigate. It was a canal, the stagnant waters of which gave off a sweetish odour. On both banks stood abandoned shells of buildings and rusting pieces of antiquated machinery. Odd pieces of soggy wood lay motionless on the surface of the water, and for a foot or so out from each bank extended a fine lacework of some emerald green plant. Occasionally, a frog would poke its glistening head through the coverlet and survey the grim world about it.

In its total loneliness and desolation, the location was not without a quiet, terrifying beauty. A young man stood gazing intently into the water from a little wood and iron sluice gate which spanned the still waters. Wrapped up in a world of his own, he ignored Gourlay's, "Braw day, eh?" Gourlay shrugged, passed over to the opposite bank, and carefully selecting a comfortable looking spot, removed his coat and lay back enjoying a cigarette.

In the quiet and stillness, it was difficult for him to believe he was in the heart of a great city. Idly, as he watched the cigarette smoke curl upwards through the warm air towards the blue sky, he looked at one spot in the sky and tried to focus on infinity, but the sheer immensity of space almost made him dizzy. He tried again, and once more his brain became befuddled at the concept of the vast nothingness up there. He sat up, closed his eyes and shook his head rapidly as if to clear it. He opened his bottle of Irn Bru and swallowed a few mouthfuls; it was warm, sweet and fizzy. He rubbed the back of his hand across his mouth and glanced over at the figure on the little bridge-like structure. The young man stood motionless, leaning forward and staring into the water. Gourlay turned his attention to his boots, and for a fleeting moment panic gripped him; his right foot appeared to have become his left! He quickly uncrossed his legs and exhaled in relief. "Goad! Whit a fleg! Damn McMinn and damn the Rabbit an' damn they buits — they'll drive me nuts yet!" He took them off and had just turned his mind to consider possible conscripts when a loud splash broke the silence. He looked across towards the sluice gate. The young man was no longer there, and a succession of concentric ripples raced after one another towards the banks. An alarmed frog leapt into the water from his tossing driftwood.

Gourlay hobbled over to the bridge as quickly as he could and peered into the dark waters. Streams of bubbles rose from the greenish depths and burst through the surface scum. The waters roiled for a moment and then grew still again; there was no sign of the young man. Then suddenly, he saw a face. It had the pallor of a fish's belly and seemed disembodied as it lay suspended in the murky depths. He watched in horrified fascination as it slowly slipped deeper and deeper until it disappeared.

With an oath, Gourlay jumped into the water. It was ice cold. Luck was with him; his foot touched the man. Quickly groping about, he managed to secure an arm, and struggling wildly, clawed his way to the surface with his burden.

The young man lay on the bank, pale as death, his chest heaving, but despite their immersions, neither was much the worse. Gourlay removed as many of his clothes as he was able without offending decency, laid them out in the sun, and placing his coat over his shoulders, turned to the young man.

"You alright therr Jim?"

There was no response. Gourlay watched as his breathing returned to normal.

"You alight therr?"

The young man opened his eyes, started at him for a long moment, and nodded.

"Take yer jaiket an' breeks off son or ye'll catch yer daith."

Wordlessly, the young man slowly got to his feet and began to remove some of his garments. Gourlay busied himself collecting pieces of wood, and soon, a good fire was blazing. He lit two cigarettes and handed one to the young man. "Here... Ah'm Gourlay, by the way."

The young man drew on the cigarette and immediately began to cough, "I'm Gordon, Gordon Rae," he said in a flat voice when his coughing fit had subsided. In silence, they sat staring into the fire.

"I'm sorry for getting you all wet," began Gordon, "the water sort of hypnotised me... It seemed to be so peaceful down there... I'd been staring at it for ages. It was so dark and still... It was the oblivion I craved... I wanted to lie on the bottom for ever... It seemed to be such a beautiful idea somehow. If you hadn't pulled me out I don't know what would have happened to me... I didn't breathe. It's funny, it's not because I was afraid to die... I just didn't want to move... Just lie there forever... It was quite beautiful, you know." He turned to Gourlay. "But you must think I'm mad..."

"No son, I don't..."

"Have you ever felt like ending it all Gourlay?"

"Oh, sometimes, mebbe... Would ye like some Irn Bru?"

"Er, no thanks." He toyed with his cigarette. "I'm a student... I did well in my first year, but am liable to fail my second... I don't know what happened. I just seemed to go to pieces... Couldn't concentrate somehow... I haven't the courage to tell my folks... They've got such high expectations of me, and think that I'm still doing well..." He closed his eyes tightly and pressed his thumbs into his forehead. Gourlay clucked sympathetically, but unable to think of anything appropriate to say, busied himself struggling into his boots. Suddenly the student's face lit up. "Here, you've two left boots!"

"Aye, Ah ken. When you've never ony money, you dinna let such details fash ye..."

"Oh. I'm sorry... I didn't mean..."

"It's O.K."

A Red Admiral butterfly fluttered past and landed trembling on a piece of wood by the water's edge.

"Daft gowk in macaroni dress. Are ye come here to shaw

your face..." quoted Gordon.

"What's that?"

"Robert Fergusson."

"Izzat right...? What's macaroni dress?"

"A macaroni? Oh, foppish, gaudy clothing in the Italian style of the day... A macaroni is a niminy pimini, a fop, I think..."

"Nice tae be educatit," said Gourlay without sarcasm.

"Maybe... But then I'm the one who jumped into the canal..."

At that moment, a large green frog appeared and devoured the butterfly in a gulp.

"Jesus Christ!" cried Gourlay in a very loud voice leaping to his feet. He raced to the water's edge and stomped up and down in an effort to kill or maim the perpetrator of this outrage, but the wise frog had already vanished into the dark waters.

"Bastert puddock!" he bawled in an anguished voice. "You just wait!"

He returned, breathless from his exertions, and sat down. Gordon stared gloomily into the fire. Gourlay held out his damp shirt to the flames. "Are you going to be alright?"

"No... I think I need help," replied Gordon flatly.

"What kind of help?"

"I think I need to see a psychiatrist again."

"That's mebbe no' a bad idea..." He turned and studied the water vainly seeking the frog.

"A couple of years ago," began Gordon, "I went to see one who works out of Hawkhead Hospital. On my first visit I arrived a bit late and his receptionist told me to go into this room and take a seat. There were about a dozen people all seated in a circle. It was weird, Gourlay... Nobody said a word for about ten minutes. I just sat there wondering which one was the psychiatrist. Then this young woman, quite pretty she was, thin, pale-faced and high-strung looking... Well, all of a sudden she started to tell us how she'd tried to commit suicide... Tried to gas herself. The horrible thing was that she talked about it so matter of factly, so casually, no emotion in her voice... Then a bloke spoke up and explained how he wanted to strangle his mother... I couldn't believe my ears. I sat on the edge of my seat, my eyes out on stalks... Then this other fellow talked about frustrations, anxieties and so on... It turned out that he was the doctor, the psychiatrist.

"The whole session lasted about an hour, and by the time it ended I was thoroughly unnerved. But later, I came to realize that I was lucky compared to most of them. After the group broke up, the doctor took me into his consulting room. Nice chap... Anyway, I'll not bore you with the details, but he listened to my story, asked a question from time to time, and then he lit his pipe, looked at me, and you'll never guess what he said?"

Gourlay shook his head.

"He said, 'Mr. Rae, you may bend with the wind, but, trust me, you'll never break!' Just that."

Gourlay watched the steam rising from his damn shirt. "Seems a pretty good assessment, Gordon... You should have a wee chat wi' a pal of mine called Quayle... I think he'd be more helpful than a whole lunacy of psychiatrists..." A sudden thought crossed his mind and he looked closely at his new-found friend. "Er, what dae ye think aboot the English in Scotland?"

"The English?"

"Aye."

"Oh them? Personally, I've no high regard for them... My fields are Scottish history and literature, so I'm alert to the way they've always used us and short changed us... Quite a few of us at uni. are pretty nationalistic... Maybe because, maybe despite the fact, that so many of our profs. are Sassenachs...

> O Scotland! that could ance afford
> To bang the pith o' Roman sword,
> Winna your sons, wi' joint accord,
> To battle speed,

And fight til Freedom be restor'd

Whilk now lies deid?"

"Burns?"

"Fergusson — or most of it is!" said the student with a quiet smile.

Gourlay put on his still-damp shirt and shivered slightly. "Your claes will take a week tae dry oot, Gordon — you'd best awa' hame an' get them dried properly."

"Right... I think I will go home... And maybe tell my parents about uni..."

"Good man... You're sure you're O.K? No more loupin' intae canals?"

"Think so... Thanks again, Gourlay... You've been a real pal."

"Nae problem... Lissen, I'd like to hear how you make out at hame... Late Saturday afternoon Ah'll likely be at the boolin' green — where Argyle an' Sauchiehall meet... See you there? An' Ah'll see aboot yer meetin' Quayle."

"Thanks... That would be great." They shook hands cordially and went their ways.

It was Saturday. Gourlay and McMinn sat on a bench at the edge of the bowling green enjoying the banter and watching in amazement at the skill of four blind men playing a friendly game.

"How the hell do they manage, McMinn?"

"See that box affair... Up near the jack?"

"Oh aye."

"It's a gadget that gies a kind o' clickin' noise, and it shines oot a wee beam o' bright light... Ye can only see the light when ye're in line wi' the jack... Them that can see a bit, aim for that, an' if they canna see onything, they use their lugs an' aim for the clickin'."

"That's great, so it is."

"Aye... Oh, here, Ah spoke tae Hector... Nae problem. He jist smiled an' said he already had Big Red's blessin', an' that we were tae call on him when we needed him."

"That's it?"

"Aye... He kennt aboot this Liberation Army already."

They sat in comfortable silence for a few moments then McMinn cleared his throat.

"Er, did you make up yer mind anent thae new buits yet? The Rabbit wis askin' like."

"Christ! Thae buits! Whit a bluidy fuss! They're quite comfortable mind, but every bugger keeps tellin' me Ah'm wearing two left yins... Ah wish folk'd mind their ane business... Ach, tell the Rabbit five bob, take it or leave it."

"You should tell folk ye've goat anither perr like that for the right feet at hame," suggested McMinn with a snorting laugh.

"Dinna be bloody daft... Here, is that the day's paper?"

"Aye."

"Sees a keek." Gourlay poured over the heavy print:

—MAN (24) FINED FOR ASSAULT...

—TWINS BORN TO PARAPLEGIC WOMAN (37)...

—TOILETS A DISGRACE SAYS PROVOST...

—NO FOUNDATION TO RUMOURS OF

 LEPROSY OUTBREAK SAYS M.O.H. SPOKESMAN...

—MAN (27) FINED FOR ASSAULT...

—MINISTER (81) DENIES HE IS FATHER OF CHILD...

—RUSSIANS BIGGEST BOMB YET...

—MAN (22) DROWNED IN CLYDE...

He drew the paper close to his face and squinted at the small print:

Police frogmen dragged the Clyde after a Mrs. Roxena Rawalpindi (26) reported seeing a young man leap off the Jamaica Bridge. A police spokesman said later that a body was taken from the water last night. The name of the man is being withheld pending further enquiries. "I thought at first it was a stunt,"

Mrs. Rawalpindi told our reporter. "Just like on television. But he never surfaced again, so I called police."

"Jesus!" exclaimed Gourlay.

"Whit?"

"Look at that..." He handed the paper to McMinn who studied it for a long moment.

"Aye. Randy auld bugger... Christ, if a man ower eighty can dae it, there's hope for us a'!"

"Naw... no that... The fella here that wis pulled from the Clyde... That might be the lad Ah wis tellin' ye aboot."

"Ach, mebbe no'," replied McMinn casting an idle glance at the bowlers. "Mebbe no'."

It grew dark and the shadows cast by the bowlers lengthened. The nearby University clock struck the hour. Sighted players gradually drifted away leaving the wide expanse of green to the four blind men and their clicking machine.

"Gourlay! Hello."

He looked up. "Gordon! Ah'm pleased tae see ye man... Sit doon, sit doon... This is my pal McMinn..."

McMinn shook hands. "Pleased tae meet ye Gordon..."

"Do you bowl yourself?" enquired the young man joining them on the bench.

"No. No' really... These old codgers are too good for us... Ach, sometimes Ah'll fill in for somebody that disna turn up," said Gourlay, "but mostly. Ah just like to watch... Ah've aye loved the click o' the bools... But here, did ye talk to your folks?"

"I did. And do you know something? I wish I'd confessed ages ago — they were very disappointed at first, but really very understanding in the end."

"That's good..." Gourlay glanced around and lowered his voice. "Oh, remember I mentioned Quayle. Well, McMinn here'll take you roon tae meet him later if ye've a mind to..."

A great shout went up from the green followed by laughter. One of the blind men had knocked over the little clicking machine with a wayward bowl. Gourlay leaned his head back and looked up at the darkening sky. It was a deep blue colour. He studied the fluffy clouds tinged pink by the setting sun.

"Here Gourlay, I owe you a drink," said Gordon. "My grant came in... Let's celebrate my salvation from the frogs! And you too McMinn, you'll join us?"

Gourlay grinned toothily. "Them's the nicest words Ah've heard a' week!" And the three strolled off easily.

CHAPTER 7

Summer or not, it had suddenly turned cold, and the City looked bleak. A shroud of fog covered everything, and even though there were a couple of hours of daylight left, cars and buses drove with their lights on. Contrasting the recent spell of glorious weather, it was depressing, and the inhabitants themselves seemed to have taken on a grey aspect to match the drabness.

The evening rush hour was at its peak and people bustled around Gourlay as he sat on a bench in George's Square. Some pigeons had gathered round an old man who was feeding them bits of bread. The buildings around the square were alive with hordes of twittering starlings which winged in every evening, after a day spent dining in the farmlands, to roost and compare notes in the warmth and safety of the City. Now they fought busy and noisy battles with one another as they competed for the best resting places while a few prattled like schoolgirls as they exchanged the gossip of the day. Even the statue of the Great White Queen was bedecked with scores of handsome birds clustered round her head and shoulders like bizarre fruits.

His crony, McMinn, had been taken to the Western Infirmary suffering from a liver complaint, and his landlady, far from being sympathetic, had taken advantage of his absence to oust him from his digs. His possessions — a large suitcase tied up with thick string, piles of books likewise tied together, and a few pathetic looking bundles wrapped in newspaper — now lay in a heap in the hallway. Gourlay recalled the times the pair of them had been forced to join the down-and-outs at the brick works at Baillieston where the great kilns retained enough heat from their day's work to keep body and soul together during the long, cruel winter nights. If O'Leary turned nasty, Gourlay thought, would it come to that again?

In an effort to raise funds for his pal, he'd been around all his debtors collecting such amounts as he was able. Only daft Harry's account was outstanding, but as nearly four years had elapsed since he'd lent him the ten shillings, he didn't hold out much hope — particularly as the miscreant was in the habit of assuming a guise of mute imbecility whenever the outstanding loan was mentioned.

The lifestyle of the pair had sustained further injury from the closing of the bakery on St. Vincent Street where they'd always been able to get half a dozen fresh-baked rolls at four in the morning from one particular man who loaded the vans in the cobbled courtyard simply by saying, "I've come for Mrs. Thompson's rolls." Some years earlier, attracted by the wonderful smell of oven-fresh bread, Gourlay had been skulking around watching the vans being loaded when one of the men said, "Can I help you mister?"

"Oh, ah, yes... Ah've come to collect, er, Mrs. Thompson's rolls..."

He was staggered when, wordlessly, the man had handed him half a dozen warm rolls. So for years they'd collected rolls, and nursing them under their overcoats to keep them warm, would walk the streets till they found a bottle of milk on a doorstep. But now the good days of the free rolls was a thing of the past...

Gourlay glanced up at the clock on the City Chambers building: five forty. Visiting hours at the hospital began at six, and McMinn had been particularly insistent that he come that evening. He set off along Sauchiehall Street at a good clip, pausing at each tram stop in the hope of being able to hop aboard while the conductor was busy on the top deck. He was out of luck. All the trams were full to bursting point and their harassed conductors were standing on the platforms ready to repel the sizeable queues waiting at the stops. He retrieved a newspaper from a litter basket at one of the stops, folded it, placed it in his coat pocket, then pulling his cap well down over his eyes, hunched his shoulders and continued on his way. For no particular reason he found himself thinking about Wallace and how the civilised English had disemboweled him and burnt his entrails before his dying eyes. "Basterts!" A tall, thin man who'd been gazing in a shop window eyed him with alarm and scurried away.

Arriving at the hospital, he went straight up to the ward where he found McMinn sitting up in bed reading a comic book. It was a large ward with beds along the walls and almost every patient had visitors.

"Hello McMinn! How's it goin'?"

"Gourlay... Whit's news?"

"Nuttin'... Whit a life! Ah had tae walk the whole way... Ah'm fair puchellt... Lucky you lyin' in yer scratcher a' day... An' Ah bet the grub's no' bad either."

"It's no' bad. Ah'm still oan a diet — fush an' chicken..."

There was a hiatus while Gourlay mentally devoured a chicken breast or two. "Did they find oot whit's wrong wi' ye, McMinn?"

"Hepatitis."

"Huh?"

"A kind o' jaundice."

"Jaundice?"

"Aye."

There was another pause. "Oh here, I brought you the paper."

"Thanks... Ah've read that Batman comic five times noo... Mebbe next time you come you could bring me somethin' decent tae read... Mebbe Hume...?"

"Right oh."

"Oh, an' lissen Gourlay, could ye do me anither favour like?"

"Nae problem."

"Weel, ye ken that bizzom o' a landleddy o' mine kicked ma gear oot?"

Gourlay clucked sympathetically.

"Ah'll be oot o' here in a week or so, an' Ah happen tae like that wee bield o' mine... She says Ah owe her three weeks' rent, an' in any case she disnae want me back because she thinks Ah'm an alcoholic..."

"Whit wey?"

"Remember a' thae empty whisky bottles in ma place?"

Gourlay nodded. "Aye, Ah helped ye finish a few masel'."

"When the auld bag — she's English ye ken — heard Ah wis in hospital wi' a liver complaint then saw a' the bottles... Onywey, the point is, Ah dinna want to flit the noo... Can ye get some cash an' see if ye can get her tae haud off for a while? Tell her it's no' ma liver but ma kidneys or something."

"Wha tellt her ye wis in the infirmary?"

"Dinna ken. But she sent her snotty son in law doon tae tell me tae get ma gear off the premises."

"Is that who brought you the Lucozade?" Gourlay indicated the half empty bottle on the bedside cabinet.

"Naw. Got that frae a fella in the next bed. Snuffed it yesterday... See that bed? It's got oxygen lines tae it... They pit these poor buggers that have heart attacks in it. Ah wis chattin' tae him just afore he croaked. He wis askin' me who won at Ibrox, then he wis taken bad an' they put an oxygen mask on him and brought in a priest... They pu'd the curtains roon the bed. Ah could see the priest's feet an' heard Latin words... Then he peed the bed..."

"The priest!" said Gourlay incredulously.

"Naw. The bluidy man, ye eejot! He peed the bed then died."

"Izzat right?"

"Aye."

"He just peed the bed then snuffed it?"

"Aye."

Gourlay removed his cap and scratched his head. "Well, Ah'm damned. Can ye beat that?"

"Efter they wheeled him away the nurse gave me his Lucozade an' his comic."

There was a pause during which both men solemnly eyed the vacant bed.

"Here," hissed McMinn, "tak' yer bunnet aff!"

"Huh?"

"Here's the matron!"

Gourlay removed his cap again and laid it on his knee. "Aw naw, it's no' her..."

Gourlay replaced his cap.

"Funny thing Gourlay, Ah fancy some grapes... Black grapes. Any chance you could bring some?"

"Grapes?"

"Black yins? Aye."

"Hoo can ye be properly siek withoot Lucozade an' black grapes?"

"Mind, Ah'll need a' the cash Ah can get for your landlady..."

"Aye, right enough," said McMinn with a little sigh. "Atweel, at least Ah've got the Lucozade... Mebbe the next bugger tae snuff it will leave me his grapes..."

The two sat idly gazing round the ward which held perhaps sixty men in beds ranged round the walls.

"It's an education bein' in hospital," said McMinn suddenly. "Sometimes ye even get a laugh."

"How's that?"

"Well, see that young fella ower there? Him wi' the green stripet pyjamas? He's a bobby. Had a collapsed lung... Thing is, the matron's awffy auld farrant and starchy like — her hair up in a bun an' that. Well, they gave him an injection — somebody said it wis pentothal — an' it made him act like a drunk. The doctor wis daen something tae his back wi' a huge needle — right here in the ward — an' the matron wis helpin' him. Well, see if the bobby startet makin' lewd remarks tae the matron: 'Did anybody tell you you've a nice perr o' tits,' an' the like. The matron just gave a wan smile an' had a look on her physog like somebody had farted an' naebody wis ownin' up... The bluidy doctor didna ken whaur tae look! An' efter he'd finished, he held up a jaur wi' some liquid in it an' we a' applauded... Aye, never a dull moment..."

The fog had more or less lifted and the pale yellow sun, which had struggled valiantly all day to make itself seen, finally retired to wherever tired suns go to recuperate. An unseasonal, raw east wind was making noses red and faces peaked and causing folk to turn up their coat collars. Gourlay, hands deep in his coat pockets, idly watched a busker entertaining a queue outside a cinema. He was a gangling, thin-faced individual in a top hat and was half-heartedly performing a shuffling tap dance while singing, "I've got a luvverly bunch of coconuts" in a pronounced Cockney accent. At the end of his routine he doffed his tattered hat and moved slowly along the line of people repeating, "Thank you, thank you." Occasionally, a coin was dropped into the hat and he would touch his forehead with his index finger in deferential salute. "Much obliged to you, much obliged..."

Pondering deeply, Gourlay moved on. In Renfield Street huddled another crowd of cinemagoers. He looked around then cleared his throat. "Ah've goat a lovely bunch of coconuts..." he sang hoarsely, tunelessly and slightly self-consciously, hopping from one foot to the other. Even above the noise of traffic, his raucous voice easily made its way to the cold ears of his audience.

"Awa' ye mug ye!" cried an unsteady voice from the queue. He stopped singing but continued his little shuffling dance as he eyed the queue through narrowed eyes.

"Awa' ye mug ye!" called the voice again.

Finally, he spotted the owner — a thoroughly evil-looking,

pimply faced fellow with a wispy, peroxide blonde dangling from his arm. The queue began to shuffle forward. Gourlay threw down the gauntlet.

"Step oot that line an' Ah'll melt ye, ye wee louse ye!"

Despite the blonde's pleas of "C'moan Billy, c'moan," fortified with cheap wine, Billy stepped forward. Brandishing a half-consumed bottle of red biddy, he looked more than capable of meeting Gourlay's challenge; Gourlay took his leave.

It was around one in the morning. The trams no longer ran and the streets were quiet. Stopping in a darkened doorway to light the stub of a saved cigarette, Gourlay mulled over various schemes to raise the cash necessary to keep McMinn's landlady at bay. In the back of a doorway, a small terrier-type dog was nosing a paper bag. Sensing that the beast was wholly engrossed and therefore unlikely to tear his leg off, he called softly, "Whit have ye got therr son?" The dog wagged its tail and stepped back. Gourlay leaned down, picked up the bag, glanced inside, and extracted a cheese sandwich. He sniffed it, and handed a piece to the dog. "Half for you, half for me son." The dog wolfed down his portion in a gulp and stood watching him expectantly.

Holding his portion between his teeth, Gourlay reached into the bag again pulling out what he thought was another sandwich, but it was an envelope containing a thick pile of pound notes neatly wrapped in tissue paper and held together with a rubber band. The uneaten sandwich fell from his sagging jaw and was instantly gobbled up by the watchful dog.

"Holy Jesus!"

He stuck his head out of the doorway, looked carefully up and down he street, and seeing no one, quickly pocketed the money, and made off as quickly as his wobbly legs would carry him. He did not see a shadowy figure across the street set off in pursuit.

In the underground toilet at Charing Cross, Wee Jummock was sitting on an upturned bucket intently studying a volume of

Tchehov's short stories. Gourlay clattered down the steps, a little breathless, but otherwise reasonably composed.

"Hello Jummock."

"Aye aye Gourlay... Whit's new?"

"Nuttin much... Whit's the cludgie situation?"

"Bloke in the end yin should be oot in a jiff."

"Thanks."

He made his way to the end cubicle, and Jummock went back to his book. The door opened and a man emerged, and just before it swung to, Gourlay caught it with his foot and went in. Thanks to a long standing agreement with Jummock, who turned a blind eye to his pals slipping in to a toilet on some else's penny, he habitually availed himself of the free facility whenever he was in the neighbourhood.

Locking the door carefully behind him, he lowered the toilet seat, sat down, and drew the wad of money from his coat. With trembling fingers he counted it, not once, but four times; eighty seven pounds in single notes! "Holy, holy Jesus!" he husked, and closed his eyes the better to savour the joys the money would surely bring. McMinn could have all the black grapes he could eat... His landlady could be paid... Ha! These left boots could be replaced..! And their embryonic Army unit would now have a small kitty... He spent little time agonizing over who the rightful owner of the cash might be — finders keepers, losers greeters. He looked upon the windfall as abundant proof of a benevolent, if often absent, force in the world.

Feeling expansive and generous with his newfound wealth, his thoughts went again to his pal McMinn languishing in his hospital bed. McMinn was his bosom crony, steadfast as Ailsa Craig, always there when needed. "Grapes be dammed," he thought, "I'll give him cash an' he can have whatever his heart desires." He nodded in satisfaction at this decision, and taking forty notes from the bundle, was about to place them in his trousers' pocket when a loud and aggressive voice echoing from tile to tile reached his ears.

"Hey you! Did a wee fella come in...? Ugly, wearin' a black coat an' bunnet?" Jummock's answer was inaudible. With his highly developed sense of self-preservation, Gourlay felt danger in the strident, anxious voice of his unseen searcher. He carefully raised his legs, crossed them on the toilet lid, and sat as silently and still as a china Buddha. The stranger moved along the row of toilet cubicles peering under the doors and shaking the handles with considerable violence. "If ye're lyin' tae me, ye cretin," he threatened Jummock, "Ah'll slit your bluidy throat!"

"Ah tellt ye, there's naebody here."

Gourlay leaned back against the cold cistern scarcely daring to breathe as the footsteps approached and stopped outside his door. The door shook. "Hey! Why's this wan marked 'Engaged'?"

"It's gettin' mairrit tae wan o' the doors in the Ladies next week!" was Jummock's dry response.

"Leave the jokes tae Lex... Whit wey is it engaged?"

"It's broke."

"You'll be bloody broke if that's a lee," threatened the man. The door was shaken violently again. Then Gourlay heard the retreating footsteps, then silence. His heart almost stopped when Jummock's small voice at the door said, "It's O.K. Gourlay, he's gone."

"Are ye sure?"

"Aye. He's gone."

Cautiously, he emerged. "You're a real man, Jummock... Here..." He peeled a pound note from the wad in the envelope and handed it to the boggle-eyed attendant.

"Thanks Gourlay! Thanks!"

"Just remember, ye never saw me — Ah wis never here."

"Right. Whatever ye say, Gourlay!" said the little hunchback with a broad grin.

Gourlay examined himself briefly in one of the mirrors above a sink, pushed his cap back to a rakish angle, and momentarily pulled a truly horrendous grimace. Then, turning to the little man, asked, "Oh, did ye give any more thought to what we wis discussin' the ither day, Jummock?"

"Ah did... Oor family lost five men in the Great War... We're from the Hielans originally, an' it wis the wan an' only time thae lads left Scotland... Ah got tae thinkin' aboot thon poor buggers sittin' in the trenches... Christ, Gourlay, it wisna their fight; they were all Gaelic speakers... Hardly a word of English between them... They must have wondered whit the hell they were doin' in Flanders..." He gave a deep sigh. "We Scots have aye spilt oor blood either fightin' the English or fightin' for them... Aye, Ah'll see yer friend Quayle ony time ye can arrange it..."

With feigned boldness, Gourlay emerged into the open air, and after a quick look round, scampered along the street and dissolved into the darkness. That the man who was looking for him was somehow connected with the money he had no doubt. As he made his way about the City he concentrated on throwing his unseen pursuer off the trail by dodging up laneways, and assuming what he considered to be effective ruses; he'd lean forward as far as he could without falling and shamble along like an orangutan. From time to time he would stand in darkened close mouths for long periods to see if he was being followed.

There was no sign of his pursuer, but he was taking no chances. He caught site of a night service bus approaching, and as he was right at a bus stop, decided to board it. It wasn't a Corporation bus, however, and it sped past him into the night its windows all steamed up. The streets were quiet. Old habits die hard, and seeing a litter basket on a lamp post, he began to rummage through it.

"Hey Jimmmy, got a light?"

So intent was he that he had not noticed the stranger's

approach.

"Er, oh, aye..." Fishing in his pocket he found a box of matches and struck a light. The stranger leaned forward cigarette in mouth. By the match's flickering light Gourlay noted the pale complexion and reddish hair of the man.

"Thanks pal," said the man. Gourlay nodded and began to turn away when, without warning, the man produced a knife and holding Gourlay by the lapels, placed the blade under his chin. "Right ya wee nyaff, where's the money?"

"Money?"

The blade was pushed more firmly into his flesh forcing his head back.

"Stop fuckin' me aboot," hissed the man. "The money!"

"Ah canna reach it!" croaked Gourlay. "Take that bluidy knife away an' ye can have yer money."

Slowly, the knife was lowered. "Hurry up!" commanded his assailant. With slow deliberation, his heart in his mouth, Gourlay went through his pockets. Noticed only by Gourlay, a policeman, torch in hand, was tugging at door handles as he made his leisurely way in their direction. Gourlay extracted the envelope from his coat pocket and as the man was about to take it from him, went berserk. A wild kick sent the knife clattering against the wall beside them and a heft punch caught the man high on the temple. "Thief! Thief!" roared Gourlay at the top of his lungs as he aimed a series of savage kicks in the direction of the man's genitalia. Numbed by the suddenness and ferocity of the assault, all the man could do was hold on. The policeman ran up as the envelope fell on the pavement scattering its contents.

"Right, against the wall, the pair of you!" He shoved them towards the wall and picked up the knife. "Whose money?"

"It's mine," said the man instinctively. The policeman scooped up the envelope and money. "It says 'James Logan' on the envelope," he said examining it by the light of his torch. "Which one of you is Logan?"

No answer was forthcoming.

"Right. You can tell your stories to the sergeant at the station... Walk slowly in front of me, and no monkey business."

The desk sergeant was sipping a mug of cocoa when the trio entered. The wall, painted institutional green, gave everything and everybody a green hue. Gourlay pulled off his cap deferentially and stood twisting it in his hands.

"I apprehended these two male persons up Maryhill Road near Queen's Cross, Sarge. They were causing a disturbance... Ginger here had a knife, and the wee fellow was laying into him something fierce. One of them dropped this." He placed the envelope on the highly polished desk. "Ginger here claimed the money was his..." The sergeant drained his green cocoa with a slurping noise, tugged his ear, and looked narrowly at Gourlay. "Were you the clown I saw dancing outside the Odeon?"

Gourlay assumed his blank look which masked some very rapid thinking. This was a dicey situation, and caution was called for.

"Dancin'?"

"That's whit I said... In Renfield Street... I wis oan a bus passin'..."

Gourlay eyed the shrewd looking sergeant. From past experience he knew that co-operation, or apparent co-operation always went down well with the police.

"Yes sir. I was feelin' happy, so thought..."

"Never mind that now," interrupted the sergeant. He slipped the money out of the envelope and counted it carefully. "Forty five pounds..." He jotted the amount into a blotter and added, 'Logan, James'.

Forty five? thought Gourlay. *Should be forty seven... No, forty six; I forgot the quid I gave Jummock...*

The sergeant turned to the pale-faced man. "And you claim

this is your money?" The man remained mute. "I suppose you're James Logan," said the sergeant heavily. Again, silence. He turned to Gourlay, "What time were you doin' your wee dance routine?"

"Er, just before the hoose went in... Nine thirty... Aye nine thirty..."

The sergeant grunted and scribbled something into the jotter. "An' why did ye attack this man?"

Gourlay's mind went into high gear. He still had forty pounds in his pocket, and, like a nervous quiz game contestant, knew that if he gave the correct answers he just might get to keep the money and remain free to enjoy it to boot. The problem facing him was, what were the correct answers? "Oh, Ah didna attack him, sergeant... He asked for a light, and Ah gave him wan... He musta burnt his fingers because he swore at me an' then we got into a wee dust up..."

"You gave him a light?"

"Aye." He produced a crushed box of matches.

"Have ye seen him afore?"

"No, never," repled Gourlay. He shook his head from side to side. "Never."

"O.K., Smiler," said the sergeant heavily turning to the pallid faced man. "Have ye anything tae sae for yersel'?" The man scowled darkly, glared at Gourlay, but made no reply.

"Right, constable..." said the sergeat, "Take him away... We've got him for disturbing the peace, an' carrying an offensive weapon for a start. Mebbe a night in the slammer will jog his memory..."

As the man was led away, the sergeant leaned over the desk and scrutinized Gourlay. "You're a very lucky lad... Very lucky for you that wee bit o' buskin' was... Logan's shop was broken into between nine and ten tonight... An' you werena there were you?"

"No sir."

"No sir... You're a lucky lad aren't you?"

"Yes sir."

"Three bags full, sir... Well, off with you... If you drop in later in the week I might, just might, get Logan tae cough up a couple of quid reward money for you."

"Verra kind of you sergeant." He put on his cap and headed for the door.

"And don't forget, my lad..." The sergeant tapped his nose meaningfully, "Keep your nose clean! O.K?"

Out in the street again, Gourlay breathed deeply. His hand went to his trousers' pocket... The money was still there. He walked along sedately, and when he had put several streets between himself and the police station, he stopped short and looked about. Not a soul was in sight. He removed his cap, placed it on the pavement, and began jumping up and down on it bawling and hooting with delight. Near the chimneys high above him, some pigeons expressed their displeasure at the disturbance.

CHAPTER 8

Gourlay had never seen McMinn's little room look so spruce. On the assumption that he'd not be returning, his landlady had cleaned it from top to bottom in preparation for a new tenant; new wallpaper (little rosebuds on a pale blue background) covered the walls, and the windows sparkled. But thanks to his pal's windfall, McMinn was back, and improvements not withstanding, his rent had even been reduced by a few shillings. While resting in hospital he'd been chatting to the friendly almoner and discovered details of the Rental Properties Control Acts, and later, when he'd talked to a helpful City official, he'd been delighted to learn that the rent on McMinn's room had been set at seven shillings and sixpence back in 1927 and that was the legal maximum his landlady could charge. The official explained that his landlady would doubtless apply for a review and permission to increase the weekly amount but that McMinn would have to be given six months' notice before any new rate could be implemented.

"Aye, you should have been therr when Ah tellt her, Gourlay! She wis fair bilin'! Jumpin' up an' doon like a wee pudden wi' her bosoms jiggling! She said she'd get her son-in-law tae chuck me oot, but Ah tellt her that if she didna simmer doon Ah'd tell her ither tenants tae pay the 1927 rate... That pit her gas at a peep!" He chortled happily and did an exuberant little jig. Gourlay wagged his head. "You're a lucky bugger, McMinn,"

"Aye... Ye should check the rent at yer ain place."

"Mebbe... But O'Leary's bad enough as it is... He'd have canniptions if his rents were rolled back... For a few bob, it's probably best tae let sleepin' dugs lie."

"Suit yersel'."

Gourlay noticed that apart from a yellowish pallor, McMinn looked none the worse for his bout with hepatitis, and was happy for his friend.

"Whit time is it Gourlay?"

"Around six."

"Hmmph... Hector's supposed tae be here... Said he'd be here after five..."

McMinn had arranged for Hector to call round, then the three of them would head for Quayle's where they'd meet up with the student, Gordon, and Wee Jummock. It had been Quayle's suggestion that the group hold its first meeting as a unit at his place.

"Forty bluidy quid! An' you're aye saying that *Ah'm* lucky!" said McMinn with a sly smile.

"Mebbe Big Red's sword has changed oor luck, er, ma luck."

"Mebbe... An' whit aboot the reward? Will you go back to the polis for it?"

"No chance! An' in ony case, Logan has paid dearly enough as it is... Here, did Ah mention that Logan's is a tool shop?"

At that moment, they heard voices on the landing below and then Hector came up the flight of stairs and into the room. "Hector! Come on in," said McMinn. "Ye'll mind Gourlay?"

"Indeed I do... We did some digging together..." He shook hands with Gourlay. "None the worse for the little explosion I see, Gourlay?"

"Naw." Dressed in his habitual boiler suit and checked cap, the little man at first glance looked innocuous, even nondescript. But a clean-shaven, angular jaw and clear blue eyes with their steady, alert gaze hinted at a strong will.

"Something tae drink, Hector?" enquired McMinn.

"Tea, if you have it thanks... No milk or sugar."

"Right... The doctors have put me off booze for a year, but Ah'm no bothered really," said McMinn as he busied himself at the sink.

"So you spoke to Quayle?" asked Gourlay turning to the little man.

"I did that... Of course, I've known Big Red and Quayle for a number of years, but this is a brand new venture." Hector removed his cap and scratched his bald spot.

"What attracts you to this Army, Hector, if you don't mind me askin'?"

"Not at all."

Gourlay noticed that his voice was refined and had an uncommonly rich timbre to it for such a small man. McMinn handed him a cup of tea which he sipped like a lady.

"You see, I've always been one for causes — ever since I was a lad... Can't explain it really... It seems as if I have spent my whole life volunteering, protesting, or marching for some cause or other..."

McMinn stretched himself comfortably on the bed.

"Know thyself," continued Hector. "That's what it's all about... No matter what the theologians say, and they have a lot to say, and I think I've heard the lot, the world is really an extension of oneself... And before you can know the world and know your fellows, you have to know yourself... Well, I happen to believe that a sense of one's national identity, one's cultural heritage, is fundamental to the process of coming to understand yourself... And we're particularly fortunate in Scotland because we are a distinct people... The knowledge that I am a Scot is a comfort to me because it helps me to define myself, to know who I am... That's a nice cuppa, McMinn... But our national identity has been under a state of siege by the English for centuries, and never more so than at present..." he broke off and smiled suddenly. "But I'm preaching, and to the converted at that... Once I get started, there is no stopping me!" Gourlay studied the little man. Maybe he really had been a monk once and had taken a vow of silence... But he was certainly making a good job of making up for the years of silence...

"We're comrades in arms," said McMinn expansively from the bed, "an' it's interestin' tae learn why folks signed up..."

"What about you, Gourlay?" asked Hector. "What is your interest?"

"Me? Well, for a start, I've only met a handfu' o' Englishmen that I really liked an' trusted... But Ah have ma reasons," he added cryptically.

"More tea anyone?" asked McMinn sitting up in the bed. Finding no takers, he lay back again. "Did you take the oath on thon big sword Hector?"

"That I did, McMinn...And very gratifying it was too..." He finished the last of his tea. "What time are we due at Quayle's?"

"If your knock's right, McMinn, it's time we were on our way," said Gourlay.

The little gathering at Quayle's could have passed for a regular meeting of some small town literary society; at least, that's the way it seemed to Gourlay: Gordon, the student, quoted Fergusson and other lesser known Scottish poets; Jummock reeled off lines of Tchehovian dialogue; Quayle tossed in occasional references to De Quincey, Johnson, Schiller, Carlyle and the like, and McMinn produced a scrap of paper and read the old Celtic oath and some Ossianic apocrypha. Not to be outdone, Hector recounted an anecdote from Kierkegaard in which a fellow walking down the street contemplating suicide had been struck on the head by a falling slate and with his dying breath called out, "Praise the Lord!" Gourlay laughed raucously while Hector and Quayle looked at him with bemused smiles.

After another round of sherry and toasts to the success of the Army, Quayle produced beautiful miniature replicas of the great sword which they all solemnly pinned to the underside of their lapels. Then Quayle explained that under Big Red's tutelage, Wee Jummock had completed a crash course on explosives and was ready for action. At this, Jummock tapped the satchel which was slung round his shoulders and smiled broadly. Hoping no one would notice, Gourlay moved to a chair farther away from the little man. Their cell, explained Quayle, had been given the signal honour of being charged with striking the first blow for Scotland's freedom. The target was an easy one, he said; a statue of Wellington in Kelvingrove Park... They were to demolish it and telephone Quayle when the mission had been accomplished so that Quayle, in turn, could inform the newspapers. It was to be done that very night...

With Quayle's, "Good luck comrades!" ringing in their ears, the group set off along the dark streets. A light rain was falling.

"Ah just hope tae fuck Wee Jummock kens whit he's daen," said Gourlay darkly to no one in particular.

"Ach, it's only a wee stachoo we're blowin' up, no' the Forth Road Bridge," responded McMinn in a low voice.

"Aye. But ye'll recall that it his instructor wis the fella who damn near blew us to hell in the tunnel!"

As they clomped along the mirky streets, Gourlay pulled his cap low over his eyes against the rain which was heavier now, and mulled over the absurdity of it all; here they were, plodding along for all the world like schoolboys on their way to a picnic. Behind them, Hector and Gordon listened intently to some yarn of Wee Jummock's. When he finished, there were gales of laughter and Hector clapped the little hunchback on the arm.

"Easy now! Easy!" cried Jummock, his Adam's apple bobbing in alarm. He shifted the satchel to his other arm. "Ah'm a walkin' bomb mind!" The laughter ended abruptly. Gourlay shook his head, but said nothing.

"How come it takes five o' us tae demolish wan wee stachoo?"

queried McMinn voicing Gourlay's own concerns. "Surely Wee Jummock could dae it on his tod?"

"I expect the idea is to get us functioning as a team, McMinn," said Gordon. "I expect that some jobs will call for a whole gang of fellows..."

At the park entrance off Woodlands Road the gallant band huddled expectantly as if awaiting further orders. It was Gordon who took the initiative.

"O.K., Jummock. You're the man with the fireworks... What's the plan?"

Jummock shifted his weight uncomfortably from one foot to the other. "Em...Well, first let's find Wellington..." They pressed on over the neatly trimmed grass until McMinn's exultant whoop stopped them in their tracks. "There he is!" And above them, on a flat, landscaped area, loomed a dark man of bronze on a bronze horse. Jummock carefully placed his satchel on the plinth and opened it with trembling fingers.

"Haud oan! Haud oan! This is no' Wellington," girned McMinn in a hurt voice. Hector managed to strike a match and leaned forwards for a better look.

Immediately, Jummock yelled out in alarm, "Jesus Christ Hector! Tak' tent! The bag's fu' o' dynamite!" Hector quickly extinguished the match.

"It's Lord Roberts... I remember now. It's Lord Roberts of Kandahar," said Gordon.

"Lord Roberts or Wellington," said McMinn huffily, "who cares? Let's blow the fucker up onywey."

"Who the hell is Lord Roberts when he's at hame?" piped Wee Jummock.

"He's not even English," responded Gordon. "He's Irish."

"Well, in any event, he's no' a Scot," grumbled McMinn... C'moan Jummock, strut yer stuff. Let's gie him a blast."

"We came to blow up Wellington," said Hector testily,

"so let's see if we can find him... Let's meet back here in five minutes..."

Their quick sweep of the park flushed out a soggy courting couple caught *in flagrente delicto*, an irate drunk, oblivious to the rain, half asleep on a bench, and a statue of Thomas Carlyle. But of Wellington there was no sign. A somewhat disconsolate group went into consultation below the brooding figure of Lord Roberts on his brooding horse.

"Let's call it a night — Let's a' go hame," suggested McMinn. "Ah'm cauld an' weet an' oot o' fags."

Wee Jummock cleared his throat. "Lissen. We came here tae strike the first blow for independence an' Ah'm no leavin' till Ah've struck it...In ony case, if ye think Ah'm taking' a bag o' dynamite hame, think again."

The rain fell steadily on the group. Suddenly, a series of whistle blasts pierced the night air.

"The polis!" husked McMinn pirouetting around in panic.

"It's the parkie... It's closing time," Gordon reassured him. "They lock the gates at 9:30... Let's get out, have a think, then come back."

In some disarray, they headed for the main gate, but the efficient park keeper had already closed and locked it. McMinn clambered up and landed heavily with an oath on the other side. Jummock swung his satchel round his head and was about to launch it over the gates when Gordon grabbed his arm. "Easy Jummock! Have you forgotten what's in your bag?" The little man paled, then holding the satchel between clenched teeth, began a careful ascent of the dripping ironwork.

They regrouped in a telephone kiosk; that is to say Gourlay, McMinn. Hector and Gordon crowded in face to face while an unhappy Jummock remained outside in the rain.

"Ye're no' comin' in here wi' that bag of explosives an' that's that!" McMinn menaced.

Gourlay produced a damp cigarette which he lit and shared with McMinn and Gordon. Ignoring Jummock's insistent rapping on the steamed up glass, they discussed their next move. "Initiative," began Hector. "That's what it's all about... We couldn't find Wellington, so we should hit another English target... Any suggestions?"

"How about Queen Victoria in George's Square?" said Gourlay. "Or isn't there another stachoo of Wellington in Exchange Square?"

"Naw. Too busy doon therr," responded McMinn between barking coughs. "But I've an idea... Whit about the B.B.C. Controller's car?"

"Is he a Sassenach?" queried Gordon.

"Naw, a bluidy Pakistani! He's bound tae be a Sassenach... Stands tae reason dunnit? He'll either be a Sassenach or kiddin' oan he's wan... Ah met his chauffeur in a pub a while syne... Nice car too. Let's dae it and we can a' go hame. What do you say lads?"

There was an immediate nodding of heads; wet and cold, they just wanted to blow up something — anything — and go home. They stumbled out to inform Jummock of their decision.

The rain continued to pelt down, but by now they were all thoroughly soaked and past caring. Despite the lateness of the hour, the parking lot at the B.B.C. was fairly full and they slunk around examining the cars until McMinn called, "Ower here!" They crowded round a somewhat elderly, large black saloon.

"Is this it?" asked Hector doubtfully.

"Aye."

"It's awffy tatty lookin'"

"Well, that's the wan I've seen Denny the chauffeur drivin'..."

Gourlay thought he detected a little uncertainty on his friend's brow, but said nothing. Muttering unhappily, Jummock fumbled with his bag.

"What's the problem?" asked Gordon.

"Big Red showed me how tae blaw up a stachoo, no' a car... Ah had just tae tie some sticks tae the cuddy's front legs, light the fuse, an' rin like fuck," he moaned. "But Ah've nae idea aboot cars..."

"Ach, stick the lot under the bloody car," advised the practical McMinn.

They gathered round with interest as the little hunchback reluctantly crawled under the car and placed the explosives on the wet ground then emerged holding two lengths of fuse. "A match... Who's got a match?" McMinn produced a box and handed it to Jummock whose trembling fingers finally managed to strike a light after half a dozen attempts. The fuse sputtered dismally and there was an immediate stampede by the five men.

Safe behind the low stone wall topped by a wrought iron fence which enclosed the area, five wet and apprehensive faces watched intently. A light drizzle continued to fall... The minutes ticked by slowly.

"Yer fuse has gone oot, Jummock," said McMinn unnecessarily.

"Aye..." The little man shook his head. They turned to him, but the little hunchback made no move. "If youse think Ah'm takin' a dander doon tae light it again, forget it!" A chorus of, "C'moan Jummock... Hey, hurry up Jummock!" left him unmoved.

"Hauf wey doon therr, an' Ah bet the bluidy thing wad go off... It couldna fail," he moaned.

Hector rubbed his wet face with his sleeve and leaned towards him. "You're the expert, Jummock — What are you going to do now?"

"Nuttin'... If any of youse wants tae try, that's fine by me; Ah'll no be affrontit."

No one took up his offer.

"Let's cut oor losses lads," suggested Gourlay. "Let's call it a day."

They had barely reached the roadway when there was an enormous "BOOM!" followed immediately by the sound of breaking glass. They turned just in time to see the wrecked and still smouldering vehicle return to the earth with a great crash. As if in slow motion, the doors fell off and a wheel rolled forlornly across the dimly-lit parking lot. Jummock, wide-eyed, uttered a shriek and a curse which more than adequately expressed his awe and fear, and took to his heels in a peculiar crab-like trot. The rest followed — Hector and Gordon in the direction of Maryhill, and Gourlay and McMinn towards Great Western Road.

"Hey! Slow doon, McMinn!" puffed Gourlay, but his crony steamed on as though the hellish legion were at his heels and vanished into the mirk and mizzle. Stopping to catch his breath, Gourlay removed his cap, threw his head back and let the cool rain fall onto his upturned face. He was soaked almost to the skin, and his toes squished in his boots. "What a balls up," he mused. "But at least we blew up something even if it wis only a rotten auld car... 'Spec Jummock will 'phone Quayle wi' the good news..." Replacing his cap, he ambled off.

Little rivers ran along the glistening tram rails and between the cobblestones. In the gutters, pieces of paper raced empty cigarette packets to the gratings. Each bead of rain round the peak of his cap held a miniature street lamp. He scowled bleakly at the scene before him. Even the consolation of finding a dry cigarette butt was denied him.

He came across a young man in evening clothes peering dismally into the engine compartment of a very large black car parked by the side of the road and watched with interest for a few moments wondering if the car was a Bentley.

"Car broke, Mac?"

"Beg your pardon?"

"Car broke doon is it?"

"Yes, I'm afraid so... Just cut out on me."

Gourlay was quick to note that the young man was cultured, well-to-do, and obviously clueless as to what to do about the broken monster.

"I say, do you know anything about cars?"

"Used tae fix tanks when Ah wis in the Army an' that... Er, you're no' oot of petrol are ye?"

"No. I just filled her up..."

As best as he could in the gloom, Gourlay studied the engine much in the manner of a consultant attempting to diagnose a patient with an obscure disease. "Hmmph... Could be the coil..." Tentatively, he extended his hand into a confusing mass of wires. "Turn it ower..." The young man slipped into the driver's seat and pressed the starter. The engine turned, but did not fire. Sparks danced along the plug leads. "O.K. Haud oan... Turn it off... It's the bluidy rain," he explained. "The wires are a' damp. Have ye got a rag or somethin' dry tae wipe them wi'?" The young man produced a handkerchief, and Gourlay noted with wonder that it seemed to be perfumed. He wiped the wires as best as he could. "O.K. Try her again..."

After coughing a few times, the engine finally spluttered into life. Gourlay pocketed the handkerchief.

"Oh, I say!" exclaimed the young man sticking his head out of the window, "That's marvellous. How can I ever thank you?"

A quid would go a long way, thought Gourlay as he closed the car's bonnet.

"Can I give you a lift somewhere? It's the least I can do on such a miserable night," said the young man brightly.

"Thanks." Gourlay got into the car. "Is this a Bentley?"

"No. It's a Daimler... Very similar in many ways... Have you worked on Bentleys then?"

"No. But Ah like them..."

The car swished through the dark, wet streets. Despite

himself, Gourlay found himself taking a liking to the well-spoken man who insisted that he call him Monty. He leaned back in the comfortable seat contemplatively sucking on the wicked looking cheroot Monty had handed him. Lulled by the hum of the engine and the regular movement of the windshield wipers, he almost dozed off.

"Can I drop you off anywhere particular?"

Gourlay attempted to clear his mind; it seemed a crime that this elegance and comfort should ever have to come to an end. As they rolled along in easy silence, he noticed that the interior of the car smelled of cigar smoke and damp leather.

"Did I hear you say you were in the Army, Gourlay?"

"Aye... Eighth Army, 30th. Corps in North Africa... 1941 on... Saw some action too..." He puffed on his cheroot. "Ah'll never forget the heat, the flies, the sand, the bully beef... An' that bugger Rommel... Clever bugger..."

"Arnold, Major Walter Arnold will probably be at this do tonight. He was in the desert... Always on about the desert campaigns... I don't suppose you ran across him when you were in the Army by any chance?"

Gourlay flipped through the diary of his memories... A collage of faces and events ran past like an old film, and then he had it; Major Arnold's face came into sharp focus... "He got wounded," he reminisced. "Shrapnel in the hip... He was invalided hame... As a matter of fact, Ah've got a picture from a newspaper of him in ma wallet!"

"Well I'll be damned!"

"One of the lads sent me it a while back because Ah'm in the picture too... The Major wis oan a stretcher an' Ah wis helpin' to carry him to the ambulance when someone took the snap... It's the only one Ah've got of masel' in North Africa."

"Well I'll be damned," repeated Monty.

"Is the Major a crony of yours like?"

"Not really. My brother-in-law had some business dealings with him... Oh, Walter turns up at the odd social do... Quite a lad by all accounts. Fond of the ladies and geegees and that sort of thing... Come to think of it, the blighter owes me twenty quid!"

Gourlay pensively studied the tip of his glowing cheroot. "He was a fine sodger an' a good leader... We a' liked him...Ah mind the time he was greetin' when a tank crushed three of his men... We wis bivouacked oot in the desert an' were in the habit of sleepin' under the tanks. But this night there was a wee sprinkle of rain and one of the tanks sank intae the sand and crushed the crew."

"Good God! How terrible."

"Funny thing, it just sank in the sand withoot warning... It wis cauld in the night... An' Ah remember shoutin' and torches an' men runnin' aboot... My buddy McMinn wis wi' that crew, but lucky for him he was on guard duty that night... Ah mind the next day seein' the Major sittin' at his wee table outside his tent writin' letters hame to the next of kin and greetin'..."

The drizzle had ceased. Gourlay looked out of the window, but did not recognize where he was. "I say," said Monty suddenly, "why don't you come along with me to this do, this party tonight? The Major will likely be there and I'm sure you two would find a lot to talk about."

"A party? Very kind of you, Monty, but Ah'm no' exactly dressed..."

"No problem, my dear chap. It's a fancy dress affair — evening togs are always acceptable, so I can go as I am and you can have my costume — something my sister looked out for me... A cat or something... It's in the boot. There will be oodles of food, booze and women; the Rawlinsons always lay on a pretty fair spread. What do you say?"

"Well, er..."

"That's settled then. Good! I'm sure the Major will greet you like an old comrade."

The car crunched up a curved driveway towards an imposing house and came to rest beside a gazebo which glistened damply under the light spilling from the windows. With Monty's aid, Gourlay struggled into the cat costume which he put on over his damp clothes. His coat and cap he left in the car. "Oh, your hanky, Monty... It wis in ma pocket."

"You look quite splendid!" said Monty with a smile. "And I do like the tail!"

Feeling ridiculous beside the elegant Monty, Gourlay followed him into the house. The guests, most of them in outlandish costumes, greeted Monty; he was obviously a popular figure, and soon, a buxom female, dressed as some Wagnerian heroine, whisked him off into the thick of things.

A side table, weighed down with cold cuts, caught Gourlay's eye and he made his way towards it through the throng. Although the mask made eating difficult, he wolfed down ham, beef, veal, and smoked salmon with equal gusto. In the mass of surging bodies he remained unnoticed and realized to his delight that wearing the costume was akin to having been granted the gift of invisibility.

"I thay puthycat!" warbled a voice at his elbow.

Invisible, my arse! speculated Gourlay. *Ah might be anonymous, but no' invisible.*

"I thay puthycat! I thee you don't have a drink. Can I get you one?"

He turned, and was surprised to see that the voice belonged to what appeared to be a stalwart female complete with ample bosoms and flaxen hair.

"Christ! An' what are you supposed tae be?" queried Gourlay.

"Thethpith."

"Sesspiss?"

"Yeth, Thethpith."

"An' who the hell is Thethpiss when she's at hame?"

"Thethpith wath the father of Greek drama," explained the contralto.

"Izzat a fact...? Hang on though; if he was the faither, why are you dressed like a wumman?"

"Well," lisped the goddess in a confidential tone, "actually, I'm Pitho, the goddeth of perthuathion, but ath everybody knowth Thethpith and nobody knowth Pitho, it maketh it eathier to thay that I'm Thethpith, thee?"

"Goad!" Thoroughly unnerved, Gourlay headed for the bar where he downed a large whisky in a gulp before daring to peek at the blonde goddess again. Nonplussed at Gourlay's abrupt behaviour, Pitho was munching maraschino cherries from a little crystal bowl.

Turning to the bar again, he ordered another double. Above the music, laughter and gay chatter, he could hear a voice calling, "Walter! Dear, dear Walter! So you came after all. It's me, Elizabeth."

Gourlay stared ahead waiting the arrival of his whisky. A hand was laid on his shoulder. "Walter!" The attractive owner of the voice gazed somewhat unevenly at him with limpid eyes. Slightly tipsy, her costume in a state of disarray, she made a very unconvincing vampire. "I knew you'd come," she breathed. He reached for his whisky.

"Dance with me, Walter," she insisted and pulled him away from the bar. Still grimly clutching his glass he was swept by the ghoul onto the dance floor. As they danced, Gourlay felt the room beginning to spin — faces and lights blended into a kaleidoscope of colour. The music suddenly stopped, the dancers stopped, but Gourlay swirled on, his boots clomping complicated rhythms on the parquet floor and his tail streaming out behind him. He fell into the arms of Elizabeth who held him steady long enough for him to drain the few drops of whisky which remained in his glass.

JAMES FINDLAY SLEIGH

Her legs wobbling only slightly less than his, she led him up the staircase and into a darkened room. A double bed piled high with coats dominated the room. She kicked the door shut, slipped the catch, and launched herself at Gourlay who fell heavily on to the bed, the vampire at his throat.

"Dear, dear Walter," she husked. "You are a very naughty boy! You've been avoiding me... Now make it up to me, you lovely tom cat you!" He closed his eyes. The whisky glass fell from his limp fingers. His groping hand found a full, firm breast... "Eat yer bluidy heart oot, Walter!" he mumbled...

The party was still in full swing when he staggered down the stairs some time later, his broken tail dangling pathetically. Supported by the newel post at the foot of the staircase, he surveyed the room through bleary, red-rimmed eyes.

"Hulloo there, Gourlay!"

He tried to focus his eyes in the direction of the voice.

"Hulloo!"

It was Monty, red-faced and collar askew, but otherwise reasonably intact.

"Good grief, old chap! What happened to you? It looks like you walked into a hurricane!"

"Aye... Here, who the fuck is Walter?"

"Walter?"

"Aye, this burd mistook me for somebody ca'd Walter."

"Could be Walter Arnold, the Major...You look as if you could do with a stiff drink, old chap," said Monty and steered Gourlay towards the bar.

They sipped their drinks and idly watched the milling motley of characters around them.

"Ah!" cried Monty. "The Major!" Gourlay saw a smallish man, dressed as a cat, and from what little he could see of his visage and from his lurching walk, it was obvious that the military man was not quite sober.

"I say! Major Arnold!" called Monty.

The Major squinted at him. "It'sh Monty, isn't it?"

"Yes… I say, do come and join us."

The Major ambled over, drink in hand.

"Do you recognize this chap?" asked Monty affably.

The Major eyed Gourlay narrowly. "No... Can't say I do... Looksh like a bloody tom cat that's been in a fight!"

"Gourlay... Major Walter Arnold, scourge of Erwin Rommel," said Monty introducing the two cats.

"Oh, scarcely old boy... Though I like to think that we gave his Afrika Korps something to think about."

Gourlay peered at him closely. Whoever the fellow was, he most certainly wasn't Major Walter Arnold... He was far too short, and the accent and voice were completely wrong.

"You were in the desert campaigns then?" asked Gourlay.

"Indeed yes. With the Eighth — 30th. Corps through all the campaigns... 'Woah-ho Mahomet!'" he warbled. Gourlay recognized it as the First Army's battle cry.

"Ah was wi' the 30th. too... Ah wis wan o' the stretcher bearers that carried you tae the ambulance when you got shrapnel in the leg... Here, Ah've got a photo of you an' me..." He groped under his costume for his wallet.

"Well, er, yes. Very good old boy..." He turned to Monty. "I say old chap, would you excuse us for a moment... We old comrades in arms have a lot of catching up to do — shop talk don't you know."

Monty, who had been trying to catch the bartender's eye, nodded and smiled easily. "Of course. I'll catch you both later."

Taking Gourlay firmly by the arm, the major steered him through the dancers, across the hallway, and out the front door into the sweet, damp night.

On the lawn, the Major drew himself up as smartly and with as much dignity as his inebriated state and cat costume would allow, and addressed Gourlay. "Now look here my good man, I don't quite know what you hope to gain by this charade. How dare you attempt to embarrass me in front of my friends? I will not tolerate it, do you hear? And stand to attention when I'm addressing you!" he snapped. For a fleeting moment, before his rational mind took over, Gourlay's limbs obeyed. His boots clicked together, his chin pushed in to his chest, and his shoulders went back... He could hear the distant rumble of gunfire, and the heavy, sweetish smell of stale sweat, cordite, and hot oily musk of the tank's interior almost overwhelmed him. In his mind's eye, he could see a broken body being pulled from under a jacked up tank... The mouth was full of blood and sand... Behind the Major, briefly silhouetted against the French windows of the house, staggered the forlorn figure of a pirate. He was brandishing a wooden cutlass and bawling nonsense in a refined English accent at some invisible foe. The shouting broke the spell and quite abruptly, the desert gave way to the dark lawn and looming rhododendron bushes, and Gourlay stood not before an officer, but a slightly-built figure dressed as a cat; Private 702138 had again become private citizen H. Gourlay Baines. He studied the bogus Major.

"You're no' Major Arnold... You're too wee, yer accent's wrong, and in any case that wis the First Army's cry, no' the Eighth's... Just who the hell are you onywey?" he glowered.

"You impertinent whippersnapper, I'll show you who I am," retorted the Major, and slapped him across the face with the back of his hand!

Blinking away the tears which were streaming down behind his mask, Gourlay sprang into action like a panther. A well-placed boot in the crotch brought an anguished soprano squeal. He lashed out with both fists, then grabbing the Major by the throat, threw him to the ground. Over and over in on the damp grass they rolled, a cursing, scratching, kicking, and punching untidy ball of arms, legs, whiskers and tails.

The pirate, who for several minutes had been lying on his back staring absently at the night sky and cursing the perfidy of all women, propped himself on an elbow and gazed bleakly at the two giant cats locked in grunting combat and fell back again with a profanity on his lips.

A panting Gourlay was in the process of strangling the unrepentant military man when he croaked, "Aargh! Wait... Money... Proposition... Give you money..."

Gourlay relaxed his grip slightly.

"I'll give you fifty quid... Fifty quid if you... If you'll just bugger off and forget... Forget that you ever saw me... Fifty quid," he gargled.

Gourlay gulped in the night air and studied his recumbent, winded opponent.

"Fifty quid?"

"Yes."

"Cash?"

"Cash."

"Done!"

They staggered to their feet and the Major extracted his wallet. "Forty quid did I say?"

"Fifty," said Gourlay icily.

"Fifty then... And you will leave right away?"

"Aye."

The major handed over five ten pound notes. Gourlay clutched them tightly and removed a blade of grass from the corner of his mouth. "Just before Ah go, who the hell are you onywey, an' who is that Elizabeth wumman?"

"Elizabeth?"

"Dressed as a vampire."

"So she came! We're old friends, that's all."

"She's in the cloakroom upstairs... She's no verra weel. She must have expected you tae come dressed as a cat?"

"Yes. As a matter of fact, it was she who sent me the invitation and the costume..."

"Just wan more thing... Why are you impersonating Major Arnold? Did ye ken him like?"

"No. Never met him... Saw his name in an obituary column..."

"He's deid?"

"Couple of years ago."

Gourlay was silent for a moment. Then looking squarely at the bogus military man, raised his index finger. "Find someone else tae impersonate... Major Arnold was a real gentleman... Understand?"

"Well, er yes... But it's not quite so easy for me to change identities, old boy... All those people," he indicated the house behind them with a sweep of the hand, "know me as Major Arnold..."

"Ah don't give a monkey's fuck aboot them," said Gourlay vehemently, "just quit using Major Arnold's name..."

"But look here, we made a deal..."

"Deal or no deal," said Gourlay clutching the money tightly, "Ah've got a photo of the real Major Arnold right here, an' Ah'm quite prepared tae gie it to Monty an'..."

"But..."

"No buts... Ah mean it, chum..."

The fake Major swallowed hard. There was a pause. "I understand," he said finally in a quiet voice.

Gourlay did not go back into the house. At Monty's car he struggled out of the cat costume, or what was left of it, and put on his overcoat and cap. He placed two ten pound notes in the glove compartment along with a note:

Monty,
The Major gave me the 20 quid
to give to you. He's had to leave
town suddenly. Thanks for a great

time. See you.

Aye,

Gourlay.

A pale flicker in the east announced the approach of dawn as he made his way down the driveway towards the road. Despite his reeling head and aching body, he smiled broadly to himself. A postman on a squeaking bicycle looked at him as he passed. "Had a night oan the tiles therr, Jimmy?"

"Aye, ye could say that," replied Gourlay.

"Haw, if ye're gaun hame tae the missus, ye'd best take aff that cat's face!" called the postman amicably over his shoulder and rode into the ditch.

Silly bugger! thought Gourlay, and removing the mask, put it in his pocket; it would make a fine memento.

Under a street lamp he checked the notes the Major had given him... A taxi ride, a good breakfast, and a packet of cigarettes would be quite in order. He strolled along pensively for a while, then halting suddenly, drew himself to attention and saluted the morning sky. "God bless you Major, Major Arnold!"

It was almost dawn. The streets were clean and fresh from the night's rain. He bought a packet of cigarettes and a morning newspaper. On the back page in a box marked 'Stop Press' he read:

**MYSTERIOUS DESTRUCTION OF
B.B.C. MAN'S CAR.**

Police are investigating an explosion which wrecked a parked car and broke several windows at the British Broadcasting Corporation's parking lot at Queen Margaret's Drive late last night. No one was hurt in the incident.

The car's owner, Dennis Douglas (47), who has been

employed as a driver with the Corporation for twenty years, said he had no idea why someone would want to blow up his car.

A telephone call to the editor of the paper early this morning saying the explosion was the work of a group calling itself the National Army for the Liberation of Scotland is believed to be a hoax.

Investigations are continuing.

Gourlay wagged his head slowly and smiled. Folding the newspaper, he ambled off in search of a taxi.

CHAPTER 9

Surprisingly perhaps, there were no repercussions with respect to the cell's débâcle. The police continued to investigate the incident and even managed to trace the dynamite used to a quarry in the Highlands, but that was about as far as it went; they had no suspects, no credible motive, and no leads.

Closing the door after the horse had bolted, as it were, the B.B.C. tightened its security arrangements to the extent that a guard now patrolled the parking lot and the doorman at the front entrance studied all visiting strangers through slitted eyes. Thanks to the press coverage of the bombing, the inevitable hoaxers made their appearance and telephoned the B.B.C. to say that an explosive device had been placed on the premises. The result was that the police were obliged to clear the building several times a day for the first few days after the car incident.

Only one man, a dedicated on-camera host, adamant in his belief that, no matter what, the show must go on, refused to budge. Valiantly, he addressed the abandoned camera on the subject of bomb scares. After a few minutes, however, he ran out of things to say and his mind became a total blank. Desperately scanning the set in search of inspiration, the merest hint of unease in his eyes, he remembered that the 'wall' behind him was filled with shelved books and decided to pick one he could read from by way of entertaining the unseen millions.

To his dismay, chagrin, and alarm, he discovered that the books were fakes; only the spines had been glued to the flats. With faltering steps, he returned to his chair, directed a brave but sickly little smile towards the camera and picked up an oversize tome the set designer had placed on the coffee table beside his anchor position.

It turned out to be *The Gardeners' Almanac for 1885*. With growing panic, he leafed through the pages until he came to a depiction of a hand radish and held it up to the camera. "Seldom," he began in a sepulchral voice, "have I seen a hand radish look more like a human hand..." Then his mind went blank again. He swallowed several times and let the book fall to the floor. He leaned back slowly in his chair, closed his eyes tightly, mumbled, "Seldom have I seen," and "Oh God...!" several times, and there he remained, statue-like, until the all clear had been given and the crew and guests filtered back to the studio.

From Quayle came word that Big Red was not at all upset; he felt the cell had done its best and shown initiative under difficult circumstances. The cell should continue its good work and embark upon another 'happening' as soon as possible.

Gourlay's little room was crowded, noisy and smoke filled. He'd laid on a bottle of whisky and some beer and the little group was making merry.

"As I understand it lads," said Hector, "we're to carry on the good work..."

"You mean blow up another Scotsman's car?" interrupted Gordon with a quick glance at McMinn.

"That's no' fair," complained the latter. "Ah'd nae idea Denny owned a car... Forby that, we should've had better research... What the hell's the point o' looking in a dark park for a stachoo that disna exist?"

Hector clasped his hands together in a little steeple and leaned back with a patient smile looking for all the world like a priest about to hear his bishop tell a good joke.

"McMinn's right," he said quietly after a pause. "Our research was lousy... We're a team," he continued looking round, "but we need a system, a hierarchy just the same..."

"Right." added Gordon. "We've got to figure out who's best at doing what then delegate... Jummock here is shaping up as our demolition expert... But as Hector just said, we need better research... Someone who can handle reconnaissance... How about you, Gourlay"

"Fine... Me an' McMinn sometimes did reconnaissance exercises in the Army, eh no' McMinn?"

"Aye, map readin' an' that," added McMinn helpfully.

Wee Jummock drained his glass, belched, smacked his lips loudly, and announced in a deep voice, "My dog eats nuts too!" They stared at him wordlessly. There was a pause, but he did not elaborate. Then McMinn cleared his throat. "Ah, say we do a bank... There must be dozens of English banks wi' branches in Glesca...An' forby, we need operatin' capital."

Hector wagged his head. "Aye. But it's easier said than done; remember the last time... The ringing in my ears just stopped last week! There just has to be an easier way of raising funds..."

"Aye. Mebbe you're right," said McMinn throatily to no one in particular as he reached out for a fresh bottle of beer the top of which he removed with his teeth.

"How about lifting a painting, an art work?" said Gordon after a pause.

"An art work?" McMinn raised first one shaggy eyebrow then the other.

"Yes. We lift a painting or two from the Art Gallery and sell them... Or give them back for a ransom..."

"Who would want to buy a stolen painting?"

"Oh, it can't be too hard... Famous paintings are stolen every day of the week... It's just a matter of finding a fence. We might even have to go to London."

"But what would stealing a painting have to do with the English?" queried Hector.

"Well, we could steal an English painting... A Constable, a

Whistler, or a Hedley Fitton or something," said Gordon lamely beginning to wish he'd never brought up the idea.

Wee Jummock tugged his ear. "It's a hinteresting idea Gordon... But whit do ye ken aboot security an' that at the Gallery?"

"Absolutely nothing," confessed the student, "but maybe that's a job for our reconnaissance unit..." Murmurs of approval followed his words.

Gourlay turned to his crony. "How aboot it, McMinn?"

"Ye mean case it oot?"

"Right... See if it's feasible... Pave the way for the gang here, an' draw up a plan."

"Fine by me."

No better ideas, it seemed, were forthcoming, so the group settled down to some serious drinking and a relaxed afternoon of gossip, ribaldry, and even mild horseplay. At one point, Gourlay's neighbour, the art student Duncanson, dropped in to borrow some tea and Gourlay took advantage of his visit to sound him out on the merits of paintings by various artists.

"Best things in the Gallery are the Van Gogh's... Stunning... There's a self-portrait... Artaud wrote about it... Talked of Van Gogh's 'lidless butcher's eyes'..."

"Antonin Artaud the playwright?" interjected McMinn.

"That's right!" Duncanson's voice showed surprise.

Used to McMinn's eclecticism and ability to store and recall arcane information, Gourlay smiled wryly and asked Duncanson what works he thought might fetch the highest prices on the open market.

"Well, the Rembrandt, no question... 'Knight in Armour' I think it's called... Very famous... Then there's a couple of Renoirs... Delicate pieces... Lord knows how much they'd fetch, but a fortune..." After the intense student had left with a few spoonfuls of loose tea in a saucer, the conversation grew animated on the subject of the monetary values of various works of art. McMinn pointed out that it would be all but impossible to fence any Rembrandt painting, and that the Renoirs would seem to fit the bill. Hector, however, put a spanner in the works by reminding them of the Auld Alliance and the fact that Renoir was a Frenchman. A thoughtful silence ensued.

"Well then," said Gordon. "Let's go for an English work."

There was some debate addressed to the paradoxical fact that while English works of art would be easier to fence, they were apparently worth far less than ones from the 'Continong.' Jummock, relieved to see that no explosives seemed to be necessary in this latest exploit, brightened considerably and had just raised a question regarding the Gallery's security arrangements when there was a knock at the door.

"Jist thought Ah'd stop by..." Looking spruce and wearing a hat which was so large that it sat on his ears, Sanny Rutherford stood in the doorway. "Young fella let me in," he explained smiling nervously at Gourlay and extending his hand.

"Come in... It's Sanny, innit?"

Sanny's quick, furtive eyes scanned the group and seemed to register mild surprise. At each introduction made by Gourlay, he nodded curtly with the result that his hat slipped lower and lower over his eyes.

"Ye'll bide a wee an' join us in a dram?" said McMinn rising to offer him a seat. The little man declined, but throwing back his head, gulped down the large tot Gourlay handed him. Gourlay stifled a laugh at the sight of Sanny's hat which had now slipped to the back of his head. He noticed that patches of his skull still showed the damage wrought by the blast in the tunnel, and his face was marked by traces of injuries inflicted by the missile which had struck him in the church hall. He wondered how Sanny knew where he lived and why he'd come.

"Having' a wee discussion on art were we?" said Sanny archly catching sight of the book Gordon held.

"Aye. Just so," responded McMinn.

"Ah wis chattin' wi' Big Red," said Sanny not at all put off by McMinn's abruptness, "an' thought it might be an idea tae drop in an' see how ye were a' doin'..."

"Oh, so ye took the oath then?" enquired Wee Jummock.

"Oath..? Oh, the oath... Oh, aye..."

"On the sword?"

"Aye..."

"You'll have the miniature then?" said Gourlay indicating his lapel.

"Er, naw..." Sanny looked at his watch. "Got tae rush... Ah'll drop in anither time when ye're no' busy, Gourlay." He straightened his hat and headed for the door. Gourlay accompanied him to the stair head, then listened attentively as his footsteps clacked down the stairs and faded before returning to the room. "Bloody funny that..." he began.

"Bloody funny is right," interrupted McMinn. "A pound tae a penny says that wee bauchle's up tae no good... Ah bet he nivver took the oath... Naw, he's fushin'."

A consensus was easily reached; Sanny was indeed up to no good, and likely wasn't even a member in good standing in N.A.I.L.S.

The meeting broke up shortly after. It was agreed that Gourlay and McMinn should check things out at the Gallery, work out a game plan, and contact the others when everything was ready to go ahead.

A few days later, feeling a little self-conscious, Gourlay and his pal wandered round the Art Gallery. In one of the salons they found what they were looking for; a splendid painting by Constable.

"Here, it's quite nice, McMinn," said Gourlay in mild surprise and tilted his head to one side.

"Aye, nae bad... Nice clouds," he allowed. Gourlay carefully examined the back of the picture. "Nae alarm wires... You could just lift it off the wall."

"Gie it a go."

With a quick look round to make quite sure that they were alone, McMinn lifted the painting clear of its hook on the wall, held it a long moment, listened carefully, then put it back.

"Hah! Nae bells! It's a piece of cake, Gourlay!"

"Mmm... But we canna just walk oot wi' it, McMinn... The, er, the fellas in yooniform... the custodians, might be simple, but they're no glaiket." At that moment a small figure flitted across the opening at the far end of the salon and disappeared.

"That's Sanny," hissed Gourlay. I'm sure that wis him." With surprising alacrity, McMinn sprinted noisily to the archway and glowered around. Gourlay joined him. "Well?"

"Bugger's gone... Wee nyaff... Ach tae hell, Gourlay, we've seen enough. Let's get oot o' here an' talk things ower."

Later, sipping cafés au lait in a pseudo-bohemian hang out, they gazed around in mild interest at the oddly dressed clientèle. At a table nearby, sucking ostentatiously on a Meerschaum pipe, a beatific smile on her not unattractive face, sat a girl. Her skimpy dress, which appeared to have been made from potato sacks, hung loose about her. Gourlay inclined his head towards the girl.

"See her, McMinn?"

"Aye... In a fuckin' tattie sack an a'... Ah'll nibble her Kerrs Pinks ony day!" He guffawed heartily at his cleverness. Gourlay examined his boots with a puzzled look. The waitress, a slip of a girl with a corpse-white face brought another two cups of coffee, and slipped away with an exaggerated wiggle of her bottom.

"What's he up to, McMinn?"

"Who?"

"Sanny... He's up tae somethin'."

"Oh aye, he's aye up tae somethin' is oor Sanny... Seems tae be followin' you, Gourlay."

"Aye... But why?"

"Dinna ken... He must've got wind that we're involved wi' something big... Jesus! Tak' a keek at thon big jessie ower therr... Dressed like a wumman..."

"I bet he never spoke tae Big Red..."

"Who?"

"Sanny, for Goad's sake!" said Gourlay, exasperation in his voice. "An' I bet he never took the N.A.I.L.S oath either... Ah should check him oot wi' Quayle."

They sipped their coffees in silence and generally enjoyed the scenery.

McMinn, as was his wont when a saucer was available, slurped his coffee from it and tried to ignore the fat girl with the beehive hairdo at an adjacent table who nudged her girlfriend and cooed, "Ooh! Café au lait from a saucer! How infra dig!" McMinn ran his tongue over his lips and blew loudly making a noise like a horse. "How dae we get it oot o' the gallery?"

Gourlay lit a cigarette and leaned forward. "Ah've been thinkin' oan it... It's easy... We get Duncanson tae paint a replica, an' we jist have tae switch them."

McMinn pursed his lips. "Aye... That's clever... But ye still canna walk in an' oot wi' a paintin' whether it's a replica or no'."

"But we'll no be strollin' aboot wi' a big paintin'... Use yer loaf! We cut the real wan oot o' its frame, an' roll it up, see... Easy."

"An' if we're stopped?"

"If we're stopped, we say we're art lovers... We carry an easel, brushes an' that, an' make sure everyone sees us paintin'... Makin' a copy of the Constable. Then we switch pictures an' saunter oot just as cool as when we wandered in earlier."

McMinn's brows furrowed. "Ach, Ah dinna ken... Sounds too easy..."

"That's the point... The simpler, the better... C'moan McMinn, let's awa' an' get organized. We can get Duncanson startet..."

Over the next few days Gourlay found himself running about busily organizing the many matters connected with the cell's latest scheme. He checked with Quayle who, in turn, spoke with Big Red, and learned that Sanny Rutherford had no official connection with N.A.I.L.S. "Tell him nothing," cautioned Quayle. "He's not to be trusted."

Duncanson was commissioned to turn out a tolerable copy of the Constable, and was delighted with the promised five pound remuneration. Gourlay assumed that the student would copy the painting from the many books on art he possessed, and was surprised to learn that Duncanson had set up his easel in the actual Gallery. Not only that, he'd walked out unchallenged with his copy of the painting under his arm. There was much discussion as to the various rôles the members of the cell were to play, but it was finally decided that Gourlay and McMinn would carry out the actual switch of the paintings while the others acted as lookouts. A complex system, calculated to cover almost any eventuality, was devised: Gordon was to remain outside the gallery and keep an eye open for potential dangers, and if, God forbid! Gourlay and McMinn were pursued out of the building, he was to discourage the pursuers by any means at his disposal. Jummock was to stand at the entrance to the salon and prevent anyone from coming in. It was agreed that he would do this by engaging them in conversation about the recently-acquired Dali painting. If he failed to detain them, or if a custodian approached, he was to whistle a few bars of a Jacobite tune. Jummock, who was almost tone deaf, agonized over this and over the fact that he wasn't quite sure which tunes were Jacobite ones and was too embarrassed by his ignorance to seek illumination. Hector was assigned to act as a messenger between the various 'stations.' Tutored on how a student of art might act, and kitted out by a helpful but unsuspecting Duncanson, Gourlay and McMinn were poised to play out their rôles as art lovers. Everything stood in readiness, and every detail of the operation had been gone over *ad nauseam*. At Quayle's suggestion, Gourlay even carried a little tin of black paint and a brush so he could paint N.A.I.L.S STRIKES ANOTHER BLOW FOR FREEDOM on the wall where the fake Constable was to hang.

The hour approached and the gang must ride... They'd chosen a Tuesday afternoon as being the quietest day at the Gallery, and jauntily optimistic after a round or two of refreshments at McMinn's, set off on their mission.

The uniformed man at the desk by the front entrance nodded in response to Gourlay's, "Fine day," and returned to the racing results in his newspaper.

The deserted salon, lit by the soft afternoon light, was magnificent, and as if they thought they were in a sacred place, the two conversed in hoarse whispers. "Here Gourlay, sees a haun' wi' this easel." In the background through the archway, Jummock hirpled to and fro in a very self-conscious manner. Now and then he would stop before a painting, and, lips pursed in a silent whistle, would study it with burning intensity. While McMinn busied himself with the rolled up reproduction, palette, and tubes of paint, Gourlay began to brush the slogan on the wall. He had just finished 'STRIKES' when a loud and tuneless whistle pierced the air. They looked up in alarm. Jummock stood in the archway arms waving frantically.

"Whit's up wi' him?" husked McMinn.

"Someone's comin'! Get crackin'... Kid oan we're paintin'"

"We canna," griped McMinn. "Ye've already pit the slogan oan the wa'... C'moan, lets' get oot o' here!" Quickly gathering up their gear, they headed out of the building with studied nonchalance. As they passed Jummock he said in a stage whisper, "Sanny an' anither fellow!" The custodian at the entrance didn't even look up from his newspaper as they strolled out with a worried looking Hector in tow. Once on the street the group huddled together in earnest discussion.

"Sanny Rutherford and another bloke... Young, tall," said Gordon. "They both went in, then a couple of minutes later the thin fellow came out and headed for Kelvinbridge."

"Did you get the painting?" queried Hector. McMinn shook his head. "We bloody near had it; another minute an' we'd have been O.K... A pox on wee Sanny!"

"Well, maybe we can have another go," said Hector helpfully.

"Naw. Too late... We already put the slogan oan the wa'," grumbled Gourlay. "It's too risky."

Somewhat disconsolately, they went their several ways. Gourlay and McMinn, still clutching the fake painting, easel, and paraphernalia, sloped off along Argyle Street. They'd gone but a few steps past a blue police box when a tall, thin man dashed up from behind, snatched the rolled up painting, and sped off. "Bastert!" bawled McMinn, and dropping the easel, steamed off in hot pursuit. Gourlay shook his head, picked up the easel and other gear, and headed home.

McMinn, he knew, was surprisingly fleet of foot over short distances, but the thin man's turn of speed was no less than wondrous.

Some time later, a glowering McMinn turned up at Gourlay's. "Lost the bastert oot by Anniesland Cross..."

"Ye ran a' the wey oot tae Anniesland?" asked Gourlay in astonishment.

"Aye... Well, naw... Ah got a caur for part of the way... Can ye believe that skinny malinky wis faster than the bluidy tram? Twice Ah got off the tram, ran efter him, then it caught up wi' me an' Ah got on again! Ah'm fair puchellt..." Gourlay comforted his pal, but McMinn, though worn out, thirsted for revenge.

"Ah'll tell ye for nothin', Gourlay, that wee clapperdudgeon Sanny Rutherford's ahint this... He's a one man leper colony! A pound tae a penny says that he set this up."

Gourlay nodded sagely. "Aye... But at least he's off wi' a worthless painting."

"We've got tae nail the wee shite," muttered McMinn darkly. "Remember that lorry load o' fags? Well, the word is that it wis wan o' Sanny's jobs."

"Get away!"

"We've got tae nail him, Gourlay," said McMinn slapping his fist into his open palm."Ah've been thinkin'... Efter a' that fartin' aboot an' pechin' up the Great Western, an' loupin' on an' off caurs chasin' that daddy longlegs, Ah didna hae a bawbee left for the caur ferr back... Ah had tae walk here so Ah had plenty of time tae think... So Ah've been thinkin'... Ah believe we could pin a rape charge oan Sanny..."

"Aw, be serious."

McMinn leaned forward. "Lissen... It's a piece of cake... Ah've goat it a' worked oot... We get haud o' a lassie, have her scream rape an' blame Sanny."

"Ach, it'd never stick, McMinn,"

"Aye, it will! She'll can pick him oot at an identification parade..."

"Dinna be daft... He'd wriggle oot o' that nae bother... Ye're haverin', McMinn."

"No, Ah'm no'... If she can prove that he wis the wan that raped her..."

"An' how, in the nemme o' the wee man is she goin' tae prove that?"

"Easy," replied McMinn with a smirk and lowered his voice to a hoarse croak. "Ah happen tae ken he's got a floo'er tattooed oan his wully..." Gourlay laughed so loudly that tears came to his eyes and his sides ached. He managed to stop braying long enough to gasp, "For Goad's sake, McMinn!" But McMinn was not to be shaken.

"He's got a wee blue rose tattooed oan his dick... Saw it wi' ma ain een... Noo, if the lassie ups an' says, 'He's the wan that raped me, an' he has a rose oan his wully...' He snapped his fingers. "Bingo! We've nailed the bugger!" Gourlay again burst into gales of laughter. McMinn studied him dourly. "Ah canna see whit ye find so funny... It's no' funny."

"It bloody well is, McMinn... Imagine a wheen o' Sanny lookalikes staunin' in a line an' a bobby askin' them tae drop their breeks and show the lassie their wullies while she saunters up an' doon studyin' them!"

McMinn's craggy face broke into a grin despite himself. "Aye... An' if the blokes refuse tae co-operate, or if Sanny refuses, he's still in trouble, deep trouble..."

Late into the night they schemed. The biggest obstacle facing them was the problem of coming up with a suitable girl. Like Caesar's wife, she had to be above suspicion, but amoral to the point where she would go along with such a bizarre, not to say illegal, act.

"Whit aboot your Jessie McGovern?" McMinn asked tentatively.

"She's no' ma Jessie McGovern; she's a mairrit wumman... Hoo mony times have Ah tellt ye we're just friends!"

Women seldom played a major rôle in the lives of the pair; they could take them or leave them, and, in general, gave them a fairly wide berth. Demobbed from the Army, Gourlay's wife had taken up abode with another, and from that time on he'd viewed all females with distrust and kept his distance. Occasionally, in his cups, McMinn would shed tears for some damsel who had apparently drowned after falling off a boat near Plockton. The sexual encounters of the cronies were usually of the hit and run variety — humping away at some anonymous blob in the dark was the rule rather than the exception. They discussed a henna-haired lady called Jemima — a sometime paramour of McMinn's — but it transpired that she was currently serving a brief spell in prison for assaulting a policeman — while Gourlay's female acquaintances, apart from Jessie, were, not to put too fine a point on it, drawn from a stable of tarts, misfits and assorted degenerates. Both, however, felt they understood the fairer sex, and McMinn was frequently heard to crack, "Oh aye, Ah ken a' aboot wummen — Ah used tae keep ferrets when Ah wis a laddie." In short, they viewed women as predatory, scheming, capricious, and wholly unreliable. "Nae point in burnin' the hoose doon when a' ye want is a slice o' toast," Gourlay expounded one day when a lady friend once broached the subject of marriage. His response brought about what he considered to be an unpardonable action; she pushed him out the door with a string of curses. Hurt and surprised by the vehemence of her reaction, he stood scratching his head and mumbling to himself for several minutes before rattling her letter box flap and bawling through the slot, "A guid wumman's like a faithful dog, an' if Ah can find a dug that can cook, Ah'll mairry it!"

McMinn clacked his teeth and grumbled resignedly, "It's a damnable shame so it is. A good idea wasted because we canna come up wi' a suitable wumman."

"Hey McMinn, mebbe Gordon has a burd that'll dae the trick..."

"Mebbe."

It so happened that Gordon did indeed know a suitable girl — Agnes — a sonsie, plumpish, dark-haired dough school student who had a crush on him. When Agnes had heard the full and slightly embellished tale of Sanny and his wicked ways, she agreed to help.

It was all delightfully simple: In the early hours of the morning, after McMinn had ascertained that Sanny was home alone asleep in his Rupert Street flat, Agnes thrust a pair of torn knickers through the little man's letter box, screamed a couple of times, and with artfully torn blouse, headed out to the street to find a policeman. Playing her rôle like an Ellen Terry, she stumbled along and almost immediately ran into a pair of burly policemen to whom she sobbed out her story.

A little later at the police station, grumpy and sleepy-eyed, the summoned police surgeon gave her a cursory examination, and agreed that a case of rape or attempted rape was at least a possibility.

Within the hour, the police were knocking at Sanny's door. Dressed in tatty long-johns, bemused and hangoverish, he invited them in. One of the officers picked up Agnes' torn undergarment from behind the door and held it under Sanny's nose, and said heavily, "Know anything about this?"

"Looks like a perr o' wummen's drawers," replied the little man apprehensively.

"You're Sanny Rutherford?" asked the second constable.

"What of it?"

"Nothing..."

After he'd thrown on a few clothes, Sanny was marched down to the station and charged. To his surprise and consternation, he soon learned that he was something of a celebrity in police circles. They had nothing definite to go on, but made it clear that they had a strong suspicion that he had some connection with the explosion under the bank and with the highjacking of a lorry carrying cigarettes. Sanny, naturally, was heated and vociferous in his denials, and as for the rape charge... Well, he'd had a few drinks at a nearby tavern and then had gone home on his own and was sound asleep when the policemen woke him.

Sanny spent a tortured night in police custody, and came to the conclusion that the police had trumped up a phony rape charge in order to get their hands on him, scare him, and grill him about the various other unsolved crimes around the City. But how much did they know? How much was bluff? What could they actually pin on him?

Around eight in the morning, he was escorted into the presence of a certain Detective Inspector Royston. The two sized one another up. "Well, well, Sanny," said the policeman affably and extended a large hand, "have a seat... A fine mess you're in eh? Like to talk about it?"

Sanny lowered his eyes and kept his peace. "Cigarette?" said the Inspector easily. Sanny reached out, then suddenly pulled back as if the proffered packet were red hot.

"Er, naw, Ah dinna smoke."

"Right." The Inspector leafed through a little pile of papers on his desk. "What we have here, Sanny, is a lassie — from a good family too — saying you raped her..." He paused, but the little man did not respond. "Says that you picked her up, invited her back to your place for a nightcap, then you raped her... Says that she can identify her assailant too... Says here that the bloke who raped her has a tattoo on his dong... A nasturtium..."

Sanny looked up in alarm. "It's no' nasturtium it's a..." He broke off suddenly when he realized that he was incriminating himself, and added rather lamely, "Ah've no' got a tattoo oan ma wully..."

"Oh, well then," said the policeman brightly, "in that case there's no problem! The police surgeon can confirm that in a jiffy, and Bob's your uncle... You're off the hook." He rose slowly. "I like it when things work out like that... Nice and clean... You know what I mean? No fuss, no bother..."

Sanny studied his boots in silence for a long moment then cleared his throat. "Er, Inspector... Ah'm wonderin' if we could do a deal..."

"Deal? Oh, come off it Sanny; you know better than that... The police make no deals." The Inspector raised his eyebrows and shook his head slowly in mock disapproval. Then he leaned forward, and clasped his big hands together. "What was it you had in mind Sanny?"

During this exchange, Sanny's mind had been racing about all over the place seeking loopholes and considering options. How the police had learned about his tattoo — a legacy from a riotous night ashore in Durban when he was in the merchant navy — he had no clue. But there it was. They'd certainly done a thorough job, what with the planted underwear and the distraught girl... As he saw it, his only way of getting out of this fix was to offer the Inspector something all good policemen crave: Information... They liked specific details, and, above all, names. The Art Gallery business was a distinct possibility, but the catch was that if the police took it upon themselves to search his flat, they'd find the stolen painting... He knew full well that Big Red was the kingpin behind the Gallery job, but the very thought of incurring the big man's wrath caused him to shudder... Gourlay Baines! Of course! Gourlay and his National Army for the Independence and Liberty of Scotland or whatever it was called... That was it!

Detective Inspector Royston listened carefully to the long, involved tale of explosions, art theft, and N.A.I.L.S which the shifty-eyed runt of a man before him recounted. The Inspector was no fool; he was quick to realize that what he had here was a tale told by an idiot which signified something... What that 'something' was, he was not yet quite certain, but his ears pricked up at the mention of N.A.I.L.S. Only a few days earlier he'd received a confidential memorandum to the effect that subversive political organizations were to be rooted out at all costs, and that a Special Branch officer was being seconded from London to the Glasgow C.I.D. and that the agent was to be given complete co-operation and any help he requested. In the complex tapestry which Sanny had woven, the shrewd Inspector could see strands of gold...

"Right Sanny. Let's go over this again... Tell me all you know about this Gourlay Baines character..."

CHAPTER 10

Wandering about after a meeting with the City's Chief of Police, Agent 28-L-5, AKA Dudley Tyrwhitt-Drake — with a hyphen — gloomily perused the ornate red sandstone buildings which lined Buchanan Street. He didn't want to be here in this dirty slum of a provincial town with its diminutive, moronic population, most of whom didn't appear to speak English; their glottal stops, distorted vowels and swallowed consonants grated on his ear, and irritated him.

His London superiors had sent him north to monitor the political climate, assess the support this so-called National Army of Liberation (or whatever it called itself) enjoyed, and make it abundantly clear to the guardians of the law and to the natives in Scotland that England would not tolerate the merest whiff of insurgency. No less a dignitary than Sir Frederick Nöel-Smythe (with a hyphen) of the Home Office had assured him that he would be welcomed with open army by officials in Scotland.

Feeling like a Crusader setting off to relieve the Holy City from the Barbarians, Dudley had taken the overnight train from Euston. It arrived at Glasgow Central at six thirty in the morning and stopped so suddenly that he was thrown unceremoniously from his bunk onto the floor.

"Glesca! Everybody oot! Glesca Central!" bawled a guard in an unnecessarily loud voice which seemed to Dudley to have in it a note of glee.

Contrary to his expectations, Glasgow's officials received him, not as some latter day saviour, but with barely concealed suspicion and resentment. What hurt most was that they seemed to regard him as an oddity, and some even snickered behind his back. Like many of his fellow countrymen, he had difficulty pronouncing his r's, and when he'd given a little speech (approved in advance by Sir Frederick) to a clutch of Glasgow's lawmen and uttered the line, "A wobbin wedbwest in a cage," he'd been mortified by the smirks, snorts, and stifled guffaws. But, by God! He would show these peasants...

The dossier on N.A.I.L.S. was a slim one, and he soon realized the local police were taking a rather cavalier attitude to the whole matter and putting it down to the work of a couple of cranks or exuberant students. Certainly, the security of the Kingdom did not seem to be threatened to any great extent, but (as Sir Frederick was fond of saying) a principle *was* a principle.

As he meandered around the City centre, he consulted a map from time to time and turned over the day's events in his mind. He would show these infidels! He would show them how things *ought* to be done; he would soon scotch this snake and return south to the plaudits and laurels of his admiring colleagues, and perhaps — Oh joy! — a pat on the back and a, "Well done old boy!" from Sir Frederick himself. Dudley insisted that he do the fieldwork himself; after all, a city was a city, and criminals were criminals.

That night in his dreary hotel room, which to his disgust lacked lampshades, he studied what little information he'd been given by the police; the file read:

H. Gourlay Baines.

Descript: Around 50, Smallish stature, rugged features, unusual gait (deformed feet?). Talks to himself — M.D. (mentally deficient?)

No criminal record. No outstanding warrants.

No visible means of support.

Honourable discharge (Army) — see file 28-3a-Gw.-1715.

Address: 274 Renfrew St. Gw. (Confirm 25/8).
Further info: See informer file 52-11OR- Rutherford, S.

Dudley rose early, bathed, enjoyed a light breakfast, and thought about finding a better hotel than the rats' nest of a place which had been recommended by one of Glasgow's police brass. A car had to be rented. But first, he wanted to see this Baines fellow... He studied his map, and immediately set off by taxi for Renfrew Street. Once there, he checked to see if there was a rear entrance to 274; there wasn't. He took up a vantage point across the road from the tenement and tried to blend in with his surroundings. In this he was not entirely successful; well-tailored dark brown suit, trilby, and tightly-furled umbrella was not really *de rigueur* in that airt.

After some time, a tall, stooped man came out of the close mouth... A dapper Asian gent went in... Then a middle-aged blonde in curlers and carpet slippers came out clutching two empty milk bottles... A grubby man wearing a sandwich board marked JESUS SAVES on both sides went by so quickly that Dudley was almost swept off the pavement... Then lo! There he was; it had to be him... H. Gourlay Baines! Dudley tried to look as nonchalant and inconspicuous as possible as the figure hobbled over the street towards him. His trained eye noted that the fellow wore two left boots.

"Looks like rain again," said Gourlay pleasantly as he went by.

"Damn!" thought Agent 28-L-5 — Dudley Tyrwhitt-Drake — with a hyphen.

"Funny carl," thought Gourlay. "Awffy weel dressed... Must be an insurance salesman... Hmmph. Looks like the kinda fella who'd drop his breeks afore lettin' loose wi' a fart..."

A little while later, while standing in a close mouth sheltering from a sudden shower, a rotund, well-dressed old lady, her hair braided into a tight knot at the nape of her neck, slipped Gourlay a florin. He was so stunned by this impulsive and bounteous act that he could only stutter, "Bless ye missus," before she'd scuttled by. He wondered what it was about him that had prompted such unexpected kindness. Was it the expression on his face? He tried to recollect how he must have appeared to the woman... Pensive? Waif-like? Sad? "Naw. Ah wis thinkin' aboot whit nice bums women have..." He practised his 'thinking-about-women's-bums' expression and resolved to assume it from time to time in the hope that further acts of magnanimity from passing strangers might be prompted by it. The rain stopped as suddenly as it had started. He turned up his coat collar and sallied forth.

A mantle of dampness hung over the City. At a window high above him across the street, a woman in a black brassiere was filling a kettle. He waved, but she did not see him. "Hey mister, it's stopped rainin'," he informed a nattily dressed gent. who was poncing along under his umbrella. The man gave him a frosty stare. "Greetin' faced bugger," grumbled Gourlay after the retreating figure. "An awffy lot o' soor-faced folk aboot these days..."

He studied a cello on display in a shop window and marvelled at the workmanship. Stepping back, he caught a glimpse of a man in a brown suit and trilby reflected in the glass, but when he turned the figure had vanished. He plodded on and wondered if McMinn might have further details of Sanny's arrest...

OSWALD STREET ZOO — ONE UP, proclaimed the sign.

"Funny place to have a zoo," he thought, and wondered why he hadn't noticed it before. His curiosity aroused, he went up the stairs. Hanging from a nail in the door a handwritten notice on a piece of cardboard stated,

Oswald Street Zoo.
Mon. to Frid. 9—5, Sats. 10—3.
Adults 6d, Children 3d.

He opened the door. The raw smell of animals and stale urine almost bowled him over. In a tiny booth, a small man, with a moustache so thin it looked as if it had been inked on his face, was sitting on a stool engrossed in a book. The book had a plain, brown paper dust jacket, but, peering round the edge, he saw it was *Mein Kampf* in English.

"Sixpence," said the man flatly without looking up. Gourlay laid a half crown on the counter. The little man picked it up, dropped it into a shoe box, and gave Gourlay one and six change — all without raising his eyes from his book.

"That wis hauf a croon Ah gave ye."

"Two bob," insisted the man.

"Hauf a croon!"

"Two bob!"

Gourlay inhaled sharply, grabbed the man by his lapels and leaned forward until their noses were almost touching. "Lissen Jim!" he hissed, "Ah gave ye hauf a croon. Gie me ma sixpence or Ah'll break yer fuckin' heid... Ah mean it!" For a long moment, both held their positions as immobile as waxworks, then slowly, without taking his eyes off Gourlay, the man extracted sixpence from the shoe box and placed it on the counter top with a loud click. Gourlay released the man, picked up the coin, and whistling tunelessly, made his way to the first of the doors. The little man watched him through narrowed eyes.

The opening of the door was the only signal needed by scores of birds in cages ranged along the walls to burst into a twittering, squawking, screeching cacophony. "Hullo the wee burds!" cried Gourlay. The volume of sound decreased immediately and dramatically. Unwilling to face a resumption of the din, he walked slowly and quietly round the cages addressing the inmates *sotto voce*. "My, my then... Whit a wee beauty... Oh, Jesus! Whit happened tae yer tail, son? Keep yer bum tae the wa' in future... Hello cocky..." He paused to pick up several bright feathers from the floor and after admiring them, slipped them into his pocket. His hand touched the remains of the roll and cheese he'd slipped into his pocket before leaving his digs. He ate the cheese, and breaking off small pieces off the roll, fed them to the grateful birds.

"Hey you! Can ye no' read? Nae feedin' the animals!" The man with the pencil moustache stood in the doorway.

"Aw, it's just a few crumbs," replied Gourlay throwing another morsel into a cage. The man rushed over bristling like a terrier. He snatched what was left of the roll from a startled Gourlay and flung it onto the floor. The birds fell silent.

"Ah said no feeding the animals!" said the man in a low, thin voice.

Gourlay exhaled as he leaned forward. "See you, Jim? See that moustache o' yours? How'd you like me to rip it off yer face and shove it up yer arse?"

The man, staggered by the unusual and explicit nature of Gourlay's threat and the note of menace in his voice, backed to the door. "You can't talk to me that way... I'm the proprietor... Who the hell do you think you are? Get out! Get out of my zoo!"

"Ah've paid ma money, Jim, so you just piddle off to yer wee box an' shut yer trap!" He raised his fist to enforce his threat and the small man, placing discretion a peg or two above valour, turned on his heel and retreated to the safety of his booth. Gourlay picked up the remains of the roll and continued to feed the birds.

The acrid stench of stale feline urine hit him like a blow as he opened the door of another room. Substantially built cages held a variety of cats and cat-like creatures. Each cage had a label giving the species and the name of the inmate. The first cage was marked LYNX — THOMAS. Thomas was asleep, curled up in a tight ball at the rear of his tiny home. His paw covered his nose, and he paid not the slightest heed to Gourlay's friendly overtures. In the next cage, what appeared to be a well-fed domestic tabby was meticulously washing his scarred face; there was no label on the cage. He passed slowly from cage to cage chatting amiably to those creatures which were in the least bit responsive to him.

An archway led to a smaller, windowless room in the centre of which was a massive cage with a rail round it. A cardboard label stating simply, LION — MOSES was tied to the bars with pieces of string. Inside, reclining sphinx-like, was a huge lion staring fixedly at the open archway. Gourlay approached slowly. The big cat did not move. Gourlay leaned lightly on the rail, looked into the pale yellow eyes, and knew fear. Slowly, he tilted his body sideways and ran his eyes along the lion's flank. Beyond the tattered mane, the ribs were pronounced and covered with sand-coloured hair. Bare patches showed a white skin. The tip of the tail was caked with dried faeces. The unblinking yellow eyes seemed to carry deep within them the stillness and vastness of the African veldt.

Throughout his inspection, Gourlay had scarcely dared to breathe. He was so overawed by the proximity of the beast that it took him a couple of minutes to realize that the lion was not only utterly still, he was not breathing. He shook his head sadly. "Poor Moses... Deid an' stuffed..." He clambered over the rail and once again scrutinized the impassive, immobile face. He stretched his hand through the bars of the cage and lightly touched the top of the great cat's head. The lion turned his head quickly and stared directly at Gourlay. He still retained his regal pose, but the cairngorm eyes, now very much alive, expressed frosty astonishment. For his part, Gourlay maintained not an iota of dignity as he executed a reverse summersault over the bar with the ease and agility of a gymnast. He scuttled backwards across the floor with a look of utter amazement on his craggy face. An age passed before he managed to gather his wits sufficiently to give voice to his terror. "Jesus Christ! Holy fuck! It's fuckin' alive!" Without taking his eyes off the lion, he got to his feet but found that his legs were trembling so violently that he had to lean on the wall for support. Moses, majestic and massive, watched him though a hunter's eyes. He rose, stretched regally, yawned, and with a final haughty glance at Gourlay, urinated violently against the rear wall of the cage. It was a spirited performance and effected with the casual panache of the true aristocrat. His territorial rights thus firmly established, Moses sat on his haunches, scratched his ear, yawned absently, lay down and continued to study the wiry little man. Realizing the lion meant him no harm, Gourlay's soul re-entered his body, and slowly the trembling left his limbs.

Cautiously, he approached the rail around the cage rubbing his crotch ruefully. "Christ, Moses! Ah think you made me pee masel!" A rumbling noise like an ancient motor turning over came from the depths of the lion's massive chest, and he playfully rubbed the side of his head against the bars of the cage. Gourlay observed the transformation from killer to kitten with growing wonder. Slowly, inch at a time, encouraged by Moses' seductive rumblings, he drew near, and, heart in mouth, leaned over the safety rail and extended his hand to the lion who sniffed it delicately and licked the tips of his fingertips with sandpaper tongue. Moses almost chuckled with delight. Soon, the bars seemed to dissolve for man and beast and Nature's social union was again established. Gourlay's only sorrow was that he had nothing to give his new-found, earth-born companion. "You're awffy thin lookin', Moses... Would ye like a bite tae eat? How aboot a fish supper eh...? Just you wait here..."

He slipped out past the little man in the booth who, to judge from his closed eyes and beatific smile on his narrow face, seemed to be dreaming of better days. The fresh air was a blessing after the musty confines of the little zoo, and Gourlay filled his lungs as he headed for Guisseppe's Fish Bar along Argyle Street.

"Ello Gourlay... Howsit going?"

"No' bad, no' bad Sep... Here, how much is oan the slate?"

Guisseppe scratched his bald pate and consulted the fly

blown ceiling.

"Eh, letta me see... Ah theenk it comes to two anda keek... Yes."

Gourlay laid two half crowns on the counter. "An' Ah'll take a fish supper, double fish, an' a puddin' supper."

"You're a hungry boy the day!"

The small man with the pencil moustache was still drowsing over his book as Gourlay slipped quietly by. Moses, too, had dozed off, his great head resting on crossed forepaws. His nose twitched as Gourlay approached, and he opened first one eye then the other.

"Hello, Moses... Hello, the Moses." Without fear, Gourlay reached through the bars and scratched the big cat's chin. "Here, Ah brought ye a wee bite... Do you want the fish or the pudden?" Moses pushed his nose against the bars and judiciously sniffed the proffered packages. "There you go, son," said Gourlay, and put the fish supper through the bars. Contrary to his expectations, the lion did not wolf it down at a gulp, but checked out this unusual offering with the finesse of a gourmet appraising an exotic dish. He licked the chips, but ignored them in favour of the fish from which he carefully removed the batter. Gourlay propped himself against the safety rail and absently began to munch the pudding supper while watching his new pal. Once finished, Moses began his elaborate washing ritual, his long tongue removing the minutest trace of his repast. That completed, he settled down to watch Gourlay with an air of friendly interest. Still chewing, his every move monitored by the inquisitive lion, Gourlay made his way to the far end of the cage. Two substantial bolts secured a large door. "Here, Moses, if Ah wis tae let ye oot for a whilie, would you behave yoursel'?" Moses responded with a genteel cough which Gourlay chose to take as an affirmative. He slipped the lower bolt and Moses rose, stretched, and meandered over to investigate. For a long moment Gourlay paused, then suddenly, his mind made up, pushed the upper bolt, opened the door a little and stood back. "Nae hanky panky, mind." Moses stuck his head out, looked from side to side as if seeking a catch in this benevolent act, then stepped down gingerly with the dignity of royalty descending from a carriage. A mild wave of anxiety caused the back of Gourlay's throat to tingle as he absorbed the massiveness of the beast before him. "Now nae hanky panky, Moses," he pleaded in a small, strangulated voice which he did not recognize as his own. Moses sniffed Gourlay's boots, rubbed himself against his legs, then stood looking around his tail swishing. From a cage marked CIVET — PENNY came a low, angry moan. Moses strolled over to investigate and Gourlay watched slack-jawed as the lion disdainfully shot a fine jet of urine into the cage of his insolent subject. "Here, Moses, here's a bit o' black pudden," croaked Gourlay in a wheedling tone. But Moses, seemingly conversant with the concept of *noblesse oblige*, was strolling augustly from cage to cage to the abject terror of the inmates. Gourlay watched the imperial perambulations of his new-found friend with wide-eyed wonder tinged with mounting fear.

He had slowly begun to grope his way backwards towards the door when his extended hand touched something large, soft and alive. His heart almost stopped and a large warm wetness seeped down his leg. Trying to keep one eye on Moses, he turned and found himself face to face with a small man in a brown suit. The man raised his umbrella in a threatening gesture, and in a single, swift, reflex movement, Gourlay slammed the remains of his pudding supper in the stranger's face. Moses ambled over, and the newcomer, seeing him for the first time, began to jabber and edge towards the door. Alive to the potential of this new game, Moses took a few swift strides to block the exit, gave a coughing growl that sounded more like the voice of a mastiff than that of a lion, flattened his ears and curled back his upper lip. The nerve of the man in the brown suit failed him completely, and with a squawk of terror, he scrambled into the empty cage. But once again, Moses was too quick. His vocal efforts becoming more leonine by the second, he rushed into the cage to face Dudley Tyrwhitt-Drake — with a hyphen — who was now crouching wide-eyed in the corner. His lips moved, but no sound emanated, and Gourlay wondered if the man were praying. Waiting till Moses' tail was safely clear of the cage door, Gourlay slammed it shut. Dudley jabbed his umbrella at Moses who showed his yellow teeth, turned quickly, raised his tail, sent a jet of urine through the bars, and uttered a snarling noise which was the least friendly sound Gourlay had heard him make to date. He glanced through the bars at the cowering man whose hat and face showed traces of black pudding and chips. A rising chorus of growls, whines, and moans came from the surrounding cages. Gourlay slipped away as quickly as his trembling legs would carry him, and all but bowled over the man with the pencil moustache who was rushing in to see what all the commotion was about. On his way past the booth, Gourlay transferred the contents of the shoe box to his pocket.

That evening he treated McMinn to a few haufs as he recounted the day's adventures. "Well Jesus! When he came oot o' his cage, Ah didna ken whit tae think... There was no turnin' back like..." He sipped his single malt reflectively. "Makes ye wunner how thae lion tamers manage, dunnit?"

"Easy."

"How?"

"Ye take a chair in wan haun, an' when the lion moves back, you move furrit. An' when the lion moves furrit, you move back."

Gourlay considered his friend's words in silence. "Aye... But here, McMinn, whit happens if the lion keeps comin' furrit an' you're right up against the bars and canna go ony farther back?"

"Easy... Ye chuck a handfu' o' shite in the lion's eyes."

Gourlay drained his glass and scrutinized McMinn's poker face, his canny grey eyes searching for the merest twinkle which would tell him his leg was being pulled. But McMinn continued to sip his whisky with stony-faced impassiveness.

"Throw a handfu' o' shite in his een?"

"Aye."

"But whit if there's no shite?"

McMinn placed his glass on the table top with a distinct movement and leaned forward his face illuminated by a summery smile. "Dinna worry aboot that; there would be PLENTY of shite!" He leaned backward in his chair and laughed immoderately at his wittiness. Then, noticing Gourlay's hurt expression, tried to stifle his laughter with an ostentatious cough.

"Christ, Gourlay, for a smart lad, ye can be a dumb bastert at times... Ye dinna really expect me tae believe ye let a lion oot o' its cage... C'moan Gourlay, this is yer auld pal McMinn, no' some glaiket English Yahoo ye're talkin' to!"

Gourlay shrugged, contemplated his empty glass with a wan smile and ordered another round. He wondered how the man in the trilby hat and pencil moustache made out...

CHAPTER 11

It was a warm, still, summer's evening. Glasgow Green was dotted with little knots of people enjoying the gentle weather. Near the main entrance a moth-eaten looking little man had set up his JESUS SAVES sandwich board on the grass and was explaining in a horrendously gravelly voice to nobody in particular how he'd given up drink and found salvation in Jesus. Small children romped and played noisy games of tag with one another. Fathers, grandfathers, uncles and friends, dark-suited and shoeless, sat on newspapers, chatting amicably. The women, seated a little apart from the menfolk, removed their shoes and discussed tribal and family matters in low voices. Few gave so much as a second glance at the group of men playing cricket by the Clyde's edge.

Big Red had called a meeting and Quayle had organized it. Here, on the Green they were safe from prying eyes and flapping ears: "Who would suspect that a group of fellas knocking a cricket ball about represented the cream of Scotland's manhood and the spearhead of the nation's liberation movement?" was the way Quayle put it. Resplendent in his white cricket boots, appropriate jersey and neatly pressed white flannels, Quayle looked quite professional. Big Red, too, was suitably accoutred. The bat looked like a toy in his big hands as he stooped almost double before the stumps. Behind him, acting as a wicket keeper, umpire, and general advisor, Quayle urged the fielders to spread out a little more. Wee Jummock, the bowler, eyes blazing and arms and legs going like fury, zig zagged along like a clockwork toy gone berserk and hurled the ball with a primal yell. Any normal mortal would have ducked or cringed, but the big man was made of sterner stuff; with a graceful sweeping motion, he contacted the ball which flew in a high, wide arc over the fielders. "Back! Back!" cried Quayle gesticulating frantically.

McMinn, the only one wearing a coat, wiped his mouth with the back of his hand and looked grim. "He's a fiend is Big Red, eh no Gourlay? There's nae chance anyone'll can bowl him oot."

"Aye... An' Wee Jummock's nae slouch as a bowler... Where the heck did he learn tae bowl?"

"Here, Ah could dae wi' a dram... Ah'm het an' drouthy," croaked McMinn.

"Take yer coat off, McMinn."

"Ah canna... Ah've got a big holie in ma breeks."

There was another loud "Thwack!" and the ball headed towards the pair.

"It's yours, McMinn!" bawled the distant Quayle.

"Oh, goody goody!" said McMinn sourly. "Might as weel try tae catch a cannonball," he complained, and positioned himself as best as he could. The ball was a high one and first appeared as a speck against the blue sky. "Under it! Under it!" yelled Quayle. There was a distinct and loud smacking sound as the ball hit McMinn's cupped hands. He gave a sharp, agonized cry and the ball slipped out of his hands and landed on his right foot. A groan went up from the players. But McMinn's performance was not yet over; almost instinctively, he flipped his foot and the ball curved towards Gourlay who caught it easily. For a moment there was a stunned silence then the whole Green seemed to erupt. Cries of "Howzat!" (from Quayle) and a miscellany of yells filled the air. Above the racket, Big Red's bull-like roars of "Well done! Well done!" could be plainly heard. Quayle called a break, and amid much good humoured banter, the group sat in a circle on the grass while refreshments were served. McMinn broodily studied his smarting fingers. "Minds me o' gettin' the tawse at school," he muttered darkly.

Big Red looked around then produced a piece of paper from his pocket. "Some business matters before we get back tae the game lads... The Army is doing well... Ye may have heard the other day that the Forth Road Bridge approach roads were blocked for nearly three hours... That was the work of an Edinburgh cell. They rented cars, blocked the roads with them and walked off leaving the cars locked while they painted our slogan on the bridge. The police couldn't get there for ages because of the huge traffic jam... Good work, good organization, and good publicity..." He drained his bottle at a gulp. "When the Special Branch takes an interest in us, we know that we have arrived... That we're a force tae be reckoned with. Well, an Englishman has been sent up to check up on us... Terry here will update us on that..."

Quayle cleared his throat. "Well, in a neat piece of symbolic action, the old lion of Scotland showed he still has teeth; the agent was mauled by a lion in the wee zoo down on Oswald Street!" Cheers and laughter greeted his words. Gourlay looked up in surprise and glanced at McMinn who raised his shaggy eyebrows. "Like it or not," continued Big Red, "there'll be others to replace him, so keep your wits about you, lads. Remember, you can only be sure of a fellow if he's wearing the wee sword... But as I said, when the English take us seriously, as they are beginning to, we know we're on the right track..." He referred to his scrap of paper. "Oh, and Sanny Rutherford is to the fore. The police gave him quite a fright so he'll be on his best behaviour for a while... But watch out for him and anyone associated with him, O.K? Questions this far?"

Gordon rose to a squatting position. "Er, for some time now I've been troubled by what might happen to us if something went wrong... I mean, I'm at university and have future plans; what support could I expect from the Army if the police pick me up for example?"

"Good question Gordon, and one that I've been asked before," began the big man. "Essentially, if you are caught, you're on your tod. However, thanks to nameless individuals and organizations, we now have a fairly substantial kitty for such contingencies so that we should be able to pay legal fees, look after dependents and the like in a modest way... But don't forget, if you want out, there's no problem... Everyone in N.A.I.L.S. is a volunteer... Some have already left; some for good, some for a while. That's healthy and makes it that more difficult for the police and Special Branch boys to keep up with us... So, Gordon, if you want out for a spell, or for good, there's no problem and no hard feelings... Now Terry has a few more words before we get back to our game..."

"I'll keep it brief," said Quayle uncrossing his legs. "N.A.I.L.S. is expanding; in fact, we really must be a success because, as you heard, we've finally got a good cell working out of Edinburgh! An' it seems that the Hielans want but the word... We'll have operational cells there in the near future... Now, just to keep you in the picture, we've got an intelligence unit set up and it's already producing results; that's how we heard about the lion chewing up the Special Branch bloke... Another thing... We're working on drawing up a list of fellows who have special skills. So if you're particularly good at something, let me know. We'll be drawing on all kinds of skills from a knowledge of Scottish geography to using a welding torch or aqualung... We've one fellow who used to be a train driver, for example, and that's good to know because if your cell needs someone to shift a train or whatever, we'd assign him to you for the duration of the operation..." Here he paused and took a deep swig from what appeared to be a bottle of whisky. But it was a devilish brew called scrumpy — a sweet, innocuous-tasting, but potent cider which the nearby Sarie Heid pub siphoned off from huge wooden barrels at a shilling a bottle or one and three if the customer failed to provide his own bottle. Quayle smacked his lips, nodded, and gazed around the group. "Anything in the works lads?" Gordon idly brushed away a stray lock of hair from his eyes and nudged Hector who shook his head and made a sign to indicate that Gordon should go ahead and say his piece.

"We, that is I," began the student in a soft voice, "got to thinking that a kidnapping might bear fruit..."

Big Red looked at him keenly. "You've someone in mind?"

"Well, er, yes... As a matter of fact I do... I figured it would have to be someone important, someone with money, and an Englishman... Well, after the cock up with his car, I thought why not have another go; I mean the Controller for B.B.C. Scotland..."

"The B.B.C. will be well guarded now," said Quayle.

"I've considered that... There's no need for us to go anywhere near the B.B.C.... We simply nab him on his way home one night... Apparently, he lives near Rowardennan... It's ideal because it's close by, yet it's pretty isolated... He's driven to his home every evening..."

"Sounds like a challenging project," said Big Red with a little smile. "What do you say, Terry?"

"Aye... Have you figured out what you'll do with him after you get him? I ask that because, in general, lifting the victim is the easy part; the hard parts are keeping him and exchanging him for cash — without getting caught."

"Leopold and Loeb in America," said Gordon, "dreamed up a clever plan..."

"Leopold and Loeb," mused Quayle. "That rings a bell... The 1920's, in Chicago wasn't it...?"

"Aye. But their plan didna work," interjected McMinn in a throaty voice. "They killt the laddie they kidnapped, and forby, were caught..."

"True," conceded the student. "But the point I'm making is that they worked out a damn clever procedure for the exchange... In the ransom note they said they'd contact the family after they knew the family had raised the cash... They contacted the family, and then the family was told to contact them using a number of telephone kiosks. Well, they had the fellow with the money running from kiosk to kiosk just right up to the time a train was about to leave... In the last call, they told him to run for a train which was about to leave the station. On the train, in a toilet I think, they'd previously left a note with their final instructions... That is, to throw the suitcase with the money in it out of the train at a certain spot..."

"Damn clever," said Big Red after digesting Gordon's tale. "The idea being that there would be no time for the police to get into the act?"

"Right," Gordon nodded.

"Well, it sounds like a good scheme... It'll be interesting to see how much the B.B.C. thinks their Controller is worth! You were thinking of the B.B.C. for the ransom?"

"We thought it would be easier dealing with the B.B.C. than with the family," explained Hector. "We've all the details to work out... But we were thinking that, in addition to the ransom money, we might be able to press them into giving the Army a plug on air..."

The group resumed the match, but called it a day when darkness began to fall. By consensus, it was agreed that Jummock was the best all-rounder; despite his peculiar crab-like gait, he had chalked up more runs and taken more wickets than Big Red.

Black night with a hint of thunder in the warm air enveloped the City. Stretched out ful-length on Gourlay's bed, McMinn studied his grubby hands. "Look at ma bluidy hauns... They're a' swole... Ah think ma thumb is broke; Ah canna move it..."

"Ach, you're an auld wumman, McMinn... It's a lassies' gemme, cricket... And English lassies at that... Ye said so yersel'!"

"Hmmph."

"Verra civilized the English... Nane o' yer rough and tumble games for them; Morris dancin', burd watchin' an' the like is whit gets the English excited..." He handed McMinn a cup of tea. "Christ man, the only wey ye ken an Englishman's sexually aroused is if his stiff upper lip shoogles a bittie..."

"Aye, aye," sighed McMinn ruefully. "Ye can gargle oan a' ye want aboot sissie English gemmes, but it disna change the fact that ma fuckin' fingers smart..." The front door rattled. "Goad! No' O'Leary again!" groaned Gourlay. But it was Gordon and Hector.

"Thought we'd drop in an make a start on the kidnap plan," said Gordon affably. "Jummock said he'd try to drop in a bit later."

After they were seated, more or less comfortably, Gordon produced a little notebook, and referring to it from time to time, outlined the plan. "It was Hector's idea really, and we've both been thinking about it... It seems that Langley — that's the Controller — lives out by Rowardennan — Loch Lomond side... McMinn's pal, Denny, drives him to and from work... He's pretty regular leaving for Queen Margaret Drive, but as I said earlier, if we picked him up and he never arrived at the B.B.C., someone there would almost be certain to phone his home and the cat would be out of the bag... The advantage of picking him up after work, especially on a Friday, is that it could be hours till he's missed... O.K. so far?" He glanced round the attentive faces.

McMinn sat up on the bed. "Whit aboot Denny, the chauffeur?"

"We'd have to incapacitate him for a while," said Hector. "One of us has to take Denny's place and drive the car with the Controller in the back... We'd have to tie up the Controller, blindfold him, till it's all over..."

"But that could take days, or even weeks, if there's any negotiation aboot the ransom money."

"True enough," agreed Hector. "Anyone any ideas?"

"Seems to me that we've a problem if we keep him, an' a problem if we let him go," said Gourlay.

"Grab the car, gie Denny a wee dunt oan the heid, chuck him in the boot an' take him along for the ride... Then when we take the Controller oot of the car an' hide him, we just leave Denny in the boot. The polis'll find the car and Denny later," suggested McMinn.

Gourlay looked at him in surprise. "Ah thought Denny wis a friend of yours like?"

"Aye. He is." McMinn smiled wryly. "Well, an acquaintance. But business is business, and Scotland First an' a' that!"

"O.K.," said Gordon making notes. "So, we put Denny out of commission — take him with us — move Langley and hide him, and leave Denny in the car... And we pull off the job on a Friday afternoon... Right?"

"One little problem," interjected Hector, "if you put the chauffeur out of action, who's going to drive the car?"

"That'll hae tae be me or Gourlay — we're the only wans who even vaguely look like Denny," said McMinn.

"What about a yooniform?" asked Gourlay.

"We'll can take Denny's"

"Haud on McMinn... We're gaun tae gie Denny a dunt, take his yooniform, chuck him in the boot an' drive away wi' the Controller... An' a' that in broad daylight!"

McMinn pushed his cap back on his head. "Lissen. It's easy... Denny usually hings aboot a' day on the off chance the Controller might need a hurl somewhere..."

Gordon, who had made many notes and deletions, looked slightly bewildered. "Well, er, we can refine that part later... Let's call that Phase One... Now we need a place to abandon the car as well as a safe place to hide the Controller until the deal's been struck and effected."

"Whit aboot keepin' him in wan o' Jummock's cludgies?" said the voice from the bed. They looked at McMinn closely to see if he was pulling their legs, but his face was iron.

"Well, it could be arranged I expect," said Hector. "And it would be a clever choice; who would think of searching one of Glasgow's public conveniences for a missing B.B.C. Controller?" Fortuitously, just at that moment, Wee Jummock arrived, and his Adam's apple jerking up and down like a yo-yo, agreed that provided he could be kept quiet, the kidnapped man could be kept secure and hidden almost indefinitely in one of the toilet's storage rooms.

"Phase Two," said Gordon after a pause, and with a flourish, scribbled 'Phase Two' in his notebook. "Now, the really tricky part is where we hand over the Controller for hard cash... The kiosk part will need some work... Big Red and Quayle seemed to like the idea on principle, so unless one of us comes up with something better, we'll apply ourselves to this kidnapping..."

"One problem is arranging the exact spot where the cash is to be thrown from the train," said Hector.

"Easy," rasped McMinn swinging his legs over the edge of the bed and dropping his cigarette butt into his empty cup. "If it's the Glasgow-Edinburgh train, for example, ye tell the mannie tae chuck the money oot the windae when he sees a bonfire on the right hand side of the train..."

"Bonfire?" queried Jummock.

"Aye... We pick a quiet spot where the road rins close tae the tracks — we'll need transport — an' get a guid bleeze gaun just afore the train's due... A signal like."

Gourlay had listened carefully to the discussion, and was impressed by the high degree of seriousness of the group. He noted that even the usually cynical McMinn had temporarily curbed his acerbic tongue and was participating very positively. There was an air of suppressed excitement in the room, and he got the strong sense that the little group had high expectations of successfully pulling off a major coup.

"It might be an idea," began Hector in a serious tone, "for us to consider every single thing which might possibly go wrong... For example, what if the B.B.C. refuses to stump up cash for Langley's return?"

Jummock looked up. "They'll pay up O.K. The polis'll tell them tae go along wi' oor demands... They aye say that, because they're pretty sure they'll get the money back when they catch the kidnappers."

Hector cleared his throat. "What if the money thrown from the train is fake? And I'm just playing Devil's advocate here..."

"Well, they'll not get their Controller back." said Gordon without looking up from his notes.

"Aye," said Jummock. "But ye'll no' be able to hae a second crack at the train business; ye'd have tae come up wi' anither system..."

Gourlay cracked his knuckles. "Jummock's got a point... Somehow we've got tae make certain it's hard cash that's chucked oot... But how?"

"Easy," said McMinn. "We tell them that if they fuck us aboot, we'll slit his thrapple."

"Whose?"

"The Controller's." After a moment's silence, Hector, his thumbs hooked into the breast pockets of his boiler suit spoke up. "Well, that might be going a bit far, McMinn... But we've certainly got to establish from the outset that we mean business... Another thing that occurs to me is that the police will be everywhere. You can bet they'll monitor calls from every kiosk in the City after we mention kiosks... And no matter how tight we cut it, you can lay a pound to a penny they're likely to be on the train too..."

"Nae problem," put in McMinn. "If we light the fire right close to the time the train's due tae pass, even if they get a message off the train, there's nae wey they could stop the train in time to do anything... An' clever an' a' as they are, they winna hae time to take a car or motorbike or cuddy oan the train tae chase us wi'..."

Aye, an' Hector's right; even gin we dinna intend tae harm the Controller, they've got tae *believe* we're capable o' it... Anyway, Hector, Ah'm sorry. Ah didna mean tae interrupt..."

"No, that's O.K., McMinn... There's a whole list of details to be worked out... Train times... And even if the train's windows open... We'll have to have a couple of rehearsals to make sure the bonfire can be seen... And that we can find the package of money quickly enough even in the dark, and that sort of thing..."

Gordon consulted his notebook and looked thoughtful. "Yes... One thing we haven't discussed is the publicity... It seems to me that N.A.I.L.S. should be able to get good mileage out of this if it's handled properly."

"We should consult Quayle on that one," said Gourlay. "My bet is that this will be a hot tattie!"

Gordon scribbled furiously for a moment. "It seems to me, gents, that we've got a good outline here — a workable outline. I'll try and draw up a list of things to be done — details. But maybe we should agree right now who is going to be doing what on the night so that I can draw up a checklist of folk and their responsibilities... Now, if Gourlay and McMinn are taking care of Denny and driving the Controller's car, then maybe they could take care of the transport and picking up the money thrown from the train?"

Gourlay and McMinn glanced at each other and nodded. "And Jummock will be Langley's custodian?"

"Right," agreed the little man.

"Hector and I will be wherever we are needed," continued Gordon, "I think we'd be wise to concentrate on Phase One first — the actual kidnapping. There'll be no big rush before the hand over... Any questions come to mind? No? Well, how about we meet again on Sunday night? Could we use your place again, Gourlay?"

"Nae problem. Provided you think it's safe enough... I've a

hunch that I was being followed a while back... Ah dinna think anyone's watching me now, but it's maybe no' worth the risk... How about we meet in the park — Kelvingrove, by the boolin' green?"

"Whit if it's rainin'?" queried McMinn.

"Then we could meet at thon wee howff up Garscube Road."

The gathering broke up. Gourlay tidied up in a haphazard sort of way, and shook his head when he picked up McMinn's cup; inside was a mass of soggy cigarette butts. "Jesus Christ, McMinn! Ye're a dirty pig so ye are... Look at ma cup!" He shoved the offensive mess under the nose of his pal who still lolled in the bed.

"Ach, whit was Ah supposed tae dae — eat them?"

"Never mind... Here, c'moan, McMinn, sees a shottie of the bed... Ye've been stretched oot on it the whole night..." Grumpily, McMinn relinquished the bed, and stretching and yawning extravagantly, sauntered over to the sink, coughed, spat, and turned on the tap. Gourlay rolled his eyes ceilingwards then sat down on the edge of the bed and looked over at McMinn who was moodily staring out of the window at something in the street below.

"Well McMinn, whit do you say?"

"Huh?"

"What dae ye think of this kidnapping business...? Think it'll work?"

"Hmmph. There's a lot can go wrong... But them fellas, Gordon an' Hector, have done a fair bit o' plannin'... That case in America — Leopold and Loeb in the 1920's that Hector mentioned. It wis a bluidy disaster... The victim snuffed it, they nivver got the money, and forby, the perr o' them wis sent doon for years an' years... They were lucky to avoid the electric chair..."

"What went wrong, McMinn?"

"Everything... As Ah recollect, the two of them kidnapped a laddie from a wealthy family, killt him, then demanded a ransom.

They hid the boy's body, but it wis found an' identified before the money changed hands..." He lit a cigarette and inhaled deeply. "The polis nailed them easily; wan o' the kidnappers had dropped his glesses near the body, and then the polis linked the typewriter used tae type the ransom note tae wan o' the kidnappers... It wis a right cock up... But the idea of chuckin' the money from the train wis smart..."

"So, you think it's a risky business?"

"It is a risky business, aye. An' if onything goes wrong, we'll be in big trouble, nae question... It's a serious offence."

"Do you think we can pull it off though?"

"Aye," said McMinn hesitantly. "Gin we ca' canny an' rehearse everything till its perfect."

Gourlay's expression was pensive. "Aye, we're no just coupin' ower a stachoo... Whit's the jile term for kidnappin'?"

"Ach, dinna fash yersel' ower muckle, Gourlay; ye're a worrier... We're a good wee group." McMinn joined his crony at the edge of the bed and studied the palm of his hand. "But Ah'll tell ye somethin' for nothin'... Ah've read a fair bit aboot forensic science an' that, an' the polis are no slow off the mark. It's a weel kennt fact that a criminal either leaves somethin' at the scene of the crime, or takes somethin' wi' him. An' that somethin' could be microscopic...They can even tell yer blood group from the sweat oan yer socks."

"Izzat a fact?"

"Aye. Even a single hair can help them. It disna tell them wha wis therr, but it can tell them wha wisna..."

"So you're sayin' we should shave oor heids an' chuck ither folks' smelly socks aboot the scene?"

"Naw. Whit Ah'm sayin' is we have tae be damn careful... If ye lent the Controller yer comb an' forgot tae ask for it back they could nail ye — finger prints, ye see. When we get startit, Ah'm using' collodion tae paint ma finger tips — it covers the prints...

An Ah'll be wearin' claes that Ah can burn later... An' Ah'll no be spittin' or leavin' fag ends... Furth, Ah'll be wearin' a disguise..."

"Jings!" interrupted Gourlay.

"Dinna forget," continued McMinn in a matter of fact voice, "we're the mugs pickin' up the Controller. Now, when we release him, you can bet the polis'll grill him for hoors tae come up wi' descriptions... Same goes for Denny. And Denny kens me, right?" Gourlay reflected. "You're right, McMinn... What kind of disguise would ye suggest?" "Beard an' moustache... Ah'll pick them up when Ah get ma stuff... There's a theatrical outfitters doon by the Athenæum..."

CHAPTER 12

The days passed in a flurry of activity for the cell; Gordon and Hector seemed to be everywhere at once, advising, checking, cajoling, and going over every detail of the proposed kidnapping again and again.

Jummock had cleared an area at the back of the bunker-like storerooms, set up two camp beds, a minuscule stove, laid on blankets, dozens of tins of baked beans, yards of rope, a hammock, towels, and rolls of tape to make gags in expectation of his guest. With Hector's help, he'd ascertained that no matter how loudly one yelled, almost no sound could be heard outside the little room. The toilets closed at 9:30, and Jummock suggested that if the Controller was brought there after that time, there would be little chance of their being seen or interrupted. He volunteered to stay with the Controller twenty-four hours a day. McMinn, on the pretext of admiring the Controller's shiny, black Humber Snipe, managed to worm the car's telephone number from Denny, and had come to the conclusion that the chauffeur's uniform would fit him reasonably well. Gordon selected Room 209 at the University as an ideal spot to entice Denny. A tiered classroom, it was currently not being used because of a dangerous looking crack in the ceiling.

Hector had borrowed, for a fiver, a somewhat dilapidated car from an acquaintance for a few days, and one afternoon he, Gourlay and McMinn had taken a run out to Rowardennan and selected a little-used roadway leading to a quarry which seemed a tailor-made place to conduct a little skulduggery and abandon a car. Hector, it was agreed, would follow the Controller's car, help with the abduction if he were needed, and drive everyone to Jummock's toilet at Charing Cross. He, too, it was decided, should be in disguise, and McMinn offered to pick out a suitable wig and beard.

Gordon had studied Murray's train timetables, and had listed every train running from Queen Street station to Edinburgh. He'd taken several trips, made copious notes, and had settled on a spot some fifteen minutes out of the Glasgow station—a derelict factory building which stood close to a slight curve in the line. Subsequent tests showed that a car's headlights flicked on and off could easily be seen from a speeding train and so it had been decided that it would be much simpler to use the car's lights as a signal rather than a bonfire. In a disguised voice, Gordon had telephoned the stationmaster at Queen Street, and saying that he was writing an article for a train spotters' magazine, learned that there was no communication system on trains whereby the police could be contacted directly. In an emergency, he was told, the crew would stop the train and telephone from the nearest station or from any of the many emergency telephones which were strung out along the tracks between the cities. The spot was a fortuitous choice; the closest station was Glasgow, and the nearest emergency telephone lay nearly a mile in the direction of Edinburgh.

The group agreed that the Controller should be worth in the region of ten thousand pounds to his employer, and Gordon had carefully calculated the size of package required to hold that amount in ten pound notes.

Phase One, Abduction Day, finally arrived. For weeks the excitement had been building in the cell as they planned and rehearsed every detail, and now, suddenly, the time for action had arrived.

Gourlay paced up and down Room 209 at the University anxiously awaiting the arrival of McMinn. The clock in the quadrangle boomed out scaring him half to death, and a few minutes later the door opened and a bizarre grinning face, which Gourlay didn't recognize, appeared. McMinn, his face blackened and wearing a fuzzy wig sauntered into the room. "He's oan his wey... Denny's oan his wey! It's workin' like clockwork!"

For a long moment, Gourlay's lips flapped silently before he could articulate his outrage. "Haud oan a wee minute, McMinn... Whit in the name o' fuck are ye doin' kitted oot as a darkie? Whit's the bluidy gemme?"

"Naebody'll recognize me," responded McMinn somewhat nonplussed by his pal's reaction.

"Ye got that right! Yer ain maw wad take ye for a muckle black deil! Ye scared the bejaysus oot o' me! Use yer noddle, McMinn; you are tae replace Denny... How in name o' Christ is the Controller tae believe you're Denny when you're rigged oot as a fuzzy wuzzy?"

"Jings! Ah didna think oan that," mumbled McMinn somewhat put out.

"Well, we've nae time to argue... Denny's oan his way?"

"Aye. He wis tellt tae chap oan the door when he got here..." They stiffened as footsteps clicked along the wooden-floored hallway outside.

"It's him!" cried McMinn. "Quick! Whaur's the club?"

The unsuspecting chauffeur tapped lightly on the door and stepped inside to Gourlay's muffled, "Come." Immediately, McMinn leapt from behind the open door and thumped Denny on the back of the head with his rough-hewn club. With a little moan, the unfortunate chauffeur crumpled to the floor. Quickly, they stripped him to underpants and shoes, and McMinn donned his uniform. Denny was soon securely trussed and wrapped in sacks, and with much grunting and cursing, especially from McMinn who discovered that the black greasepaint on his hands was rubbing off on the sacks, they struggled along the hall and down the stairs to the car. Not one of the passing students gave the odd pair as much as a second glance as they placed their bundle in the boot.

"O.K., McMinn?" asked Gourlay somewhat breathlessly. "We hivna forgot onything?"

"We forgot tae gag Denny. What if he comes roon an' starts makin' a main..."

"Ye gave him such a dunt I doubt he'll hae muckle tae say for a whilie... Christ, McMinn, ye look like a bogle! Whit possessed ye tae disguise yersel' as a darkie? Ye daft bugger ye — whit'll the Controller say when he sees ye?"

Before the latter could retort, there was a discreet 'Toot toot' and they turned to see a strange figure getting out of a tatty-looking little car with a carpet tied to the roof. Resplendent in auburn wig, matching beard and dark blue serge suit, Gourlay didn't recognize him until McMinn gave the man a thumbs up sign and said, "It's Hector... Right, Gourlay, I'm off. See ye doon therr..."

Gourlay joined Hector and they followed McMinn on the short drive to the B.B.C. parking lot. Hector pulled up outside the actual lot but within sight of McMinn in the Controller's car.

"Thought I'd choke when I saw McMinn in his rig... I wondered who the hell he was at first," said Hector with a little smile.

"You're in full fig yersel' Hector wi' yer copper nut an' a'!"

"McMinn's choice... But you've not bothered with a disguise yourself, Gourlay?"

"Naw... Ah came tae the conclusion that Ah'm nondescript, and thought that a disguise would just draw attention tae me... This wey, Ah'm damn near invisible!"

"You might be at that," replied Hector, sticking a pencil between his wig and scalp to ease an itch.

Periodically, they glanced through the railings at McMinn who sat bolt upright in the driver's seat and stared ahead with stoic expression. He arranged the interior mirror so that he could see the door through which the Controller would appear. He was momentarily startled at the sight of a black face staring back at him. "Well, hello dere! How is ebberyding gwine today den?" he said in a *basso profundo* voice to the leering face. He bared his teeth and was fascinated by their whiteness. He pulled a few faces and grimaces and in a low rumble had just managed a couple of 'Doo dah doo dah's' when he caught sight of the Controller, briefcase in hand, newspaper under his arm.

As he strolled towards the car Mr. Langley's mind was on many things, not the least of which was something that had happened at the beginning of the week and still puzzled and troubled him deeply. Passing through his elderly secretary's, Miss Bogue's, office, he'd accidentally dropped his glove which fell into the wastepaper basket at the foot of the new-fangled copier machine, and when he'd leant forward to retrieve it, couldn't help noticing the strange design on a scrap piece of paper. Idly, he'd picked it up along with his glove and perused it as he went into his own office.

It was mid-morning before it struck him with an impact that was almost physical that what looked liked a Rorschach test was, in fact, a mechanically reproduced copy of a female pudendum. The rest of the morning he valiantly fought to retain some vestige of composure even though the realization of what he had found came close to unhinging his mind. At eleven precisely, Miss Bogue brought in his tea and two biscuits.

"I wonder, Miss Bogue," said he in his beautifully modulated undertaker's voice, "if you would be so good as to draw up a list of persons who have used the copier machine this past week."

The neatly typed list of names was of no help at all; only a handful of silver-haired, spinsterish secretaries had availed themselves of the machine, and his personal assistant, Mr. Fielding, could shed no light on the matter either. The most disturbing aspect of the affair was that he now found himself compulsively glancing at the rear ends of the female employees wondering whose bare buttocks had been squatting on the cold glass plate of the copying machine... It was all most irregular and unnerving...

The Controller strode towards the waiting car, got in, glanced at the driver, saw broad shoulders, cap, and white neck — fortuitously, McMinn had omitted to blacken the back of his neck — and opened his paper at the crossword. McMinn, readjusted the mirror, started the vehicle, and drove carefully out of the parking lot to join the rush hour traffic heading out of the City. A few cars behind, he could see Gourlay and Hector following in their battered machine.

"You're very jumpy, Gourlay."

"Naw... There's a spring in the seat that keeps jabbin' ma bahookie... Is this wreck going to get us there an' back?"

"No problem..."

"He's a big bugger."

"Who?"

"Langley, the Controller."

"Aye," said Hector with a wan smile. "But there's three of us... And he'll probably be flabby from living the good life."

"What exactly does he do, Hector?"

"The same as any executive I'd imagine; hangs around and acts the part! Seriously though, I suspect his main function is to keep the Scots from thinking about themselves too much, and reassure the English that we're nonthreatening."

"How do ye mean?"

"It's a bit like Al Jolson in blackface... Folks are a bit scared of Negroes, so what better way to reassure the Whites than to have a Black man who is not really a Black man but a White man made up to look like a Black man..."

"Oh aye," said Gourlay, not fully comprehending.

"Our Scottish Al Jolsons are the singing shortbread tins... I'm not saying Andy Stewart, for example, has no talent — he has — but the White Heather Club and Andy, warbling away about tartan, kilts, heather and haggis is a nice way of presenting us as harmless clowns to the English... An', of course, Harry Lauder was an expert at that... Broadcasting is a powerful tool in getting someone, or even a nation, to think or not think in a particular way... It's no accident that the first thing revolutionaries do is seize the radio and television stations... How many hours a week do you suppose the B.B.C. in Scotland devotes to us Scots?"

Gourlay shook his head. "Nae idea."

"We're about a tenth of the population in Britain, and I'll tell you, my friend, we get nowhere near a fair proportion of the programming... Not only that, the bulk of the programmes they call Scottish have no true relevance to us at all... All we get are some plastic folk dressed in tartan singing a few songs... Plus some sports. How often do you see a Gaelic programme on television, for example? And the sods will actually rehearse a play in London then ship all the actors up to the studios here just so they can say that it's a Scottish production — did you ever hear of anything so underhand...? An' another thing," added Hector warming to his subject, "did you ever once see anyone discussing our independence on the air in a fair and balanced way? Not a bloody chance... Ah, don't get me started, Gourlay... I just think it's a black disgrace that's all. And to add insult to injury, we pay the same licence fee to watch television as the English..."

In the Controller's car, all was quiet but for a low moaning sound coming from the rear of the vehicle. McMinn glanced uneasily in the mirror, but engrossed in an anagram the great man was oblivious. At the appointed spot, McMinn swung the car up a track, brought it to a halt, and switched off the engine.

"Why have we stopped?" enquired the Controller in his rich voice. McMinn turned to face him.

"Why, hello dere massa!" he said rolling his eyes and giving a great toothy grin.

"Upon my soul!" exclaimed the passenger. "What on earth...?" But before he could continue, the rear door was whipped open and a slightly built man with a shock of red hair dragged him out by the shoulders, pushed him to the ground, and sat on his chest. McMinn held his legs while Gourlay struggled to pull a sack over the astonished man's head and torso. Easy living or not, the Controller put up a spirited struggle; he scratched, kicked, thrashed about and even managed to bite McMinn's pinky.

"Ye English bastert ye!" cried the latter and dealt the unfortunate Controller a horrendous blow to the top of the head with his fist.

Soon, it was all over. The Controller, bagged, gagged, trussed and rolled up in a length of old carpet, was placed in the rear seat of Hector's car, while a moaning and mumbling Denny was lifted into the Controller's car. McMinn joined the Englishman in the rear while Hector, with Gourlay beside him, reversed down the track to the road and headed back into the City.

A light rain began to fall and Hector slowed down. "Wipers kaput... Can't see properly," he explained.

"You dere, haud still!" said a deep, gruff voice which carried a whiff of both Alabama and Govan.

The rest of the journey was uneventful, and the trio kept conversation to a minimum lest they inadvertently give some clue as to their identities. But they needn't have worried; wrapped in the carpet, which smelled horribly of cats, the Controller was oblivious to anything but his acute discomfort and the fact that his life recently seemed to have become a series of nightmares consisting of female pudenda and leering golliwogs.

It was still light when they arrived at Charing Cross. Hector parked the car as close to the toilets as he could. For a long while, they sat in silence watching the steps leading down to the Gents. Gourlay and McMinn shared a cigarette. "Aw. Ye've blackened the end o' it wi' your warpaint, McMinn!" whined Gourlay. In response, McMinn placed a black finger to his lips pointed to the carpet-wrapped bundle.

Various men ascended and descended the steps including a sinister figure with an attaché case. The man was, or at least closely resembled, the lunatic knifeman of the toilets. Gourlay shuddered. Then after a lengthy wait, Jummock appeared at the top of the steps. He looked around in an exaggeratedly furtive manner, gave a wave to signify the way was clear, and disappeared down the steps again.

"Right lads," said Hector, "let's go!" With much cursing from McMinn and Gourlay at the weight of their burden, the three lurched through the traffic, across the cobbled street, and stumbled down the steps. Jummock held open a door marked 'Storage — Employees Only.' Once inside, they unwrapped their package. The Controller, half suffocated and covered with a fine dust, looked ghastly, but the consensus was that he'd survive. They quickly blindfolded him and tied him securely to a chair while Jummock lifted his gag and made him sip a cup of water.

"Right. He's all yours, Jummock. Your sure you can cope O.K.?"

"Aye."

"Don't get into any discussion with him — keep talk to an absolute minimum," added Hector *sotto voce*.

And so, with a brief telephone call to the police telling them where they could find Denny, Phase One of the operation ended, and at Quayle's the participants celebrated noisily into the early morning hours. Jummock, relieved by Gordon, dropped in and announced that the Controller had recovered somewhat from his abduction and was demanding to be set at liberty forthwith.

They gathered round in silence as Quayle placed a call to the B.B.C. and read a carefully prepared statement. It was late at night and the sleepy janitor, assuming that he had some nut on the line, at first refused to take him seriously. Finally, however, he called the Duty Engineer to the telephone and Quayle had him write down his statement word for word:

The National Army of Independence for the Liberation of Scotland has struck another blow for freedom. The Controller for B.B.C. Scotland is in our custody. He will be returned safely in payment of a ransom, and after a N.A.I.L.S. announcement has been broadcast verbatim.

All future communiqués from N.A.I.L.S. will contain the code 'Tattie bogle' thus ensuring authenticity. You are now to appoint an intermediary and place his name, telephone number, and the message "Call Head Office" on the Central Station blackboard. Leave it there for twelve days. Await further instructions.

Gourlay felt weary after all the exertions and excitement of the past weeks, but there was little rest because planning and rehearsals for the next phase of the operation were racing ahead. Having successfully pulled off Phase One, the group could almost taste complete victory. Gourlay realized that for perhaps the first time in their checkered lives some of them had found a cause — something they could really believe in — and that helped to make the cell a cohesive, dedicated unit with an almost fanatical hunger for success; it suddenly seemed to be of the utmost importance that each member prove to his fellows, to Quayle, Big Red, and indeed, to himself, that he was totally dependable. Gourlay had rarely seen McMinn sustain such single-mindedness of purpose about anything before. Indeed, the pair of them, usually of a sceptical turn of mind, were, for the first time since their Army days, unreservedly and enthusiastically throwing their full weight behind the team.

Careful not to be seen expressing too much interest because he knew plainclothes policemen would be watching, Gordon noted the name J. T. Fielding, a telephone number, and the message "Call head office" chalked on one of the boards at the railway station. Gourlay suggested that because McMinn could speak some German and could therefore easily assume an accent, that he should be the one to place the call to the B.B.C.

Crowded in a steamed-up telephone kiosk with Hector, Gordon and Gourlay, McMinn assured Fielding that the Controller was safe. Reading from a carefully prepared text in a mangled accent which had Gourlay fighting back paroxysms of mirth, he informed the B.B.C. man that Langley's safe return would cost £10,000 in used Bank of England ten pound notes securely wrapped in one packet. In addition, a N.A.I.L.S. communiqué would have to be included on the evening television news. Fielding kept trying to interject, but McMinn ploughed on and when he'd finished his statement, said, "Goot Nacht," and hung up.

After several such brief calls, made from different kiosks, Fielding said that arrangements had been made to broadcast the communiqué and that payment could be made in a day or so. Firstly, however, he demanded proof that N.A.I.L.S. did indeed hold the Controller and that he was alive and well.

The police, meanwhile, were not simply sitting around in their various stations swigging tea, smoking, and discussing football scores, current events, their pensions and the like; Dudley was back heading a special task force of hand-picked men. His face bore a neat pattern of scars where Moses the lion had toothed him and gummed him, and in places, tufts of hair were gone forever from his scalp. It was Dudley who urged a B.B.C. committee be set up specifically to deal with the crisis and insisted that, initially at least, they co-operate with the kidnappers. Rapping the board room's mahogany table with his knuckles in an accompanying rhythm, he said, "We'll get your Contwoller back safely... And the wansom money too," he announced crisply to the concerned grey-headed ones, "I'll have this so-called Liberation Army behind bars in a twice — mark my words! I stake my weputation on it."

Dudley went on to implement all the routine things — all calls to the B.B.C. were being carefully monitored, cold-eyed plainclothes officers quizzed Denny relentlessly, dusted the Humber Snipe for fingerprints, and after McMinn's contact with Mr. Fielding, put a recording device on the latter's telephone. Anyone who as much as glanced twice at the blackboards in the railway station was questioned closely. A linguist at the University was consulted as to the accent of the caller, but could make little of McMinn's 'German' accent.' "I could be wrong, but he sounds like a Lowland Scot who has spent some of his life in the Urals," said the expert.

Thus, despite Dudley's efforts, and the flurry of police activity, nothing concrete emerged. Adding to the confusion, after interviewing Denny, at Dudley's insistence, two gigantic Ethiopian medical students, a Nigerian-born trolley bus conductor, and sundry other non-white residents of the City and had been subjected to many questions and mild verbal abuse by the police. The Glasgow Police, a fine body of men with great understanding of the City and of its inhabitants, both good and bad, was not normally given to such crass tactics. But under the imperious direction of Agent 28-L-5, otherwise known as Dudley Tyrwhitt-Drake, the members of Glasgow's finest had no option but to play the heavies. Most of the force was sceptical about the very existence of a National Liberation Army, while a minority felt it might exist and indeed were even mildly sympathetic to the notion of bunch of nut cases giving their Sassenach overlords a hard time of it.

In due course, following the evening news, a plummy-voiced television newsreader intoned the brief N.A.I.L.S. communiqué:

And now here is a special report: Further to our earlier report that the Controller, B.B.C. Scotland had vanished after leaving his office on Queen Margaret Drive last Friday, we have just received the following communiqué from a group calling itself the National Army for the Independence and Liberty of Scotland. The group claims to have kidnapped Mr. Langley, and has asked us to read the following which the British Broadcasting Corporation now does on the advice of Glasgow's Chief Superintendent of Police:

'The National Army for the Independence and Liberation of Scotland has but one mandate: to free the Scottish nation from the yoke of foreign domination. In the forthcoming struggle to regain our independence, we ask for your support...'

Most of the group, for one reason or another, missed the broadcast, but word of it soon spread and there was quiet jubilation.

All things considered, Wee Jummock wasn't having too bad a time of it. After an initial period of struggling, threatening and pleading, the Controller settled down and resigned himself stoically to whatever these maniacs had in store for him. He found that Jummock's rambling discourses on Tchehov helped relieve the monotony of the long days in captivity. The little man was a walking enclyopædia *vis-à-vis* the life, times, and works of the Russian writer, and the Controller listened with genuine interest as he recounted details of his meeting with an elderly lady in Glasgow who had actually attended school with one of Tchehov's relatives. Langley appreciated the fact that his little jailor made every effort, short of removing the blindfold and the various ropes securing him, to ensure his comfort, and, despite the rough treatment he'd received when he'd been abducted, he no longer believed that his life was in danger.

One day Jummock announced, "Ye've got a visitor the day, Mr. Langley... Just bide quiet, and lissen tae what he's got to say." The visitor was Gordon, and to Jummock's astonishment, when he spoke his voice was high-pitched, nasal, and seemingly very English.

"I have to prove that you're alive and well, Mr. Langley. If you'll co-operate, you'll soon be given your freedom. Perhaps you'd like to tape record a message to your wife...?"

Agent 28-L-5 and the Controller's assistant, Fielding, went through the revolving doors of the Ivanhoe Hotel and hovered near the telephone booth in the foyer. Dudley, carrying a wrapped packet, sauntered in turn into both bars, ran a shrewd eye over the clientèle, then rejoined Fielding who was perusing a fine etching of Sir Walter Scott (Bart.). The telephone rang shrilly and they stumbled over each other as they tried to enter the booth at the same time. Dudley got to the receiver first.

"N.A.I.L.S. 524," said a crisp, thin voice — Gordon's. "When you come out of the hotel you will see a laneway facing you on the other side of Buchanan Street. Take it. It leads to Queen Street station. Take the Edinburgh train from platform 4... Get your ticket on the train. In the second carriage back from the engine, taped under the sink in the toilet, you will find a note. Follow the instructions to the letter... You have just under 4 minutes to catch the train..."

The line went dead. "This is it," said Dudley. "Follow me! We're taking the twain to Edinburgh!" As they ran out into the street Dudley hissed, "Edinburgh twain, *now*!" to a plainclothes officer who was fiddling with a broom on the pavement outside the hotel.

Some miles away, Gourlay, Hector and McMinn sat in their car and studied Hector's turnip watch. "Eight minutes to go... In any event, a minute or two either way is of no consequence," said Hector. "The next train is the one."

To their left as they faced the City, a steepish bank ran up to the railway line, and to their right loomed the great dark shell of an abandoned factory. The lights of the City in the distance gave the night sky a dull orange glow. All was perfectly quiet but for the subdued crooning of some pigeons perched on the building's window ledges. "Right lads," said Hector, "to your positions!" Dutifully, Gourlay and McMinn got out of the car, and clutching torches, headed towards their prearranged positions along the embankment. Gourlay screwed up his eyes and peered into the darkness for a sign of the train. Higher up the bank in the car, he knew that Hector enjoyed the best vantage point and would most likely be the first to see it. His heart thumped and the hairs on his neck tingled and the feeling reminded him of the nights he'd spent under fire in the desert.

It was not long before Hector gave three toots of the horn to let them know he'd spotted the train. Some of the pigeons took to the night skies at the outrage. "Don't take your eyes off the second carriage — that's where the money will come from..." Gordon's words ran through Gourlay's head. The car's headlight's began to flash, and suddenly, with a great rumbling, rattling, and clouds of steam, the train was upon them. On the bank above, it seemed monstrous. Then framed against the light from a compartment window in the second carriage, he saw a figure. The window was lowered and a parcel arced towards him. Above the roar of the engine he called, "I got it! I got it!" and flashed his torch in the direction of the car. Followed by McMinn, he stumbled up the bank through the long weeds, and after a brief search, there it was. The train rolled off into the darkness. "Good for you!" said McMinn, and together they clambered up to the car calling out the good news to Hector. Breathless, Gourlay husked, "Here, sees your gully, McMinn." The latter produced a black-handled jack knife and handed it to his pal who cut the string securing the packet. In the torchlight Gourlay fumbled with wads of notes. "It's real! An' it looks as if it's a' here! Haud on... What's this?" He held up a shiny button-sized object which fell from one of the bundles of notes. "Hey, McMinn, whit's this?"

McMinn shone his torch on the object and peered at it closely. "It's a fuckin' radio transmitter... A fuckin' radio transmitter, that's whit it is!" He took the object and flung it back along the path where an opportunistic pigeon with excellent night vision gobbled it down. The car horn tooted and Hector called down to them, "Hurry up! The train's stopping... Hurry up!" As soon as the pair were safely in the car, Hector raced back towards the City.

"We got it! We got it!" said McMinn still panting from his exertions. "An' there wis a wee radio transmitter in the money Hector — Lucky we spotted it..."

"Clever move that! Where is it?"

"Chucked it awa'... An' Ah think a bluidy doo et it!"

Hector laughed so loudly the car nearly left the road. "My gosh, that'll keep them busy! They'll be trying to get a fix on it for weeks!"

"Here, McMinn... Shine yer torch here a minute," said Gourlay, and he began to checking the notes. As prearranged, he divided the money into two bundles and placed them into paper bags. "Right, Hector, that's the money sortit."

It had been agreed that it would be best not to put all the eggs in one basket, and because they felt the police would not be slow to set up road blocks, it had been decided that Gourlay and McMinn should take charge of the ransom money and get out of the car separately and as soon as practicable. So, on the City's outskirts, the two got out of the car, and hearts pounding, went their separate ways to catch bus or tram. *En route* to his flat, McMinn gave his bag of money to The Rabbit for safe keeping; if he had the temerity to abscond with it, McMinn had argued, a one-legged man should be easy to catch. Gourlay handed his bag over to Quayle and gave him an account of the evening's goings on.

By eleven that night, Jummock had been informed of the night's events, and Gourlay, McMinn, Hector, and Gordon celebrated over a dram at McMinn's.

"It went like clockwork, like clockwork," said McMinn for the umpteenth time. "They stopped the train right enough, so the polis must have been oan the train... But it was near a mile doon the track when it stopped, eh no' Hector?"

"Closer than that... But when I saw it stop I was a nervous wreck in case they'd get to you before we could get off our marks."

"And you say the money didn't appear to be marked?" asked Gordon looking at Gourlay.

"No' as far as we could see... An' it was a' used tenners, just like we tellt them... Quayle will be able to tell us; we just saw it wi' torches..."

"Aye, but used notes or no', they'll have made a note o' the serial numbers," opined McMinn in his raspy voice.

"Quayle said he'd take care of that," said Gourlay draining his glass. "An' he said wance the money wis laundered, as he cried it, we're a' tae get a few quid tae oorsels."

"Let's drink to that!" smiled Gordon reaching for the bottle. Like schoolboys who have executed a successful prank on their dominie, the group celebrated its victory. Around midnight, the ever thoughtful Hector suggested that someone should take Wee Jummock a dram. Gordon immediately volunteered.

Within a couple of days, Quayle had all the money, Mr. Fielding had been contacted, and arrangements were well under way to effect the return of the Controller. In many ways, Langley's return was anticlimactic. He had ropes running from his feet up inside his trouser's legs through the pockets to his wrists. Over the gags and bandages which blindfolded him he wore a rubber gorilla head.

Backed up by Gourlay and Hector, who were operating an elaborate scheme for signalling all was clear, McMinn and Gordon, wearing false beards, led the unfortunate captor up out of the toilet at a late hour, frog-marched him for several blocks, then hailed a passing taxi. The three piled in. The Controller had trouble sitting because the tight ropes made it hard for him to bend his knees. McMinn leaned forward to the driver and husked,

"Right Jimmy — Cowcaddens underground."

At the entrance to the station he and Gordon got out of the cab. Gordon gave the driver some money and said, "Take our friend to the B.B.C. studios at Queen Margaret Drive… He's appearing as a guest on a programme…" As the taxi drove off, the pair headed down the long steps to the platforms, removed and discarded their beards, took a train to George's Cross, then strolled easily to the toilets at Charing Cross where they helped Jummock remove all signs of Langley's sojourn.

Agent 28-L-5 was in a foul mood. For days and nights he'd led a squad in pursuit of an uncanny radio signal which led them on a merry chase back and forth from various derelict buildings on the Glasgow to Edinburgh railway line. He refused to call it a day and rejected outright the suggestion that their quarry must be a bird. Innocent citizens throwing crumbs to the host of birds in George's Square in the City centre were shaken down and two abandoned factories almost demolished, but still the ubiquitous 'beep, beep, beep' continued until Dudley Tyrwhitt-Drake — with a hyphen — was almost reduced to babbling idiocy. In the privacy of his hotel room he gave vent to his pent up frustration; he howled at the walls, flushed the toilet incessantly, repeatedly banged his forehead on the bedside table, and vowed he'd get to the bottom of the maddening and elusive beeping and bring this damned tartan army to heel if it was the last thing he did...

CHAPTER 13

The euphoria over their successful venture was slow to wane. For a fortnight the friends relived every moment with relish, congratulated one another, guffawed loudly at the retelling of minor incidents, and with their cash bonuses, generally made very merry indeed. Big Red played host to the cell for dinner at a posh south side hotel and presented them all with miniature gold hearts to go with their swords. He explained that he'd had a limited number of them cast and that their cell was the first to receive the highest honour N.A.I.L.S. could bestow.

A few years earlier, on a visit to the ancient seat of the Douglas family — the halls now stood in ruins because the family had deliberately dynamited the roof in order to avoid paying the extortionate rates which were based on a number count of a building's windows — the old caretaker, noting the big man's passionate interest in Scottish history, had produced a blackened heart-shaped block of lead and placed it in his hands.

"You have in your hands the heart of Robert the Bruce, King of Scots," announced the caretaker solemnly.

"Well, of course, at first I didn't believe him," recounted Big Red. " 'Pull the other one,' I thought. But you know what? Years later, reading the preface of one of Walter Scott's novels, I discovered that James, the Eighth Earl of Douglas, was taking Bruce's heart to the Holy Land when he was killed in Spain in 1330... Well, they took Jamie's bones back to Scotland for burial..."

"That's right," interjected Gordon, and staring fixedly at the ceiling began to quote Barbour's lines:

"The banys haue thai with them tane,
And syne or to their schippis gane:
Syne towart Scotland held thair way..."

"But there's no word of what happened to Bruce's heart," continued the big man as if there had been no interruption. "Aye in those days if a nobleman hadn't been on a Crusade, it wasn't uncommon for family and other folk to lap his heart in lead — after his death that is — and hump it to Jerusalem... And right enough, when they howket up Bruce's bones in the 1800's, the rib cage had been sawed open... More than possible that Bruce's heart ended up in Douglas's home base..."

But pleasures are indeed like poppies spread, and all too soon the cell's moment of glory and celebrations gave way to more mundane pursuits. Hector drew up and distributed a list of suggestions for further activities; an exploratory raid into England; capturing Edinburgh castle; a visit to Eire to see the I.R.A. in action; a trip to the Highlands to drum up new recruits for N.A.I.L.S... McMinn and Gourlay perused the list at the former's flat.

"Hmmph," grumped McMinn removing his pince-nez; a recent sixpenny acquisition from a Barrowland stall, they were gold-rimmed, delicate, utterly incongruous, and seemed to add more than a whiff of villainy to his rugged face. "Hmmph," he repeated. "Raid England eh? We hivna done that syne the days o' the Border rievers... He's livin' in a dream world is oor Hector so he is... Capture Edinburgh castle? Mebbe we could... But it's a wheen like a dug chasin' a caur; if he akshully catches it, whit the fuck did he *dae* wi' it? Naw, it's a daft idea..."

"Mark you, McMinn, it wad be grand if we could take it an' haud it..."

"Ye've hit the nail oan the heid, Gourlay; we might take it, but we'd never haud it." McMinn placed his glasses on the end of his nose again and studied the list. "Visit the I.R.A? That's mebbe no' a bad idea..."

"They're a bunch o' hard men, McMinn... Pit a bullet in yer heid or kneecap as soon as look at you."

"True. But by Goad! They get things done... They got their independence... Aye, they've got balls the Irish; we're a bunch o' pansies by comparison... We can talk, but nae action syne the days o' Charlie... We're too busy argy-bargyin' amang oorsels."

"Pansies? Oor cell?"

"Naw, the Scots! Ach, we're O.K. fightin' under an English banner — ye ken that weel enough from North Africa — but it's as if we've tae be led, as if we need the English tae tell us whit tae dae... We're queer folk right enough..."

"How dae ye mean, McMinn?"

"We're a divided nation — Papist/Protestant. Highlander/ Lowlander, an' the like... A Glesca keelie wad as lief pit the buit tae an Embro man as tae a Sassenach... But the Irish," he continued with unwonted eloquence as he carefully polished the lenses of his pince-nez, "the Irish, mebbe *because* of their Catholicism which unites them, are *wan* folk... The I.R.A. has aye enjoyed support we'd never get in Scotland... Unlike us, the Irish are no' too busy lickin' English boots tae get on wi' things..."

"A trip tae the Hielans then?" said Gourlay tentatively.

"Hmmph... We tried that wance, mind..?" He smiled thinly. "But an organized trip wad gie us a wee brek forby mebbe drummin' up business... Aye, it's the best o' a bad lot, eh no', Gourlay?"

"Tell ye what, McMinn..."

"Mmm?"

"Yer glesses have gi'en ye the gift o' the gab!"

"Izzat right?"

"Aye... Nae need for you tae go tae Ireland tae kiss the Blarney chuckie!"

"Ach, Ah'm just feelin' good aboot oor wee success... It wis Jummock gave me the idea for the glesses... He wis tellin' me that Tchehov aye wore them, an' bugger me but on Setterday Ah seen a few perrs oan a barra. Tried them on, an' this perr really worked... Ah can see the wee print oan labels an' can see tae squeeze ma plooks an' the like..."

In honour of their success, Gourlay had treated himself to two packs of Passing Cloud cigarettes and the pair indulged themselves with the peculiar, oval, pastel-coloured cigarettes.

"You know, McMinn, that wee bauchle o' a Sassenach is still following me — or wan of his flunkies is." Gourlay was right; Dudley harboured the deepest of suspicions about him and was so filled with a thirst for revenge that he spent most of his spare time attempting to shadow Gourlay. He could have, it is true, had Gourlay picked up on a number of charges related to the lion incident, but had decided to leave him free to roam in the hope that he might lead him to bigger fish in the N.A.I.L.S. pool. Professional or not, Dudley had never had so much trouble shadowing a suspect, and even the shrewd and experienced Glasgow C.I.D. lads he delegated to follow Gourlay usually lost him.

Slowly, Dudley began to get wise to some of Gourlay's disappearing tricks, but remained totally baffled how the little beast could vanish without a trace from a platform in any underground station; he hadn't boarded a train because no train had passed; he hadn't crossed the tracks and exited on the other side — Dudley had tested this theory by posting men at all exits; and he hadn't appeared to have run up any of the tunnels... What he didn't know was that Gourlay had discovered that below the platform in every station was a niche which held a stretcher and other emergency gear and first aid equipment. He'd found that he could dreip over the side of the platform and worm his way to the rear of the niche and become lost to the world. It was a dangerous trick; there were

James Findlay Sleigh

only inches to spare between the side of the platform and a passing train. He easily avoided the ticket collectors because they were invariably in their little booths when no trains were at the station. Occasionally, he climbed out from his hideaway under the very feet of a startled passenger, but he was never questioned.

For Dudley, it was an exhausting business — the little man kept weird hours, was totally unpredictable in his movements, operated to no discernable patterns, and lived a very nomadic life. What infuriated him most was the taciturnity, cunning and smugness of Gourlay's acquaintances; from them he had learned nothing of consequence. Adding to his misery was the covert smirking of the Glasgow Police. On the advice of the C.I.D., Dudley had cultivated Sanny Rutherford and pumped him for information but had never come to trust him; certainly, he did not like the furtive little man. The feeling was mutual; all the pair had in common was a burning desire to get even with the members of N.A.I.L.S.

"Bloody Sassenach! He's the slyest wee shite," said Gourlay to his crony. "Ah aye seem tae manage tae shake him off, but Ahm' nervous that Ah'll lead him here or somewhere..."

"We'll scupper him an' that wee bauchle Sanny... Aye, mebbe a wee waft tae the Hielans will dae the trick."

"How do you mean?"

"We'll make it easy for yer man, or yer man an' Sanny if he's wi' him, tae follow us, an' wance we get them tae the back o' beyond, Phhhttt..!" Here, he rolled his eyes and sliced his forefinger across his throat.

Jummock, too, felt a jaunt to the Highlands and Islands was in order, and Gordon, still recuperating from his exhausting involvement in the kidnapping caper, readily agreed that it was a fine idea.

At clandestine meetings held in all manner of places, the group hashed out its near-future objectives:

1. Rest and recreation. ("Drink like fuck then sleep it off," was how McMinn put it.)

2. Give Dudley Tyrwhitt-Drake — with a hyphen (and Sanny, if he showed up) a severe drubbing.

3. Organize a cell or cells.

4. More rest and recreation.

As the Highlands covers a fairly extensive geographical area, there was much debate about where a base should be established, and finally they turned to Jummock to arbitrate because he was the only one on the group who claimed to have any connection with the locale.

"The Isle of Skye," said the little man without hesitation. "It's handy for the mainland an' it's handy for the ither islands. Forby, ma mither's folk came frae Skye."

His words were accepted as a *pronunciamento*; Skye it would be. The preparations taken by the gang were as bizarre as they were diverse. McMinn, whose knowledge of the area was coloured by his familiarity with Dr. Johnson's *A Journey to the Western Islands of Scotland*, seemed to labour under the impression that the land was peopled with Erse-speaking savages. He acquired a massive oak cudgel, a tattered booklet called *Brush up your Gaelic in Six Easy Lessons*, and half a dozen bottles of Zonobrone cough mixture and expectorant. Sensible Gordon, following discussions with an uncle who'd spent a fishing holiday between the Wars in the Highlands, bought oilskins and angling gear. Hector insisted on keeping his boiler suit, but in honour of the occasion, purchased a tartan bonnet and stout walking shoes. Jummock, who was soon claiming his ancestry had it roots in the Macdonalds of the Isles, went one better and bought a used and oversized kilt in what he'd been informed was the Ancient Macdonald tartan. McMinn hotly disputed this and claimed it was the Lindsay tartan. Then Jummock borrowed a book on the Scottish tartans and learned to his chagrin that it was actually the Sinclair tartan. No one had the heart to tell the little man that he looked ludicrous, although Hector tactfully suggested that if the garment were shortened by about a foot it would be far more becoming. Jummock took the advice, and simply sliced off a broad strip from the bottom of his kilt with a breadknife. Unfortunately, as the bottom edge frayed, the kilt soon became progressively shorter and shorter until it bordered on the indecent. Gourlay, who had his own ideas about what to expect, purchased several jars of an evil-smelling liquid which a herbalist had assured him would keep the voracious Highland midges at bay. Additionally, he purchased Wellington boots, a bright yellow oilskin jacket, and an outsized souwester which would fit over his bonnet. By consensus, they decided that camping would give them the greatest flexibility, and accordingly, Jummock bought a huge striped tent at a knockdown price. Its size and colour suggested that it might well have seen service with a circus or travelling fair. Gourlay and McMinn, whose Army experience had included sleeping under canvas, drew up a list of necessary equipment and utensils, and in due course, these were purchased.

With the vast tent and all the bric-à-brac safely in hand, their next task was to find a way of transporting it and their good selves northwards. For seventy pounds cash, Hector came up with the solution; an ancient but pristine Rolls Royce hearse complete with shiny oak coffin.

"God, it's a beaut!" enthused Gordon. But Jummock eyed the monster with some alarm. "Did ye check tae see if there's a corp in the kist...? Whit in Goad's nemme is this ye've got us Hector?"

"Looks O.K. tae me," growled McMinn. "An' ye nivver get a cheep oot o' the passengers," he added with a grin and jerked his thumb towards the coffin in the rear of the vehicle.

Gourlay was enthusiastic; a life-long Rolls and Bentley admirer, he couldn't wait to get, "a wee shottie at the wheel."

Early one Sunday morning, its coffin packed with gear and food, the hearse slid majestically out of the City with its five outlandish passengers while at a discreet distance, two scar-headed gents in a grey car followed. Tartan bonnet at a rakish angle, Hector was at the wheel humming contentedly. Beside him McMinn intently studied the petrol gauge and announced in his gruff voice, "Ah've been watching that wee dial an' the needle's movin' like the meenit haun oan a knock..."

"Yes, she's pretty heavy on petrol," agreed Hector unconcernedly. Wee Jummock, his apology of a kilt barely covering his frailties, lay stretched out in the rear alongside the coffin. He was nursing a fearful hangover and mumbling over and over something about "needin' a guid piss an' a gless o' mulk." Gordon and Gourlay, on the bench-like seat behind the driver, were engrossed in their own thoughts, and idly watched Glasgow's leisurely Sunday morning life through the spotless windows and occasionally returned nods to the odd gent who raised his hat as the hearse glided by.

They spent the night in a field near Fort William. In the semi-darkness they cursed the endless folds of canvas as they tried valiantly to raise the tent. Finally, nearing exhaustion, they gave up in disgust, and with many dark, muttered imprecations, settled down for an uncomfortable night's rest on top of the beast. To add to their misery, a gentle rain began to fall.

"The tent wis a mistake," stated Gourlay flatly with a sour look at Jummock and pulled his souwester over his ears.

"We'll study it in daylight; I'm sure we can master it," came the muffled voice of Hector.

"You an' yer bluidy bargains, Jummock," whined McMinn. "Did ye no' think tae speir aboot ha'en a dug an' barkin' yersel'?" rumbled McMinn cryptically. "Hiv ye ever saw such a bunch o' eejots... Sleepin' on top of a folded tent, an' in the bluidy rain forby...?"

Gourlay stifled the impulse to laugh. "Aye, we're eejots, McMinn. But harpin' oan aboot it winna mend matters... Can we try an' get some shuteye?"

There was a series of mumbles and general vocalizations one associates with disgruntled people, then a long silence before Jummock sat bolt upright and announced: "Ah ken it's ma faut, an' Ah'm sorry... But Ah canna thole this ony mair... Ah'm cauld... An' Ah'm weet an' fed up..." He got to his feet and accidentally trod on Gordon's arm. "Oh, sorry. Wis that you, Gordon? Sorry... Ah'm gaun tae kip doon in the hearse." As he stumbled off into the darkness, a throaty voice called after him, "Hey, Jummock! Jist as ye're aboot tae drop off, the coffin lid'll open an' a cauld haun'll come oot and grab ye by the thrapple!"

"Tae hell wi' ye, McMinn!" rejoined the little man as he vanished into the darkness. They heard the car door open then shut, and then all was quiet. The rain stopped and a mist fell. As they dozed off in the wet, lumpy canvas, a snore or two broke out. Suddenly, there was a muffled yell from the hearse, a door slammed, and a distraught Jummock skittered across the wet grass to rejoin his comrades.

"Ah tellt ye a haun..." began McMinn.

"There wis a chappin' an' scartin' at the windae," blurted the terrified hunchback. "Somethin' wis trying' tae get in, or get oot! Ah got sic a fleg that Ah louped up an' dinged ma heid oan the roof... Then the coffin lid came off... Ah swear it!"

"Ach, ye were dreamin', Jummock," said McMinn dismissively. "Like as no', ye coupit the lid yersel'."

But Jummock was adamant. "Ah tell ye, there wis a chappin' at the windae... That's what woke me up."

There was a muted discussion, but despite their best efforts to assure the little man he'd simply had a nightmare, no one took up Gordon's suggestion that someone should take a torch and check out the hearse. In the darkness and stillness of the misty night, an air of suppressed hysteria grew as a dim glow seemed to flicker momentarily near the hearse. Nerves taut, they peered into the gloom. McMinn suddenly cried out, "Fuck! Whit the hell's that?" and lashed out with his cudgel. The oaths that followed almost lifted the mist, and Gourlay hopped around nursing his left shin. "Ye glaiket bastert, McMinn! That wis ma fuckin' leg!"

"Jeeze, Ah'm sorry, Gourlay... Ah thocht Ah saw something movin' under the canvas..."

"Ye did," moaned Gourlay. "Ma bluidy leg!" The mist thickened, and gradually, punctuated by Gourlay's groans, relative peace again prevailed.

"I believe we could all do with a dram, gentlemen," suggested Hector quietly. A chorus of voices sang out in acquiescence, but Jummock put a damper on the enthusiasm when he said flatly, "The whisky's in the hearse." In the torchlight they looked at one another as the implication of this sank in.

"Ach, Ah'll go," offered McMinn clutching his cudgel. Impressed, they watched as his torch bobbed across the field to the parked monster. The interior light came on throwing an eerie glow over the damp grass as he raked around. Then the light went out, they heard a door slam, and the torch sped towards them. A slightly breathless McMinn spluttered, "Oor gear's scattered... The coffin's open, an' some of oor things are oan the grun'."

"Did you get the whisky?" queried the ever practical Hector.

"Aye..." The bottle was passed around and they took eager swigs. Even Hector, not normally given to drink, took a mouthful. "Not much point in sleep now," he said. "It's nearly dawn." Sure enough, a metallic glimmer had begun to silhouette the hills to their left, and some time later, the mist gone, full daylight filtered through the low cloud cover and found a forlorn empty bottle lying on the glistening grass and five cold, wet, stiff, bleary-eyed, tetchy men squatted on a mound of soggy canvas.

"I have two suggestions to make gentlemen," announced Gordon solemnly. "One, let's check the hearse for clues as to the person or persons responsible... Two, let's practise putting up this dratted tent in daylight, and three, when we leave, one of us should hide by the side of the road while the rest drive off... We can pick him up later...That way, we'll find out if we are being followed."

No one argued, and in the early morning light they brewed up some tea and examined the car and surrounding area. It did indeed appear that someone had hurriedly rummaged through their belongings and strewn them about.

"The English copper or Sanny," said Gourlay, gently massaging his leg which still smarted.

"Bluidy Sanny!" hissed McMinn vehemently as he threw the dregs of his tea on the grass. "We'll nail him yet... An' the Sassenach, if he's wi' him... They'll pey for oor lost sleep!"

The frustrating job of erecting the tent was complicated by the difficulty sorting out the many poles which came in various lengths. Once it was up, Gordon used a pencil to code each pole to make things easier the next time round.

"It's bloody huge," remarked Jummock. "We'll can haud a dance in it ony time."

"It's got nae flerr," whined McMinn. "We'll a' get piles sleepin' in the glaur!" The tent came down quite easily, and soon it was wrapped and stowed in the car along with their other paraphernalia and they were ready to take the road.

"I'll bide if ye like," offered Gourlay. "Drop me by the yett there..."

They stopped, Gourlay got out, and the hearse purred off into the distance. Scarcely had he concealed himself by a boulder than a small grey car drove past. "Sanny Rutherford an' the Sassenach!" breathed Gourlay. "Basterts!" Hector completed a quick circuit of the nearby village and arrived back at the track leading to the field. Gourlay clambered in.

"That Special Branch bloke an' Sanny Rutherford... In a wee grey car... We can easily shake them off..."

"Na, na," replied McMinn. "Let them follow us; we'll gie them their fairin'."

As they headed westwards, the day brightened. Hector drove steadily while the rest of the crew tried to catch up on their lost sleep. Now that they knew they were being followed, it was obvious to Hector. Dudley was skilled in such an art, but on the quiet roads that wound through lonely glens and over trackless moors, it was not at all easy to follow and remain unseen. Hector drew up at a hotel courtyard to fill up with petrol and someone suggested having a late breakfast or an early lunch.

The bar was not exactly crowded when they traipsed in; in fact, only two old timers — shepherds, to judge from the collies at their feet — were sucking on their pipes and sampling mine host's best.

"Fine day... What can I do for you chentlemen?" asked the big man behind the counter. One of the dogs ambled over and sniffed Gourlay's trousers' leg. Satisfied, it rejoined its master.

"Whisky?" said Gordon glancing at his companions. They nodded.

"On holiday are you?"queried the barman as he poured the drinks.

"Aye," replied McMinn. "A wee jaunt tae the Hielans... Jummock here is frae this airt." A shrill female voice called from the depths of the hotel and the barman wandered off.

"Well, well, iss that so?" said one of the old fellows in a genial tone that suggested that the news came as a pleasant surprise. "A Nicholson is it you are, or a MacLeod... We're nearly all Nicholsons and MacLeods here, issn't that so, Alasdair?"

Alasdair raised his shaggy eyebrows. "Aye... And there's a few McSweens... Who are your people then?" he asked looking at Jummock.

"Macdonalds of the Isles," announced Jummock proudly, then added, "My people are from Skye..."

There was a lull, then Gordon spoke up. "Have you any Englishmen hereabouts?" The two locals glanced at one another uneasily; bluntness and directness were alien to their ways.

"Oh, there's a few right enough," offered Alasdair tugging at a hairy ear. "My daughter iss married to one..." His crony, John Alec, found this immensely funny and laughed wheezily.

"And do you still speak Gaelic?" queried Hector.

"Oh yes," responded John Alec after a final wheeze. "We still have the Gaelic... But we don't speak it at home any more."

"Why's that?"

"Och, the children don't like to speak it at all... One of my lads is a doctor and the other is in astronomy... But they understand it well enough though..." The group absorbed this in silence.

To Gourlay, it was all rather sad somehow. Since an early age he had fostered a clear image of what Highlanders were supposed to be like; warrior poets speaking an ancient tongue. It was a Romantic ideal, but never put to the test by him until that moment. Murdo's scrawny bitch suddenly began to scratch furiously, her hind leg thumping on the wooden floor. "Away out of that!" grumbled her owner in a very loud, gruff voice raising his arm in a threatening gesture. The thudding stopped and the dog rolled its eyes. The barman rejoined them. The atmosphere was almost sullen. Had they discussed the weather, the crops, the fishing, or other innocent subjects, the *rencontre* would have doubtless retained a watery conviviality, but the directness of the southrons was always something of a shock to these quiet-spoken, diffident, taciturn Gaels. McMinn, sensitive to the situation, but uninhibited to the last, ploughed on. "So, some Englishmen live up here then?"

"Aye," said John Alec hesitantly, "the landlord here is English..." Antennae extended, McMinn thought he detected a hint of something negative in the man's tone. "Good landlord is he?"

"Aye, verra fair..."

McMinn pressed on and came at the subject from all manner

of oblique angles. But the natural caution of the Highlander *vis-à-vis* anything considered to be a personal matter was not easily pierced. Gourlay noted that every time he was about to make a gain, the shepherds quickly changed the subject. Then Hector had an inspiration: he ordered two double whiskies all round. The old fellows protested mildly at this lavish act.

"Ach," said Alasdair draining his glass in a gulp, "Colonel Bacon, the landlord, iss no' a bad fellow at all... But he can be abrasive at times all the same..." They waited expectantly for him to elaborate, but nothing more was forthcoming.

"Abrasive?" asked Hector after a pause.

"Well, he can be merciless, yes merciless chust, if we as much as lift a single salmon from the river... Duncan Post got a six month suspended sentence for lifting two wee fish last autumn..."

"The Colonel iss also the local magistrate," added John Alec by way of explanation. It was Gordon who finally broke the ice, as it were. He slipped out to the hearse, returned with his fishing rod, and explained that he was hoping to catch a salmon or two on his holiday. John Alec and Alasdair exchanged wily smiles.

"No, no laddie!" said the latter with a wink. "There's only one way to lift a salmon or two... Issn't that so, John Alec?" Several rounds of drinks later, the roof and rafters still didn't dirl, but Gourlay noted that there was now an appreciable measure of bonhomie in evidence. Colonel Bacon, it transpired, had retired from the Indian Army and had purchased the estate shortly after arriving back in civvey street with a very comfortable pension. He did not fish himself, but was relentless in his detection and pursuit of poachers; the time-honoured tradition of 'one for the pot,' which crofters had enjoyed for centuries, was anathema to him. What particularly irked the locals was the fact that while they were forbidden to shoot or fish on the extensive estate, hordes of the Colonel's friends from south of the border descended on the place every summer and wreaked havoc by their indiscriminate slaughter of fowl and fish.

By mid-afternoon, the friendship between the parties had blossomed to the extent that Alasdair and John Alec had agreed to provide boat, nets, sundry equipment, and instructions so that the 'Glascu chentlemen might enjoy a good night's sport on the river.' Not only that, Alasdair positively insisted that they pitch their tent on his croft, and gave them explicit directions how to find it.

The gang spent the rest of the day coasting around the glorious countryside. From time to time, they caught a glimpse of the grey car. Alasdair had described the boundaries of the estate, and as they travelled, its considerable acreage became apparent; mountains, lochs, rivers, moor and grazing land all belonged to Col. G. S. Bacon (Retd.).

Their bellies full, their clothes dry, and the previous night's stiffness ameliorated by the mixture of good whisky and warm sun, the group felt in fair fettle after their initial disappointment with Gaeldom.

"They're funny buggers," muttered McMinn.

"Who?" Gourlay asked.

"Thon Hielanders... Difficult tae nail them doon aboot onything..."

"That's their wey... An' in ony case, ye canna judge a whole race by twa auld shepherds an' a barman..."

"Hmmmph."

The stunning scenery became even more beautiful as the setting sun's orange glow spilled in from the Western ocean. The purr of big car's engine had a soporific effect on the occupants, and there was a long, comfortable silence.

"We Gaels is naturally polite," began Jummock breaking the spell, "an' quiet-spoken..."

"Like yersel'," guffawed Gourlay.

"We Gaels is naturally polite," repeated the hunchback as though no one had spoken, "an' circumspect in a' oor dealings wi' strangers... Christ, ye've only tae look at the times we've been betrayed by furriners — including the Scots in the south, who are also kennt as Sassenachs — an' ye'll can understand why..."

"Call me a Sassenach again an' Ah'll melt ye!" spluttered McMinn.

There was much growling, but as darkness approached, things quietened down and they decided to head for Alasdair's field and set up camp for the night.

CHAPTER 14

Nestled by the dark mountains rising behind it, the wee cottage on Alasdair's croft rested alone in a quiet glen. A tarred, corrugated iron roof sat atop massive stone walls, and it was easy to imagine that not so many years earlier the roof had been thatch. A few hens scratched and clucked in a desultory way round the door, and on the little plateau above the house a few cows grazed or chewed the cud in their easy way. A plume of smoke rose from one of the house's two chimneys and curled high into the brisk evening air in promise of a fine day to come. Hector nudged the car into the field, and the curious bovines meandered over for a closer look.

"Fuck off, coos! We're no' needin' ony shite the day! Shoo!" cried McMin almost before he was out of the car. The obliging beasts sauntered away.

Thanks to Gordon's marks, the poles were soon sorted out and the tent up. With its garish stripes, it looked intensely alien in Alasdair's field.

"Ah bet they bluidy coos'll be ower tae rub their fat arses oan the tent in the middle o' the night," stated McMinn dourly to no one in particular. They lit a fire and the billycan was coming to the boil for tea when Alasdair chugged up on his tractor. He removed his cap respectfully and edged slowly away from the coffin, which, lid off, lay alongside the tent.

"It came with the car," said Hector by way of explanation.

Only slightly reassured, Alasdair joined them by the fire but kept stealing glances at both coffin and hearse during his entire visit. "And did you enjoy your run, chentlemen?"

They assured him that they had. After tea, liberally laced with whisky, they chatted about this and that and the crofter began to relax a little.

"Now in the trailer I've brought you a rubber boat, two good nets, some gaffs and the like... If you follow the river up past the track by the kirk I wass telling you about, there's a good spot for fishing not two hundred yards upstream from there... But be on your guard for Bacon or one of his bailiffs. In emergency, chust forget the nets and head for the opposite shore... The nets are a couple I got from a tinker fellow for a few bales of hay... You'll be knowing how to use them I'm thinking?" They turned to Gordon who gave a slight nod.

"Now, if there's anything else you think you might be needing, you know where I live..."

As the crofter left, they organized the bedding and generally made the tent's interior ship-shape. Later, at Jummock's suggestion, Hector drove him and Gordon back to the hotel for a nightcap. Gourlay and McMinn decided to stay behind and take a nap. Night fell. After the others had left, they built up the fire and lay back on their blow-up mattresses.

"Thon coffin's fair spooky in the firelight."

"Ye're an' auld wumman, Gourlay; it's just a kist." He took a cigarette, passed one to his pal, and they lit them from a glowing twig. "Ah'm nackered," mumbled McMinn sinking back. "Need ma night's kip... Last night wis a disaster."

"Aye... Here McMinn, dae ye think Gordon really kens how tae use a net?"

"Ah hae ma doots... But it canna be awffy difficult. The fush are headin' upstream at this time o' year, so a' ye dae is fix wan end o' the net tae the shore, an' tow the ither end up the river wi' the boatie in a kinda circle..."

"Mmm... Why did Alasdair gie us two nets then?"

"Nae idea... Mebbe he thought we might lose wan..."

The night was chilly but clear. Above them, seemingly close enough to touch, the stars glittered. A peculiar chattering noise in the distance followed by a single "Twannnggg" as if a gigantic guitar string had snapped broke the stillness.

"Whit the hell's that?"

"A burd?"

"A burd? Whit kinda burd wad mak a main like that, an' at this time o' night, McMinn?"

"A hoolet... A gled... Jesus, Gourlay, Ah'm no' an ornitholologist... Ah've nae idea... Mebbe it wis a tod... Mebbe it's Hector an' them trying tae gie us a fleg... Mebbe it's Sanny an' the Sassenach; they canna be a' that far away."

"You think so?"

"Aye," said McMinn flicking his cigarette butt into the fire. "They'll likely have followed the hearse tae the hotel... But ye can bet the perr o' them are wonderin' whit the fuck we're up tae!" He brightened suddenly and rubbed his hands together. "Hah! Mebbe the nicht's the nicht for nailin' them!" The fire slowly died and they dozed off. All too soon, the hearse's headlights swept across the field and came to rest on the sleeping figures.

"Whit time is it?" asked McMinn in a thick voice. "Musta drifted off."

"Nae idea."

Hector and the other two staggered over, and McMinn squinted up. "Ye've been knockin' them back a' this while?"

"Aye... A rerr wee crowd in the bar, eh no' Hector? Verra nice folk... Generous wi' the drams," said Jummock tipsily.

"But barely a hint of anti-English sentiment," added Hector. "Peculiar really... But you know, I have the feeling that they are just too gracious and reticent to publicly admit to being anti *anything*."

"Meaning?" asked Gourlay.

"Meaning," responded Gordon with an inane little smile,

"meaning that the meek don't inherit the earth; the meek are walked over and shat upon from a great height... The English are not meek people," he continued with a slight slur and addressed his pals as if they were a sizeable crowd, "they are takers..."

"Aye, just as we Lowlanders are takers... We take from them too, Gordon..." rumbled McMinn.

"Two wrongs don't make a right though," added Hector. "You're confusing the issue, McMinn... You might well be right; we've been as guilty as the English at eroding Highland culture, kicking out folk and replacing them with sheep and the like... But one thing at a time... Our mandate concerns the English, and if we start arguing amongst ourselves, we're done for."

"Aye, you're right, Hector," said McMinn simply. He produced his pince-nez from an inside pocket and examined them as best as he could in the darkness.

"Did youse sort oot the fushin' gear," asked Jummock and staggered a few steps before falling down on the wet grass.

"Bloody marvellous innit!" complained McMinn as he helped the little man to his feet. "You blokes hauf pissed an' us aboot tae set sail oan dark waters!"

Jummock drew himself to his full height as best as he was able, put his hand on McMinn's shoulder and intoned solemnly:

"We are na fou, we're nae that fou,
But just a drappie in oor e'e..."

Catching the words, Gordon giggled, wagged his finger at McMinn and recited:

"O laith, laith were our gude Scots lords
To wet their cork-heel'd shoon
But lang or a' the play was played
They wat their hats aboon..."

They looked at him in amazement as he doubled over and gave a series of soprano barks.

"Ach Christ, here we go again! The bluidy literary society is in session," moaned McMinn.

Hector cupped his hand over his mouth and whispered to Gourlay, "We were chatting in the pub and Gordon said he's never been in a small boat before and has no idea how to handle a net..." Then in a normal voice he added, "From the fellows at the bar, I gather that this river is no wee burn... It's a bloody great river and can be treacherous too... Not only that, if Bacon or his bailiffs catch us, we could end up doing time... It's not worth it. I say forget the whole thing."

McMinn turned to him, "Aw, bugger that, Hector! Ah wis dreamin' aboot salmon... A nice piece o' caller fush wad be grand for breakfast. Forby that, Alasdair's gone tae a' that trouble for us..."

Hector shook his head. "Yes, but did it never occur to you that he has his motives? He gets a chance to get back at Bacon with no risk to himself... You can't take the breeks of a Highlandman... What do you say, Gourlay?"

Gourlay hesitated. What Hector said made sense; it *was* a high risk venture, and for what? A fish? Fiddling about on a dangerous river on a dark night with a bunch of drunks held little appeal. But he didn't want to offend McMinn. He scratched his head. "Well, er, Ah'm no' sure... Mebbe it would be an idea to postpone it... There's a million rivers we can try, McMinn... Wad ye no' settle for a nice piece o' clabby doo or a black puddin' meanwhile?" But McMinn remained adamant. "Ah'm for gi'en it a wee whirl. Wha's wi' me?" he demanded almost belligerently.

"Me! Me!" cried Jummock thickly. He stood up, swayed, and promptly fell down again, his kilt flapping up around his scrawny, thighs.

"Me too... I'm all for a turn on the river," lisped Gordon. The student brewed a large pan of strong tea on the embers of the fire while McMinn and Hector stumbled about in the dark getting the gear ready. They managed to raise and secure the boat to the roof of the hearse, emptied the coffin and placed the nets and other gear in it before lifting it into the back of the vehicle.

There was a hint of frost in the clear air, and a ghost-pale moon rose above the dark hills throwing a blueish light over the land. From somewhere high above them came the plaintive call of some unseen night creature.

A few miles away in his comfortably built mansion on a hill, Colonel G. S. Bacon poured himself an unsparing measure from the crystal whisky decanter and was gazing reflectively at the log fire when the doorbell chimed.

"Drat!"

"I'll get it!" called his daughter, Angela. "It'll be Rupert for me..." She was a tall, gangling girl, good looking in a horsey sort of way, and had that vague chinless look one usually associates with the English upper classes. Every vowel and diphthong announced clearly to the wide world, "I'm true blue upper crust; if there is a royal function, I am almost certain to be invited; I never miss Ascot, Henley or Glyndebourne; I'm rather partial to things French — Pagnol, Camus, Disque Bleu cigarettes, and Cannes during the season... Sex seems common somehow and doesn't really interest me... Rupert is probably a homosexual, but he's well-connected and he's rich..."

But it wasn't her beau; the visitor was a wispy Anglo-Scot from Edinburgh called Pringle who ran a pottery and crafts shop on the estate. After a brief period of braying and honking in that odd, affected way unique to the English when they put on the dog... ("So sorry to drop round so late har, har..." "Not at all; we're not early bedders har, har...") Angela ushered him into the parlour.

"So sorry to disturb you at this late hour, Colonel."

"Not at all, Mr. Pringle. Come in, do... What can I do for you?"

Mr. Pringle had worked very diligently to ingratiate himself with the Colonel and his circle. In an effort to gain acceptance, he had emulated the Colonel and his English friends as closely as his skills and finances permitted. He had bought a shooting brake just like the Colonel's, had begun to attend Evensong, taught himself bridge, helped out at amateur theatricals, vociferously supported the many charities espoused by the Colonel's wife, and made a concerted effort to mimic the speech patterns, accent, and intonations of the southrons. Eventually, his efforts began to pay off, and the Colonel now permitted him certain liberties. But an invisible line remained, and Mr. Pringle was alert to the pitfalls should he inadvertently overstep it. Despite his endeavours, however, he came to realize he would probably never attain the exalted position where he could address the great man by his first name. As he stood before the Colonel now, for example, it did not escape his notice that he was offered neither seat nor whisky. "A little bird told me that there is to be some action on the river tonight," began Mr. Pringle in a precise tone. "A group of Glasgow roughnecks is in the area, and there is talk to the effect that they might try their hand with a net on the river." The Colonel's eyes narrowed and a pinched look came to his face. He drained his glass and put it on the mantlepiece with a loud click. "What else do you know about this, Pringle?"

"That's it, I'm afraid," answered Pringle amost apologetically. "An acquaintance of mine was in the hotel bar tonight and overheard..."

"Well, thank you," interrupted Colonel Bacon politely but firmly. He subtly indicated that the interview was now at an end and that Pringle should now leave. With a few bows, scrapes, and har har hars, the Edinburgh man headed for the door. Outside, he dabbed beads of sweat from his upper lip and wondered if the day would ever come when the English *côterie* treated him as one of their own.

Alone again, the Colonel replenished his glass. He tried to place a call to his factor, but the line was busy. "Blast!" he said, and went off to fetch his shotgun and cartridges from the gun room. He put on a heavy coat and Wellingtons, returned to the parlour, filled his glass yet again, drained it, and stalked out into the night.

A short distance away, Dudley Tyrwhitt-Drake — with a hyphen — and Sanny Rutherford were enjoying a cup of tea and a biscuit with the matronly Miss MacLeod with whom they'd taken lodgings. Innocent lady that she was, she'd believed them when they'd told her that they'd come to the area for a few days to study moths.

"Most kind of you, Miss MacLeod, but I couldn't take another dwop," said Dudley gallantly as the good lady picked up the teapot. "We weally must be off on our hunt... We apologize for keeping you up so late... We'll twy the wivver banks tonight shall we, Mr. Wutherford?" he said turning to Sanny with a meaningful look.

"Such nice men," thought Miss MacLeod smiling a little smile to herself as the front door clicked behind them and her guests stepped out into the darkness.

The hearse nosed its way carefully along a rutted track which ran through clumps of trees by the river's side.

"This looks about right, Hector," said Gordon who'd been peering out of the side windows. "Can you get turned here?"

Under the lemon-coloured moon, the river ran darkly and silently at this point, but they could sense its power and depth. Gourlay threw a piece of broken branch into the water and was surprised how quickly it was swept away.

Dudley had seen the lights of the hearse turn off the road and head towards the river, and after a few moments, he drove for half a mile or so past the turn off and parked the grey car on the verge.

Sanny turned to him with a puzzled look. "Whit are they up tae? They dinna hae the gear for poachin'."

"No idea, old boy. But I'd like to get a closer look."

They got out, and after Dudley had put on his Wellingtons, he led the way, torch in hand, down the treed slope towards the river. As they headed downstream along the river bank, a dim figure stepped from behind a bush and levelled a shotgun at them. "Hold it right there!" ordered a crisp English voice. Dudley fumbled for identification. "Look here, old chap, you're making a ghastly mistake..." He got no further. Without warning, Sanny leapt forward, grabbed the gun's barrel and yelled, "Naebody, Ah said naebody, points a gun at Sanny Rutherford!" The two figures swayed back and forward in the gloom, then suddenly, the gun went off with a tremendous roar. For an instant, all three men froze, then Dudley stepped in to help Sanny subdue the gunman. Soon it was all over. Sanny wrestled the gun from the Colonel, for it was he, then, with Dudley's help, pushed him to the ground and sat on his chest. Again, it was Sanny who took the initiative. "Let's chuck the bastert in the river!" In view of the fact that the man had pointed a loaded gun at them, it did not seem a totally unreasonable course of action to Dudley, and together they heaved the apoplectic Colonel into the river as if he were a sack of potatoes. The current swept him away.

"Are you alwight? You're not shot are you?" enquired Dudley.

"Naw. But ma lugs are ringin'... You O.K?"

"Yes..."

The Colonel was fortunate; after a few minutes an eddy beached him on a sandbank where he lay gasping and cursing. Sanny threw the shotgun into the water.

"Good God!" said Dudley breathlessly as the enormity of the deed sank in. "What have I done? We don't even know who he was."

"Dinna fash yersel'. Ye canna go poncin' aboot in the mirk wavin' a loaded gun at folk no matter who ye are... Good riddance to bad rubbish... C'moan Jim, pu' yersel' thegether... Let's see what oor lot are up tae." He headed off.

The distant shotgun blast had an immediate and salutary effect on Jummock. He scrambled to his feet, danced around in a tight circle, and cried, "That's a bluidy gunshot! Let's get the hell oot o' here!"

"Probably a poacher after a rabbit," said Gordon with a little titter. Hector turned to him. "In this light? Not very likely." McMinn pulled his cap down over his brow and reached for his cudgel. "Youse yins cairry oan here... Ah'll awa' an' see whit's up." He sloped off and was immediately swallowed by the darkness. Gourlay looked off in the direction his chum had taken, and despite the chilly night air, felt sweat beads forming under the band of his cap. This was folly. Jummock was right; they should clear off while the going was good.

In the darkness ahead, McMinn thought he detected something. He crouched behind a bush and waited. A short figure headed towards him. "Sanny!" he husked under his breath. As the little man passed, McMinn sprang to his feet and lashed out with his club. Sanny gave a little sigh and sagged to the ground in a heap. McMinn felt his victim's throat — there was a healthy pulse — then he unceremoniously dragged him away by the feet.

Unaware of Sanny's fate, Dudley crept forwards keeping the river to his right. It occurred to him that the man with the shotgun, English accent or not, might have been some kind of sentry, and if that were the case, he reasoned, then it looked like something important was on hand. That the unfortunate man with the gun was an Englishman and, to judge from his accent, a fairly aristocratic sounding one at that, troubled him; what would a man like that be doing mixed up with a gang of Glasgow louts? He cursed himself for not checking the man's pockets before they threw him in the river... And where was that ignowamus Wutherford? He'd told him they were to stick close to one another...

"Whit have ye got therr, McMinn?"

"Guess whit?" said McMinn stepping back as the group gathered round the forlorn heap on the ground.

Jummock peered down. "Sanny! Christ, ye've killt him, McMinn!"

"Naw, A wee ding oan the heid..."

Suddenly, Hector cupped his hand to his ear the whispered urgently, "Ssh! Lissen..."

"Doon! Get doon!" urged McMinn throatily. They strained their eyes and ears, and in a moment a figure emerged from the trees.

"Aw fuck!" exclaimed Jummock as he accidentally flicked on his torch. The figure immediately took flight and disappeared.

"Efter him!" cried McMinn, and they all stumbled after the fleeing figure. They soon caught up with Dudley, and once again, McMinn's cudgel was brought into play and a semi-conscious Special Agent was soon laid alongside Sanny.

"Now what?" queried Hector. "Now that we've got them, what do we do with them?"

"Chuck them in the river," growled McMinn.

"Leave them be an' let's get oot o' here... Pack up wir tent an' go!" pleaded Jummock,

"Gie them a wee hurl in the coffin," suggested Gourlay. "It'll gie us time tae pack up an' move oan... Pit them in the kist, an' pit the kist in the river..." For a long moment they looked at each other, then without further discussion, they lifted the two men into the coffin, placed the lid loosely on top, then slid the coffin into the river where it settled to within inches of the surface and floated away into limbo. McMinn rasped out the 'Last Post' through pursed lips. He wiped his lips on his sleeve then rubbed his hands together.

"Right lads, now for a bit o' quiet fushin'." There was an immediate howl of protest from his peers, and after a moment's reflection, he capitulated. "O.K. O.K. Keep yer wigs oan... C'moan then, forget the fushin'and let's get loaded up..."

Soon, the hearse was picking its way up the track to the road and Hector made a wrong turn. Realizing his error, he was looking for a suitable place to turn when Gourlay spotted the grey car. "The Sassenach's car! Let's hae a keek inside..." The car was locked, but it was the work of a moment for him to get the door open. "A perr o' shoon," he announced. "Mebbe they'll fit you, Jummock..." The only other thing of interest they found was a little leather-bound notebook which turned out to be a log of the cell's movements since leaving Glasgow. "The bugger's nemme is Dudley Tyrwhitt-Drake," said McMinn with a snigger. "La dee bloody dah!" He pocketed the book and Gordon let the air out of one of the rear tyres.

Back at the tent there was a brief discussion and it was decided that under the circumstances, it would be best to move on to pastures new right away.

"Whaur the fuck are we onywey?" Gourlay asked.

"No idea," responded Hector. "Where's the map?" He spread the map on the car's bonnet and poured over it with the aid of a torch. "We've wandered off course a bit... But we could head for Glenelg or Kyle, and maybe reach Skye tomorrow... Aaargh!"

"What's wrong, Hector?"

"Look... Here's the river here... Just back from the sea a bit... And here, it's marked 'Waterfall'..."

"So what?" said Gourlay.

"It's headed right for the waterfall!"

"Bugger them," said McMinn. "And if they're no droont, they'll be bluidy clean! C'moan lads, sees a haun wi' this gear — we'll drop it off at Alasdair's..." Gourlay sucked his lower lip, and perused the map. "Ach, the river's almost at sea level... An' in ony case, look at the contour line here…" Hector leaned forward and peered. "Aye. I think you're right Gourlay… It's likely just a wee drop. They'll be alright."

Gourlay turned to Jummock. "Here Jummock, gies a haun' wi' this damn tent..."

CHAPTER 15

The arrival of the hearse at Kyle, the main ferry point for the Isle of Skye, caused a minor stir. By way of salutation to what was assumed to be a native son's return home for burial, the little ferry boat gave three mournful blasts that set the seabirds wheeling and screaming and the crew deferentially removed their caps as the big black car was ushered to the head of the queue and boarded the craft. With much rattling of chains and commands in Gaelic, the boat cast off for the short trip to the island. Hector rolled down the window and the bracing sea air heavy with the scent of wet seaweed filled the hearse. To their left, the walls of an ancient ruined castle lowered above them. The island was mist-shrouded and a gentle drizzle was falling.

"Gloomy place," said Gordon. "No wonder they call it the Misty Isle."

As the car rolled off the ferry Jummock exclaimed, "We made it! Skye!"

Gordon turned to him with a quirky expression. "Hmm... Savage mountains, savage flocks, and savage folk..."

"What makes ye say that, Gordon?"

"I didn't; Burns did."

"Awa' wi ye! Burns was nivver oan Skye!"

"True. But he did visit the Highlands, and he did say that..."

The tops of the mountains were obscured and the rocks glistened wetly as the hearse swished along the puddled road. McMinn peered morosely out of the steamed up window. "Hmmph... Sam wis right," he mumbled half to himself, "Rocks and water..."

At a lonely spot at the base of the Coolin mountains Gordon supervised the setting up of the tent. The mists swirled around the jagged peaks, but every once in a while their full immensity and grandeur could be glimpsed. A blackened billycan of steaming, strong tea, fortified with a tot of usquebaugh, soon restored both circulation and spirits and they set to work.

Later, as they relaxed before the little fire which spluttered and fumed in the damp air, Jummock cleared his throat and looked at his chums. "Weel gents, whit's oor next move?"

"Mebbe we could try the hotel we passed? There'll be a pub..." suggested McMinn jerking his head in the direction of Sligachan.

Hector nodded. "Most likely full of English tourists though... Why don't we try the little town, Portree is it? If we're seeking recruits, that's probably the best place to be. Maybe we could give it a try once we've rested up and had a bite."

The little town on a damp mid-week evening in late summer seemed to be deserted as they drove in. Despite its pretty setting and handsome stone buildings, there was a certain bleakness, a sense of desolation about it; "The whiff of Calvinism," Hector put it, "permeates the very stonework."

In spite of, or perhaps because of, the oppressiveness, the bar they found on the quay was lively, even roisterous. A thick-set, swarthy man, his eyes closed, an unlit cigarette dangling from his lips, was urging out spritely tunes from a melodeon. No one took the slightest notice as the gang entered and squeezed themselves around a table in the corner. Two German youths, their huge rucksacks at their feet, stood at one end of the bar explaining to an old salt, "Chermany hez scheep dogs too" but that "zey do not run so fast as the scheep dogs in Schottland." Hector elbowed his way back from the bar with a round of drinks and as he took his seat an old man with no teeth turned to him and said, "An deachaidh do chumail air is?" Hector smiled wanly and plucked Jummock's sleeve. "What did the old fellow say?"

"Mmm?"

"The Gaelic... What did he say?"

"Nae idea, Hector... Ah didna hear." McMinn leaned forward, smiled at the old man, raised his glass and said, "Wie geht es Ihnen?" The old gent shook his head and cupped his hand to his ear with a quizzical expression.

"Wie geht es Ihnen?" repeated McMinn loudly.

Slight alarm in his eyes, one of the German lads stared at McMinn and the old man showed his gums and lisped, "Well, well, but you have the Gaelic fine, well, well..."

Gourlay sipped his whisky reflectively and ran his eyes round the room. Many of the men wore waders folded down over their thighs — fishermen off the various boats riding easily at anchor in the little harbour. There was a sprinkling of crofters, strong-backed, stocky Celts with tufts of hair in their ears, and the odd tourist trying to savour and absorb the local colour.

A lanky, black-haired young man came to the table and leaned over to the toothless one. "Ciamar a tha Shiv an diugh a Seumas?" As he pressed forward to shake hands, the lapel of his jacket flapped open and Gourlay was astonished to catch sight of a little silver sword pinned to the underside. He nudged McMinn.

"Look at that fella's lapel... Oan his jaiket!" he husked out of the side of his mouth.

McMinn looked. "Bugger me!" he exclaimed simply. As the man straightened and turned toward the bar, Gourlay tugged his sleeve. "Er, excuse me, but Ah think we've met somewhere before..." The man looked at him squarely and Gourlay noticed that his eyes were as black as coals and seemed to glow. "My first allegiance is to Scotland..." whispered Gourlay surreptitiously turning his lapel.

"Well, well, it's yourself!" said the young man slightly self-consciously. "And how have you been?" He extended a bronzed hand. "The name's Donald," he said in a lowered voice. "Meet me aboard the *Agrippina* in the harbour in half an hour." He gave a quick smile, turned on his heel, and was swallowed up by the crowd round the bar.

"Who was that?" queried Gordon.

Gourlay put his finger to his lips. "I believe it's my shout gentlemen," he said loudly. "Whiskies all round?" A few rounds later they stood on the quayside outside the pub.

"Whit's up wi' youse?" whined Jummock. "Whit's the rush? Ah wis fair enjoyin' the music an' drams..."

"That fellow is wan o' us," explained Gourlay. "The young fella wi' the dark hair... He's wearin' the wee sword... We're tae meet him on his boatie... The *Agrippina*." They all peered across the harbour wall into the semi-darkness.

"Goad! There's dizzens o' boats," moaned McMinn.

"How do you know he's genuine?" Hector asked.

"We'll find oot soon enough," responded Gourlay. "An' there's five o' us... We'll can sink his bloody boat, an' him in it, if he's wan o' Dudley's men..."

A little unsteadily, they made their way along the quay and peered down at the many fishing boats and pleasure craft. Yellowish lights lit up the interiors of some of them and spilled across the water, while others were dark and lifeless.

"We'll never find it," muttered Jummock tugging his kilt towards his knees. "Hauf o' them that Ah can see dinna hae names... An' if we do find it, hoo are we supposed tae get oot tae it...? Whit wis it cried again?"

"The *Agrippina*."

"Here it is!" called out Hector who had wandered ahead. They joined him and stared down at a large, but tired-looking boat, which in its halcyon days might well have served time as a puffer lugging coal to the isles. Gourlay leaned over the low wall and called down, and after a moment Donald appeared on deck.

"Friends of yours?" he asked.

"Aye."

"Welcome aboard, gentlemen... There's a ladder... To the left."

They clambered down a steep narrow stairway after him, and Donald averted his eyes as Jummock descended. At the end of a narrow passageway was a tiny cabin.

"Make yourselves as comfortable as you can... And welcome again aboard the *Agrippina*," said Donald expansively as if he were welcoming them to the state room in a luxury liner.

They squeezed into the cramped space, and introductions were made. The cabin was painted a dirty yellow and smelled strongly of diesel fuel and bacon. A single minuscule porthole looked out seawards over the dark waters of the harbour. The rivetted bulwarks reverberated to the throb of a generator. They sat below a wire-covered light which cast its pale rays on the assembled company giving them all a sickly pallor. Donald explained that he'd recently been down to Glasgow to pick up some spares for the boat's engine and had stayed with his brother who was an active member in one of the N.A.I.L.S.' cells. He'd been introduced to Quayle and formally inducted into the Army. On his return to the island, he'd put out feelers regarding possible candidates, but while there was no lack of interest, to date, no one had actually been officially recruited. He produced a bottle of whisky and an assortment of glasses and after filling them, proposed a toast to the success of N.A.I.L.S. Gourlay rose a little too abruptly and his head clunked against the grillwork making his teeth rattle. He cursed under his breath.

"So you think, given time, you'll have no trouble organizing a cell here?" Hector asked.

The slim man swept his black hair from his forehead. "Aye... The climate is quite good. They're mostly Liberals here right enough, but there's a new generation coming along who are more aware of their heritage and fed up being second class citizens in their own land... The biggest problem will be selecting lads who can keep a secret."

"How so?" Jummock asked politely.

Donald smiled wryly. "In a tight little community like ours, everybody knows everybody else's business; it's not easy to keep a secret here."

After a lull, Gordon asked Donald if he thought there was any anti-English sentiment on the island.

"There always has been to some extent... But for a little island, we've quite a few divisions. For example, to this very day the MacLeods give pride of place in their castle to a picture of Stinking Billy — the Butcher Cumberland — who put the wounded to torch and bayonet after Culodden..."

"Whit for would they dae that?" interrupted Jummock.

"Well, they were, and probably still are, Hanoverians... And, of course, we've a class system here that even the English themselves haven't seen in centuries."

"How's that?"

"For example, I'm a crofter as well as a fisherman... I don't even own the land I till, and probably never will; I lease it from the estate... From a hereditary land owner..."

"And the land is owned by a southron?" put in Gourlay.

"Yes, well no, not exactly... It's worse; he's what you might call an Anglo-Scot... The only illustrious thing about him is his noble Highland name... English-educated, and his values are a hundred and ten percent English..." He sipped his drink reflectively. "Peculiar how a people always seems to pick up the worst of their overlords' attributes... The Redskins in America got into booze, the Incas got chickenpox... And we Scots always seem to do our damnedest to ape that which is least admirable about the English and their values... Their arrogance, class consciousness, their posing... They're a nation of poseurs..."

"Bloody right!" interjected McMinn banging the table with his fist. "They say the Krauts are arrogant, but yer average Kraut canna haud a can'le tae yer Sassenach as far as arrogance is concerned..."

Donald nodded absently. "Mmm... Peculiar really; put one Scot with six Englishman and he'll be quick to mimic the English, but put one Sassenach with six Scots and they all end up talking like and behaving like Englishmen..." He puffed out his cheeks and made a "phutt" sound. "I'm of the generation who were beaten at school if we dared to speak our native tongue in the playground..."

"Gaelic," confirmed Gordon.

"Gaelic... But now, to hell with them!" He ran his burning eyes round the company.

"Aye," said Gourlay. "But we've aye had oor ain education system in Scotland, so how can ye blame the English for that?"

"Oh, some of us are so keen to ape the English that many of their values filter down... I went to Secondary School here, and I learned more about English history than Scottish... Aye, even our education system is polluted by the English... They're like fleas on a dog..." Hector cleared his throat, and Donald glanced at him before continuing. "If you don't believe me, just try a head count of faculty members and administrators in any college and university in Scotland and you'll be staggered by the percentage of English... It's all out of proportion... And even here, on Skye... they're into everything from the council to businesses... Aye," he concluded, "we're badly needing to scour the English hence..."

Hector nodded sagely. "Hear, hear! With a full parliament in Edinburgh, we might not be much better off, but could we be any worse off than we are?"

The clatter, drinking and table thumping lasted into the small hours. At one point, during a lull, a ferocious-looking bearded face bobbed into sight from the sea-side of the vessel and peered in through the porthole for a moment before vanishing.

"Jesus Christ!" exclaimed McMinn who was seated closest to the opening. "Whit in the name o' fuck was that?" The face appeared again, leered in, and then a hand came into view, and in an elaborate pantomime, indicated that its owner was in desperate need of liquid refreshment.

"It's only Duncan Mac," said Donald reassuringly, and opening the porthole, passed out a full glass of whisky to the eager, hairy face. "Tha mi trang Duncan... Now bugger off," he said good naturedly to the face and closed the porthole again. "Duncan Mac," he said by way of explanation. "Simple lad, but harmless... With a half bottle in him he aye sings,

I'm Duncan Mac o' Stormy Hill.

I never worked an' I never will.

He wanders around doing a bit of this and a bit of that, lifting a salmon or whatever... He must have scrounged the use of a boat tonight... Lives in a house without a roof up Stormy Hill... I remember one snowy night when we left the pub together and he was telling me that he'd have clean sheets on the bed that night!" He chuckled at the memory.

"Ah hope he's no' a prime candidate for your cell," grumped McMinn who was still somewhat unnerved by the sudden appearance of the fierce face at the porthole.

"Well, no. But he could be a very useful fellow just the same — he knows everybody and every move they make..." Donald leaned over and opened the porthole again to try and clear the pall of cigarette smoke which hung over the cabin. The soft lapping of the waves against the hull could be heard. "I was surprised to see you on Skye... What's up? A special project?"

"Naw," replied Gourlay. "We just felt like a wee brek efter the B.B.C. job..."

"Ah, so it was you lot! Quayle said it was a N.A.I.L.S. job, but, of course, mentioned no names... Are you planning to pull something off while you're here?"

They looked at each other for a moment then Hector spoke up. "Not really. We did think of trying to drum up some new recruits, but you're obviously better able yourself..."

Chatting amicably, they sipped their drinks. McMinn surreptitiously studied his Gaelic booklet then suddenly announced loudly, "Cunnaic mi cù dhu aik an dorus!" They stared at him in astonishment. Donald smiled broadly. "Good on you, McMinn! You'll be fluent in Gaelic in no time at all!"

"Aye, oor McMinn's a talented chiel," said Gourlay. "He can speak German like a native forby." His pal beamed and busied himself polishing his pince-nez on his shirt tail for a moment or two then said, "When in Rome... But ye ken, Donald, it might be an idea for us tae hae a wee go at a project... An' you could maybe recruit a few blokes on a trial basis, probational like..."

Donald mulled over the suggestion. "That's a very fair notion, McMinn... Does any one have any ideas?"

Wee Jummock pulled down his kilt for the thousandth time and stroked an imaginary beard. "Ah noticed a big van earlier on... a travellin' bank, an' thought it might be an easy mark..."

"I'm sure it would," smiled Donald. "But I can think of a couple of things against pulling that off: You'd never get off the island... The first thing the police would do is seal off the ferries, and with two, no, three, ferry points it would be easy for them..."

"But if your boatie could make a run for it," interrupted Jummock.

"True. But don't underestimate the local bobbies... There's virtually no crime on the island, so all they have to do is chase drunks and try to catch poachers... They'd just love to get their teeth into a real crime... Aye, we could make a run for it alright, but it wouldn't take them long to check the movements of every vessel on the island... And another thing: the travelling bank doesn't carry all that much money... Oh, and it's not even an English bank!"

Hector stuck his head out of the porthole and sucked in

lungfulls of air before turning to face the company. "How about the ferry itself, Donald?"

"What about it," asked Gordon.

"Well, the day we crossed, I noticed a fellow collecting fares... And isn't it an English company that runs it?" He looked directly at Donald for confirmation, but the latter shrugged.

"Ach, it'd be daft, Hector... Like haudin' up a tram," said Gourlay.

"There's a holiday weekend coming up," continued Hector unabashed. "On Monday, the banks will be closed and they'll likely to have to hang on to the takings until Tuesday... Now, if we could find out where they keep their cash, we could easily knock it over..."

"Mmm... It might work," said Donald dubiously. "They use a little shed at Kyleakin — at least they did when my dad worked for them years ago — and I expect the money would be in a box or safe there... But there's a catch... You couldn't get the cash until the workers left, and they only leave after the ferry ties up for the night. That means you'd have a problem getting off the island..."

A loud snore, like a chain saw starting up, ripped the silence which followed Donald's words; Jummock, his head forward on his chest, had fallen sound asleep. McMinn jabbed him in the ribs with his elbow and immediately the little man raised his fists, gave a loud snort, and in a high nasal voice cried out, "Ah'll melt ye! Ah'll melt ye...!"

"Hey, hey, hey Jummock! Take it easy! It us. Ye're wi' friends," said McMinn soothingly. The distraction and laughter which followed seemed to act as an indicator that the evening had come to a natural conclusion.

As they rose to leave, Gourlay noticed a naval chart of the Sound of Raasay, the strip of water which separates Skye from its smaller neighbour. In deep water he discerned a cross and the words, 'Arms Dump'... "What's this Donald?"

"What's that?"

"On your chart here... see. 'Arms Dump.' "

"Och, that's an old chart... Very handy when you're at the lobsters though; it gives the depth in fathoms at regular intervals."

Gourlay jabbed a grubby finger at the cross. "Aye, but whit's this marked 'Arms Dump' here?"

"That? Och, I believe it's where they dumped explosives and the like after the Great War... That's the deepest part of the Sound."

"Explosives?"

"Shells, bombs, ammunition, mustard gas, I would guess... Typical that the English would dump dangerous stuff like that in Scottish waters! Just like they tested anthrax in the last War up here..."

Gourlay looked pensive as they filed out of the cabin.

Agreeing to meet the following day, they took their leave and headed along the quay towards the hearse. The dark waters of the harbour reflected ribbons of light from the buildings and from the few anchored boats which showed signs of life at that late hour. From one of the boats came the sound of a melodeon or mouth organ and drunken laughter.

"Why's the boatie's ca'ed *Agrippina*?" mumbled Gourlay more or less to himself.

"One of Nero's wives," said Hector. "He kicked her when she was pregnant with his child... Both Agrippinna and the unborn child died."

"Nice chap!"

Dawn saw Hector up and about. He sloshed some clear, ice-cold water from the burn on his face and filled a pot for their morning tea. After persistent efforts, he managed to get a fire going, and soon the tea was brewed. His bawling and beating on pots eventually bore fruit, and one after another his chums emerged from the tent, red-eyed and blinking in the hard morning light.

"Nivver again," groaned Jummock shaking his head in an attempt to clear it of the army of demons who were having a noisy party inside his skull. "Whisky disna agree wi' me..."

"It's no' the whusky, it's the amount, Jummock; ye're a right wee guzzler," said Gourlay quaffing his tea noisily.

"Gonna be a stoater o' a day," offered McMinn squinting up at the clear sky. "Here, this tea's no' bad, Hector."

Hector accepted the accolade with a little smile; coming from the laconic McMinn, that was high praise indeed. Gordon viewed the jagged peaks of the mountains which swept up and stood out starkly against the lightening sky. "Bet there's some good trout lochs up there..." Hector produced the map and they both perused it.

McMinn peered over their shoulders. "Hmmph! There's nae lack o' rivers and lochans oan the island, Gordon... take yer pick; there's a thoosand places tae try guddlin' for troot..."

"You know," said Hector, "we're going to have to be extra careful with any stunts we pull off here..."

"How's that?" queried Jummock.

"Well, according to the map here, there are police stations at Broadford, Portree, Dunvegan, and that's the ones that are marked; it might well be that every clachan has a bobby... And it looks like you can only get off the island, here, and at Uig... And that's no good because from Uig you can only get to the outer isles... And another thing — judging from the roads on the map here, there's hardly anywhere to hide the hearse... What I'm trying to say is that the police could seal the island and check out every mile of roadway in a blink..."

Gourlay squatted down, drained his mug and threw the dregs over his shoulder. "Aye. But Ah thought we were just masterminding' ony schemes an' that Donald's men wad be daen the akshull wark..."

McMinn sniffed noisily and spat into the fire. "We're a'

worryin' ower nothin'... Huh! We hivna even got a scheme, and, in any case, as Gourlay says, we can set things up an' step back."

They lazed the morning away. Jummock dozed fitfully in the tent until the blow-up mattress he was lying on deflated suddenly and he was almost asphyxiated by the resulting alcoholic fumes. He staggered out spluttering and cursing all and sundry until it came to him that it was his own boozy breath which had burst out of the mattress.

Gordon fished in the little burn nearby and was delirious with delight when he landed a tiny trout. After they'd all admired its beautiful speckled colouring, he put it back in the water. Hector filled a bucket of water from the burn and, humming contentedly, washed down the Rolls while McMinn, pince nez at the end of his nose, studied Gaelic phrases, and complained to anyone who would listen about the language's tortured syntax. Gourlay brewed more tea, then poured over the map marvelling at the mix of old Norse and Gaelic place names.

Towards noon, Donald clattered up on a vintage girder-forked motorcycle, and despite the earliness of the hour, produced an almost full bottle of whisky. After admiring the hearse and tent and they'd observed the social niceties, they got down to business. The Highlander had drawn up a list of islanders he felt he could call upon for any scheme the cell came up with. He ran his dark eyes round the group. "Did you have any further thoughts on doing the travelling bank or the ferry?"

They looked at each other for a moment, then Gourlay piped up. "Well, no' in ony detail, Donald... It did occur tae us that we'll need tae be extra carefu' this bein' an island an' a'... We'd need tae ken how mony men ye've got afore we can get doon tae details."

"Five, maybe six... And that includes me."

"Weel then," said Jummock, "why no' knock off the ferry *an'* the bank at the same time... It would keep the polis loupin'."

The idea was taken up and discussed. Donald pointed out that, theoretically, it would be possible, provided that the ferry job was pulled off early on the Tuesday morning before the takings had been banked. The travelling bank, he pointed out, did a run from Portree to Broadford on Tuesdays, but that there wouldn't be much money aboard at that time.

"We're talking about raids in broad daylight then?" asked Gordon.

Donald pursed his lips. "Well, er, yes, now that you mention it... But it would be early morning... I mean, the ferry could be hit before dawn, but the bank van doesn't leave Portree till about half seven in the morning... We could knock off the bank after that..." Gordon smiled. Donald was beginning to sound like Humphrey Bogart with a Highland accent. And indeed, Donald's knowledge of the world of crime came from American gangster films which were shown in Portree's drill hall. The projectionist, a dyed in the wool Free Kirker, didn't seem to be troubled by films which depicted violent acts, murder and general mayhem, but the merest glimpse of a female in a state of undress was enough to set him off; following a shot of a lady's thighs, for example, he'd been known to rave non-stop for a good half hour about the hellish legion of women and the evils of the flesh, and once, a picture of Bridget Bardot in a bikini caused him to fall to his knees in a swoon mouthing lengthy prayers. He acted as the little town's self-appointed censor by the simple expediency of not showing any reel of a film which he felt might tend to corrupt the morals of the picturegoers. That omitting to project a couple of reels of a film sometimes had the effect of rendering the story line totally incomprehensible, seemed to bother neither the projectionist nor the audience, and it probably never occurred to either that while the little screen provided a window on the world, that world only rarely included Scotland, and it certainly never included any portion of female anatomy which might tend to corrupt the morals.

It was finally agreed that Donald should head up the team —

four members would suffice — and that the ferry terminal should be tackled before dawn. After that, the team could have a crack at the bank van *en route* home should conditions be propitious. The visiting cell members would take no active rôle other than acting as advisors. Despite his innocence in such matters, Donald proved to have a shrewd head on his shoulders, and as the afternoon wore on, and the whisky levels in the bottles dropped, many details were thrashed out to his satisfaction. Planning, speed, and surprise, it was agreed, were the essential elements needed for the outcome of the venture to be successful. Donald was giving brief biographical sketches of his chosen desperadoes when a sudden thought struck him. "Ach! It's just hit me that we've a transportation problem... Neither of my lads drives, and I've only got a motorcycle licence... There's no way we could do all that running about without a car..."

"The hearse is too obvious," said Hector.

"Can't you get your hands on a car or van, Donald?"

After some consideration, a slow smile spread over Donald's handsome features. "Aye... John Angus owes me a favour and would surely lend me his old car no questions asked."

"It'll hae to be wan o' us who drives it," said Jummock. "How about you, Gourlay?"

"Fine." He turned to Donald. "Tell me when and where, an' Ah'm yer man." Donald nodded, then his face clouded over again as another thought struck him. "But there's another wee problem... His car's a bit of a wreck; I would chance driving it here, but Kyleakin and back... I don't know..."

In the days which followed, plans were discussed and refined under Donald's capable tutelage. Meanwhile, Gourlay and the others relaxed and took several sightseeing trips. McMinn was fascinated by the numerous Iron-age brochs and duns, and every time he saw one, he'd mark its location on the map. After a few days, he solemnly announced that as none appeared to be located in the southern part of the island, they must have been built as part of a defence network against a northern foe. None of them felt inclined to dispute his findings and let him ramble on to his heart's content.

One overcast afternoon, they dropped Gordon off at the Storr Loch where, to the plaudits of his comrades, he fished till evening and produced half a dozen beautiful brown trout. In search of his ancestors, Wee Jummock took a trip to Roag. His enquiries were fruitful; touched by the kindness and hospitality of the local crofters, he returned with his pockets stuffed with scones, crowdie, home-made jam and scraps of paper upon which he had scribbled the plethora of information he had gleaned about his forefathers. Hector, who was now alternating driving duties with Gourlay and McMinn, was struck by the sheer number of ancient monoliths, Pictish remains, prehistoric barrows, and centuries-old strongholds. For a time, they were all as happy as they had ever been. The countryside was truly glorious and the timelessness of the island cast its spell upon them, and gave them, for perhaps the first time in their checkered lives, a sense of wellbeing and inner peace.

But all too soon, the long evenings round the campfire began to lose their magic; good natured bantering occasionally gave way to bickering and little spats and the jokes became stale, the tales less droll until, at times, a brooding silence would fall over them. It occurred to Gourlay that they only functioned well under adversity, mild forms of imagined or real persecution, or in the face of a challenge. They needed something, some project, some scheme they could get their teeth into while they waited to get cracking on the ferry and bank van business... And then, suddenly, it hit him; of course, the arms cache!

McMinn, the first he broached with the idea, was not impressed. "Be like findin' a needle in a haystack. Forby, there'll surely be naethin' left but some rusty bits an' pieces o' airn efter a' this time, Gourlay."

Gourlay tried to salvage what he could of the notion. "Aye, mebbe so... But mind the wey the army shipped parts tae North Africa in the War — a' coated wi' grease, wax, an' happit in oilcloth... Goad, thon stuff wad last a thoosan' years even in saut watter."

"Hmmph... Mebbe."

Hector, however, seemed amenable to the idea. He reasoned that whether or not they dredged up something from the depths was neither here nor there; a day trip on Donald's boat would do them all a power of good and perhaps put an end to the bickering. Like Hector, Gordon was in general agreement with the idea. But with his recent experience of explosives still fresh in his mind, Jummock had reservations. "Howk up Christ kens whit from the depths — it's madness, Gourlay."

Donald thought that they were crazy, and pointed out that even if the naval chart was accurate, their chances of retrieving something other than seaweed from the seabed were very remote. But, since carrying out minor repairs to the boat, he was keen to take her out to sea, and happily organized grappling hooks, extra long lines, and other necessary equipment.

The *Agrippina* slipped away from the quay at first light on a crisp morning and headed past the black rock which guards the harbour entrance and chugged and chortled her way round the Ben Tianavaig headland and into the sound of Raasay. McMinn nudged Gourlay and pointed to the flat-topped mountain on Raasay. "Boswell danced a jig oan the top therr..."

"Wi' Sam?"

"Naw. Sam couldna be trachellt wi' the climb, an' he'd had enough of mountains by then."

Donald called down in Gaelic to James, his 'engineer,' and the boat juddered to a stop. The sea was calm, cold, and grey.

"Right lads. Here we are... It's as close as I can make it...

We'll drift over the area; it's too deep to drop anchor, so once in a while, I'll have to start her up and adjust her position..."

All morning, over and over again, they dropped a stout line with grappling hooks at the end and then winched it up. By noon, their total haul amounted to masses of kelp and seaweed and the remains of something which resembled an ancient sewing machine. With the exception of Donald who was in his element, they were all wet, cold, tired, raw-handed, and close to calling it a day. The afternoon wore on, and then, as the winch groaned, James called out, "We've got something!" They gathered round and leaned across the rail peering into the grey-green waters which roiled for a moment before a barred metal frame broke the surface. Donald stopped the winch and studied the object which appeared to be the top of a cage-like structure. "Losh knows what it may be, boys... But you'd best take cover till I get it clear." Dutifully, they sought shelter as best as they could and waited with bated breath while he cautiously manoeuvred it aboard.

After the masses of seaweed had been carefully cut away, it was soon apparent that it was indeed a cage-like container crammed with a variety of items from canisters to long, barnacle-encrusted boxes. Glistening under the pale sun, rusty, covered with seaweed and mollusks, they looked innocuous, but when McMinn pointed out that the canisters might contain phosphorous, chlorine gas or some other unstable and noxious chemicals, they suddenly took on a more sinister aspect and they all backed off a pace or two.

"Well, chentlemen," said Donald, "now you've a sample, what do you want to do with it? But I can tell you that if it was up to me, I'd be throwing this lot back into the sea again." Finally, after much debating, they decided to take their finds back to camp and sort them out there.

Back at the camp site, they gingerly unloaded the cage from the hearse and placed it a safe distance from the tent. The canisters were sealed so there was no way of telling what they contained. They declined to follow Jummock's suggestion to, "Chuck a couple oan the fire, rin like fuck, an' see whit happens." The disintegrating oblong boxes contained the remains of what Gourlay and McMinn recognized as spare parts for machine guns. Other smaller boxes held cartridges, while two larger ones were packed with hand grenades which appeared to be in very fair condition. Steel lockers, which crumbled when they tried to open them, were packed with large shells and flares. "So what do we have after all that fiddling," asked Gordon rhetorically. "Some hand grenades which look as if they will explode at any moment, some bullets, shells, and a few canisters of Lord knows what..."

"Hmmph," grunted McMinn noncommittally.

CHAPTER 16

The time appointed for the ferry heist duly arrived. In the small hours of the morning, the silence by the campfire where the warriors lolled was shattered by an extraordinary noise; the racket, which sounded as if dozens of empty biscuit tins were being kicked down a rocky mountainside, was punctuated by a series of dull explosions.

"In the nemme o' the wee man, whit the fuck is that?" said Jummock sitting bolt upright. It was Gourlay, James, and Donald in a truly ancient car.

"Good grief, Gourlay!" exclaimed Hector as the machine spluttered to an uncertain halt alongside the tent. "Is that the best you could come up with?"

"Aye, it is," replied Donald in a hurt voice as he stepped out and gave the bonnet a pat. "John Angus has been driving her around the Skye roads since I was a laddie... Very proud of her is John Angus."

"It's a scrap heap, Donald," muttered Gourlay. "Ah think only two of her fower plugs is firin'."

Two gangling young men stepped out of the car and were introduced by Donald. "You've already met James... And this is Murdo," he said simply. The two looked slightly ill at ease and gave the group around the fire the distinct feeling that they'd rather be downing drams somewhere else — anywhere else. Gourlay, too, looked less than happy; a vague, nagging sense of doubt as to the wisdom of the venture, the taciturnity of Donald's cohorts, and the miserable excuse of a car, all contributed to his feeling of unease.

The hours slipped by in anecdotes, jokes and clatter, and even James and Murdo brightened when a bottle of whisky was produced. But their joy was short-lived; Donald permitted them only a mouthful each with the *caveat* that they'd need all their wits about them in the challenging work ahead. However, as James noted sourly, that didn't stop 'himself' from taking great swigs from the bottle each time it passed his way. A couple of hours before first light, Gourlay started up the car, and to a chorus of shouted farewells and wishes for success, the foursome clattered off on their way to Kyleakin.

For the most part, they travelled in silence, but as they approached the ferry terminal Donald once more ran over the details of the job which lay ahead. Gourlay peered through the dirty windscreen into the gloomy night and cursed the single miserable functioning headlamp which threw out a half-hearted watery yellow light on to the dark roadway. As the car muttered and groaned its way into the sleeping village, a cold, blue-grey light began spreading from the east. On Donald's instructions, Gourlay nosed the vehicle between two parked lorries and switched off the engine which, to his alarm and disgust, rattled on defiantly for a few seconds as if it had a mind of its own. Gourlay remained in the car and watched with interest as the three, wearing home-made masks, headed for a small wooden shed that rested at the top of the slipway leading down to the sea. He smiled at the elaborate pantomime of their approach; they reminded him of villains in a second-rate silent film. Donald rapped on the door and waited, half-expectantly, while James and Murdo lurked in the background. There was no response. Again, Donald knocked, louder this time, but still there was no sign of life within. He shook the door, but it was tightly secured. Gourlay watched as the three went into a conspiratorial huddle and guffawed as all three put their shoulders to the shed. "Eejots! They'll never budge it."

But he was wrong; the hut rocked wildly a few times, then suddenly tipped over and fell into the heaving sea below. The interior furnishings remained *in situ* like a set in a theatre with the sea and outline of the distant mainland making a splendid backdrop. Gourlay almost choked trying to suppress his laughter; sound asleep in an upholstered chair lolled a fat man. "For Christ's sake!" He giggled in falsetto as he wiped the tears from his eyes. He watched intently as Donald approached the sleeping figure with stiff-legged caution, and saw him relax at the whiff of whisky fumes and beckon to James and Murdo. The pair, urged on by Donald, extricated a large metal box from the clutter and lurched back to the car with it.

"Start her up, Gourlay! We're on our way!" called Donald as he ran up behind his men. As they humped the box into the boot, Gourlay pressed the starter switch and a horrible whining and grinding noise set his teeth on edge. "C'moan ye auld whore! C'moan!" To everyone's relief, the engine finally caught just as Donald and his men breathlessly took their seats.

It was daylight as they headed across the moors and round the edges of cold-looking sea lochs.

"We're askin' for trouble runnin' aboot wi' that kist... Gin that auld fart wakes up and cries the polis, we're done for," bawled Gourlay above the din of the labouring engine.

Donald looked thoughtful. "You're right... We should open it now and dump the box... Pull over..."

James and Murdo lifted the box on to the roadway. The box, which resembled an army footlocker, was stoutly constructed, and two outsized padlocks secured the top. Murdo kicked it in a half-hearted way and said softly to no one in particular,

"It's ferry strong."

"Wait you now..." said Donald, and he rummaged in the boot and produced a length of tarry rope. "Tether this to the back bumper," he instructed James, "and put this end round the handles of the box..." This done, they got back into the car and drove off. Gourlay glanced in the mirror and saw the box bouncing and jumping along the road behind them like a wild thing. After one particularly high leap, it slammed into the tarmac, paused for a millisecond, then as the rope became taut again, sprang into the air again and vanished. For a long moment he could see nothing but the rope stretching skywards, then there was a tremendous crash as the box whammed onto the roof of the car and broke open scattering the contents. "The Good Lord preserve us!" exclaimed James rolling his eyes piously. With an oath, Gourlay brought the car to a juddering halt, and they all clambered out to inspect the damage. There was a substantial dent in the car's roof, and the box, or what was left of it, lay on the grass verge. Hundreds of papers were either blowing in the wind or lying strewn over a wide area. A brief look around by the foursome confirmed that there was no money. "Not a tam penny," muttered James redundantly. "Not a tam penny."

"Oh my God!" lamented Donald, "John Angus will be in tears when he see the roof..."

They untied the remnants of the box, discarded it in the ditch, and were clearing up some of the papers and coiling up the rope when James gave a warning shout. "Car coming!" A flurry of activity followed. Gourlay lifted the bonnet and pretended to fiddle with the engine while the others rushed about gathering up some of the papers and stuffing them into the boot of the car. Slightly out of breath, Murdo joined Gourlay and peered into the distance. "It's the bank! The mobile bank!"

"Do we put on our masks?" cried James.

Donald closed the car boot. "No, no... It's too late... Act normally."

The van drew up and a friendly red-faced man rolled down the window. "Well, well Donald, it's yourself is it? And the car's broken down then?"

He ran an interested eye over the scene.

"No... Just the fan belt," said Donald. "And how's Mary?

"Fine, fine... Much better... And did you get all your hay in, Donald?"

"Aye. Most of it... We're needing another wee dry spell though."

"Aye, chust."

From under the bonnet, Gourlay bemusedly ran his eyes from one speaker to the other as the conversation about family, crops, and weather ran its course. The mobile bank, he gathered, was on its way, moneyless, to a garage in Broadford for its annual service. From the exchange he also gleaned such snippets as Donald's father's asthma was still troubling him, his uncle Iain was very poorly with his gout, Donald Hamish's goat had eaten holes in the old man's long johns, Cuddie Mackinnon had found his long lost telescope, Eppie's daughter, Murdina, was planning to go to India as a missionary, and the police had charged someone nicknamed Ally Pally with driving his tractor while under the influence. He heard how Ally Pally habitually jolted over his boulder-strewn fields singing lustily and, thanks to a skinfull of John Barleycorn, feeling no pain whatever. On a tractor with a dram taken, he was, it seems, not only victorious over all the ills of life, and, while on his own land, immune to police prosecution. However, to reach one of his fields he had to cross a public road, and it was here, apparently, while crossing the little township roadway, that he'd been nabbed by an officious young constable on a pushbike...

"Madness," repeated Gourlay for the umpteenth time to his cronies who were seated round a good-going fire and occasionally taking a swig of whisky from a bottle. "A' that pissin' aboot an' bugger all to show for it... They musta taken the wrang kist frae the shed... An' the bloody bank wis empty — not a bawbee... An' how that driver nivver seemed to notice a' the papers blawin' aboot Ah'll never know... But what have Ah been missin' here?"

"All quiet on the home front," rumbled McMinn. "It's that quiet here, Ah heard ma blood moving in ma heid so Ah did..."

"Aye," confirmed Jummock, "it's quiet alright... Ah'm missin' the hurly-burly of auld Glesca!"

But if life on the island was peaceful to the group, elsewhere there were stirrings: The waterlogged coffin swirled towards the edge of the little waterfall and slammed into a projecting rock. Sanny revived, and as soon as he realized his predicament, bawled and raged like some wild beast. The din brought a glimmer of consciousness to Dudley, and he too began to wail. Seconds later, the strange craft wobbled violently and launched itself over the rim of the falls. Happily for the two, the drop was not very great and the coffin took most of the impact.

After a great deal of flapping, swearing and splashing about in the roiling waters, they managed to drag themselves to the safety of the bank. No sooner had they coughed the water from their lungs than they began cursing and blaming each other for their sufferings. As they sloshed their way along the roadway to the car they came upon a fat, forlorn, wet figure — Colonel Bacon. The old soldier gazed at them mournfully, raised his fist, and croaked, "Bloody Scots!"

Back in Glasgow again, Dudley and Sanny went their separate ways to rest up and plot revenge on the cell. Sanny sent round the burning torch as it were, and with the aid of some cash advanced by Dudley, had soon assembled a veritable army of cutthroats and ne'er-do-wells, and within the week, three chartered buses marked 'On Tour' were wending their way northwards with their drinking, singing, squabbling passengers.

For his part, heartily sick of playing the rôle of cockshy to the cell, Dudley turned to London for help, and the very next evening two smartly dressed agents checked in to the Ivanhoe Hotel and joined him for dinner. They were more than a little taken aback by their colleague's appearance and demeanour; vivid gashes on his head and scalp — the result of his *contretemps* with the lion — contrasted the more recently-acquired purplish weals and blotches. The erstwhile steely glint in his eyes had been replaced by a restless, almost shifty, quality, and adding to his existing mild speech impediment were periodic hesitations which amounted to a full-blown stutter. As he outlined his plans, the two agents sensed his bitterness and suppressed anger and looked at one another and shook their heads almost imperceptibly.

Next morning, however, as the trio drove out of the City they noticed that he seemed to have perked up a little. "I want to catch them in *flagwente delicto*," he confided. "I want a w—w—watertight case against them... Sanny Wutherford and his h—h—h—halfwits can s—soften them up for us, then w—w—we'll move in... There will be no s—s—slipping away this time!"

Word of something in the air was not long in reaching the large, hirsute lugs of Big Red, and he immediately contacted Quayle, who, in turn, gathered information by every means at his disposal.

"So it's true, Terry?"

"Aye. So it would seem... Three coach loads of Sanny's Yahoos an' a few Special Branch lads in a car all headed north..." The big man stroked his bearded lantern jaw reflectively. "What the hell have our lads been up to?"

"God alone knows... It was supposed to be a rest and recreation trip... I finally got hold of Donnie Macdonald — our man on Skye — on the phone, but he wasn't much help really... He's all hot about the Stone..."

"Huh?"

"I don't know what to believe," continued Quayle, his brows wrinkled. "He claims he's on to the Stone of Destiny..."

Big Red's jaw fell. "The whit?"

"The Stone of Scone... The Destiny Stone... Frankly, I'm not sure what the hell is going on up there... All I know is that Donald says he knows where it is..."

"Good Lord! And that's what Sanny is on to?"

"No. From what I gather, our cell has somehow mortally offended both Sanny and the Special Branch lad... The Stone is an added complication..." The big man tugged his beard thoughtfully, and after a moment came to a decision: "There's only one way to get the true picture, Terry... We'd better round up a few lads an head up to the Hielans..."

Before sundown, in a fug of blue smoke, two single-decker buses, their destination screens reading 'Private,' rumbled out of Glasgow and headed northwards.

On Skye, it was a still evening with wisps of mist on the Coolins. "Ahoo — hoo — hoo ye basterts!" wailed McMinn swirling his bonnet wildly round his head. He hunched up his shoulders, pulled the collar of his jacket up over his head and placed his bonnet on top. Sitting almost on top of the smouldering fire near the tent, he continued to growl like a angry bear. The jacket formed a kind of cowl over his head giving him a neckless appearance, and a passerby would almost certainly have taken him for a raving lunatic, gnome or monk who had lost his reason. But McMinn's sanity, such as it was, was quite intact; his problem was midges. A million or so of the minute pests had suddenly appeared from nowhere and put to flight the little group who'd been seated round the fire. To judge from the slapping noises and cursing from within, not even the tent provided a safe haven. In desperation, McMinn sprinkled his bonnet with the Zonobrone expectorant, lit a Woodbine and puffed furiously in a vain effort to disperse the cloud of insects around his head, and then from the tent came a new refrain: "In the nemme o' Christ! C'moan,

Gourlay, gie us a brek for Goad's sake! Awwww... Christ...!"
Gourlay had remembered that he'd packed his 'insect repellant'
mixture and had liberally doused himself with the potion. To
say that it was evil-smelling would be to understate matters;
the stench was overwhelming and indescribable. Jummock was
beside himself, and the stink of the potion seemed to give him
the strength of ten, for the tent door flap opened and Gourlay was
ejected. He picked himself up, shouted a few profanities over
his shoulder at the little hunchback, then ambled over to join
McMinn who, almost exhausted from his efforts to destroy the
island's midge population, was seated by the fire. "In the name
o' the wee man, Gourlay, whit the hell's the pong? Is that what
got Wee Jummock a' worked up?"

"Midgie repellant..."

McMinn made a gesture to indicate that Gourlay should
remove himself to the other side of the fire.

"Christ, ye could repel the whole Afrika Korps wi' that
stuff, never mind a few midges... Ye smell like a badger's arse.
Here, hae a swig." He passed over the remains of a half bottle
of whisky.

"Thanks... Here, whit's the pong on your bunnet?"

"Zonobrone... Cough mixture"

Gourlay rolled his eyes in disbelief but said nothing.

Night fell, a little breeze blew in off the sea nearby, and the
midges slowly evaporated. Gourlay and McMinn were joined by
the others who emerged cautiously into the cool night air. The
fire was stirred into life and they opened another bottle. McMinn
let his jacket slip back to its normal position, replaced his cap
and lay back looking up into the starry sky. "Aw, this is the life,
lads! A guid dram, guid fire, guid company, and nae midges...
Musta been the stink Gourlay an' me pit oot that scared them..."
He stretched out full-length and gave a deep sigh. Gordon idly

poked the fire while the others sat quite still absorbing the peace and calm. Gourlay turned his head and listened intently for a long moment. "Jings! That's Donald's bike... Lissen..." Sure enough, in the distance they could make out the machine's distinctive clatter and then the pale yellow beam of the headlamp swept into view.

"Well, Donald, it's yourself," called Jummock somewhat unnecessarily as the machine spluttered to a halt. Weaving almost imperceptibly as if he already had a dram or two taken, the tall Gael strode towards them rubbing his hands together. As he joined them beside the fire, his eye lighted on the empty whisky bottle. "By God it's cold on the bike this night... If I'd thought of it, I'd have brought along a dram..." Taking the hint, Gordon, who was closest to the hearse, slipped off without a word and returned with a fresh bottle. After he'd drunk long and deep, Donald smacked his lips in an exaggerated way to show his appreciation. They sensed he had something important to say, but knew better than to ask him directly; in the circumspect, polite way of the Highlander, Donald would come to the point all in his own good time. Thus, for a while, they talked in generalities before the guest said quite casually, "Oh, I was talking to Quayle on the telephone... Here, what's that awful smell..?" He pulled long and hard on the bottle before continuing. "My, but that's a grand whisky just... Aye, it appears that a fellow called Sanny Rutherford is headed this way with a gang of men — yobbos or Yahoos I think Quayle called them — he said he'd been having words with Big Red, and when I told him where you were camped, he said maybe it would be best if you got away out of sight of the road a bittie... Quayle said they'd be up here just as soon as they could round up a few fellows..." Studious silence greeted his words until Jummock got to his feet and in a high voice demanded that they up and move right there and then.

"Calm down, Jummock," said Hector reassuringly. "Let's

not rush into anything... I'm sure Donald can point us in the right direction..."

"I can that," replied the Gael. "Up the Dunvegan road there to the left... Not a mile up, there's a wee track. Once you get over the hillock, there's a glen with plenty of flattish ground... There's a burn there too. The hearse should make it no bother... But you'd be as well waiting for daylight I'm thinking."

Gourlay cleared his throat noisily and spat into the fire. "Bloody Sanny!" he said expressively.

"Ah'm gonna put his gas to a peep," added McMinn vehemently banging his fist into the palm of his hand. "You see if Ah dinna!"

Donald stood up suddenly. "Here, Gourlay," he said with studied nonchalance, "give me a hand." Gourlay sensed the excitement in Donald's voice and shadowed the taller man over to the motorcycle. Strapped to the pillion was a large object wrapped in potato sacks. Only when he helped Donald to lift it off the bike did he realize why he had asked for a helping hand; whatever it was, it seemed to weigh a ton, and it took all their combined strength to heave it off the machine.

"In the name, Donald! Whit is it? A boulder?" Breathing heavily, they lugged it over to the fire and placed it on the ground with a few final grunts.

"What do you think this is?" asked Donald breathlessly but with obvious pride.

"Felt like a big fuckin' rock," rumbled Gourlay turning to reach for the bottle of whisky. Eyes dancing, Donald produced a big knife and cut the bailing twine holding the sacks and with a flourish pulled them back as they gathered around.

"It *is* a fuckin' stane! Ah wis right!" cried Gourlay ruefully.

Sure enough, before them, illuminated by the flickering fire, was a black, oval stone. The top was highly polished and slightly concave while the sides were ornately carved with what appeared to be snakes, broken arrows and curiously interlaced designs. Some fresh earth clung to the carvings. For some reason, perhaps because of the firelight, it reminded Gourlay of a great lump of coal which had been mined, hewn, worked and polished.

"It's very beautiful," said Gordon simply. "Where did you get it?"

McMinn adjusted his pince nez and gently laid his hand on the polished top. "Jesus!" He withdrew his hand as if he had received an electric shock. "The bloody thing is warm! How's that, Donald? Whit the hell is it?"

"Gentlemen," began Donald drawing himself up to his full height and speaking in a tone usually reserved for delivering eulogies, "this is the true Stone... This, my friends, is the Stone of Destiny!"

Flabbergasted, they stared at him open-mouthed.

"Wha...Whe...?" said Hector, at a loss for words.

"Awa' ye go, Donald — we werena born yesterday," said McMinn who was the first to find his tongue. But his voice held little conviction. "How dae ye ken it's the real stane?"

Hector motioned for McMinn to hold his peace and sit down. One by one they sat down and occasionally stole long glances at the black stone as Donald told his story.

"Angus Og of the Isles is a direct ancestor of mine, and it was to him that Robert the Bruce, King of Scots, gave the Stone for safe keeping when Edward's army was slowly heading northwards burning and destroying everything in its path... Angus, you see, had galleys, and Bruce knew the English would never take on the West... We never spoke about the Stone very much in the family, but I grew up knowing that we were its custodians and that one day, if I was spared, I would be entrusted with its care... Now, in the Spring, my uncle Ewen was taken poorly — his heart — and he gave me a sealed letter which he said I was to open at his death. Well, he died in the early hours of this morning..." He paused. "Here, I need another dram!" The bottle was passed to him and he drank deeply before continuing. "The letter — it was in Gaelic — asked me upon my honour to keep the Stone in trust until Scotland was free and ready to receive her rightful king... And it described the spot where the Stone was hidden, buried. Well, me being me, nothing would do but I just had to see if... Well, a wee bit digging, and there it was! Oh, losh, but the thirst is on me!" He put the bottle to his lips again. "I was about to bury it again, but who should chance by but Duncan Mac... The hairy faced lad at the porthole... I quickly sat down on the Stone and told him I was burying a dog and didn't need a hand... Thought he'd never go away... Duncan Mac might be a simple fellow, but he's not completely daft, and it suddenly occurred to me that he was a liability and that I'd be wise to find a new home for the Stone... And who best to guard it meanwhile, thought I to myself, but the N.A.I.L.S. cell?"

Despite this signal honour, the members of the cell looked rather pensive, even glum. Jummock rose and stood over to the Stone peering at it as if he expected it to explode in his face at any moment. "If this is the true Stone, Donald, what the hell have the English got in Westminster?"

"Well, think about it," began Donald taking another quick swig from the bottle, "the Scots are sitting around Perthshire and Edward's army is slowly heading their way. They can't stop him this time, and they surely know that he will cart off anything of value, or anything of significance to the Scots. So what so the Scots do? Easy... They quickly turn out another stone, a replica... And you'll note that the Stone in Westminster Abbey is just a big, plain hunk of red sandstone..."

"Aye, there's plenty of that in Perthshire," interrupted McMinn.

"Exactly... And the true Stone here is magical... I mean, just look at it... It probably fell from the heavens... a meteorite...

Don't you see? They thought the old pagan gods sent it..."

"And the kings of Scotland sat on it," began Gordon.

"No, no, no... They held it above their heads."

"Get away!" chipped in Gourlay. "It's that heavy that you and me could scarce lift it between us..."

"Surely, but I managed to get it on the back of the bike myself... You're forgetting that our kings in the old days were mighty warriors too — powerful men..."

"What you are saying makes a great deal of sense," said Hector solemnly, "and I don't disbelieve you... But how could anyone ever prove that this is the true Stone of Destiny?"

Donald got to his feet rather unsteadily and with infinite dignity declared, "You have my word of honour as a chentleman and a Macdonald... The blood of Angus Og runs in my veins: I do not lie." After a long moment, he drew himself to attention, saluted the company, and said, "I shall return... Meanwhile, gentlemen, I charge you to keep the Stone and..." He burped, staggered, then weaved his way over to his motorcycle. He swung a long leg over it, managed to kick it into life, and immediately, both rider and machine fell over sideways. McMinn switched off the engine and they extricated Donald from under the bike and helped him to his feet.

"Forget it, Donald... You'll bide with us this night," said Gordon softly.

Fuzzy-headed, they were all up at first light, and after a quick wash in the burn, a shave and tea, began taking down the tent and preparing to move camp. Gourlay idled over to Donald who was staring at the Stone with an expression of mild puzzlement on his swarthy face. "Whit's up, Donald?"

"I thought I dreamt it," he said quietly. "But here it is! The true Stone... Can you believe it? How did it get here?"

"Oan the pillion of yer bike."

"Oh, good grief!" The taller man ran the back of his hand over his eyes.

McMinn ambled over slurping his tea from an enamel mug and jerked his thumb in the general direction of the explosives. "Whit aboot thon stuff?"

"We'd best take it wi' us," Gourlay said.

"Aye. Ah wis afraid ye'd say that."

"Tell ye whit, McMinn," said Gourlay with an engaging smile. "Efter we've moved, you can drive ower an' pick it up on yer tod. That wey, if it goes 'Boom!' we'll just lose you an' the Rolls an' no' the hale bloody Army!"

"Thanks pal." McMinn bared his teeth in a mock smile.

The tent was soon set up in the new location and with unwonted caution, then McMinn dutifully took the hearse and retrieved the substantial load of explosives, and canisters. As he drove up Dunvegan road at a sedate pace, his dusky face blanched as he caught sight of a police car parked by the little stone bridge spanning the Sligachan River. He had no option but to drive on and as he passed, the young policeman at the wheel gave a little nod by way of respect.

Back at the new site, he pulled up well clear of the tent and carefully stacked everything in a neat pile. The tent stood in the basin of a glen whose upper reaches vanished into gigantic black outcroppings of basalt and gabbro littering the base of the mountains. A little burn threaded its way round massive boulders as it descended towards the sea. When McMinn mentioned the policeman to Donald who was fiddling with his motorcycle, he told him not to worry — the police were always poking about keeping an eye on things. It was assumed that Donald, being more than a little hangoverish, would leave them and go about his normal business, but with the impending visit of the Glasgow heavies in the air, he had no intention of missing out on the fun.

In the early afternoon, the coaches containing Big Red,

Quayle and an unkempt gang of rowdies pulled into the courtyard of the nearby hotel and the occupants piled out and headed directly for the public bar. Discreet enquiries made of the barman by Quayle elicited the fact that his boys had decamped but their new ground was only half a mile or so up the road. He ordered another round for the mob and turned to Big Red. "Will I take a wee dander up the road?"

"No. It's O.K. Terry. You carry on here for a while... I'll take a wee stroll up... The lads can have another round after this and then see if you can herd them up to this new camp."

"Look! It's himself!" croaked Gourlay as the unmistakable figure of the big man hove into sight. He noticed for the first time that for all his size, he moved with great grace — like a shepherd or hunter used to the hills. The group formed a little line by the tent as if they were about to receive royalty. Warm greetings were exchanged and the big man announced, "Quayle and the boys are on their way up... When they get here, don't offer them any more to drink... God knows but they've been knocking them back since we left Glasgow... Any sign of Sanny yet, lads? He's on his way with his hard men."

Hector shook his head. "Nary a sign."

Big Red turned to Jummock and a faint smile creased his face. "What's wi' the kilt, Jummock?"

"Ach, the fellas keep raggin' me aboot it. But Ah've Hielan blood in ma veins like." He tugged at the bottom of what remained of the garment with an embarrassed little smile, but it remained obdurately high above his knees.

"And how are they treating you, Donald?"

"Very well, very well indeed... Did Quayle tell you about the Stone?"

"He did that, yes..."

"Would you like to see it?"

"You mean you have it *here*?" said the big man in surprise. "Aye."

They all gathered round the Stone which rested nearby covered with its sacks. Donald pulled then aside and the big man stooped low over it and gave a low whistle. "My God! It's beautiful!" he said in an awed whisper. "How did you come by it?" Donald recounted his tale, and it was obvious from Big Red's reactions and from the way he regarded the Stone that he entertained no doubts as to its authenticity. Donald had washed it earlier with pail after pail of water drawn from the burn and, still wet, it glistened in the sunlight like some gigantic jet-black jewel. The big man straightened up and as he did his shadow flickered across the Stone and for an instant it seemed to Gourlay as if the strange carved figures round the edges had come to life. "It's very beautiful Donald," he repeated. There was something almost hypnotic about the Stone and they stood round it in a tight little circle and gazed down at it for a long while in silence.

"Donald wis tellin' us that the Scottish kings in the auld days didna sit oan it, they held it aboon their heids," said McMinn.

"That is so," replied the big man absently, then inhaling deeply, he suddenly squatted down, grasped the Stone in his huge hands, swung it above his head then slowly and majestically drew himself up to his full height. Massive and powerful though he was, the great weight of the stone caused his extended arms to tremble and his face took on a hue to match his hair. Despite himself, McMinn gave a little grin. "Reminds me of Sisyphus who's just got fed up rollin' his chuckie up the mountain," he whispered to Gordon who nodded without comprehending. Like the others, the student was awed by the sight before him. For several long seconds, eyes red and bulging, the veins at his temples throbbing, Big Red stood like a Colossus.

"Holy fuck!" said Jummock in a throaty whisper. "Holy fuck!"

The faint but distinct wail of bagpipes broke the spell and they looked down the glen as first the piper then Quayle then a rag tag mob stumbled into view and headed towards them. "Good Lord!" murmured Gordon.

Earlier, Dudley and his cohorts had made frequent halts *en route* northwards in order to make telephone calls to the various county police forces and had eventually learned where their quarry was located.

Passing through the lonely grandeur of Glencoe, the three agents were affected by its beauty and eerie desolation. A gentle drizzle was falling and the rock faces high up the mountains glistened. Above the swish of the tyres on the wet road and the squeak of the windscreen wipers came the moan of bagpipes echoing dismally off the rock walls of the cutting through which they were passing. They emerged into the open glen again and saw a lone figure in full Highland dress, seemingly oblivious to the rain, standing on a rocky outcrop screwing his pipes. Dudley pulled the car to the side of the road and rolled down the window.

"Why..." began one of the agents.

"Shush!" His colleagues looked at one another uneasily and the agent in the rear tapped his temple with his index finger. The music stopped and Dudley got out and approached the piper who had removed his Glengarry bonnet and was shaking his head in the manner of a swimmer clearing water from his ears. He gazed down at Dudley with red-rimmed eyes as the latter extracted a florin and held it out. "What was the name of that tune you were playing?"

"The Floo'ers o' the Forrest, sir."

"The Floo'ers o' the Forrest?"

"In memory of Scottish manhood killed fighting the English at Flodden," said the piper pocketing the coin and replacing his bonnet.

"You have a sad history..."

"Mmm?"

"Scotland has a sad history... You have a sad history..."

The piper laughed. "Not me sir; I'm English."

"But..."

The piper climbed down from his rock. "I'm a waiter at a hotel in Brighton. This is my annual holiday... I get a change of scenery, meet new faces, and even make a few bob tax-free!"

On the bleak moorland road north of Fort William, they came upon three parked buses. The passengers were pouring out and relieving themselves against the wheels and sides of the vehicles. A small man stepped out and waved at Dudley to indicate that there was plenty of room to pass.

"Sanny!" exclaimed Dudley. The two men exchanged cool greetings, and after some pleasantries, Dudley informed him that if he scouted around the Sligachan area on Skye he'd find the N.A.I.L.S fellows.

The sounds of merrymaking filled the glen. Gourlay recognized some of the men from the memorable night in the church hall. Big Red sought out Quayle. "What do you think, Terry? Sanny's lot is liable to show up at any time... Is this a fair place to meet them?" Quayle swept his eye over the rock-strewn plateau and up to the jagged peaks and back down to the burn below. "It'll do... I'll try and get the lads into some kind of order..."

"Fine... The Stone'll make a grand rallying point... Could we get the lads into three groups? We can take one each and put one of the fellows in charge of the third..." He caught sight of McMinn who was engrossed picking his ear with a stalk of grass and called him over. "Right, McMinn. I'm giving you a squad... Form your men up over there..."

The hours slipped by, the daylight faded, but there was

still no sign of Sanny. From their position by the tent where McMinn's group slept, lolled, drank or squabbled, McMinn and Gourlay glanced over to their flanks. Plumes of smoke rose into the evening air and from time to time raucous laughter came faintly to their ears.

"Hey McMinn?"

"Hmmph?"

"Whit'll happen when Sanny's lot arrive?"

"If an' when they come, they'll come ragin' up from the road doon therr... Then Big Red'll blaw his whustle or whatever, an' we'll go racin' doon an' there'll be a right stushie..."

"That's it?"

"Aye... Whit mair did ye expect?"

Before dark, a shout went up; a vigilant picket had spotted a white face peering at them from behind a boulder. The cry was taken up, and in the three emplacements those who were able, roused themselves and prepared to do battle. The face belonged to Sanny who, realizing he'd been spotted, ran back down the slope and rejoined his men who were milling around just above the roadway. He gathered his lieutenants around him and they tried to instill a measure of order and cohesiveness. Their task was not easy; some of the men were drunk, some very drunk, and some were dead drunk and lying on the wet grass in glazed-eyed stupor. Those who could, bore a great variety of weapons from sticks and hatchets to chains, and open razors, and one enterprising dwarfish fellow wielded a sawn-off shotgun.

"Right lads!" cried Sanny valiantly trying to make himself heard above the clamour of singing, cursing and yelling desperadoes.

"Head straight up the burn... Keep the burn tae yer left, an' head for the big stripet tent..."

A disjointed howl went up and they surged, hobbled and

stumbled forwards.

Sanny was knocked to the ground and was yanked to his feet again by Valentino of the luxuriant moustaches and a little cross-eyed man he did not recognize. Head swimming, he heard the tiny fellow with the shotgun bawling repeatedly, "Nae prisoners! Nae prisoners!" Perhaps twenty or so actually made it to within sight of the tent; in the failing light some had fallen in the burn, some had tripped over rocks and stunned themselves, and some had become too winded to continue, and a handful, uttering wild cries, had charged off up the Dunvegan road in error. Dudley and his two men, nervous lest they be mistaken for Big Red's lot and hacked to pieces, followed at a discreet distance.

"Here they come!" warned McMinn with a growl and clutched his cudgel tightly in both hands. Beside him, Donald squared his shoulders and clenched his fists in anticipation. "Haud fast lads!" boomed Big Red. But as the first wave of Sanny's gallant band neared the tent, the men on the flanks could no longer contain their excitement and, without waiting for an order, rushed in to do mischief.

A buzzard, finger-like wings stretched to catch the last of the day's air currents, soared above the plateau, cocked its head the better to see the madmen below, then with a disdainful cry, made an abrupt turn and headed for the safety of the mountains.

As Sanny's men attempted to press forwards towards the tent, which even in the fading light provided a clear focal point, Big Red bellowed commands which remained unheeded. Somewhere in the gathering darkness, a shotgun roared. Although the men, under McMinn, rose to the challenge and advanced steadily to meet the foe, Gourlay, thinking it best to sleep in a whole skin, remained where he was, alert to every danger. The yelling grew louder, the shotgun boomed again and was immediately followed by a tremendous explosion and dazzlingly bright flash. The tent vanished as if by magic, the heavy hearse rocked wildly, and

Gourlay was thrown backwards with great violence. For several minutes the cache of explosive kept up a series of cracking and thudding noises as ammunition and canisters continued to explode and a dirty yellow carpet of chlorine gas rolled slowly downhill and enveloped the combatants in its lethal, evil-smelling fumes causing them to drop, flee, retch, or utter obscenities of the most terrible kind.

Dazed and deafened, Gourlay sat up and marvelled at the fact he was still alive and appeared to have all his limbs. He looked around, but everyone seemed to have vanished. A flare spluttered into life, arced high above him and shed a bright, intermittent blueish light over the desolate landscape. To his left, a movement caught his eye and he stiffened. His nether parts invisible in the creeping fog and every red hair on his head and chin standing on end, a gigantic form stumbled towards him, then reaching an area relatively free of the noxious fumes, sat down heavily. Gourlay rose, took a few tentative steps towards the big man who sat rocking to and fro, his face buried in his hands. Gourlay then pulled up short; his mind numb, he could think of nothing appropriate to say. As he ran his eye over the weary-looking giant, he noticed that he was, quite oblivious to the fact, sitting on a smouldering rag-covered hump — the Stone of Destiny.

Just before the flare died and the darkness of twilight descended again he thought he saw the familiar figure of McMinn heading to safer ground up the slope of the mountain. Silently, Gourlay made a wide detour to avoid the nauseous stench of the gas which lingered over a wide area and headed for the nearby hotel for a drink. As he limped over the starlit moor he wagged his head and muttered over and over, "A parcel of rogues... A parcel of rogues..."

Finis.

Coy about his age, Dr. Sleigh will only say that he hacked away at his novel (which began life as a series of short stories) for close to 60 years… As with his doctorate, which took him decades to earn through part-time study, he says, "Both demonstrate, if nothing else, that I'm thrawn (dogged)."

Growing up in Rhodesia, Kent, Glasgow, and the Isle of Skye, he believes that what he lost in formal education, he gained by experiencing the values evident in disparate cultures.

These days he splits his time between Skye and Canada living in the hope he will live to see Scotland free again!